BLOOD & TEARS

ICEFIRE TRILOGY BOOK 3

PATTY JANSEN

CAPRICORNICA PUBLICATIONS

GET FREE EBOOKS

Visit pattyjansen.com
to sign up for Patty's mailing list. You get four series starter ebooks
for free!

CHAPTER 1

$\mathcal{I}$T WAS WELL PAST midnight when the truck stopped at the gate of Sady's house. Orsan got out of the seat next to the driver, walked around the side and opened the door for Sady, who let himself down, pulling the sides of his cloak together against the biting wind.

"Thank you," he said to the driver.

"My pleasure, Proctor. Get some rest. I'll be back here tomorrow morning, as usual."

Sady nodded. Thank the heavens for faithful staff.

He walked through the gate, where Orsan exchanged a few words with the young guard Farius. Then across the path flanked by meticulously-clipped bushes, up the steps to the front door.

The night was darker and even more quiet than normal. Low scudding clouds stopped any moonlight reaching the ground, and ever since the bell had rung, the people of the city kept indoors. For the first time in Sady's memory, the famous street lights of Tiverius remained unlit.

The only light in the hall was the lamp that Lana lit every day after dark and that normally burned all night. By its flickering light, Sady turned to Orsan.

"Any word from my house guests?"

Orsan shook his head and fixed him with an intense stare. "Sady, they can wait until morning. Get Lana to make you some soup and go to bed. I'll be out at the gate if you need me." He gave a customary bow and left.

Sady couldn't argue with Orsan's reason. Soup sounded great. Bed even better, although he suspected that once he lay down, sleep would be the last thing that came to him.

After the skirmishes in the refugee camp, he had gone back to his office to deal with the polite unhappiness of the senators, and with the much more rude complaints of the citizens, who told him bluntly that they did not want *this southern menace* in their city. Mercy, could these people just explain to him what they would have done with all those refugees? Turn the trains around and send the poor wretches back to their ravaged country?

He took his cloak off in the hall, and with it, the stoic façade of strength. He let his shoulders sag and dragged his hands across his stubbled face. He didn't think he'd ever been so tired in his life.

But even here, in the comfort of his house, he still saw the people on the platform. He saw the stack of bodies. A tangle of arms and legs, coated in indescribable filth. He saw the wretched survivors with weeping sonorics wounds. He smelled the incredible stench. He saw the angry faces of the refugees in the camp. They only asked to have the bodies of their dead relatives returned to them to observe the proper rituals. They'd been robbed of all dignity, and clung onto what little they had left. But all those bodies would have to be burned to stop contamination. He didn't look forward to dealing with the aftermath of this necessity. From what he understood, burning your dead amounted to sacrilege in the south; burying them was even worse. It made sense how the southerners left their dead for animals to eat, so that the people could eat the animals in turn. But you just couldn't *do* a thing like that in Chevakia's climate. Not to mention the uproar it would cause to the citizens of Tiverius.

How could he possibly solve this?

Bed, Sady, go to bed.

But first, something to eat.

He walked into the kitchen where a single light burned against the back wall. The benches were empty and clean. A bowl of fruit stood in the middle of the table.

"Hello? Lana?" He expected to hear a voice from the pantry, *I'm in here! Wait a moment. Do you want roccas or some soup?*

Now that he came to think of it, he was more than hungry. It could be the reason why he felt so ill. He couldn't even remember his last meal.

"Lana?"

The pantry door was closed. The back door into the laundry was closed. The corridor to the servant quarter was dark.

That was strange. Lana was always here. He couldn't imagine that she had gone to bed; she never did before he was home. But then again, it *was* very late, and he *had* told her repeatedly to go to bed if he was late. He was just . . . disappointed that she seemed to have taken his advice on this night, when he needed to talk to someone calm and sane.

He left the kitchen and knocked on the door to her private room. "Lana, I'm back." She would want to know; she would worry if he stayed out too long.

There was no reply.

Neither was there a sign of life from anywhere else. The noise he made should have brought out Serran, because he was responsible for the grounds, or the young Merni, because she was a gossip, and would make sure that she didn't miss anything.

Where was everyone?

Sady walked into the dark living room, feeling stupid. Here he was, the great leader of the country, and he was unnerved by being alone. Unnerved by feeling so *strange* in his own house.

The living room window looked out onto the courtyard, where he could only see a stone bench lit by a lantern on the patio, a little island of light in the dark. There was a statue in the middle of the yard, of Eseldus han Chevonian, one of his great forefathers. Today, Eseldus was only a dark silhouette.

The windows in the guest wing to the right hand side of the courtyard were dark. The surgeons must have already gone home. He was relieved about that; Sady had no desire to become more intimately acquainted with women's business than absolutely necessary.

He could still see the woman's bruised and red-blotched abdomen. The thought made him shiver. He hoped she survived. He hoped the child survived. That would be one point of light in this misery. He'd never thought that this was the way his house would ever see a baby.

He went back to the kitchen and scouted for some food, cringing at every noise he made. The clank of a plate on the stone bench, the rummaging in the cutlery, the rumble of pouring coal into the stove, the hiss of the flame under the kettle, it all sounded incredibly loud. He found some bread and a bit of goat's cheese, which crumbled all over the bench when he cut it up into clumsy, too-thick slices.

He sat down and ate, listening to the silence of the house.

And the sounds of the day. The ringing of the bell. The yelling of the men in the camp. He didn't understand their language, but he could feel the despair and anger in their words. It brought back many bad memories of his youth. Hundreds of people crammed into a cellar for days without food. The stink of too many bodies in a confined space. There had been that boy, a bit older than himself at the time, who projectile-vomited on those around him.

Sady could still smell it. He could still see the mother's embarrassment, her despair. Her son was seriously ill with sonorics, and yet her immediate concern was the irritation of the people around her.

Sady could still hear her, and the boy's muffled cries. And the ringing of the bell. He would never forget that. Today, the bell had rung again, after more than ten years of silence.

Somewhere in his mind, he registered that the water was boiling and probably had been for a while. Now, where did Lana put the teapot?

As he pushed up from the seat, there was an enormous crash at the back of the house, and the breaking of glass.

He froze, heart thudding. What in all of mercy's name was that?

"Lana?" he called at the door. Surely, that crash would have woken the whole house up.

But again, there was no reply.

He ran into the living room, unlocked the cabinet in the corner and took out the powder gun. It was a solid and heavy thing given to him by Milleus back in the days when they used to go hunting. He hadn't taken the weapon from its cabinet for a long time, but now the metal barrel lay cold against his arm. Comforting. Familiar. He pulled out a box of bullets, inserted two in the gun and slipped a handful into his pocket.

Still, none of the staff had come to investigate.

He made his way through the corridor to the back of the house.

His footsteps echoed loud in the silence. His mind churned, trying to come up with innocent reasons for the breaking of glass. Maybe the family had been scared by a door they couldn't figure how to open. He'd travelled in the southern land, and everything was so much more primitive there.

He opened the door to the guest wing. All dark. No signs of movement. The lamp in the hall was out.

"Hello?"

His heart was pounding.

The only reply was the soft keening of a whistling ground squirrel out in the garden, an unpleasant, creepy noise that made his skin crawl. The damn things were a menace, destroying plants and digging holes everywhere, dislodging tiles and cracking walls. He'd remind Farius to put out some baits.

A fresh breeze stroked his skin, making the hairs on his arms stand on end. There should *not* be a breeze here.

As quietly as he could, Sady walked into the living room, clutching the gun.

In the washed-out light from the lamp in the courtyard, broken shards of glass glittered in the window frame. More glass lay on the ground. A chair lay upside-down on the carpet. Then . . . there was a human-looking shape on the floor, a few paces into the room. Booted feet of a man, face-down on the carpet, surrounded by a dark stain.

Sady ran across the room, and crouched next to the prone form. The man was dressed in thin trousers and a jacket that could be white or some other light colour. He was wearing thin gloves. Sady grabbed him by the shoulder. The weight was heavy, with no sign of movement. He didn't recognise the face. As Sady turned him over, a metal instrument fell out of a breast pocket. This had to be one of the surgeons. With a huge gash across his stomach where his bowels spilled out. The man's open, staring eyes spoke for themselves. Nothing he could do for this man.

Just inside the window was another body. Another man, on his side.

Sady recognised the jacket in han Chevonian maroon with gold piping before he could make out the man's face. Serran, the off-duty groundsman who should have been asleep in his room. He would not be going anywhere ever again. Rivulets of blood had run from deep gashes across his lower back and soaked his jacket and the carpet. Sady pushed him on his back to see that his chest had been cut to the bone. His eyes were glassy and open.

Next to him, another unknown man in white shirt, arm ripped to shreds, the side of his tunic slashed open to reveal a dark mess of blood and intestines.

Sady rose, feeling dizzy with the cloying scent of blood and death.

Was anyone left alive in this room?

Where were the southern woman and her family?

One of the beds had been taken from the bedroom into the middle of this room, and stripped of blankets. It was covered only in a bottom sheet, neatly tucked-in as only nurses and soldiers could. Next to the bed stood a surgeon's kit of instruments. Unused, as far as Sady could tell. There were towels and sheets. Clean.

But someone had used the bed. There was a dark patch of something wet that wasn't dark enough to be blood. And a wet patch on the floor with in the middle a glistening heap of . . . something that looked like a disorganised bunch of dark entrails.

Sady's stomach churned.

On the floor, on the far side of the bed, was another body, this one a woman.

Sady's insides went cold as he recognised the bun on her head, the dress, and the apron, the sturdy shoes and the chubby arms and dimpled hands that had so often brought him tea.

Mercy, Lana.

"No," he whispered. For a moment, his vision went black.

No, Lana!

He dropped to his knees, put the gun down and reached for her as if in a nightmare.

Her shoulder felt limp and lifeless.

Her face was a bloodied mess. He couldn't even see her eyes for the blood. Half her cheek had been ripped off.

"No, Lana." His voice came as a rough whisper.

Sady took her arm. It was barely still warm. There was no pulse. The room blurred before his eyes.

Lana, and her cheerful jokes. Lana, who would not go to bed before he came home. And he'd been eating in the kitchen, maybe even while she was bleeding to death and he could still have saved her.

The silence of the room, the smell of blood and the staring eyes of four bodies made him dizzy.

He breathed slowly through his mouth, trying to think. He needed to get guards out here, to comb the grounds to find out who had done this.

Where were the southerners? The pregnant woman and her family. There was no sign of them, although a fur cloak lay draped over the back of the couch.

He said, as loud as he dared, "Hello? Where are you?"

There was a sound in the garden.

Sady froze. The killer might still be out there. For all he knew, the killer might *be* one of the southerners.

He pushed himself up, picked up the gun and went to the broken window, walking over the carpet so that his footsteps didn't make any noise.

The bushes in the garden looked like big angry trolls against the dim sky. Old Eseldus was like the king in their midst.

The sound came again, a snort, from somewhere in the yard.

He cocked the gun, once, twice to fill both barrels.

Click-click. Loud in that heavy silence.

"If you're out there, give yourself up. I have a gun." His voice echoed in the courtyard.

There was no reply.

He slowly stepped through the broken window, avoiding shards of glass, into the garden. His boots crunched more glass. A couple of bushes had been ripped out of the ground, their stems broken. A trail of dark spots led down the paved path, but stopped before they reached poor Eseldus.

There was that snort again. He raised the gun, holding his breath, his finger on the trigger and stood like that, as quiet as he could, until the need to breathe overwhelmed him. Nothing moved.

On the other side of the garden was a pavilion which the architect had probably intended as a garden room, but which, in absence of the large family that would normally live in a house like this, the staff used as storage.

The door stood open.

The door was not normally open.

He crossed the yard and looked inside, but it was far too dark for him to make out anything.

"Hello? Anyone in here?"

Something moaned softly in the darkness. It wasn't an angry or a dangerous sound, but the sound of an animal in pain.

Clutching the gun, he stepped into the pavilion. Years of accumulated dust crunched under his feet. It was so dark in here. There were stacks of unused furniture in here somewhere but he hardly ever came in this room, and couldn't remember where exactly they strood. And if only he was looking into the light, he might have been able to see some silhouettes. Still holding the gun poised, he waved his left hand about and shuffled forward, feeling where he went.

"I'm here. I have a gun. Don't try any funny business." He hoped it sounded confident, because he didn't feel confident. Somewhere in the back of his mind, it occurred to him that it was probably an exceedingly stupid idea to pursue this alone, and that he should go and find Farius or Orsan.

The sound came again. This time, it was clearly a human voice. A woman. He couldn't make out the words, but she sounded distressed.

He found the owner of the voice in the far corner behind some garden furniture. He remembered the garden table, the big one from Milleus' house that had a candle well in the middle. He could see the table in his mind the last time he'd come in here, and remembered that there was wax in the well which no one had bothered to clean out. He ran his hands over the table, found the well and lit the wick. The paltry smoking and sputtering flame revealed that his quarry was the southern woman, legs pulled up against her chest, hugging herself.

She blinked against the light, her eyes intense blue. Her cheeks were wet with tears. She said something in her language.

"Hang on, I don't understand a word you're saying. Do you speak any Chevakian?"

She only responded to that by crying.

"Come, let's get you some place safe."

He clicked the safety back on the gun, looped the strap around his shoulder and bent down to help her up.

Her hair felt wet and the naked skin on her shoulders cold and clammy. The muscles in her arm shivered when he pulled her up. Her belly was blotched and bruised, but floppy. Her thighs were smeared with blood and she left a puddle of it on the floor. She almost fell and he put a steadying arm around her waist. She was completely naked, and her arms had multiple scratches and if she'd crashed through the bushes.

"Where is your baby?" Because clearly, the child had been born. He made a cradle of his arms and pretended to rock an infant, but he'd never had children, and maybe they didn't rock their infants in the south, in any case, she didn't understand him, and his first priority should be to get her out of here.

"Can you walk?"

He pulled her towards the garden. She stumbled and said some more words in her language, crying. Rivulets of blood ran down her legs. It was clear that she couldn't walk. Not well, anyway. Also, she wore no shoes and there was glass in the courtyard.

"Come." Sady looped his arm under her shoulders, put his other arm around the back of her legs and lifted her up.

Carefully, he walked through the garden to the guest pavilion. She was heavy, and her legs were wet and slippery with blood, but she clung onto him like she was a little girl. Curly hair tickled in his face.

He made his way back into the guest pavilion, past the bodies still on the ground.

When he entered the corridor, Orsan came the other way in big strides, carrying a torch.

"Proctor, what has—" He stopped. Looked at the woman and the broken furniture in the living room. "What happened here?"

Sady explained quickly, to Orsan's increasingly horrified expression. "Did you hear the window break?"

"No, but I thought I heard the side gate open. What has happened to her?"

"No idea. Have you seen her baby?" Sady asked. "Have you seen the rest of the family?" There should be two other women, and a man.

"No. I was at the front gate."

The woman moaned. Her face was wet with tears.

Orsan said, "Give her to me. I'll take her to the domestic wing."

"No. Take her to the second bedroom." The one next to his. "She needs a physic. She's bleeding."

Orsan took the woman from Sady and his arms thanked him. He was no athlete.

"Sady!" Fast footsteps in the corridor announced Merni. She came into the room, skirt flapping. Her hair was messy from bed. "What happened? I can't find Lana—" She stopped. Her gaze found the booted feet of the surgeon. Her eyes widened. She clapped her hands over her mouth to stifle a scream. She stumbled about, her eyes popping wide and dropped onto a bench, where she sat, panting. "They're dead, they're dead, they're *dead*."

Sady sank down next to her and put a hand on her shoulder.

She jerked towards him, her eyes still wide enough for the whites to show on all sides, and let out a scream.

"Shhh, calm down. It's all right."

"No, it's not all right There's *dead* people in there. How can you call that all right?" She screamed again, and clawed at her face. Her eyes were so wide, he wasn't sure if she even saw him.

"Shhh—screaming is not going to help them, or the guards looking for the killer."

"You mean there's a killer still out there?" Her voice spilled over, hysterical. "You mean he's going to come back and kill all of us, too?" She screamed again, shrill. Her nails left red marks on her cheeks. Sady felt like clamping his hands over his ears.

"Quiet!" he shouted, perhaps a bit louder than he'd intended, but the screaming jangled his nerves. He grabbed her hands, so she couldn't scratch herself again. The muscles in her arms were tense and fought him. "They're dead. They're dead!"

He tightened his grip. "Merni, stop it!"

She looked at him, breathing fast. Tears tracked over her cheeks. He mouth quivered. "But . . . but they're dead."

"I know, but screaming is not going to help anyone."

Her chest moved in rapid expansions, as if she'd burst out screaming any moment. But she kept her mouth shut.

"Calm down, breathe slowly, that's it."

She was young, much younger than Lana, and had started working at his household last year at Lana's recommendation, but Sady had found her excessively formal and nervous.

Her breathing slowed somewhat. "That's it," he said, trying to sound as soothing as possible, even though he didn't feel that way at all. "Now, follow Orsan and look after the poor woman."

"Yes," Merni said, and she nodded, clamping her lips to stop them trembling. "Yes, certainly."

She rose and ran off, leaving Sady with the bodies. He slumped on the bench. What now?

Where was he going to get a physic and an interpreter at this time of the day during a level one sonorics warning? The physics held emergency clinics, he'd heard, but he had never been to one. At the hospital, he assumed. He had to—

There was a sound behind him. He whirled around to see that the door to the guest wing's bedroom had opened and three people were coming out. There was a man, a hairy, unshaven fellow in a woollen robe, a middle-aged short and squat woman and a teenage girl, presumably their daughter, cradling an infant in a sling. Ah, that solved the issue of the missing baby.

The girl advanced into the room, her grey eyes wide. The baby started crying, and she patted it on the back.

"You . . . live here?" she said in heavily accented Chevakian.

"I am the owner of this house." He couldn't believe it. He'd spent all day looking for someone who spoke Chevakian, and all the while such a person had been in his house? "I sent you here. What happened here? Is that the baby?"

She backed away when he pointed at the child in the sling, putting a protective arm over it.

"I only wanted to know if the lady's child was safe."

"Is my child." She stuck her chin into the air.

At her age? No way.

"Mine," she said again. Her grey eyes blazed with protectiveness.

"Then where is the lady's child?"

He had to repeat the question before she understood.

"You not see it?"

"No. I found the lady, but not the child. Where is it?"

She shrugged. "We go in." She pointed at the bedroom door. Her mother said something and the girl replied in a sharp tone.

"You didn't see any of what happened?" he tried again.

"We hear . . . Whaaa . . . Whaaa." She waved her arms presumably to mimic screaming and panic. Her mother again commented. She returned another sharp reply.

"Didn't you go and help?"

She spread her hands. "I . . . not . . ." She rolled her eyes at the ceiling.

Sady struggled on for a bit longer, but clearly her Chevakian was inadequate to tell him the full story. He did get that her name was Myra and that Dara and Ontane were her parents. The pregnant woman's name was Loriane, and he didn't think she was related to the family.

Orsan returned, carrying a plank and a hammer. He leaned the plank against the couch and put the hammer down on the seat.

"For the window," he said when Sady raised his eyebrows. "I just spoke to Farius at the gate. He says he heard the side door, too. I'm going to take a light into the yard and see if we can find out where the killer went."

"You may need to find a newborn baby."

Orsan nodded, his face grim. "I thought it was the child the girl carries, but it's too old. Merni showed me."

"What would someone want with a newborn baby?"

Orsan shrugged. "We'll have a look if we can find the bastard."

Sady made a decision. "I'm coming."

"Do you think that's wise? It could be dangerous—"

"I'm coming. I'm not letting you go out there by yourself." His voice was definite. Better in danger than sitting inside grieving over Lana's death. There would be time to get the family's story tomorrow, or whenever he located a translator. "It could be a while before the guards are here. The trail will be long cold by then."

CHAPTER 2

A ROUGH MAN'S voice woke Isandor from his sleep. It was a shout, garbled words that his brain couldn't process in its sleepy state, somewhere close outside the tent. He looked around, to find that he wasn't, in fact, in the tent, but he'd been sleeping on the passenger bench of the truck. Well, that explained why he felt hot and stuffy.

It was still dark outside, and the orange glow of firelight flickered through the cabin, lighting the seat backs and the wheel and dashboard.

He now remembered Milleus suggesting that two of them sleep in the truck, for safety, while the third person guarded the goats against refugees desperate for milk or, heaven forbid, meat.

He sat up, feeling sweaty and shivery. The seat had been none too comfortable, its leather sweaty. His neck was sore, his back was sore and he had lost feeling in his left hand.

Jevaithi sat in the front passenger seat, her cloak drawn around her. By the way she held her head up, she was awake.

Outside the front window dark shadows moved in groups, all going down the hill. The firelight was not from the campfire—which had gone out—but from people carrying burning torches. There was purpose and aggression in the way they moved.

He saw a memory of a mob of young men, most older than himself, running through a snowy street. Setting fire to limpets.

Shouts, and fights. The night sky lit up. That had been the night that the Outer City burned, the night they had fled.

"What's going on?" he asked. His voice was croaky. By the skylights, his neck really hurt.

Jevaithi's face looked pale in the flickering firelight. "I don't know. A lot of people are going down there. None of them coming back."

"Where is Milleus?" Isandor had seen him earlier that night, when he'd come to relieve Isandor from his guard duty in protecting the goats. Isandor had been stiff and cold, sitting on the trailer's railing, with the goats asleep behind him, all piled half on top of each other, because there wasn't enough room in the trailer for all of them to lie down. Isandor had sat there, with the metal railing biting in his back-side, clutching the gun, jumping at every sound. And Milleus had come out of the truck for a change of guard.

"I haven't seen him. He should be outside," Jevaithi said, just as Isandor had reached that same conclusion.

Isandor pressed his nose against the glass. There were so many people going down that road. Their shouts sounded muffled through the glass, and he couldn't make out the words, but the voices were rough with anger. He thought of all the young men he'd seen yesterday, standing around bored and angry, attracted to wherever there was an argument. The goats were bleating and jumping around, and their movement rocked the truck. Surely Milleus was out there somewhere.

"I'll go and have a look," he said.

"No." Her eyes were wide, with little bright spots where the torchlight reflected in them. "Don't go outside."

"How else can I find out what's going on?"

"Please. I'm scared. This is just like the night . . ." She didn't need to finish the sentence. He knew. The night he'd rescued her from the Knights, and they had escaped the blue giant of a servitor. The night that the Outer City erupted in fights.

"If there is trouble, I need to help Milleus."

Jevaithi's eyes met his. She didn't argue with that. "Please, be careful. If something happened to you . . ."

"You'll be fine." She'd be completely lost without either of them. "Just stay here, all right? Don't talk to anyone. Don't let anyone into the truck."

She nodded, her eyes wide. "What if those hunters come back?"

"Lock the door after I've gone. You'll be fine." He repeated it to convince himself. By the skylights, he really didn't like the look of what was happening outside.

He rummaged around in the back of the truck and found a length of wood that Milleus sometimes used as a walking stick. "Here."

She took it from him. The determined expression on her face made him cringe. She would be nothing against trained Knights even if she had a gun. They had only one gun, and Milleus had it, or so he hoped.

He retrieved his cloak, dragged it over his shoulders and opened the door. A gust of smoke-scented wind blew grit and ash into his face. People were talking in nearby tents. Agitated voices. Somewhere in the darkness, someone started a truck engine with a hiss. He looked past the side of the truck.

"Milleus?"

No reply.

He let himself onto the ground, shut the door and walked past the truck. The goats stirred.

"Milleus?"

Milleus wasn't sitting on the trailer bar, where he had been when Isandor went to sleep. The truck's tool box stood on the ground, open, but the truck's panels were all closed, and there was no sign of Milleus fiddling with the engine. The canopy had been pulled over the trailer as if they were on the road. Two goats stuck their hairy noses out between the bars of the railing, one of them curling its tongue to get hold of a piece of rope.

"Milleus!" Isandor's heart thudded. Jevaithi's heart, in his chest. Through it, she would feel everything.

"I'm here!" came a voice from behind him. Isandor whirled. A group of people stood between tents. The light was too feeble to distinguish faces, but the thought he could pick out Milleus' old vest.

Isandor made his way between packs and vehicles, dogs and guy ropes. It wasn't easy with his wooden leg. He almost tripped over a pack and had to steady himself against a tent pole, and a man inside shouted at him. Dogs started barking.

Milleus stood in a group with three men and a woman. The woman was saying, ". . . and I heard from my brother that the Mekta

Road is very busy but still moving, but he's not been able to get a word from Tiverius."

One of the men said, "The lines are down."

The other said, "All this newfangled telegraph technology. Pigeons would have gotten through ten times."

And the woman, "You did well to get through at all."

They stopped talking when Isandor joined the group. The woman raised an eyebrow at him. She was a middle-aged woman with the soft, pale-skinned features of an administrator. "This is the young man you were talking about, Milleus?"

"Yes," Milleus said.

She eyed him up and down, but said nothing. Isandor thought her face was disapproving.

"What's going on?" Isandor asked.

"He speaks Chevakian well," the woman said, looking at Milleus as if Isandor wasn't there.

"He's a fast learner."

"You did well, teaching him. Theirs is such a strange language."

"Excuse me, what's going on?" Isandor asked again. Why did these people think that because he was young and not Chevakian, they could talk over his head?

"We'll be moving soon," Milleus said.

"But it's still dark." And where were they moving to, anyway?

"Some young fellows have cut a hole in the fence and we're moving through. They say that a lot of the tents in the camps are empty, and wondering what the hold-up is. We'll be travelling through the camp now, before someone can come and stop us. We'll be at my brother's house in the morning."

Isandor looked from the truck—and the open tool box—to Milleus. "You gave them the wire-cutters, didn't you?"

"It was a ridiculous place to put a fence. Come on, let's go."

Isandor guessed that meant yes. Strange. Milleus had struck him as being someone who liked rules.

The woman and two men left and Milleus and Isandor went back to the truck, where Jevaithi was watching, a pale face behind the window. All around, people were busy dousing fires and packing up tents. Isandor grabbed the hay people had brought yesterday and stuffed it into bags Milleus had for that purpose. The goats could smell it and thought they were getting fed. They jostled each other to be in the position closest to Isandor. He scratched the animals behind the ears.

At the bend down the hill, the first trucks already started moving.

Isandor helped Milleus fire the furnace. All around, people were talking in eager voices. Hurry up, let's get going. After days of being stuck here, they were moving again; they were doing something. Just like in the Outer City and in the Knights' Eyrie, people got up to all sorts of trouble when they were bored or frustrated.

Soon, the convoy was rolling again, very slowly at first, and there was a long wait before the way ahead was clear enough for the truck to join the downhill convoy. While they waited, Milleus leaned his elbows on the truck's wheel, and talked about his brother, who worked gathering information about the weather. Isandor hadn't known that Chevakians made such detailed observations of weather patterns. He didn't know that icefire rose and waned in cycles. He had known that Chevakians could measure it, but didn't know that it determined so much of their weather.

Whichever way Isandor looked at it, there could be no peace between the two countries unless icefire was controlled. If the Knights, as he had seen, were experimenting with it, that could upset the entire climate in Chevakia and it would become as cold as the City of Glass. That would be a disaster.

In the City of Glass, people could hunt and eat meat—this habit of eating bread was very strange to him anyway—but Chevakia had no ocean where Legless Lions could live, and without their meat, the people would starve. They had camels and goats, but they ate grass and there would be none of that, either.

Their houses were also too flimsy for the cold. If the climate changed, many people would freeze before new houses could be built. And that was even without any of the deadly effects icefire itself had on Chevakians.

The truck before them jolted into action, and Milleus followed, still at walking pace, but soon going faster.

At rounding the bend, an amazing scene unrolled before them. The column of trucks moved through a large opening cut in the fence, with the wire mesh rolled away in both directions. The camp down the hill was dark, with just a few lamps burning between the tents. Further down the slope, the camp merged into the streets of Tiverius: lights in neat rows and the dark outlines of square buildings.

Tiverius, the legendary Chevakian capital. Isandor had often wished, but never truly believed that he'd ever come here. As butcher's assistant in the Outer City, he'd been too poor. As Apprentice Knight, he would have been unwelcome.

Milleus steered the truck through the fence, held open by a couple of youths waving to the passing trucks.

Onto the grassy plain of the camp. The convoy chugged towards the tents.

Jevaithi leaned on his backrest; Isandor could feel her breath in his hair. She'd been quiet. For her, Tiverius would mean getting back to her old life. She could run from her heritage, but she would never be free from it.

The truck in front slowed down and then stopped.

"What now?" Milleus muttered.

Someone ran past the truck from the direction of the camp, shouting something Isandor didn't catch. The first person was followed by two more people.

Someone else came running after them. "Stop, stop! Go back or I'll fire!"

That man was joined by a second person, carrying a torch. Both wore uniforms Isandor had seen a few times on their drive from Milleus' farm. Soldiers of the Chevakian army.

Milleus opened the door on his side and slid out of the truck. "Stay here."

He walked past the front of the truck and said something to the soldiers.

"Get back into your vehicles, and turn around where you came from immediately," the Chevakian soldier shouted back. "You are not allowed here."

"We are refugees from Ensar and are on our way to Tiverius." Milleus planted his hands at his sides, as he did when arguing. "We've been waiting on the other side of that fence for more than a day, and we're fed up. We demand to use the road, which is a public road for all Chevakians. We will not go back there and wait. We can't turn the convoy around. Too many vehicles are still coming from behind.

Food is running out. Some people here have nowhere to stay in the city. They need to stay in the camp. They're fed up with waiting."

The man replied, but Isandor didn't hear it because a number of people ran past at such speed that one crashed into the soldier with the torch, and stumbled before regaining his balance. The soldier yelled at him and the skinny youth ran for the truck. From the sounds and rocking, he had climbed onto the trailer. The goats scrambled and bumped into the side rail.

"Hey, you!" Milleus shouted. "Get off! You're scaring the goats."

Isandor opened the door on his side. "I got to go and help him. Stay here." He jumped onto the grass.

A couple of other youths had arrived, and while the soldiers fought his mates, the youth on the trailer inserted his hand in between the cover and the mesh sides. The goats were bleating and jumping around trying to get away.

Isandor grabbed the youth by the back of his coat. He yanked. The youth lost his grip on the trailer and fell back.

Isandor jumped onto the railing to shield the goats with his own body. "Get away from my goats."

The youth scrambled up, looked as if he was going to fight, but then his mouth fell open. "The . . . the Queen's champion?" He spoke the southern language and those words took Isandor back to a time he'd almost forgotten. Flying on the back of an eagle, a time when his only worry was Carro's unusual behaviour.

Yes, he had won the medal, and that had been the beginning of all this misery.

"I'm Isandor," he said, and his voice sounded strange even to his own ears, having spoken Chevakian to all others except Jevaithi for so long. "How did you get here?"

"Like everyone else, on the train." He used the old southern word for train, one that had been in use at the time of the old king.

"What train?" Isandor used the Chevakian word.

"The one that brought us here. You didn't come on the train?"

"No, we came with a Chevakian farmer. These are his goats." He grabbed the bars of the railing. The press of the warm and hairy bodies against his hands was comforting. They had become *his* goats as well.

"We came on the train, and the Chevakians put us here."

"How many of you?"

"All of us. The whole camp."

Isandor let his eyes roam the hillside dotted with tents. There were thousands of people here.

More even. Now he understood. Milleus had assumed the camp was for refugees from the Chevakian border regions. But it was for southern refugees.

"Why did you flee?"

"There was a massive explosion. They say the Knights messed with the Heart of the City, and the Heart took revenge. Some say there was a war. Some say the Knights did it on purpose."

"Hey, guys!" Another youth called out to his mates some of whom still jostled with the Chevakians. "Hey, come here, guys. The Queen's champion is here!"

A couple of people came running out of the darkness. A boy of about ten, a girl and a young woman. They looked dirty, pale and emaciated. Their furs were filthy and matted.

"We all thought the Knights had killed you," a girl said. She was about Isandor's age, but her face was scabbed and oozing fluid. Her eyes were wide with pure adoration.

Isandor felt sick. While he had been eating well and frolicking with the Queen, the people of the City of Glass had suffered a terrible disaster. The next moment, panic clawed at his insides. *Mother.* Where was she?

More people came running towards the Chevakian convoy. "The Queen's Champion is here!" The shout was repeated by people across the grassy field. "The Queen's champion! The Queen's champion!"

"Go back to your tents immediately!" a Chevakian soldier shouted. There were only two soldiers, and at least thirty southern people. Isandor recognised the emotions in their faces from that night in the Outer City. They were hungry, desperate, frightened, bored, all recipes for a riot.

Isandor didn't want to start a riot. He wanted to know where his mother was.

One of the Chevakians from the truck convoy joined the soldiers, and yelled at the southerners, "If anyone touches any of us, I'll shoot."

Isandor shouted at the southern youths. "Go, before there is trouble."

The group made a half-hearted effort at retreating, but didn't go very far.

Chevakian men gathered next to Milleus' truck. Isandor remained in the shadow, feeling their angry gazes on him.

One man said, "So Destran gives all this to southern scum while we have to wait outside and get nothing?" Isandor recognised the driver of the truck in front of Milleus'.

"And why close off the road?" another said. "That is the most stupid thing I could think of doing."

The first man said, "Why isn't there a camp here for us? We have nowhere to stay."

"And no money to pay for their expensive inns," another added.

"Now you people here, listen." The grumblings grew quiet at the sound of the clear male voice of a Chevakian soldier. He looked to be of senior rank, with glittering buttons on his uniform.

"I'm going to have to ask you to turn back. I don't know how you got in, but—"

"We made a hole in the fence, that's what," Milleus said.

The soldier looked at him, briefly raised his eyebrows, and went on, "You have to leave for your own safety. There was a disaster with sonorics in the City of Glass, and these people have fled—"

"We have fled, too," a woman said, and some people cheered.

"These people are contaminated and a risk to your health."

"Any more of a risk than starving to death?" someone yelled.

Several others agreed.

"You have to go back the way you came," the soldier shouted over their voices. "Turn your trucks around immediately and go back the way you came. Follow the Mekta road into the city."

"Where we will find what? Have you got something set up for us, too or is this just another way to keep us out of your hair? This camp looks good enough for us."

"We can't allow you to go through here. Return where you came from. That is an order. Disobey and you risk being fired at." The soldier's voice rose.

"Come on, mate, you wouldn't really shoot at a fellow Chevakian." This soothing voice was Milleus', and he pushed his way through the group. "That is against the army's mandate."

The officer turned his head to him, swallowed visibly, clutching his gun. "Who are you?"

His nostrils were wide, and his chest moved fast.

Isandor knew the type; he'd seen them in the lower ranks of the Knight officers. They had some responsibility but didn't have the experience or aptitude for higher command. They were used to having their orders obeyed and panicked when they were not. He wished he could tell Milleus to watch out. Such men could do strange things at no notice and this one looked at the end of his rope.

Milleus put his hand on the man's shoulder and said some quiet words that Isandor couldn't hear.

The officer's eyes widened. He sprang into a military salute. "Honoured to meet you, sir."

Milleus said something else.

The officer listened, and then said, "The command won't like that, sir."

"No," Milleus said. "They probably won't, but they'll like the alternative even less."

The man nodded and they spoke more. Milleus gestured at Isandor to get into the truck. By the skylights, it looked like Milleus was actually going to convince them to let the convoy through.

Isandor made his way towards the truck when there were fast footsteps and more Chevakian soldiers arrived. They spoke to their comrade and Milleus.

Milleus protested.

One of them said, "It's our orders to keep the camp sealed and remove these people."

"Let's be realistic. There is nowhere for them to move to," Milleus said, his voice calm. "The road is blocked with too many people still arriving. People out there are angry and hungry. Let us pass through to clear up the jam. Seal the fence afterwards."

And so it went on. Milleus argued in favour of common sense. Someone in the Chevakian army had given the order to remove the Chevakians from the camp, and some soldiers thought it was all right to interpret that as letting these people out on the other side of the camp, and others said it was not.

Over their heads, Isandor noticed that southern people were gathering further down the hill. Some were pointing at him.

Another group of Chevakian guards arrived and tried to shoo the southerners back to the tents. Isandor heard shards of shouting, some mentioning his name. Milleus was still talking to the other Chevakians.

A scuffle broke out further down the hill.

"Be calm! Don't fight!" he shouted in his own language over the heads of Milleus and the soldiers. His voice sounded thin on the wind.

Voices shouted back. "Champion, champion."

"Don't fight. They will kill you!"

"Champion, champion, champion!"

Now several of the Chevakians civilians of the truck convoy turned to Isandor.

"That's one of them," Isandor heard a woman say.

"What is he doing here?"

"I saw him with the old man."

"He's the one who gave us milk." This was a child's voice. "I like him."

Down the hill, the scene descended into chaos. Isandor spotted a man in a Chevakian uniform beating a refugee on the ground. Some southerners threw rocks at that soldier. Other Chevakians went after the rock-throwers. Most of them ran up the hill to the shelter of the Chevakian trucks, where Isandor spotted one man clambering in the back of a trailer, and one crawling underneath the vehicle. Another climbed on top of the wood stack. The truck's owner who had been tending the boiler yelped when he found a stranger behind him.

Chevakian soldiers walked past the column inspecting each truck. They caught the southern youth hiding in the trailer, dragged him down and kicked him.

In all that chaos, Milleus came back to the truck in great angry strides.

"Get in," he said to Isandor.

"But they're beating up my—"

"Get in. Now."

There was no arguing with that voice. Isandor climbed into the back, where Jevaithi put the gun aside and clamped her arms around him. Her skin was clammy and cold.

"The people in the camp are all southerners," he whispered. "They're refugees from the City of Glass."

"Oh!" Her eyes were wide, but she said nothing else. She stared into the distance and he could only imagine what she felt.

"Don't be afraid," he whispered.

"There will be Knights."

"If there are, they'll have me and Milleus to deal with, but I haven't seen any."

"You don't understand what they can do if they don't get things their way."

"We'll be fine. Milleus is with us." But he understood very well. *He* knew what the Knights could do. The pain of having his very essence sucked into an icefire sink was not something he'd forget easily. Now that the Chevakian barriers had failed, they were no longer immune from icefire.

He kissed Jevaithi on the lips.

From his position, he could see four or five Chevakian soldiers, walking past the trucks. One yelled and swung his baton, clanging it against each truck. "Move, move, move! Turn back!"

The truck in front jerked forward in a cloud of steam, stopped with squeaking brakes to avoid running over a youth who was being chased by a couple of Chevakian guards, and then completed the half-circle and went off back up the hill. A couple of southern youths chased after it and jumped onto the back.

Chevakian soldiers ran after them and tried to pull them off. One of the youths fell and was besieged by Chevakians. A fight broke out.

Milleus had started the engine.

More and more trucks from the front of the column were now driving back towards the hole in the fence, many with people hanging off the back. Chevakians tried to pull the hitchhikers off. They didn't get all of them. The Chevakian soldiers were too few in number to stop the fights that broke out. Isandor could do nothing but watch, clutching the edge of his seat, while Milleus waited for boiler pressure to build.

"Are we going back?" he asked.

"No way. We'll be sleeping at Sady's house tonight."

Now that the truck in front had gone, Isandor had an uninterrupted view of the camp, where more and more people were streaming out, up the hill, many carrying burning torches.

A soldier came to the window. "Move please, sir." He flapped his hand in a general uphill direction and said a few words Isandor didn't catch.

Milleus grumbled, "Old man? I'll show you who's an old man." With a sharp clink, he dropped the truck into gear. "Hold on, youngsters."

The engine roared, blowing a cloud of steam by way of a threat. The soldier didn't move.

"Get out of the way!" Milleus shouted out the window.

"Sorry, sir, you can't pass. Proctor's orders."

"And do you know what you can do with that dishrag of a proctor?"

He cranked the truck into reverse, shot back as far as they could without hitting either of the two trucks that were still following, and made a sharp turn to the right, over the edge of the road, ploughing through the grass and past the soldiers. The goats in the trailer protested with the jerky movements.

"Hey, hey! Stop!" The soldier ran beside the truck, but he couldn't keep up. There was a loud bang.

Milleus gunned the truck as fast as it would go. "Did you hear that? They fired at us! They shot at honest Chevakian citizens. Hang on, this will be a rough trip."

Isandor grabbed the handholds on the side of the door. Jevaithi clung into him. Milleus steered the truck around bumps and gullies. He seemed to enjoy himself. They rolled down the hill faster and faster and soon Isandor couldn't see the running soldier anymore. He glanced over his shoulder.

Jevaithi's eyes were wide.

Isandor held her. He was scared, too.

The truck bumped and creaked and clanged. They kept going downhill, getting closer to the first line of tents. There were no longer other trucks in front. The sky showed faint blue at the horizon, and the glow lit Milleus' determined face. He muttered obscenities to himself.

The truck clunked back onto the paved road with a sound that

Isandor hadn't heard before. The engine roared, but they were not going as fast as Isandor would have expected.

Milleus swore. "They shot the tyres."

A few loud bangs echoed over the field, these ones further away, presumably aimed at the trucks trying to follow. The truck laboured down the road. They were now coming up to the first of the tents. Refugees thronged at tent entrances to watch the spectacle. People of all ages, all southerners in fur cloaks. Skinny, filthy refugees. Many of them were wounded. There were hundreds, thousands.

While they progressed slowly, some of the refugees cheered. Children ran with the truck, barefooted.

"I wish all these people would get out of the way," Milleus muttered. He glanced over his shoulder, where a group of Chevakian soldiers fast caught up. "The old lady can't pull much with a couple of flat tyres. We'll probably have to stop soon, when they catch up with us. You're ready?"

"Ready for what?" Isandor couldn't run with his wooden leg.

"We're likely to get arrested by the soldiers, and they'll take us into the city. You'll have to come up with a story that will convince them that you're no southern spies."

Isandor met Jevaithi's wide eyes.

"Whatever your reason for being in my shed, it can't be political or have anything to do with the government of the City of Glass."

By the skylights, were the Chevakians that scared of the south?

Jevaithi's breath was coming fast. Her face glistened with sweat. Isandor held her tightly, and could feel his heart racing in her chest.

If there were any Knights in the camp, this wouldn't end well. If they were caught by Chevakians, this wouldn't end well.

A Chevakian soldier caught up with the truck, jumped on the outer step, yanked the driver's door open and half-pulled Milleus from his seat. The truck stopped abruptly when Milleus' foot left the accelerator.

Jevaithi let out a squeak and buried in Isandor's arms.

Milleus struggled to free himself of the soldier's grip, cursing, but the soldier was stronger and dragged Milleus from the cabin.

Champion, champion, champion, the southern people were chanting.

Some of them climbed onto the front of the truck. Soon, they would come inside, and then . . .

"What do we do now?" Jevaithi cried. "It's over. We're lost."

"No, it's not," Isandor said.

Something clicked in Isandor's mind. The people he'd talked to briefly were Outer City people, because people from the City of Glass proper would never have recognised him. It made sense that if something had caused an explosion of icefire, most of the refugees would be from the Outer City. Knights would have eagles, and he'd seen none. Maybe there *were* no Knights here. He had to take the risk.

The Outer City people he knew well, and those people loved the Queen. Jevaithi had another protection: her name.

"Wait." He released Jevaithi and turned to the door.

"What are you doing?" Her voice sounded like a squeak.

"Wait. Come out when I ask you."

"No, Isandor."

"Yes. I have an idea."

He pushed the door open. The scene outside was utter chaos. People were fighting the Chevakian guards, or each other. Three people were on the trailer, trying to get it open. The goats were bleating and jumping about. Milleus had vanished in the seething mass of people.

Still in the door opening, Isandor pulled himself up onto the truck's roof, his trembling hands slipping in the layer of soot and dust that covered it.

He put his fingers in his mouth and whistled as hard as he could.

"Stop. Fighting!"

Not that it made much of a difference. The wind carried his voice and the words were lost in the chaos.

But then a man yelled, "There is the Champion! See? I told you so."

A woman replied, "Our Champion!"

"That can't be. The Knights killed him."

Isandor yelled, as loudly as he could, "I'm not dead, as you can see."

Fights stopped. A few people laughed.

Cheers went up all around, and all the southerners in the vicinity of the truck gathered to watch. Isandor spotted Milleus with the Chevakians at the back, also watching.

He asked. "Are you all from the Outer City?"

A woman replied, "Most of us, yeah."

"Are there any Knights here?"

"If there are, they're keeping their cowardly heads down." The man who had spoken was dressed in black, and when he spoke, voices quietened.

By the skylights, since when had the Brothers of the Light been so visible? There must be truly no Knights here. "Are you the leader of these people?"

"I'm Simo," the man said. He was perhaps in his thirties. He had a thin beard and a balding patch at the top of his head. "Leader is probably not the right word, but we are leaders, of some kind, for the freedom of the people of the City of Glass. I'm glad to hear that you survived. The last we saw you was when you were being taken away by Knights."

That time seemed like years ago. The man must have been in the audience at the arena for the ritual killing, like most of these people here.

Isandor bent down and stuck his hand into the window. "Come out."

Jevaithi stared at him, looking into the window upside-down.

"Come. These are good people, from the Outer City. They won't harm you. They'll protect you."

He could see the whole world go through that frightened expression in her eyes. Did she want to go back to being their queen? She had said she didn't, but she'd been very quiet the last few days whenever the subject came up. She was scared, and lost, and too groomed for the position to do anything else.

She came out of the truck, took his hand and let him haul her on top of the roof, where the grey pre-dawn light silvered her face and her no-longer-white bear skin cloak.

There were gasps, and a stunned silence.

Then someone cried out, "It's the Queen!"

Several voices repeated the cry. "It's the Queen, it's the Queen. The Queen lives."

Isandor met Milleus' eyes over the heads of the crowd; his mouth was open. Isandor mouthed, *I'm sorry.*

Men climbed up on the truck and lifted both Isandor and Jevaithi onto their shoulders.

From his position, Isandor glimpsed a whole convoy of Chevakian trucks still coming into the camp through the broken fence, and soldiers trying to turn them around. Fights were again breaking out on the edge of the camp, and the Chevakian soldiers, too few in number, retreated. The southerners were throwing up barricades. Fires burned in some places, sending clouds of smoke through the camp.

But there was nothing Isandor could do about any of that. The people carried him and Jevaithi into a large tent, where many people sat on the ground. Mothers and children, older people, all huddled under cloaks. In here, it smelled of bodies and damp earth.

The young Brother Simo yelled, "Listen to me, people. There is good news! We have the Queen. The Queen is back!"

CHAPTER 3

SADY GUIDED the southern family in the direction of the main part of the house. He could hear Merni's voice in the kitchen, much calmer now. She would tell them what to do. Hopefully the bedroom in the guest wing was unaffected, and they could still use that. If they could sleep at all.

He went to get his dark winter coat and returned to the yard. By that time, Orsan had returned from taking the southern woman Loriane into the bedroom. He had also stocked up on weapons: he carried not just his guard's gun, but had retrieved his pistol. Sady and Orsan started combing the courtyard by walking in a grid pattern so as not to miss any clues. Farius joined them a bit later, carrying a torch in one hand and a pistol in the other. He was only a young fellow, an apprentice under Serran, twenty at most and with a face that retained some of the angles and bony corners of an adolescent. He would have had little practice with the weapon.

"Look here," Orsan said from the darkness.

Sady and Farius went to where Orsan kneeled on the pavement of the path that led to poor old Eseldus' statue. Sady had seen the dark trail of spots when he went out here, before he found the woman Loriane in the pavilion. Sady kneeled and reached out, but Orsan said, "Don't touch it."

"What is it? Looks like blood to me."

"Could be. Could be poison. We don't know until we investigate. Best to be safe."

Farius followed the trail which went halfway to the pavilion and stopped there.

Orsan crouched and examined the grass and the path and the small hedge and rockery adjacent to the path.

"See anything?" Farius asked.

Orsan shook his head. "It looks like he's just vanished at this spot."

"Didn't you hear the side gate?" Sady said. The gate was on the other side of the courtyard, with no clear sign of how the killer had crossed that distance.

Farius went over to the door and tried the handle. "It's locked." He hit the wood; it sounded solid. The door was fairly new; Sady remembered it being replaced about five years ago.

"That's strange. I swear I heard the door." Orsan's bushy eyebrows knitted together. "Any other way out?"

Farius raised the torch. The wall on the side was too high and there were no trees or features that would allow someone to climb it easily, or at least not without leaving tracks.

Farius searched the pavilion where Sady had found the southern woman and found nothing except the puddle of blood she had left. The pavilion had only doors into the garden and no access to the street.

"The only way someone could have escaped without having to go through the house is over that wall," Orsan said.

"Look, we're losing time," Sady said. "Let's just assume he got out over the wall without worrying about how he did it. Let's have a look on the other side."

Sady pulled out a key and turned the lock on the side gate. It creaked; the door was only opened when a lot of material needed to be carried into the garden and that hadn't happened since the end of winter.

The alley on the other side led past the walls and gates of neighbouring houses. In the past, these alleys were used by servants who, in those days, were not allowed to enter their family's house through the main door. These days, people used the side entrance only to cart rubbish away.

A wind gust tore between the buildings and blew all his hair to one side. Mercy, this biting wind didn't feel like summer at all.

Orsan and Farius came out as well. By the light of Farius' torch, they examined the paving and walls, but could see nothing that wasn't supposed to be there.

They were wasting time here. The killer would long since have fled. "Let's assume that he fled into this alley, which way would he have gone?"

"That way." Orsan gestured to the east, where low hills rose over the surrounding houses. "Any criminal would probably flee out of the city, rather than into it." He came out of the side gate, and shut the door behind him. Sady registered the noise, and tried to remember if he'd heard it earlier that night, when he'd been sitting in the kitchen. He didn't think so.

They walked through the alley. Farius with the light, Orsan clutching his pistol and Sady between them, his hand on the grip of his hunting rifle.

It was dark. The wind howled around corners and blew sand and leaves through the street. Farius' torch made long eerie shadows on walls. There was no sign of life anywhere on this night. Even the ground squirrels hid in their infernal burrows. The wind carried distorted sounds of the bell tower's hour chime. Then a single strike of the bell, the continued warning for Tiverians to stay indoors.

Sady remembered that before he left his office, he had been keen to look at the sonorics measurements for tomorrow morning. All things going well, the contamination should be going down now that the southerners and the trains had been cleaned.

Somehow, the world of the office and the doga seemed incredibly far away.

They continued through the deserted streets, seeing nothing and no one. A feeling of darkness grew inside Sady's heart. The killer had obviously long since fled, and walking around here was useless; they would not find him tonight. He was just about to suggest that they turn back—he was feeling guilty about not being at home at a time he could probably be more useful there—when there was a sound of footsteps in a nearby yard, and a bolt being shoved back.

Orsan held up his hand.

Farius slammed the dimmer over his torch and ducked into a

shaded alcove. Sady followed, pressing himself against cold stone. Orsan hid in a corresponding alcove on the other side of the alley. Sady heard the click-click of the cocking of Orsan's gun.

A bit further down the alley, a door opened. Two men came out, talking in relaxed voices just outside Sady's hearing. They wore long cloaks such as commonly worn by men from Tiverius' well-off families. Sady could only catch the occasional snatch of conversation. *Have to have a meeting . . . and . . . says it should be ready for review soon . . .* One man pulled the door shut behind them and they walked off, away from Sady, Orsan and Farius, all the while in oblivious conversation.

When they had gone, Orsan gave the sign to keep moving again.

"Who were they?" whispered Farius.

Orsan said, "People are allowed to use these alleys."

"But, there is a level one sonorics alarm active. People should avoid going outside."

"*We* are outside."

Point made. And Farius was right, too. It was strange.

They walked past the gate where the men had come out. Lights blazed in the yard and lit those parts of the house visible over the wall. The wind also carried the sound of many voices talking and laughing. Who would have a party on a night like this?

"Wait—isn't this the Lady Armaine's house?" Sady asked.

"Yes, it is."

Hadn't Orsan been turned back at the Lady Armaine's house because *she was away?* He stopped, studying the wall. The gate where the two men had come out was a double door, wide enough for a cart, but made from solid wood. "Any way we can look into the yard?"

"You'd have to climb the wall and we can't do that without a warrant," Orsan said.

"And who signs warrants?"

Orsan's eyes met his. Everything about his stance with his hands at his sides, the muscle moving in his jutting jaw and his heavy brow screamed defensiveness. "Aren't we here to find a killer?"

"Do you think we'll find anyone? Wherever he is, he's long gone."

"The city guards won't like if you go over their heads."

The city guards were the ones who normally applied for warrants, and the proctor approved them, not the other way around

"You are a member of the guard. You have a warrant as of now. If you want an official one, I'll write and sign it in the morning. Get me up on that wall. Over there, near the tree."

It was Farius who helped Sady climb up. Orsan stood back and watched. It was too dark for Sady to see his expression, but his silence probably meant that he didn't like it.

Dear Orsan was way too fond of the rules. These people had become so reliant on their inflexible bureaucracy.

Once he could see over the wall, Sady recognised the house with the large garden room where he'd met the Lady seated at her huge desk.

The room was brightly lit, and the doors wide open as they had been during Sady's visit. All the furniture had been moved to the sides to make place for rows and rows of chairs. There were a lot of people on these chairs, talking to each other, all of them wearing warm clothing as if prepared for the cold. They obviously knew of the Lady's propensity to have all doors and windows open. Sady recognised many people. Merchants, the doga's chief accountant and some of his staff. Destran, Alius, and a couple of young people who were probably students. Many in their work clothes, some dressed in dark clothing. So as to sneak in and out of the house through the back entrance without attracting attention?

Something happened at the back of the room that made people cheer and clap. A thin figure in a powder blue robe walked along the aisle between the seats, her hair piled in an enormous bun on top of her head. While she walked, Lady Armaine spread her hands, and many people reached out to touch them. She smiled and talked to them.

She reached the front of the room, faced the seated people and bowed. A man Sady didn't recognise wheeled a small table towards her. He was a young fellow, dressed in a black robe. He wore his hair tied back at the nape of his neck. His thin beard hung halfway down his chest. Sady couldn't see what was on the table he had brought, because two people at the side of the crowd blocked his view. They stood watching the proceedings, hands clasped behind their backs. The lady's guards, he guessed. They also had beards.

The lady lifted a gold-coloured cloth off the table. The object underneath radiated such a bright glow that washed colour from the surrounding furniture and people. What was that thing?

People cheered and clapped.

The guards shifted, and Sady saw that the table held a brightly glowing sphere on a stand about waist high.

He had seen these types of light in the houses of the rich in the City of Glass.

They were, his guides had explained to him, remnants of old technology that had been common under the reign of king Caldor. His guide had said these words with much disapproval on her face.

One by one, the people in the room came forward to touch the globe, bow, kiss their hand and return to their seat.

What was this strange group? Why would all these people care? They were Chevakians. Half the important senators were here.

Sady watched, but the queue was long and it didn't look like anything else would happen soon. He was getting cold, Orsan and Farius were waiting, and they had a killer to find, so he let himself down, his head reeling.

It seemed the Lady Armaine had her fingers everywhere in Tiverian politics.

"Anything interesting?" Farius asked.

"Puzzling," Sady said.

"Not the murderer," Orsan said.

Sady met Orsan's eyes, emotionless. Orsan had tried to dissuade him from looking in the yard. He had a discomforting thought: did Orsan know this party was going on? Did Orsan know why these people met here?

Sady's heart pounded. Doga guards worked for the doga, and not for individual senators. They swore to secrecy to protect the privacy of the senator they served. If that senator was preparing to challenge, his guard could not go to the rival senators and talk about any of the senator's recent meetings. Guards knew a lot, and never said anything, unless presented with a summons to a formal interview. And Sady was going to have to order such an interview. It troubled him especially that Destran was there, because that would make any investigation political in nature.

An uncomfortable silence lingered.

Farius said, oblivious to the tension, "I don't think we're going to find a trace of the killer tonight. It's much too dark, and he's been gone a long time. Maybe even went into the other direction."

"I agree," Orsan said.

"Yes, let's go." Sady's heart pounded. Interrogations were not his favourite. Orsan had been with him for a long time. He *should* be trustworthy.

"Home?" Farius asked.

"Yes. Lead the way," Sady said.

Farius uncovered the light and he and Orsan started walking.

At that moment, there was a muffled shout that came not from Lady Armaine's yard, but from the other side of the alley.

Sady stopped and whispered, "Orsan!" as loudly as he dared, and gestured for them to come back.

But Orsan and Farius had walked down the alley and didn't hear him.

They'd just passed a gate into the yard, this one a lacework of metal. Sady remembered glancing in, but had noticed anything out of the ordinary. Just the standard courtyard with central statue and clipped hedges.

Sady ran back, and was followed a moment later by Orsan. "In there," he whispered, and tried the gate. I was open.

"No, I go first," Orsan whispered and he gestured to Farius, who came with the torch.

Both men went into the yard, and Sady followed. There were no sounds other than the burbling of a fountain.

Then another snort, a cough and a sniff.

"Who's there?" Orsan lifted his gun.

Farius held the torch higher.

Long shadows trailed over the yard's walls. Clipped bushes made eerie shapes on the stuccoed walls.

"There," Orsan said, pointing to the far corner.

Behind the backs of both men, Sady saw little, but he could feel the tension in Orsan's voice. Farius raised his gun. Someone tried to run away, judging by the sound of shoes slipping on stone.

"Don't move," Orsan said.

Farius ran forward, and held his torch higher. "Here he is!"

In the corner of the yard stood a man who resembled a walking skeleton. Half his hair was missing, his skull a mess of weeping scabs.

His only remaining hair, a patch around his right ear, hung in dirty dreadlocks down the side of his head. His face, deathly pale, had deep scratches from which blood flowed freely. His shirt may once have been white, but now it was grey in parts that were not soaked in blood. In his hand he clutched a knife. In place of his other hand, he had a golden claw.

He stared into the light with wide eyes, his chest moving quickly in shallow breaths.

When Orsan came closer, he turned around with a panicked whimper, and tried to clamber up the wall. It was far too high and smooth for a healthy person to climb, let alone one as crazy and injured as this.

Orsan and Farius closed in. The man lunged at Orsan with the knife, but the attack was jerky and clumsy. Orsan avoided and deflected the slashing knife with ease. One hit with the butt of Orsan's gun and the knife clattered onto the paving. Sady bent to pick it up, but the hilt was slick with blood, so he pushed it with his foot, well out of the man's reach.

After a short struggle, the two guards had him tied up with the sleeves of his own shirt pinning his arms to his sides. The prisoner made no effort to fight or talk. His eyes were expressionless, the pupils tiny, and whites showing on all sides.

His ghost-like face made Sady shiver.

"I think we have our killer," Orsan said, pushing the man in front of him. He was barely panting. "Who are you?"

The man said nothing, and continued to stare out of those blue eyes. Southern. His felt trousers were definitely southern.

Orsan checked the man, rifling through pockets and patting the front and back of his pants. The prisoner didn't object to any of Orsan's searching. Orsan found nothing.

"Come on, who are you?"

The prisoner responded with silence.

Orsan snorted and picked up the knife and swung it in front of the man's face. "It this what you used to kill all those people?"

Nothing.

"Come on, come on." Orsan pushed him in the chest with a flat hand, and Orsan's hands were enormous. "Answer me when I ask a question."

The man stumbled back, but made no sound. His face showed not fear, but the distant, haughty arrogance of a madman. Not someone who regretted his deeds.

Orsan pushed him further back. "Who the fuck are you, and what were you doing sneaking around like this?"

Nothing.

Orsan hit him in the face. "Talk to me when I ask you a question. Why were you sneaking around with a knife, looking like you just killed someone?" He grabbed him by the collar of his filthy shirt—

"Wait," Sady said.

Orsan turned to him, and relaxed his grip on the prisoner's collar. His face glistened with sweat, his eyes were wild with anger. It was not a good time to be reminded of the fact that Orsan was half Sady's age, two heads taller and twice the width. Nor of the fact that prisoners often died "accidentally" in interrogations. Nor of the fact that Orsan, and other members of the guard, would certainly have had their fair share of involvement in those "accidental" deaths. And that these deaths were, if not entirely condoned, certainly not questioned by the doga.

Sady breathed out tension. "This man is southern. It's likely that he doesn't understand Chevakian. We should take him to the courthouse and let the guards interrogate him in the presence of an interpreter."

"What is there to interrogate? He has a knife and is covered in blood."

"I'd like to know: how did he get out of the camp, and why did he target my house in which southerners happen to be staying?"

Orsan gave an impatient snort, and shrugged.

"We don't know, and he can't tell us what he knows when he's dead. I want him in the courthouse prison, and I want him interrogated."

Orsan sighed. Some of the wild anger went out of his face. He wiped his upper lip with the back of his hand, and nodded. "Yes. Let's take him there." And a bit later, "I cared a lot for Serran, that's all."

Sady nodded, and the sadness of his loss again settled over him.

"Come," Sady said to Farius, whose young face showed a wide-eyed expression. He was probably afraid that he had been about to witness his first killing. "Let's take him to the jail."

He met the prisoner's eyes and noticed that he didn't look so arrogant anymore. He was sure: despite his southern appearance and attire, this man understood every word he said.

Sady, Orsan and Farius went home after having made sure that the prisoner was securely locked up in a solitary cell.

The jail, that place of death, made Sady's skin crawl. One single corridor of cells for an entire city of criminals. Average stay, five days—he had seen the figures. Next stop, the court, and then the gallows room. High numbers of death sentences made sense in times of food shortages, but railways and farm machines had made life better for over thirty years. Nobody had thought to adjust the law.

All lights blazed at the house and two city guards stood at the porch before the closed door.

When Orsan pushed the gate open, both turned around. "Oh, there he is."

The guards turned to Sady with polite nods. "Proctor."

"You just arrived?" He was sure the guard had been called before he left the house. Had they taken this long to show up?

"Yes, sorry, Proctor, but we've been very busy tonight."

Sady remembered windblown and empty streets and was tempted to ask if that busy-ness involved games of dice, but he bit his tongue. He'd spent enough time feeling annoyed at the misguided "independence" of guards. "How long have you been waiting here?"

"Not too long."

The other guard nodded, but Sady had the impression it was longer than both wanted to admit. Where was Merni?

"Well," he said, trying not to let his worry show through. "We've had four people killed by what appears to have been southern madman. We've done the work for you, because we found him. He's already in the courthouse prison."

He almost enjoyed the shocked look on their faces. Served them right, playing games while on duty.

"Now all we need to do is find a newborn baby. I'm sure you can manage that."

"Sure." The guard completely missed Sady's sarcasm. "Could we see the scene of the disappearance of this baby?"

Sady led the men through the house to the guest quarters, where someone had lit a couple of lamps, although there was no one in the room. The harshness of full lighting made the horrors worse. There were smears of blood on the carpets, furniture and walls. The glistening blob of unidentified tissue on the floor looked like bloodied entrails. One of the guards told him that it was, in fact, an afterbirth. It seemed that the child had been born normally and that the madman had come afterwards.

Then a chilling thought: what if the madman had been part of the family? The large window had shattered outward because most of the glass was in the yard. Sady had asked for Loriane and the members of her family to be taken to the house. He'd thought it was the right thing to do, rather than splitting them up. He thought there had been the woman, the man, and the girl and the infant. But he could not be entirely sure. He'd been too busy to take note.

The thought made him sick and made him realise that he did not understand these people and their strange habits.

And because he'd thought to be *charitable*, four good Chevakians were dead.

He sat on the couch, clenching his hands in his pockets, staring at the form covered in a sheet that was Lana's body, while the guards combed the room.

Mercy, if they were dead through his fault.

He stared at the carpet, his eyes sore with fatigue or tears or both. Somewhere in the distance, a man and a woman argued.

The guards studied everything, and wrote down notes. They asked Sady what he had seen, which wasn't much. They approved for the bodies of the surgeons to be taken away.

Farius came in not much later. "The people from the hospital are here."

Sady rose, feeling dizzy. Farius had held up remarkably well, seeing his young age and inexperience, but now his face looked pale and haggard.

"Go to bed as soon as you can," he said.

"Do you think I could sleep?"

Sady let the question hang between them and sighed.

"Try for the sake of the household," Sady said. "We'll need you more than ever."

"Yeah," Farius said and his eyes glittered briefly. "Merni's not so good."

Pieces clicked into place. "That was her shouting a little while back?"

Farius nodded. "She refused to make the southern family tea. It was their fault that Lana was dead, she said. I tried to calm her, but she's hysterical about it."

Sady closed his eyes. "That's not . . . particularly helpful."

"No. I said that, too. Didn't make her listen, though."

"Where is she?"

"She went into her room and slammed the door. Hasn't come out, not even to open the front door when the guards came."

Great. One more thing to deal with. "I'll deal with the hospital people first."

Farius left and two men and a woman came into the room, the woman and one of the men in hospital uniforms. The other man carried a rolled-up stretcher.

The woman bowed and greeted him. Her face was anxious, her eyes brimming with tears.

"I'm sorry for the loss of your colleagues," Sady said. He felt helpless. Tomorrow, he'd have to face Lana and Serran's families with the same news.

She nodded, pressing her lips together. Her chin trembled.

Sady put a hand on her shoulder, not feeling so steady himself. "If there is anything I can do . . ."

"Is it true you caught the killer?"

"We think so."

"Why would anyone do something like this?"

Sady shook his head, thinking of the mad youth and his unfathomable black eyes.

"It's just . . . incredible. We don't have many people like them," she said. "We can't miss their experience, especially with all those refugees in the camps. Why would someone kill people who are doing so much good work?"

Sady spread his hands. He didn't know. He didn't understand either. Yet the look in the woman's eyes was accusing, as if it was his fault that her colleagues were dead. And to an extent, it was. *He* had brought the southerners here; *he* had insisted that the surgeons treat the woman. To add insult to injury, his intervention appeared to have been unnecessary because the child had been born normally.

He felt fragile, crumbling under pressure and fatigue. *I was only trying to help.* Why? Because he'd met the woman Loriane's eyes across a seething, disgusting mass of people on a crowded train platform, and had *felt sorry for her.*

The three busied themselves putting the closest body on the stretcher.

Having nothing more to do, Sady slouched down the corridor to his bedroom. Tears rolled over his cheeks.

CHAPTER 4

CARRO STARED out the window in a little bay off the wide corridor of the farmhouse that was the Eagle Knight's base. Large rooms to the left and right were dormitories, each with eight or ten beds. His fellow Knights slept there, in stuffy rooms designed to sleep only two or three people, but he had been tossing and turning on his mat until he grew too annoyed to pretend he was asleep.

The courtyard outside was dark and quiet. Eagles slept in their shed, a low open-walled building on the other side of the courtyard. Carro couldn't see them from here under the dark overhang of the roof.

He'd made this little alcove his work space, with a flat piece of wood that looked like it had started life as a door for a desk and two narrow shelves for the books. It looked homely and tidy, and reminded him of his sleeping shelf at home in the Outer City. Except that little homely space no longer existed, and the books stashed under his bed were gone, those books he and Isandor had risked much to acquire. The books his sister scoffed at, and his father—no, he meant the merchant—had threatened to burn.

Just what had happened in the City of Glass?

A candle flapped with the draught that came in through the cracks where the window didn't close properly.

He'd been sitting here since midnight, going over the documents that Rider Cornatan had given him in preparation for future negotiations with the Chevakians. The books about Chevakia were interesting, although he could not hope to remember everything about the Chevakian council—doga they called it.

He had more trouble with the hand-written notes from Rider Cornatan.

They said things like, *The Eagle Knights have been destroyed by this disaster, and there are but a few left.*

"That's a lie," he had said to Rider Cornatan while walking in the courtyard that evening.

Rider Cornatan had stopped and faced him, so that the light from the lamps around the farmhouse's courtyard lit his eyes. "The Chevakians don't know that."

His father smiled, and his expression held pity. He stood in his typical proud position, with his thumbs tucked in the metal loops at the chest strap of the riding harness. Another disconcerting fact Carro had found out since coming to Chevakia: his father did still ride. He had a magnificent bird that parted the air like the sharpest sword and had never been housed with the other eagles and therefore Carro had never seen it before. He flew it steady as if he'd been born on the back of the bird, with just the stirrups and reins. The saddle weighed the bird down too much, he said.

And it made Carro feel inadequate and clumsy. He needed the saddle.

He pushed the books aside, heaving a sigh.

Was he meant to accept these lies without comment? Was there any truth in anything Rider Cornatan said, even to his own son?

Go to the Chevakians, pup. Pretend that you're the most senior Knight left. Tell them lies as if they're idiots.

Carro leant his head in his hands.

Lies, lies.

He didn't want to be a leader, not even a fake one. He hated to be told to do things he didn't understand, or things he didn't want to do. Or things he understood how to do, but didn't understand why he had to do them. Or things he could do but disagreed with why he had to do them. Not just disagreed, but thought they were fundamentally wrong.

There, up on the wall opposite the window bay was the Eagle

Knight's crest with the motto. *Obedience, honour, honesty, humility and silence.* Those five words haunted him to no end.

What was the honour in killing people who couldn't defend themselves, like Isandor and Jevaithi? Where was the honesty in hiding yourself behind a fake leader who had no real power, but whose only function was to give an impression of weakness? And where was the humility in assuming you were worth more than others, like the people from the Outer City, who were in the Chevakian camps? That you were worth so much more, that you could disregard their lives as if they were rats. Silence, there was plenty of that. Codes of silence amongst the Knights were everywhere. You did not tell on your mates. Not even if they did terrible things.

Obedience was the one that worried him most. All his life he'd obeyed. He'd obeyed the merchant by changing the books for the sake of the tax collector. He'd obeyed his father in going with the hunters, and helping them set fire to the houses of innocent farmers. In his sleep, he heard their screams. Obeying had given him nothing but trouble. Obeying had made him betray the only person who had ever cared about him, because he hoped that his father would be genuinely happy with him.

Yet, did he have a choice? That was always the question.

"Hey, there's not much privacy in those dorms, huh?"

Carro gasped and turned around.

It was Nolan, sneaking up from behind. The bluish light from outside silvered his curls and made his eyes glitter. He pressed himself against Carro's back and gently folded his arms around Carro's shoulders. "We see so little of you these days. I miss you whenever we fly out. It gets boring watching Farey and Jeito fool around."

"Yeah—uhm—I've been really busy. What have you been up to?" He wished he could fob Nolan off with some sort of excuse. He wished he never, ever said yes to his advances.

"Not much. Keeping an eye on this crowd of Chevakians where the Queen is. Can't do anything until they're on the move again. Maybe not even then. She'll be in the city. Too many people there. But we'll keep an eye on her. Me, I've been patrolling. On foot, by the skylights. Talk about boring."

The camps. Someone in the Chevakian army had thought it was a good idea to build a camp for the refugees who had come on the trains from the City of Glass. Trouble was, they'd built it in the middle of the road that led to one of the southern provinces. And those silly Chevakian vehicles were too heavy to travel on sand or anything that was not a paved road. For days, the Chevakian refugees had built up on the other side of the fence. They all knew that Isandor and Jevaithi were in that crowd, protected by a mass of Chevakian people and out of the Knights' reach.

"Come. Enough talking," Nolan whispered and pulled Carro up.

Carro cringed; his skin tensed with dread for what would happen next, anticipating the touch of Nolan's sweaty fingers under his shirt.

Obedience. He could not say no without consequences worse than what he wanted to avoid, but oh, how did he want to avoid it.

Nolan led him to the linen cupboard where it was dark and musty and where it smelled of soap and freshly-washed sheets. He lifted Carro's shirt over his head and let it whisper to the floor. "I really want you."

His breathing sounded loud in that silence. He pulled Carro into his embrace. His mouth closed over Carro's. He tasted like cheap bloodwine and smelled of sweat. There was nothing tender about his kiss. Nolan's wet lips slobbered over what felt like half his face. Carro fought to repress his desire to shove Nolan away, a feeling that became stronger every time Nolan touched him.

"You seem so quiet when we meet these days," Nolan whispered.

Carro glanced out the door of the laundry cupboard into the corridor. He hoped someone would come. "I guess I'm nervous. We're not alone in this place. What if someone comes? Are you sure it's the right thing to do?"

"Why do you always bring that up? I've told you so many times: no one cares. This is how we look after each other. Like wolves."

Once, Carro had found that term interesting. Now, the word made him sick. He had enough of being pestered by Nolan every night. Were you allowed to say that you found sex disgusting and smelly, and that it felt too much like rape to be nice or comfortable, that it flat out didn't interest you?

"Come on, relax." Nolan's hand found its way between Carro's waistband and his skin. His hands went over his naked buttocks. He pushed Carro's pants down and pressed himself against Carro's back.

Carro felt the slimy hardness of his cock. A wave of despair washed over him. How could he stop this without appearing soft, without making an enemy of Nolan? He'd asked himself that question so many times, and had not yet found an answer. He liked Nolan, but not like this. He hated how his body betrayed him and feigned emotions he did not feel. Regardless of how much he hated the invasiveness of Nolan's touch, there was always a point where what he wanted no longer mattered as long as Nolan made him come, and Nolan was good at that. But afterwards, when the high ebbed and Nolan whispered soft words of love and believed that he enjoyed it, the shame set in. He didn't know how to break that cycle.

There were fast footsteps in the hallway. Someone called out, "Carro?"

"Shit," Nolan whispered and ducked into the back of the laundry. Carro hoisted up his pants, slipped out of the cupboard and sat down at his makeshift desk, his heart thudding. He recognised the voice: his father. He had never been able to work out whether the Knights condoned or punished sexual relationships between each other. His gut feeling told him that it didn't fall under *honour*, and that, if a superior didn't like you, it could be used as a reason for punishment. But that it usually wasn't. Only that rape was used *as* punishment, and that some superiors enjoyed it.

"Working hard?" Rider Cornatan joined Carro in the alcove. If he noticed the door to the store room moving, then he didn't show.

"Uhm—yeah." His heart was still going like crazy.

Rider Cornatan leaned over the makeshift desk and leafed through the book on Chevakian government. "Interesting, isn't it?"

"Uhm—yeah." Carro struggled to remember what he'd been doing.

Rider Cornatan turned around and fixed Carro with a penetrating stare. Carro felt like his father looked straight through him, saw his weird relationship with Nolan, and disapproved. All sorts of excuses were on his tongue *I don't want it either*, and *He came to me, and I didn't ask him*. But they felt like that: excuses, making him look like a spineless dud, which, by all accounts, he was.

"We may be moving in sooner than we thought."

Moving in? Moving where? Rider Cornatan made it sound like a military operation. They had no hope of gaining control of anything with the few Knights at the farmhouse. There might be a few hundred of them, but that was not an army. "I thought you wanted me to go and talk to the Chevakians."

"Yes, but the time is not right for that now. There is no reason why the Chevakians would want to talk to us. We need to give them a reason first before you'll get the talk you're so looking forward to. I have another job for you and your hunters to do first."

By the skylights, another job with the hunters? He'd barely seen Jeito and Farey since they had arrived here. He'd presumed that part of his task was over. Jeito would kill him if he came too close to her.

"We have reliable reports that the Queen is indeed in the refugee camp and has made herself known to the people. Unfortunately, a large percentage of the camp population is made up of rogues."

"Uhm—rogues?"

"The Brotherhood of the Light. The trains that came from Fairlight are full of them."

That made sense. Most of the survivors from the explosion were from the Outer City. "But I thought you said that the Chevakians had isolated the camp and we didn't need to worry about those people?"

"The Chevakians did, but there has been a development overnight which is unexpected and we might call interesting. A number of Chevakian civilians broke into the camp from the south. The official line is that they thought the camp was for them and grew tired of waiting to be let in. But since we have good evidence that the Brotherhood has its fingers through much of the Chevakian doga, I wouldn't be surprised if the so-called southern Chevakian refugees included a good number of Brotherhood supporters."

Carro nodded. His close examination of the farm's accounts had shown that. By all evidence, the manager had sided with the Brotherhood and that was why he had left the place in chaos as soon as the Knights had arrived, taking the important financial records with him. "But I still don't understand why Chevakians would support them. Icefire kills them."

"You tell me, son, I have no idea either, but clearly, over the years that the ex-royals have lived here, they've built up quite a following and have convinced a good number of important Chevakians of the amazing things that can be done with icefire. It would sound stupid that Chevakians would believe that, except there are now claims that they have found some sort of medicine that allows Chevakians to withstand icefire." His voice was grave.

"Isn't that a good thing? I mean—if it doesn't kill Chevakians anymore then we don't need to worry so much about it?"

"Have you learned nothing from all I've told you?" Rider Cornatan's voice was fiercer than it had ever been, even when Carro had deserved a scolding.

Carro retreated outside the immediate pool of light cast by the lamp. He could imagine Nolan trying to stifle laughter in the cupboard.

"Think of it, son," he said, his voice low. "Us Pirosians are at a disadvantage because we can neither see nor use icefire, so the Thilleians can use it against us without our notice until it is too late. Chevakians, with or without medicine, can also not see it. Now their barriers have broken. If the Chevakians allow the Brotherhood to start using icefire, they won't care, because it no longer harms them, and they don't believe that icefire is more than the energy in air particles which they can measure. Everyone might live peacefully for a while, but ultimately, someone starts using icefire for the purpose of gaining power again. For making servitors who do their master's bidding. Icefire is an excellent device for changing someone's mind. I hope your reading about Chevakia has at the very least impressed upon you that their society relies on people speaking their minds." Oh, he was angry now. He took in a deep breath through flaring nostrils and continued, "From all reports, it looks like we will be unable to return to the City of Glass for some time, so this affects us, too. The Chevakians simply won't know what hit them, and we will be too few to fight this evil for them. The important Chevakians will be under the influence of those who can use icefire and will side with the Brotherhood. Son, those barriers that were broken after the explosion need to go up again as soon as possible or the entire of this country, as well as our own, will be our enemy."

"But if they have this medicine, the Chevakians won't need the barriers anymore."

"Exactly, and that's why we can't wait any longer. We must act against the Brotherhood now. Before that medicine is a reality."

Act? Like how? A chill went over Carro's back, as he imagined

Rider Cornatan's plans, most of them involving innocent refugees' lives, and none of them nice.

"And this is where your task comes in." Rider Cornatan licked his lips. "We've had a problem with communication."

Oh?

Again, Rider Cornatan waited for what seemed a long time before continuing. "A messenger was supposed to have come in by now." He looked into the corridor, which was just as empty as it had been before, and his gaze lingered on the half-closed door of the linen cupboard, as if he realised that it was usually wide open. "We are not the only surviving Knights. There are a lot more of us. I ordered other units to hide at our field bases, because to bring this many of us into Tiverius would arouse the suspicion of the Chevakians. But now, with the new developments in the camp, we'll need all of us here."

"How many have survived?" Carro thought of Jono and Caman and the other bullies he had left behind in the City of Glass, and he had assumed dead. There had been thousands of Knights at the Eyrie.

"Most of us were able to get out, thanks, in part, to the fact that a good number of us were on duty at the Newlight festival."

And that was not a coincidence, wasn't it? Carro had spent a lot of time thinking about the machinery he had seen in the dungeons below the city, and what Rider Cornatan had been doing there. And the fact that no one seemed keen to explain what had caused the explosion.

A chill went through him. Ever since the fall of the king, the Knights had tried to destroy the Heart of the City, first by taking apart the machine—which they couldn't—and then by dragging it underground and encasing it in sheets of metal. But it was a self-containing energy source, even when disconnected from the wires that fed it. Having failed to dismantle the machine, Rider Cornatan had decided to experiment with the power. Had it exploded during some sort of experiment?

"The other units of our army are spread over a couple of locations, the most important one of which is directly south of here. However, I haven't heard from them, and we should have, by now."

He unrolled a piece of paper on the desk. It was a map with marked on it, Chevakia's southern border, the mountainous region with the cliff-surrounded town they called Solmeni, and a couple of black connecting stripes that were train lines. Rider Cornatan pointed. "They should be here. I sent some scouts to check up on them a while ago, but haven't heard from them either. I want you to go there." His finger rested on a town called Twin Bridges. "And then track south from there. Look for a small abandoned woodcutters' village surrounded by forest. Last we heard was that there were storms and fires in that region. They may have kept the eagles inside to stop them panicking."

But Carro could hear in his voice that he didn't believe that. A well-trained eagle didn't skitter that easily. Somehow, the messengers had not come through. They might have fallen into the hands of the Chevakians. Or something else . . .

How far away was this, and where was the location where he had seen the giants made of fire before falling from his bird?

He couldn't possibly tell his father about them. Pirosians were not meant to see things like that. But that had to have been much further south and surely, icefire wouldn't reach this far into Chevakia.

"I want you to go there and return with the army." Rider Cornatan met his eyes with a penetrating look.

Carro tried to read the meaning in those grey eyes, but all he could see was the hardness of his expression and the cold calculating look.

CHAPTER 5

ITHIN MOMENTS of Isandor and Jevaithi having entered the tent, Simo started ordering people about. Some men dragged a mat into the middle. Two other men placed a crate on top, which they covered with furs.

Simo bowed. "Here you are, Your Highness. We don't have much, but we give you the best we have."

The crate made a cosy little bench. Jevaithi sat down, and Isandor followed, with the weight of many stares on him, as if the people questioned his right to sit next to her. He took her hand, cold and clammy. His heart beat like crazy in her chest.

Her gaze darted over the seated audience, as if she expected Rider Cornatan to emerge from the crowd any moment.

Several people dressed in black stood out in the audience, the men with beards. They were, like Simo, Brotherhood of the Light.

It felt absurd, sitting here while he could hear fights going on in the rest of the camp.

She went on in Chevakian. "Who are these people in black?"

"The Brotherhood of the Light. They run schools and orphanages in the Outer City. They are known to support the old royal family. They often sell and collect old things from the palace."

She frowned. "Is Tandor one of them?" Still in Chevakian.

Isandor shrugged, feeling uncomfortable. He didn't know for certain either, and disliked to be reminded of Tandor. What *did* the

Brotherhood do, other than teach poor orphans things that the Knights didn't think they should learn? He'd considered them to be a quaint relic of the old royal family in a quiet, unassuming sort of way.

Meanwhile, people streamed into the tent. Simo yelled at them to sit down around the makeshift throne. Jevaithi sat with her back straight. Isandor wondered where Milleus was. People raised their eyebrows at him, whispered to each other while looking at him. Simo gave him annoyed glances.

Soon, the questions came.

How had Jevaithi escaped, since the palace itself had been completely destroyed?

Did she know the whereabouts of Rider Cornatan and the senior command of the Knights?

Were there any other southern refugees with the Chevakian convoy?

"Quiet!" Simo yelled over the cacophony. "Her Highness will answer questions one by one."

Isandor wondered what gave Simo the right to boss everyone around. It seemed like everyone in the camp accepted him as leader. Was it because he was loud, and no one else had volunteered, or for some other reason?

"I would like to ask you some questions first," Jevaithi said, and although she hadn't spoken loudly, talk stopped immediately, and all those people fell into an expectant silence. Many faces displayed bright expressions of hope.

Simo bowed. "By all means, Your Highness."

But Simo's voice betrayed a measure of annoyance. Maybe Simo hadn't expected Jevaithi to return at all, and he was irritated at her taking his leadership position.

Jevaithi asked, "Are there any Knights in the camp?"

"We don't think so, Your Highness," a woman said. "The guards are all Chevakians."

"There was a Knight at the station," a man said. "We chased him off."

Some people laughed.

When it was quiet again, Jevaithi said, "Some Knights have survived. I've seen them, they've been following us. A group of hunters tried to kill me."

Several people in the audience gasped.

Isandor wanted to say, *But not all Knights are like that. I was a Knight, and most of them are honourable.* Instead he jammed his hands between his knees and said nothing as the ex-citizens of the City of Glass recounted wrongs done by the Knights. He thought of Carro, who would probably be dead by now, and was sure Carro was honourable, or had been honourable, under his veneer of despair to be liked by others.

The perimeter of the tent had filled up with people, and extra onlookers were trying to cram into the tent entrance, but there was no room for anyone to move and still more people were trying to get in. People lifted children onto their shoulders, held lovers on their laps, and leaned on others while standing on tiptoe at the back. Everyone looked at Jevaithi. By the frowns on their faces, everyone wondered who Isandor was, and why a *cripple* ex-Knight should be with *their* queen. Isandor wanted to run. All this *Your Highness* business was starting to get on his nerves.

It was time for Jevaithi to tell her story. In that clear-voiced way of hers, she told the people how the Knights had been worried about something afoot in the palace on the morning of the explosion, of secret dialogue between Rider Cornatan and his senior-ranked officers. She told them how she was sure that the Knights were doing something unusual. That was because she could feel icefire, but she didn't tell anyone that. She told them how none of the Knights would tell her what was going on, and that Rider Cornatan hadn't wanted her to go to the Newlight festival.

That was because the Knights had *wanted* Jevaithi to be killed, someone in the audience yelled. Because they knew the explosion would happen and they expected Jevaithi to be one of the victims. There was much cheering after this, and Isandor grew more angry. That was just *not* true. The Knights adored Jevaithi.

Next she talked about her life. How she lived practically in a prison, of turning sixteen and how she'd been wanting to escape from the palace to dance with normal boys during the Newlight Festival. She showed them her missing hand. That earned some gasps, but many others said that they had always known. Those people were mostly Brothers in black.

Simo said, "We have saved many children. There is not one family in the Outer City that isn't secretly mourning an Imperfect-born child." After some cheers, he concluded, "This idiocy has to stop."

Several people shushed him and urged Jevaithi to keep talking.

She told them of Rider Cornatan's refusal to hand over power and to let her sit on the Knights' Council. Of his insistence that she wear stupid, gauze-thin clothes that made the Junior Knights drool over her body. Of his constant threats to rape her.

Everyone went very quiet when she said all these things.

A woman at the front cried and said they'd never known. She would have done something had she known.

"No one could do anything," Jevaithi said. "I was surrounded by Knights all day."

Then she told them how she'd wrangled the trip to the Newlight Festival out of Rider Cornatan, of attending the races and of that confusing night in the Outer City, when, after choosing the champion and the escape of the Legless Lion Isandor was meant to kill, she couldn't go back to the palace because the bears and the driver of her sled had been murdered. She told them how an unseen form, a blue-skinned servitor, had tried to kill her, and how she had escaped, with the young apprentice Knight whom she had chosen as champion and his servitor Legless Lion. At this point everyone looked at Isandor and their expressions showed that they had added up the facts.

There was no icefire here to hide the fact that he was Imperfect. They stared at his leg, and increased the size of the circle around him. He was sleeping with *their* queen. They didn't want him. It was acceptable for the Queen to be Imperfect, but a random boy—no. But to his surprise, someone said, "Hurray for Isandor."

A number of people cheered, and some clapped, and a man behind him put a meaty hand on Isandor's shoulder. Isandor turned and saw that the man was a Brother, dressed in black. His eyes twinkled with mirth. "Anyone but that shrivelled prune will do as father for the next queen. I hope you gave it your best."

He laughed, but Isandor felt angry. So that was it, now? That was his function? As Outer City boy, they probably thought he was not smart enough for anything else. He wanted to tell them that he knew how to read and speak Chevakian, but that would make him look stupid.

While Jevaithi told the listeners how they had come here with

Milleus and what had happened on the way, he drew his knees up to his chest and looped his arms around them, feeling the wood of his missing leg bite into his buttocks.

The people, mostly citizens of the Outer City or Bordertown, told their stories, of a massive explosion in the City of Glass, of a ring of icefire expanding outwards, of the shattering of the Chevakian barrier, of the forest fires, and the harrowing trip in the train.

People held conflicting opinions about what had caused the explosion.

"It was the Knights," one said.

"No, it was a servitor," someone said, and others argued and suggested that cycles of icefire happened by themselves.

"There were many servitors," a woman said. "Big shapes made from icefire, destroying everything in their path."

"Those were not servitors," a man said, and people argued about what exactly servitors were, which no one seemed to know, apart from the fact that they had no hearts and obeyed their masters blindly.

"The city is a mess," one man said. "Most of the buildings were destroyed that I could see. No one will be going back there in a hurry."

"But why were you not safe even in Bordertown?" Jevaithi asked.

"After the explosion, these . . . people, servitors, things, whatever you want to call them, made of icefire came out of the ground. They formed a bubble of icefire that expanded outwards."

A woman said, "Yes, and those things were still following us off the plateau. Setting fire to the forest."

Jevaithi looked at Isandor, her eyes wide. "I don't even understand what they're talking about. Shapes of icefire?"

Isandor shrugged. His knowledge from books failed him. He'd never read about anything like that.

Simo took up a stance with his hands behind his back and his legs slightly apart, as if he was teaching. He said, "We're fighting icefire itself. Through the Knights' trying to stifle it, it has become so strong that it has burst from the ground and has taken possession of people's bodies. Somebody did something to those people and they're angry with us."

The woman said, "And these monsters have taken possession of our city? Are they ever going to leave?"

"We may have to fight," Brother Simo said, spreading his hands in a grandiose gesture, as if fighting was something glorious.

A man said, "How would you fight beings of icefire anyway? You can't."

Isandor was tempted to jump up and tell them that all knowledge on icefire held in the City of Glass was based on myth and that there was no proof for any of the things in Simo's conclusions, but he had no proof to the contrary either, and he was sure most of these people here would support Simo. Who'd listen to a boy whose only task was to fuck the queen and get her pregnant?

The debate carried on around him.

Simo said, "Someone unleashed this power, so there must be a way it can be defeated. Icefire can be collected. Sinks do that. We need sinks. Lots of them."

Then there was debate about what sinks were. It was all so futile. They didn't have sinks, and if icefire was strong enough to blow up buildings, no number of sinks of the type the Eagle Knights had was going to have any influence.

Isandor glowered over his drawn-up knees at Simo's back and the people seated around the makeshift throne. Faint sounds of shouting and crashes came from outside. He wondered where Milleus was.

Jevaithi's eyes met his briefly. Her expression looked resigned, and that made him even more angry.

"What he says is all rubbish," he said to her in a low voice, in Chevakian. "Milleus' brother knows more about how icefire works than these people."

"These Brothers have a lot of support," Jevaithi said, her eyes wide.

"Yes, these people believe anything. Just because a Brother says so doesn't mean it's true. We should say something."

"Please, let's make sure we are safe first—"

"We can't be safe until this type of idiocy ends. We have to speak out or they will be just as bad as the king was, or the Knights—" All of a sudden, his voice was the only one in the tent.

Brother Simo had turned around and everyone watched Isandor. Their looks were suspicious. A worthless Outer City boy was one thing, but a worthless Outer City boy who spoke Chevakian to their Queen? Outrageous.

Yes, he got the message.

He unlooped his arms from his knees and rose, awkward because he placed his wooden leg on someone's boot and he nearly tripped.

In the silence, he said, "We should not make up our minds while no one knows what is going on and what caused the explosion. I think there is someone who may know more about it. The master of the blue servitor that killed the bears and the driver is a middle-aged man named Tandor. He does not live in the City of Glass, but he poses as a travelling merchant." Tandor, his mother's lover. He saw a sudden flash of his mother coming out of the door to the inner room of the limpet. The expression on her face was one of worry. Emotion threatened to overwhelm him. He finished with a lame, "Has anyone seen him in the camp?"

An older Brother near the entrance said, "I think I know the one you mean. Wasn't he the fellow collecting old stuff in the Outer City?"

"That would be him," Isandor said. "Have you seen him since leaving the Outer City?"

"No, sorry."

"I think he was on the train," a woman said.

Another said, "No, I know the one you mean, but I didn't see him."

"Yes, he was here," the original woman said. "But he was badly burned. He was with a family, and they got taken away to some medical place, I heard."

"That can't be him. Tandor doesn't have a family," Isandor said.

Simo sniffed. "How can one man make such a difference?"

"He asked me to be his apprentice." People gave him odd glances. Some expressions were clearly annoyed. Feeling the situation slip from his control, Isandor continued, "Before all this happened, he came into the Outer City with a servitor, and tried to recruit me for his plans."

"Why you?" Simo asked, in a who-do-you-think-you-are kind of way.

"Because he saved the lives of many Imperfect children put out on the ice floes. I'm one of those he saved."

Simo held his gaze briefly, and those eyes were full of pity, before turning away to talk to Jevaithi about people in the camp, and how her wish was his command.

Jevaithi answered him politely. Why didn't she see that Simo had no intention of giving up his position?

What did she know, having been locked up in the palace all that time? Knights or Brothers were all the same: they only wanted power. Failing power, they'd suck up to someone who had status, just so that they could grovel their way up.

He pushed himself off the bench. Why ever had he introduced Jevaithi to these people? Why had he even agreed to come with Milleus? There was no need for them to flee advancing icefire. They should have let Milleus go alone. Offered to look after his farm, so that they could learn to be farmers.

"Where are you going?" Jevaithi asked.

"Out," Isandor said, and he knew he sounded angry and Chevakian was an excellent language for being angry.

"What's going on? I thought you agreed with these people?"

"These people are idealists, and they won't stop poking the Knights until they hit back."

"I thought you'd been betrayed by the Knights."

"I was betrayed by *one* Knight."

"I can't believe you're saying this, after Knights tried to kill us. The Brotherhood is for the people."

"And who is to say they won't form another group that will end up just as evil as the others? I want to know what they stand for. What do they believe in? What do they want?"

"Who cares? All of those ideals are useless if we can't go back to the City of Glass. The Brotherhood wants to help us."

"They don't. They want power. They're annoyed that we've turned up."

"That's nonsense. They're helpful and courteous."

"You're too trusting. The Knights aren't the only ones with dicks to rape you."

Her eyes widened and Isandor cringed. That was a tactless remark, but, her naivety was so infuriating.

"You are so suspicious."

"That comes with living on the streets. You should try it once."

Her nostrils flared. "Are you saying that I am dumb?" Her eyes flashed with true anger that made him feel chilled inside.

"No, I'm not. I'm just—" Although in a way, that was the translation of what he'd implied. She was so innocent as to be a danger to herself. She had always been protected by Knights.

"Yes you are. Don't you think that living with the threat of being raped every day does nothing to you? Do you think that I have been living an easy life?"

"I never said that." But she'd known no hunger, no worry of disease.

"Yes, you did. What do you want us to do then? We can't be farmers. We can't hide. These people need our help. They are *our* people."

"I never said they weren't and that we shouldn't help."

"Then what? What is your problem?" She spread her hands in a frustrated gesture.

People watched. There was sure to be someone who understood some Chevakian.

Isandor started to say *I don't like being treated as a nobody* or, *I'm not just a dick with a pair of eyes* but that sounded stupid and selfish, and it wasn't really that. It was that he didn't like all the men in black, and didn't like their mysterious organisation. They had the crowd just as much under control as the Knights had, only people seemed to willingly subject to them, and he was angry about that, because he'd thought people would be smarter than that, after so many years of repression by the king or the Knights.

Jevaithi repeated, louder now, "Come on, tell me, what is your problem?"

"Shhh, calm down," he said.

She whirled to him. "No. I've had enough of being treated like I'm a toddler."

"All right, all right, I'm going." He gave a mock bow. "Your Highness." He left the tent, but his legs were trembling and his heart—her heart—was beating like crazy. Why couldn't she understand him?

CHAPTER 6

WHEN THE LARGE mob of southerners carried the youngsters off amongst the tents, relative quiet returned to the hillside on the south side of the camp. With no illumination, and a heavy cloud cover blanketing the sky, it was pitch dark.

The remaining Chevakians gathered by the light from their trucks. Squally wind brought cheers of many voices, presumably from the southern tents. News came that the soldiers had repaired the fence, although the soldiers appeared to have vanished. Milleus could make out a faint glow of light uphill, at the spot where they had entered the camp. He also thought he could hear the sounds of wood being chopped. So someone had finally used their brains and was cutting a road through the forest, or more likely, widening an existing track, so that the people behind the fence could move. He was unsure how many Chevakians had made it into the camp with him, but the vast majority had turned around. The sight of soldiers had frightened them off, or maybe it had been the thought of contamination, or the fear of "magic" folklore ascribed to southern people. It disappointed him that so many people lacked the courage to push on.

For the remaining foolhardy Chevakians, too few to force their way out of their situation, there seemed nothing else to do but to stay put for what remained of the night. They arranged the trucks in a circle and pitched tents inside this circle. Some people had dogs, which they tied up on the outer periphery. As for himself, he had to fix the truck's tyres before he could do anything, but that didn't take long.

And then there was nothing more to do except pay homage to that old Chevakian saying, *If all else fails, make tea.*

"We're not going to sit here and do nothing," Milleus said.

They had gathered around the pot bubbling on the fire. Orange light danced on attentive faces. There were about thirty of them, twelve trucks besides Milleus', men and women, old and young, all of whom had been on the road for days. It was a mixed crew: there was a family of five with a child that needed medical attention, a young couple who had no money and knew no one in Tiverius, and were afraid of the cost of staying there, an elderly couple whose truck had a trailer that contained at least a hundred chickens, and two sisters who were looking for a brother who had travelled ahead of them on the Ensar road, but whom they had been unable to find in the crowd.

"Then what can we do?" said the man who had introduced himself as Artan, the owner of the chickens. The days on the road had left him with grey-flecked beard.

"We're going into Tiverius. Or at least any of you who want to come."

"But aren't you afraid that the soldiers—"

"The soldiers can go polish their guns and shine their boots. They cannot stop us travelling in our own country."

"Maybe not, but they have the guns."

"They will not fight Chevakians. It's in the charter of the army."

"How do you know that for sure? I'm not keen to be a test case."

"Because they will listen to me." And when everyone's eyes were on him, Milleus added, "Because I used to command them."

Milleus took the pot off the stove, added tea leaves and stirred, aware that everyone around the fire looked at him.

A man whispered, "Milleus han Chevonian?"

"The very one."

The man smiled, and some of the people started laughing.

"Milleus han Chevonian? In a southern refugee camp? With goats?" There was more happy laughter, and cheers.

"How did you end up here?" a woman asked.

"I run a farm now, and I'm rather attached to my goats. You won't find better milking goats anywhere in the country."

"Hey, let's drink to that!" A man called.

Someone brought glasses, and a bottle was passed around.

When it came to him, Milleus shook his head, the previous time that he'd drunk still vivid in his mind. At that time, he'd almost lost the youngsters. "I don't drink, thanks. But I do have some tea."

Glasses and cups were shared and a man carried an elderly grandmother to the fire. The old lady turned out to have been a great supporter of Milleus back when he was in power. "Best ever, best ever," she said, moving her lips with great flexibility in her toothless mouth.

Milleus smiled awkwardly, because hadn't been the best ever, and by being stupid when Sady came for him, he'd missed an opportunity to make a difference.

"So," said Artan. "How are we going to get out of this camp?"

"It was my plan to simply go up to the lower camp gate and tell the guards who I am. I guess they are likely to let me through. It may not be easy, and we may need to create a fuss, but they won't want to keep us in here, because the news that we're here will get out as soon as the others reach Tiverius and there will be a lot of questions about the mismanagement of this situation in the doga. So they will let us out, it they want to or not. And then when we're free, I'm going straight to the doga. I'm fed up with their incompetence. They are too disorganised to make sure emergency supplies of suits and salt pills were available in the regional towns, but no, keeping those supplies up-to-date would have been too easy. And now this debacle." Mercy, he was angry, about everything. Why were there no soldiers here to keep order? Why had they closed the road? Why had no one built a camp for the Chevakian refugees?

A woman asked, "Do you think anyone in the doga will listen? They're too busy with their regional squabbles, especially those from the north."

"They will listen, or I will make them. Before all this happened, my brother came to ask me to return to the doga. He said he had the necessary votes. I said no, let the past be the past. I should never have let him leave, but I should have gone, and we might not be in this mess we're now."

"You changed your mind?" The man sounded hopeful. He was older, and would remember Milleus' time in office.

"I had no idea of the severity of the situation."

A man said, "Destran is an idiot, letting all this happen. If the army can't control a couple of unarmed refugees, then what have we come to."

"It's not quite as simple as sending in the army. It is not an invasion of a foreign army. These are refugees. Everyone still alive from the City of Glass is here. Something happened there that destroyed the city."

"Their filthy magic," whispered a woman.

An uncomfortable silence followed. Many people glanced at Milleus, knowing that during his term, the doga had tried to stamp out the use of the word magic. Magic was fear. Magic was unknown, something no one understood. The Scriptorium had progressed to a different stage with sonorics. They understood it now. They could measure it. Sonorics was *not* magic.

But he had no energy for that debate.

"Magic or no, it doesn't matter what name you attach to it." Was this him talking? They must think he'd gone soft. "I don't know what else is going on, but I'm planning to push on into Tiverius, maybe tomorrow when we can see where we're going, and go into the doga. This camp, and the guards, is a shambles. Either the army keeps the refugees under control, or they don't. They'll need someone who makes the decisions."

One of the men clapped. "And get the southern knights out of our country. There have been too many sightings for them to be untrue."

"Shoot them down. Let the whole lot go back to their own country."

"We'll come with you."

"Tomorrow," Milleus said. "When it is light."

This satisfied the Chevakians, and people retreated to their trucks and tents to sleep.

But dawn was not that far off and Milleus felt too restless to sleep.

In the distance, he could see the city lights, turning the heavy cloud cover a sickly orange. He leaned on the railing of the pen and sighed. The hurt that started with the revelation that the delicate Nila was really the Queen of the City of Glass refused to go away. She was not just an innocent highborn girl. Both of the youngsters had played him, and he had been too dumb to see it, and worse, now he'd lost them and they never even found out who he was.

Both he and she could have put their contact to better use. What a waste of opportunity.

And damn it, he *still* liked the two of them.

To his right, a bit further down the hill, the sound of many voices came from the big tent. Well, they had what they wanted, although it was unclear to him exactly why they had fled. It didn't matter anymore. They were safe, and with this many people around, whoever had tried to kill the youngsters would not get a second chance.

It was just that . . .

To be honest, he wanted to return to the farm.

He didn't look forward to going back to Tiverius. There was too much unfinished business for him to attend to. Andrean and Kalius would have a few things to say to him, none of them nice. How he'd walked out on them, how he'd driven their mother to kill herself and then failed to even put up a plaque at her alcove where the jar with her ashes stood. Trouble was, he couldn't think of anything suitable that was also appropriate. He'd wanted to say, *I never loved you as much as you deserved, and I should have set you free.* But at the time, he couldn't stand the thought of Sady, young, smart and cocky Sady, getting his hands on her. While he was away, his brother was screwing his wife. So Suri was dead and Sady had never married. Had Sady ever touched a woman since?

He did *not* want to deal with this.

He stood there, leaning on the fence. The goats were all settling down for the night. The lights in the other Chevakian trucks and tents winked out one by one.

If he wanted to be gone tomorrow, he should go to bed. The time that he could work through the night unaffected had gone with his youth and his strength. Bluff aside, there was no guarantee that he'd be able to talk his way out of the camp, and there may still be long days of dangerous negotiations and riots ahead. Heck, the soldiers might even decide to take them to jail for disobeying their orders.

He *should* go to bed.

He straightened and turned to the truck. As he put his hand on the door handle, a cold gust of wind tore over the hillside and blew all his hair to one side. The air was humid and cold as winter. This weather got more strange every day.

Then, a screech that echoed over the hillside made him shiver deep in his bones. Whatever that was, it sounded close. He peered in the direction of the forest. A huge shape flew low overhead, lazily flapping huge wings. It came straight overhead. For a moment, Milleus saw a dark form, a leathery belly lit from below by the glow of the few remaining lights.

It was as if the wind stopped, the sounds from the city stopped and the whole world turned to silence. Then a gust of warm air followed in the creature's wake.

What in mercy's name was that thing?

Milleus stood quiet, watching the sky. None of the other Chevakians appeared to have seen the creature, at least no one seemed to be awake still. And why was it so hot all of a sudden?

CHAPTER 7

TANDOR ACHED like he never ached in his life. Not when he became engulfed in icefire, not when Loriane peeled burnt skin away from his face, not when his hands thawed out after the long ride through the snow, had he felt like this. It was as if a piece of his soul had been ripped out of him. As if Ruko's mind had grown roots inside him that had been torn out when Myra and Loriane cut the bonds. Yet he had still managed to maintain the merest wisp of a connection with Ruko. He could still feel Ruko's presence, and see shards of what he was doing.

After his escape from the tent, Ruko had simply vaulted the fence and the Chevakians hadn't even noticed. Now, he was running with the same superhuman strength through the Chevakian country, on his way to join his friends. Whenever he needed to eat, he'd steal a pigeon or duck from a farm and eat it raw, annoyed at the weaknesses of his body that needed food.

He ran, and ran, and ran. All he wanted was to find the other children. Once he reached them, he would discard his mortal form and become one of them once more. With him as their leader, he would push them into revenge. They'd seek out the Knights, and find Tandor, and punish all of them for hurting his girl.

The hatred was so strong that it burned in Tandor's mind.

But Tandor could do nothing to stop the visions coming. And he could also do nothing to stop Ruko reaching his goal.

Tandor himself had been lucky to escape the refugee camp once he confused the camp guards by swearing at them in Chevakian. Claims about his membership of a good Tiverian family were not lies, and when the soldiers left him to confer with their superiors, he'd simply walked out without being questioned; the Chevakian army was that short on personnel.

He'd even been lucky to have overheard where Loriane had been taken. He'd managed to climb into the yard of the senator's house and waited outside the window of the house's guest room, hiding behind a hedge under the cover of gathering darkness. The room had flimsy doors with large panes of glass. He studied them so as to break in quickly, after everyone had gone and the lights were off. After the child was born. He could taste victory. He'd grab the child and take it to his mother's house. If the books were right, it wouldn't take long before the child's first turning. Then he could start to repair the damage, defeat Ruko, sweep up the expanding field of icefire and bring the plan back on track.

For now, he waited and listened to the Chevakians talking. There were two men, in medical gowns. By the skylights, why would this senator go to the expense of getting in surgeons?

What did a Chevakian care about Loriane? She was Tandor's princess. When all this was done and fixed, and the Thilleian family once more held the throne, she would be his queen.

He remembered a hazy flash of memory from yesterday. Loriane shouting at him *I hate you*. She did that often, when he visited her, but she never meant it.

Then there was a ruckus inside the room. Loriane cursing. And then her voice again, a beastly cry that made Tandor shiver deep inside. He tried to imagine Loriane's face, but could not. He could only see Maraithe, grabbing her swollen belly. In his mind, he heard Maraithe's cries. And the voice of the nurse, *By the skylights, this one is Imperfect*.

And panic. He had to save her children, both of them.

So when Maraithe slept, and the Senior Knight came in to take the boy to be left on the ice floes, Tandor jumped out of the wardrobe and overpowered the man, put on the man's uniform and took the baby to a safe place. And of course, he had been caught when he returned to the palace. By now, the Senior Command knew that

Maraithe's baby girl was Imperfect and understood that the young Chevakian merchant whom they'd deemed safe company for the Queen was not what he claimed to be.

If the Chevakians thought their courthouse prison was bad, they hadn't seen the prison under the palace in the City of Glass.

Tandor remembered lying naked on a table, the feel of rough wood against his naked back. He remembered the Supreme Rider grabbing a handful of his manly bits. He remembered the glint of a knife—

—and he tried to push away those memories as he sat there hiding behind the hedge, and tried to listen for signs or sounds that Loriane's child had been born, and that the surgeons had left. But there were no clear sounds—Loriane said screaming was for first-time mothers; she had told him often enough—so he risked looking over the hedge.

The light was still on in the room. Loriane sat propped up against pillow in bed. A serving woman brought tea to the surgeons. There was also a guard in the room. Tandor could see a basket next to Loriane's bed, but he couldn't see inside it.

By the skylights, what if, for all his calculations and study, the child was *normal*? His mother would kill him.

He was flooded with memories from even further back, when he sat on the little stool in his mother's big garden room, surrounded by luxurious furniture he wasn't allowed to touch—because little boys only make things dirty. She would tell him of all the riches in the City of Glass. He would ask why the City of Glass was no longer rich, and she'd say that the Knights were stupid. She said that he was a prince and that all those riches were his.

And he believed all of it.

Except when he mentioned at school that he was a prince, the Chevakian kids just laughed. Then he would try to make sparks with icefire as his mother had taught him, but he couldn't do it while they watched. Icefire was too weak in Tiverius anyway, even before the barriers went up.

And then the kids would laugh even more, and he got called into the teacher's room and this big fat Chevakian man would rant at him about how there was no magic. Tandor tried to throw sparks at the teacher, too, but it didn't do anything either, except earn him a cuff on the ear.

There was a shout and the light went out in the senator's guest room, casting the courtyard in deep darkness.

A low, sibilant sound came from the room. Someone shouted and another said, "It must have been the wind."

Where before, there had been no wind at all, there was an icy breeze which found its way through the gaps in Tandor's clothing. The air tingled with icefire.

He rose and grabbed his dagger, and headed for the darkened room, but before he reached the door, and before he could force his way in, a terrible hiss came from inside, and then a muffled scream, cut off suddenly. Another growl and hiss. Tandor couldn't see anything inside that dark room, where there were now crashes and growls, and the sound of breaking crockery, and the splintering of wood.

The window exploded outwards and a huge shape emerged, shaking broken glass of its back as a bear might shake water from its pelt. It moved in a stealthy way like a sabre wolf, with powerful strides like a huge predator. Its neck was long and its head was an extension of the neck, without ears. It had no hair. It walked on powerful claws, but soundless like a lion.

It unfurled its leathery wings. Tandor leapt forward, onto its back. The skin was rough and scaled like a snake's, and was incredibly *warm* under his hands. The creature bucked to try to throw him off. Tandor held onto the place where the wings joined the body. He threw all icefire he could muster at the animal, but it wasn't much, and it sank into the skin without trace. Tandor cursed.

The dacon turned its head and regarded Tandor with an angry blue eye. Then it snorted and jumped into the air. The power of those wings!

While it flew over the courtyard wall, it shook its shoulder blades and rolled. Tandor did his best to hang on, but his clawed hand couldn't get a grip on the creature's back, and he slid off. Fortunately, he landed in bushes, where the Chevakians had found him.

After discovering him in the yard, the three Chevakians, a doga guard, a family-employed guard and a higher-placed man, had taken him to the Tiverian courthouse jail, where the guards had locked him into the dungeon. He was accused of killing four people. He saw no point in arguing; they wouldn't believe him anyway, not until they saw that locking him up wouldn't be the end of the killing. They tied him to a crate with bonds so tight that he couldn't sit down without the rope cutting off circulation in his arms.

Meanwhile, the dacon was loose in Tiverius, and it was only a matter of time before it killed again. It needed lots of food.

He needed to find the hybrid, and fast, because crossbreeds lived one day for a normal person's year. Even when healthy, the crossbreed would not last to see the end of summer.

Once Ruko re-joined his fellows, he would send the children on a rampage of revenge. Maybe Ruko would seek out the crossbreed in order to kill it, which meant Loriane was in danger, too. But Tandor was trapped in this stupid prison by unbelieving Chevakians, and weak from the trip without much food, and still aching from where Loriane and Myra had cut the bonds with Ruko.

"In prison, tied to a fucking crate," he mumbled to himself, and laughed so that he wouldn't cry, and his laugh developed into a wet, hacking cough. He spat out phlegm, wishing for a drink.

Tandor fought a tickle in his throat that wanted to become a cough. His breath rattled with stringy phlegm. He tried swallowing it, but couldn't so he spat. And then coughed up more phlegm.

He peered into the darkness. There was only one small oil lamp at the far end of the corridor, and it cast the feeblest of light by which he could just make out the bars to the opposite cell.

It grew cold in the cell. Tandor was mortally tired but couldn't lie down. He dozed a bit only to find that his arms became painful where the metal bands clamped around them. The scabs on his face itched, but he couldn't scratch. He also needed to pee, and he hoped someone would come and untie him before he embarrassed himself.

But no one came.

He could feel a whisper of a cool breeze stroke past his skin. There was a vent somewhere, and where there was air, he had access to icefire . . . if it was strong enough . . . if the guards untied him and he could get near the vent.

Then he was back at the palace in the City of Glass, and relived that moment where his Imperfect children walked out of their prison into the corridor. With stone sinks embedded in their bodies, they would not listen to his commands. Those sinks also stopped him making them his servitors. They were walking towards the Heart of the City, and he should have killed them, knowing that they would absorb the icefire and that something disastrous would happen.

But those children had been the only people he had really cared about. Not his mother, with her scheming plans and her shady money and her large band of supporters who would all abandon her as soon as they realised what she wanted. Not his merchant stepfather who had been as clueless as he had been rich. Not his haughty half-sisters, who took after his mother and only cared for money.

Having lived the life of a scrawny bullied kid with the fake hand, he wanted those kids he saved to have good lives.

He enjoyed bringing them presents and organising parties for them. He loved the smiles on their faces, even though he knew they thought he was a bit creepy and he didn't know how to be nice to them. He enjoyed seeing them fall in love with each other. Like a dirty old man, he had spied into lofts and rooms watching them fumble making love.

He wanted them to live, and have lots of Imperfect children. Apart from Myra, two other girls had fallen pregnant. He couldn't possibly kill them.

But he should have, because now their bodies had been filled with icefire, and they had slipped from his control. And now the only thing that could control them—the hybrid child—was about to slip from his control as well.

I cared too much, Mother. He'd hoped to give the children the childhood he'd never had.

How to get out of this cell to salvage whatever he could of his plan? He had to change his tactics, and talk to the guards, convince them that they had the wrong person, if they could still be made to change their minds.

Icefire was still very weak in Tiverius. All the way down here under the ground, it was far too weak for him to get rid of the metal manacles, but there was one thing that didn't require so much power. He closed his eyes, and blinked, and blinked again. Ideally, he needed a mirror to do this, and he hoped that just thinking of brown eyes would be enough.

By the skylights, that exhausted him.

He must have dozed, because suddenly there was the jingle of keys and the creak of the cell door, and two guards came in, one of them carrying a torch.

"What do we do with this one?" one of the men said. He carried a slate. "Wanted for quadruple murder, needs a translator."

"I'd say he needs the rope," the other man said. He held the torch close to Tandor's face.

Tandor's eyes watered from the brightness of it, and he could not make out more than the men's outlines and brown Chevakian uniforms.

"Urgh, he looks like a troll. What has he done to himself?" The glow from the torch moved across Tandor's face.

Tandor took a deep breath and plunged in, hoping his disguise, feeble as it was, had worked. "Please, untie my arms." His voice wouldn't cooperate and it came out as a rasp.

The guard cursed. "He speaks Chevakian. Did anyone know he speaks Chevakian?"

"Who cares? It makes the matter more simple. We have a trial today and hang him tomorrow."

"Please. I'm a Chevakian citizen," Tandor said. "I have the right to a fair trial." Not tomorrow. He needed more time before icefire was strong enough for him to escape.

The guard laughed. "You murder four people and dare talk about rights?"

"I did not murder anyone. It was all a misunderstanding."

"A misunderstanding that involved a knife and a lot of blood, huh?"

"The blood was mine." And it was. Scratches from when he'd fallen into the bushes. "Please. I think it was an Eagle Knight. I was trying to stop him by jumping onto the bird. I couldn't hang on and I fell off."

The guards glanced at each other with an expression that said *Eagle Knights?*

"Hmm," one said. "I wonder why you didn't say anything before."

"Because I fell off. I was dazed."

They continued their non-believing glares.

"Please," Tandor repeated. "Untie me. I'm an honest Chevakian citizen. I won't try anything funny. Only for a short while." Only to untie his pants and piss. His bladder was so full that it hurt.

"I don't know about that. You don't look Chevakian. Why do you speak Chevakian so well?"

"Because he's a spy," the other said, and understanding dawned on the first man's face. By the skylights, not only were they obnoxious, they were stupid as well.

"Please," Tandor said.

The man looked at him, his face sneering. "Why should we trust you? We should tell the doga about you."

No, not the doga. His mother had ties all through the doga. They would report him to her. And he didn't want to face his mother before he had the hybrid, or Ruko, or preferably both.

"I'll do whatever you say. Please."

"I don't think so," the guard with the torch said. "Come, let's go." He went to the cell's entrance.

The other man followed, then stopped, turned and hit Tandor in the stomach.

Doubled over, Tandor heard his voice come from far off. "That is what we do with traitors."

When the pain subsided, Tandor felt the cold of piss having soaked his pants.

From elsewhere in the prison came a voice, rough and gravelly. "Hey, new guy, what'd you be in for?"

"Nothing. I don't belong here." Even to his own ears, his voice sounded too cultured.

A couple of men laughed.

Another voice said. "That's what they all say, the first day."

"Ha, ha, until they are taken into the gallows room." Another voice joined. "And then they'll say whatever the guards want to hear, and the guards don't care, because they love hanging prisoners. We can hear them scream from here."

Tandor shivered. Without the dacon, he couldn't prove his innocence, and the court would have no trouble finding him guilty and the hangman would come quickly. No use in wasting resources on people who killed.

"I stole Lady han Silvanian's jewels," said the first man again. He seemed proud of it, too. Thievery carried the sentence of deportation to one of the labour farms outside the city. Some destitutes stole simply to get a roof over their heads.

The other laughed. "She has too many jewels anyway."

"Yeah, fat cow."

"Will you shut up!" came a voice from further away.

A brief silence, and then the thief said again, "Don' listen to him. He's the one who raped the Vinalissi girl and then killed her when she screamed too much."

"Yeah, he'll be hanged real soon."

Tandor felt sick. In here, status mattered nothing. If he didn't get out, he would be remembered as worse than them. Much worse.

"So, new guy, what did you do?"

"Nothing," Tandor said again.

"Whoa, a cranky one," the talkative prisoner said. "Yeah, all right. Suit yourself. Just trying to be friendly that's all. Good night to you sir."

There was some rustling and grunting and creaking of benches and it grew quiet.

CHAPTER 8

$\mathcal{I}$SANDOR PUSHED his way out of the tent, past the crowds cramming in to see the queen, past the self-styled guards, into the darkness.

"Hey, where are you going?" someone asked.

"I can go wherever I want," Isandor said. By the skylights, he was angry. As if the Brotherhood had suddenly taken over ordering people about when the Knights had gone. And Jevaithi believed them, by the skylights.

The stupid civilian guards had no authority to boss him about, and no one was going to stop him seeing Milleus. But when the guard held the lamp up and Isandor could see his face, he realised that the youth was younger than him.

"By the skylights, it's the champion," the other guard said, this one a woman.

"Really?" the boy said.

"Hey, you," someone else called from further down. "Didn't Simo say that we had to guard the tent?"

"That's what we're doing," the woman called back. She gave a derisive snort.

"So, Simo is pretty much the boss here?" Isandor asked. He tried to make his question sound as casual as possible.

"Pretty much," she said, shrugged, and then let an awkward silence fall.

They were afraid to say more, Isandor guessed. Afraid to be on the wrong side of whatever the Brothers wanted. He asked, "What's your name?"

"Kenna. This is my brother Zito." The boy looked about thirteen, and he had a dirty bandage around much of his left arm.

"Are your parents here?"

Kenna shrugged. "My father sells fish. He was away to get supplies." There was no need to say more. The fish markets were closer to the City of Glass proper than to the Outer City.

"Are all people here supporters of the Brotherhood of the Light?"

"I think so." Kenna looked over her shoulder, but the third youth had vanished. "Not that I've talked to any and know much about them. You know what they were like, quietly going about their business. You're from the Outer City, too, aren't you?"

Isandor nodded. He knew. The Brotherhood school was for orphans. No one cared much about what went on there, except the young people who left the school were usually very smart and did well for themselves in a quiet, unassuming sort of way. None of those people, the merchants, the administrators, the teachers, ever mentioned that the Brotherhood stood for anything, except education. It seemed people were glad the Brotherhood was looking after orphans, so that no one else needed to worry about them.

"When did they start coming out so openly?"

"When we were on the train. There were more and more people in black. Not just men with beards, but women, too. They were saying things like that this was our chance for freedom, and that we could defeat the Knights."

"A lot of people liked that," the boy said.

"Did they say how they planned to defeat the Knights? Did they have any real plans, or were they just saying things because they sounded good? They do know that just because there are no Knights here, it doesn't mean that they're all dead?"

She shrugged. "I thought they meant to recruit people to fight. They set up an army, and gave people tasks to do. You could join the guards or the cooks or work in the supply tent. Everyone joined these groups. I mean—there is nothing else to do here, and it sounded like a good idea because no one else was organising anything." She cast him a nervous look. "I mean—you *did* get banned from the Knighthood, didn't you?"

Isandor let the uncertainty hang between them. "Have you spotted anyone using icefire?"

"But we're in Chevakia. There is no—"

"Not anymore. The barriers broke and now it's everywhere." Isandor held up his hand and let a spark dance over it. Young Zito's eyes widened.

"No, I haven't seen anyone use it," Kenna said.

"What about Simo?"

They both shook their heads.

"He yells a lot at people," Zito said. "People are scared of him."

"He knows Chevakians," Kenna said.

"Chevakians?" Isandor frowned at her.

"Yes, I saw him with some of the ones who came into the camp. They seemed to know each other well."

Isandor glanced uphill where the remaining Chevakian vans were clustered around a fire. He recognised Milleus' truck. "Any of those Chevakians?" It didn't look like they knew anyone in the camp. Milleus had told him he hadn't met any southerners for many years.

Kenna peered. "I don't think so. A lot of Chevakians left."

The fence had been repaired and he could see fires and tents on the other side. The group still on this side sat around the fire, where people were talking. Milleus was one of those people. Isandor didn't see him, but he saw the familiar truck, and the trailer and goat pen. He ached to go there, but the Chevakians would probably think the was an intruder, and he didn't want to lead Brotherhood thugs to Milleus, so he sat with his knees pulled up to his chest and watched from a distance until the meeting with Jevaithi in the large tent broke up and people streamed out talking to each other, oblivious to him sitting in the darkness. He caught a snatch of conversation about how pale Jevaithi looked.

An older man in black strolled past, semi-casually, but Isandor didn't miss glances at him and at Kenna and Zito who stood on both sides of the tent entrance, not moving and not saying anything. When everyone had left the tent, two new sentries came, both dressed in black, and Isandor finally got up.

Both glared at him as he walked past into the tent, but didn't challenge him.

The people had turned the throne room into a makeshift bedroom by draping Chevakian blankets over upright planks, which partitioned off half of the tent. An oil lamp sputtered, about to go out, on a table in the other half of the tent. A couple of crates and boxes formed chairs and a table.

As he stood there, a cold chill went through him, tugging at his senses. Something above the tent, in the air. He froze, looking uselessly at the tent's ceiling. For a moment, it seemed the world had died. But the feeling passed, leaving the air warmer and without the edge of icefire.

By the skylights, the Knights were flying over the camp with their sinks. No Knights here? Who believed that? They were hiding, waiting to attack.

On the other side of the partition, Isandor found a bed covered in furs. Jevaithi lay there, already asleep.

Isandor undressed and lay down next to her, pulling the fur covers over him. The skins smelled grimy and retained a lingering scent of animals. Cocooned in the smell, he lay staring into the darkness. He liked Milleus and his rational way of dealing with people. He liked the way Milleus looked at something, and tried to understand it. Milleus did not judge based on beliefs or birth. He did not discount facts because they were provided by his enemies.

Isandor realised he had become a lot more Chevakian since being with Milleus, and he liked it. No one in Chevakia had questioned his wooden leg. They'd just assumed it was from an accident, and, unlike the people from the City of Glass, didn't judge him any less for it.

Jevaithi loved her adoring masses, but he felt more comfortable with getting knowledge. He'd always been like that, wanting to question what people told him. He wanted proof, not beliefs or rumour. It was, he thought sadly, something that his mother had taught him.

He could still hear her voice. *I've seen so much stupid belief about birthing babies, and a lot of girls would be dead if I didn't speak out against it.*

By the skylights, where was his mother now?

He nodded off and woke with a shock to the screeches of an eagle in the distance. He jumped out of bed, still in the dark, but when he checked outside, he could only see the side panel of a trailer moving in the wind, and the flapping of a tent awning. It was pitch dark. There was no one to be seen. Even Milleus had gone to sleep.

He went back inside, shivering with the cold, too worried to sleep. Too many things went on in his head. Daytime would come soon.

He re-lit the oil lamp and sat at the table, wondering if he should go outside and find a fire and make tea. Didn't know if it was safe to do so. The camp had gone quiet, but there might still be trouble-makers about. Southerners or Chevakians, he didn't know. Who could he trust, anyway?

He wondered how many people they had displaced in this large tent and what the poor people of the City of Glass had given up just so that the Queen cold have her own tent and big bed with furs. Jevaithi accepted it without question. She was used to being given things without asking for them.

The table was clearly a Chevakian thing, being made of wood, but the crate that formed the seat was something different. In fact, it looked like someone's travel luggage, very old and very Chevakian. He wondered what it was doing here. When he lifted it by one handle, the contents slid against the far end of the chest. By the skylights, it was heavy.

Curious, and because there was nothing else to, he tested the lid and found that the lock was damaged, and open. The lid creaked. The golden light from the oil lamp lit a jumble of clothes and books all thrown in at random, as if someone had searched the chest.

There was a large stopper of the type of jar his mother would use in her practice, but the jar was missing. Whatever had been in it must have been stored in some kind of spirits and must have broken during travel, because the smell still lingered in the chest.

The clothing was mainly men's felt underwear, southern style, but there were some long-sleeved felt shirts and a leather vest.

They were southern clothes, too. Well enough made to belong to a rich person. The chest also contained a variety of pots and stones and metal instruments like rulers and a quadrant, and some instruments he didn't recognise and . . . very old books, with dusty and worn spines.

He took one of the books out and opened the silky pages of vellum. It seemed a diary of some sort, in a very old style of hand-writing. Southern, and dating from before the Knights. This was something he would once have paid a lot of money for, when he collected this sort of stuff with Carro.

The writing was hard to read and loopy. The entries were dates, and the text detailed such things as meetings and things that needed to be done, many unfamiliar to him. What, by the skylights, did *temper the feeder lead* mean?

He leafed through and was about to put the book aside when he came to the last entry, scrawled sideways across the page in a hasty hand.

They are at the door. My son and his wife have hopefully fled the palace. Look after them. My life will be short.

By the skylights, he noticed the date, fifty years ago. And the seal depicting the leather-winged creature, some mythical all-powerful figure called a dacon, which was the symbol of the Thilleian house. This was a diary of the old king himself. This travel chest must have belonged to Tandor.

There were two more books, one equally old and incomprehensible, and one full of notes and calculations. There was a diagram with maps and numbers, using a Chevakian word: motes? What did that mean?

He turned a few pages read of a chamber outside the City of Glass, where one could control the thing called the Heart of the City. Someone had made elaborate notes on setting and levels of all kinds of elaborate levers, similar to the ones Milleus had on his truck. The type of work the Brothers did, with very detailed instructions. By the skylights, it looked as if Tandor had been messing with the Heart.

At the end of the book, he found a diagram in tiny writing spread over two pages. It held names and birth dates. None of them older than himself. His name was on the scheme as well.

Tandor x Maraithe—Jevaithi and Isandor.

He read the line several times. Underneath his and Jevaithi's names was a date of birth. Jevaithi's. He'd always been told his birthday was a day earlier.

He stared at the text, while the diagram blurred before his eyes.

Tandor had betrayed them all. He *was* Isandor's father, the mysterious man who had fathered Maraithe's children while the Knights were bickering, the merchant in disguise. Jevaithi was his twin sister. They were both the old king's great-grandchildren.

CHAPTER 9

$\mathcal{M}$ILLEUS ROSE at first light, much earlier than he would have liked, and still feeling tired after a few measly hours of sleep. Mercy, he was way too old for these night-time escapades. Outside, the light was still dawn-blue, filtered through a grey-blue haze. The air smelled of fire, although from his position, any evidence of the fights from night before was well-hidden. The tent entrances were shut, and the alleys between tents were empty, except for a few black-clad sentries by the large tent, hands in their pockets. The Chevakian tents, too, were still closed.

Heaving a sigh, he opened the door and let himself down from the truck. As soon as he set foot on the ground, the goats started jostling each other to the corner of the pen, clanking their hooves in the food trough.

He ran his hand over the hairy heads, while they pushed their noses into his palm, bleating and shoving each other out of the way.

"Shh, Ladies, people are sleeping."

He found the milking stool and started the daily process of milking with hands that had become unused to the task. At home, he had the milking machine, and since leaving the farm, this had been Isandor's job, with his stronger hands and more supple back, and there was a kind of sadness in the fact that he now needed to do this. But there was no point in complaining. He'd been on his own for ten years, after all. Still, his fingers felt sore and stiff and the joints ached from the weather. More than anything, he was so *tired*.

He was well into the job when a voice said, "Can I help with the goats?"

Isandor. In the faint morning light, he looked exactly like Milleus felt: tired and weary. Had the boy slept at all? He'd noticed activity in that big tent until he had fallen asleep.

The boy clambered over the railing. Blue eyes met his with an expression of concern. "Are you all right, Milleus?"

"I'm just a grumpy old man. A very tired and grumpy old man with weather in his bones."

"I don't like the weather either. It looks like there is bad weather coming. In the City of Glass, the sky goes like this when there is a snow storm on its way."

He was right. The ill-defined, low-hanging clouds were typical for snow. At least, they were in the southern highlands. It didn't snow in Tiverius.

Isandor picked up the bucket.

Milleus heaved himself off the too-low milking stool and let Isandor take his usual spot. They fell into the familiar routines, milking, feeding, changing drinking water and brushing the goats, including passing milk to waiting people. All those were Chevakians who had been around the fire last night. There were not many, so they had milk left over, which Isandor poured in two cups, took one himself and handed the other to Milleus. They drank, leaning on the railing of the goat pen.

Artan and his wife had come out of their tent and were now cooking breakfast, and a few others were starting to pack their tents. It wouldn't be long before the Chevakians would leave. And Milleus, damn it, had promised to lead them. Yet, seeing Isandor's young face made him doubt that the youngsters would be up to all the trouble they might face here. He had so little time left to tell them all he wanted to say. He didn't even know where to begin.

"The Queen, huh?" Milleus said.

Isandor shrugged. "I'm sorry. I didn't want to lie to you, but we were running away from the Knights and she wanted it like that."

"Why did you run?"

"Jevaithi is scared, for a good reason. She had nowhere to go."

Then he went on to describe a life locked up in the tallest tower in the City of Glass, kept away from the people who adored her. A life of constant put-downs and threats. A life where the young princess had seen her mother slowly wither away, both in mental and physical strength, locked up in the tower for her protection by the people who controlled every aspect of her life. And he told of the mystery surrounding Jevaithi's father, and how the Supreme Rider Cornatan, the regent, kept telling her that he would rape her so that he could have his own blood on the throne.

While Isandor was talking, he met Milleus' eyes, through a curtain of ratty and greasy black hair. "Tell me, knowing all this, wouldn't you have fled?"

"I guess so." Milleus couldn't imagine a life of hardship like this. "But if she lived so protected, how did you become involved?"

Isandor spoke of how he'd been an Eagle Knight, how he flew in a race, won and how Jevaithi had crowned him her champion. The first time they met each other's eyes, they had felt a connection. "We're both Imperfect." He glanced at his wooden leg. "But soon after I won, my friend betrayed me. Imperfects can't be Knights."

"Just because you have a part of your leg missing, you are considered inferior, and are not allowed to sign up?"

Isandor nodded.

"Mercy, in Chevakia you'd be branded a hero, an invalid having beaten more able men."

"Imperfect," Isandor said.

"Well, that's pretty much the same as invalid, isn't it?"

Isandor shook his head. "Imperfect means not just that we are missing parts of our arms or legs, but also that we can feel icefire."

"Sonorics."

"Icefire. Sonorics is what Chevakians call it. Chevakians don't understand it."

"It's the same thing."

"No. When Chevakians say sonorics, they only mean the parts they can measure. The things they can't explain are called magic. And magic is something that's not real, no? And something people don't believe in."

The intense look in his eyes gave Milleus a chill. For years, the doga had waged a public campaign to weed out the use of the word magic, because it made people fearful where they didn't need to be. Sonorics was *not* magic. You could measure it, and make it harmless. Sonorics was under control, and did not need to be feared. But understand it . . . he suspected not even the Most Learned Alius fully understood it.

Isandor continued, "Imperfects are Imperfect, because we can feel icefire in the air."

Milleus knew about the southern resistance to the effects of icefire, but now apparently their bodies had built-in sensors? He thought of the sonorics meters he had seen Sady carrying around, big clunky boxes that contained magnetised strips of metal that attracted the motes, which were then fed into a gel-filled tube, which then needed to be processed in the dark by rolling it over a sheet of silver-paper. It was a cumbersome process that made the bellows air-pressure meters look like child's toys. Was he saying that these Imperfect people could do that within their bodies? "What exactly do you mean by *feel*?"

"Like . . ." Isandor raised his hands and let them fall again. "Feel. It's in the air."

"Here and now?"

"Yes. Not much, but there is some. We can . . ." He held out his hand, palm up. A tiny spark lit up, like a miniature bolt of lightning. "It's very weak."

Milleus stared at Isandor's palm, now very normal and pale-skinned. "You did that?"

"Yes. I told you."

"And everyone can do that?"

"Only Imperfects. Ones with arms or legs missing."

That meant both the youngsters. "And what can you do with it?"

"Not much, unless you know a lot about it, but that kind of lessons are forbidden. Normally, if an Imperfect baby is born, the Knights leave it on the ice floes for the wild animals to eat."

Milleus stared at Isandor's leg, hidden under his trousers. "Yet the Knights allowed you to become one of them?"

"Yes, I . . ." Isandor looked down. "When I think hard about the leg I don't have, it seems that people don't notice that it isn't there."

Magic. Illusions, ghosts that were said to roam the southern slopes as far down as the barrier. Insubstantial beings that ripped apart livestock that strayed onto the southern slopes. He remembered his own struggle keeping goats safe from what he had always thought were sabre-wolves, but he had never actually seen a sabre-wolf. Magic beings, magic people. He shivered. "Surely you did something to cover up your wooden leg." It wouldn't be that hard, since he had his knee. A good prosthetic on a boy who was young enough to learn to run with it might be barely noticeable.

"I have a shoe that fits the end of the wood."

"There you go." But what a brave kid he was to have enlisted regardless of the threat that he'd be punished severely if found out. Milleus tried to remember his own sons at that age. Andrean insecure and shy, Kalius thought he knew it all and was popular with the girls. Compared to this young man, they'd lived such luxurious, protected lives.

"You don't believe me." Isandor lifted his trouser leg. "I'll show you."

The skin on Isandor's leg was unbelievably pale, with sparse black hair. The wooden stump was tied to his leg below the bony knee, but an insubstantial white veil marked the place where Isandor's calf would be, had his leg been complete.

Milleus stared and blinked, as if that would make the illusion go away.

"Feel it."

Milleus did. His hand went straight through the illusion, but the wispy form made his fingers ice-cold.

"Mercy."

"It's not very good. It was a lot stronger yesterday."

Not very good? This was scary. Some form of optical projection of light. The white veil slowly faded.

Was there another word for this other than *magic*? "I still don't get it. If they were intent on killing you, why did you sign up for the Knighthood?" He cleared his throat, because his mouth seemed to have gone dry.

Isandor shrugged. "They seemed . . . honourable, and noble. I thought, because no one said anything about my leg . . . that it didn't matter anymore. All those persecutions of Imperfects were a long time ago. I thought people no longer cared." He let a small pause lapse. "Also, I like animals."

Milleus nodded; he'd noticed that, too. "But once you were in the Knighthood you found out it wasn't as you thought?"

"A lot of bad things happen there. The Knights are so afraid of the supporters of the old royal family that they punish anyone who has items that used to belong to the royal family. But a lot of people have those things. After the king was killed, people went into the palace and stole everything the royal family owned. Between the Knights, at the Eyrie, superiors use beatings and rape to keep new recruits under control. Everyone is afraid of everyone else. I had a friend . . ." His eyes looked distant. "His name is Carro."

"The one who betrayed you?"

He nodded. "The Tutors singled him out for punishment. I don't know why, but he's kind of awkward. He always says the wrong things to people, and seems to think everyone conspires against him. And then he does things like telling the superior what the Apprentices got up to last night just so that the superior will be pleased with him."

"Some friend."

"I don't think he can help it." Isandor blew out a breath. "He's probably dead now."

Milleus felt sick. "What a barbaric world." He had known this, of course, but it had always been a distant thing. "How did you two even get to this age?"

"The Knights couldn't kill the princess, because the people love the Queen and would have rebelled. About me, I never knew why I'd been saved."

"Surely, someone must think that this is barbaric. Isn't there anyone who does anything for these poor invalid children?"

"Yes, there is a group called the Brothers of the Light, who run orphanages. They save Imperfect children, sometimes. Not me." His expression was intense.

"So what about you, then?"

Isandor's face went tense. "I wanted to show you. I found this last night." He slowly drew a couple of books from inside his cloak. "I found these in a travel chest that's in the tent. I'm not sure whose they were." Isandor put the top book into Milleus' outstretched hand.

Milleus turned it over, studied the very southern leather cover, and opened the book with its soft vellum pages. He ran his fingertips over the page full of curly southern letters. He didn't know the language well enough to easily read it, but the recognised that certain lines were dates, which, in the south, went back to some past war. "A diary?"

Isandor nodded.

Milleus turned another page. The vellum was of extra-ordinary fine quality. He didn't even know they made things like this in the south. Spread over two pages was an intricate drawing of a strange creature. Its body was vaguely wolf-like in shape, but it had no hair and its skin was grey and wrinkled. From its shoulder blades sprang two huge leathery wings, with claws on the end. The drawing showed it slashing sharp nails at a white bear. The white fur was bathed in blood. A small diagram in the corner showed the creature in flight. He froze. That was the thing he'd seen last night. Or was it?

"What is this thing?"

"It's a . . . dacon. This is the symbol of the royal family." He pointed to a stylised representation of the creature, arranged within the border of a circle that looked like a family seal. "If the Knights find this symbol on anything, they take it off you. Any old cups and plates, and books, and things that came from the old king's household."

"Could I . . . could it be possible that I saw one of those creatures?"

Isandor turned sharply to Milleus. "It would have been an eagle."

"I felt . . ." Milleus put his hands together. "First, the air was cold. Then I heard this beastly cry. I saw a creature fly over. It wasn't an eagle. I've heard those. I've seen those, too. This creature was dark, and had no feathers. When it passed, the air became warm."

Isandor nodded. "I felt that, too. But, this creature . . . people in the City of Glass say it's just a story. It doesn't exist."

"You're absolutely certain of that?"

Isandor met his eyes, but said nothing. He let a silence lapse before continuing. "Anyway, I wanted to show you something else. It's on this page." He flipped through the pages, until he reached the two-page diagram with lines of what looked like names.

Milleus looked at it, silently.

"They're all names—"

"I can read those," Milleus said, running his finger down the list. "Just not very well or fast." And he was clearly meant to find Isandor's name. Indeed, there it was. *Maraithe x Tandor: Jevaithi and Isandor.*

Milleus looked into Isandor's eyes and said nothing for a long time. A tear tracked over Isandor's young face. He sniffed.

"This changes everything," Milleus said, slowly.

Isandor nodded, and wiped his cheek. "This is bad—"

"Bad?" Milleus raised his eyebrows.

"Bad for me. They only want the queen, and they only want her to shut her mouth and do as they tell her. I have too many opinions. The Knights will kill me. The Brothers won't know what to do about me. They already think I'm trouble. They'll try to kill me, too, if they can. They just want Jevaithi to be their puppet queen. They don't want anyone to interfere." His eyes were wide.

Milleus nodded, slowly. "Possibly, but have you considered—"

"And Jevaithi will be angry with me."

Yes, he could understand that. "She couldn't have known?"

Isandor shook his head. "Tandor was always telling everyone how he'd lost his . . . manly bits and couldn't be my father—"

Milleus winced.

"He lied to everyone." He let a silence lapse. A tear rolled over his cheek. "I slept with my sister."

"But you didn't know she is your sister." And then he had to suppress a shudder because of the implications. In Chevakia, it would have been a punishable crime. He hoped the City of Glass didn't have such laws. After all, if no one knew who their parents were, then it was bound to happen more often. He continued in a low voice, "You can only do one thing."

"And that is? I have to tell her, and then she'll be upset and then everyone will know. And then they'll kill me because they can imprison a Queen, but they're afraid of another king."

"Yes, you have to tell her. But you also have to find a way to use it. You will be stronger together than she can be alone."

"But no one listens to me. I'm only an Outer City boy. No one listens to a boy. No one listens to the queen, even. They don't even want us here. I bet they were disappointed when we came into the camp."

"No one listens to an old man either, but you'll have to make them."

There was a clang of tent post and the squeal of children as one of the Chevakian tents came down.

"You're leaving, aren't you?"

Milleus sighed. "We are, I'm sorry. I am hoping that the guards will let us through just to be rid of us. Then we'll go to the doga and demand that they deal with the situation, that they let all the Ensar people through, or clear the road, and take them to a different camp. I'll be back with help, I promise."

Isandor's mouth twitched. "I would have loved to go to Tiverius."

"You can come with me."

Isandor pressed his lips together but then sighed and shook his head. "I have to stay here, and Jevaithi couldn't come, even if she wanted. I have to stay with her. I think she trusts these people here far too much. Because they're not Knights, it doesn't mean that they won't try to use her in the same way the Knights did."

Milleus nodded. He didn't look forward to leaving the youngsters behind. "It would have been a lot easier had you told me who she was. I could have prevented most of this from happening. For one, I would never have taken the main road, so we would now be safely at my brother's house." He would have been able to take her into the doga, and it would have helped his standing, too. Never before had there been much of a relationship between the Proctor, or indeed anyone in the doga, and the southern royal family.

"If I'd told you, you would have handed us over to the local army post."

Milleus thought back to a time that felt like it was years ago, when he did everything to avoid being public figure and taking responsibility for the district in which he lived. "Maybe." A bit later, he added, "Probably, yes."

Not much later, the Chevakians had finished packing, and the convoy was ready to go. Milleus climbed into the truck, alone, and found it horribly quiet and empty in the cabin.

Mercy, if only the youngsters had told them who they were earlier, he would never have gone into the camp—but no one had known that the inhabitants were southerners. He would never . . .

He sighed. He must do his best to make sure that they were safe and to make sure that no fanatics got control over the camp, and that, for once Chevakia and the people of the City of Glass spoke openly and worked together.

The column of trucks started moving downhill.

Milleus closed the escape valve and his truck jumped into motion. Isandor and Jevaithi waved.

"I'll be back as soon as I can," Milleus called out the window. He tried to sound optimistic, but oh, how he wished to take the youngsters with him. They were only children, and this camp seemed a hotbed of conflict, even within the southern population.

The large tent and the gathered onlookers, and Isandor and Jevaithi slid from view.

The convoy rolled down the hill, past tents that had been taken down, past the burnt-out remains of the feeble barricade that would never have been adequate to hold back the Chevakian army. Milleus was sure: the Chevakians had been ordered to retreat. Possibly because they had no interest in the conflict, or because they had established a more effective perimeter to isolate the riots. And what had the fights been about, anyway? Just southern refugees being frustrated and angry, and Chevakians being frustrated and angry.

There was no one in the lower third of the camp. Whatever tents had not been pulled down had been divested of their contents. Beds, blankets and whatever sparse furniture had been dragged to the top of the camp, leaving the ground dusty and muddy with occasional black spots. There would be trouble in Tiverius over this. The people would say that the southerners didn't deserve their support if they started burning things provided by the Chevakians. They should be more grateful and have respect. He could almost hear the voices in the doga. That self-righteous prick Janus, if he was still alive.

Ahead were the camp gates. The two metal-barred panels. Closed. Milleus slowed down, and then stopped. The trucks behind him did the same. He had expected to have to argue to be let through, or to be arrested. He'd expected a fight. Whatever he had expected, it was not this.

He honked the horn, but no one came, so he opened the escape valve, parked the truck in neutral and let himself out of the cabin.

There was no one in the gatehouse.

Mercy, what stupidity was this? Milleus rattled the gate. Through the strips between the bars he only saw the Ensar road snaking down the hill.

He banged his fist on the metal. "Hey, is anyone here?"

Artan came up behind him.

"What's going on?" he said.

"I have no idea," Milleus said. In his day, the army didn't just abandon a job. He banged on the gate again. "Hey! Can anyone open this?"

No one came. Artan peered through the gate and the restricted view it offered of the world outside the camp. "I guess we could use your wire-cutters again."

The other Chevakians had also come out of their vehicles and inspected the gate and fence. Several men rattled the gate. Others discussed how they could possibly open or break it, or cut through the fence.

Others suggested they go back to the south side of the camp.

"The gap we made has been closed," someone said.

"But can easily make another one."

They discussed this for a while. Other people had also noted the activity of trucks in the forest and concluded that someone had made a route through the forest for the traffic on the Ensar road to escape.

"Hey, someone's coming!" Artan said.

Everyone crowded at the gate, or prised aside the tightly-strung cloth that covered the fence on either side.

A small panel opened in the gate, and a man said, "What's going on here?"

Milleus was dismayed at the young and innocent voice. This was only a junior officer. He was wearing a sonorics suit over his uniform, complete with hood and visor.

"Let us through," Artan said, and his call was repeated by some of the others. He gestured for Milleus said, "We're Chevakians and we got stuck in here last night. We ask to be let out."

"I'm afraid I can't allow that, Sir." His voice sounded muffled under the mask. "The camp is to be sealed off. General's orders."

"Finnisius?" Milleus said.

"Yes. General's orders. Chevakian or southern, everyone in the camp is contaminated. You'd endanger the population."

"Rubbish," Artan muttered. He held out a bare arm. "I don't feel anything."

Milleus said, "Surely what little sonorics these people contribute is not going to make a difference to overall levels within Tiverius."

"The Chief meteorologist says differently. The General has ordered the camp sealed off, Sir. I cannot speak against my orders."

What? Sady had given the orders? Sady would not do such a thing as isolating people unless it was warranted. Just how badly contaminated were the southerners? What again were the early symptoms of sonorics illness? Surely sore joints were a symptom of old age, or were they?

"I am here on the invitation of the doga." He groped in his pocket, but the letter with the signatures was in the truck. "We need to get through, for the safety of the Chevakian refugees."

"They are being dealt with."

"By mercy's sake, use some sense. Let us out."

But it was a waste of breath. The man was too junior to argue with, and would never make a decision on his own. Milleus knew that too well.

"Can I speak to your superior officer?"

"I'm afraid, he's not available, Sir. You will understand that we are very busy."

"Then go and get him. Tell him Milleus han Chevonian is in the camp and wants to have a word with him. He's an old mate of mine." Not quite. Finnisius had been a junior officer, a bit of a self-righteous prick if Milleus remembered correctly, one of those people with slavish attention to rules.

The man flicked his eyebrows in a kind of *is that so?* way. But he didn't respond, and Milleus had an awful feeling the soldier didn't believe what he said.

"Look, just get him here, and let me do the talking."

"Sorry, Sir, he's busy. We're all busy."

The man turned and walked away.

Several of the men banged on the metal panels of the gate. "Hey. Let us out."

The soldier came back. "I'd advise you against cutting through this fence. We have a perimeter set up over there, in that line of bushes over there. Anyone coming out will be seen as a threat to Tiverius, and hostile to us."

They were actually going to shoot at Chevakian citizens? "You have to be kidding."

The man met Milleus' eyes for a moment, turned on his heel and went back to his truck.

What now?

Artan was looking at Milleus, and he wasn't the only one. They all expected him to know what to do.

Milleus shrugged. "Guess the only thing we can do is go back and wait until a senior officer comes into the camp."

CHAPTER 10

"SADY." There was a voice in his dreams, a voice that wanted him to come into a dark mire. He couldn't see the speaker from where he stood, hesitating, on a tall wall, surrounded by mist, with no idea how he'd managed to get up there. Everyone he loved, his parents—long dead—Milleus—missing—Suri—killed herself—was down there and wanted him to jump. But the water—and the dark substance underneath the mist must surely be water—was cold and there were weeds that would drag him down.

Another voice called from behind him, "Sady!"

This voice he recognised as Lana's, except the woman who had spoken wasn't her. He didn't know where she came from, but this was a dream and things happen like that in dreams. She looked like an old shrivelled prune of a woman, probably twice his age. She was wearing a wedding gown and carrying a wilted bunch of flowers. He had promised he'd marry her, but he couldn't possibly, not like this—

"Sady, wake up."

Sady woke with a shock. Opened his eyes in bleary morning light. Recognised that there had been someone calling him for real.

Sady said, "What?" Only it came out like a croak, and his mouth felt like sewerage.

The remnants of the surreal dream fled his mind.

The voice belonged to Orsan, who stood in the doorway, poking his head into the room. Bright daylight peeped between the curtains. What was the time?

Orsan continued, "Sorry, Sady, I'd like to let you sleep, but there have already been two messengers from the doga for people demanding to see you."

"What for?" But the moment he said that, reality rushed back to him. Lana dead. The trashed guest quarters, the four bodies, the deranged killer. They'd be the victims' families, or other people attacked by this deranged youth, or people from the hospital protesting the loss of two surgeons, or—

"Give me a moment. I'll be there soon—and Orsan, wait."

Orsan came back into the room.

"Any clue about where the baby is?"

"No. Not yet."

Orsan left, and Sady rose from the bed. He'd slept in his clothes, too, and they smelled of sweat and dust, and blood stains marked the front of his shirt.

No time for a bath.

He retrieved clean clothes from the wardrobe, raked a comb through his hair and shaved as quickly as he could. It made him feel slightly better, but did not dispel the dirty feeling.

In the kitchen, he found the southern family eating breakfast at one end of the table, and Farius staring into a cup at the other. Merni stood at the stove, stirring the pot that Lana used for making roccas.

The southerners looked tired. Sady presumed the city guards had interviewed them last night, presuming they had been able to find someone who could translate.

No one said anything when Sady came in, but the southern girl rose from the table, the baby still in the sling, and gave an awkward bow. "Thank you, thank you."

Sady wasn't quite sure what he was to be thanked for, but he returned a polite nod and sat at the table, feeling empty and bleak. Lana's absence was like a big hole inside him.

Merni gave Sady his breakfast. Her eyes were red. Yes, Lana would do this normally. Serran would be at breakfast, too.

Sady smiled at her, but her expression was hollow, and she turned back to the stove without saying anything.

"It's not fair," Farius said, in a low voice. "He was like a father to me. What do I tell his family?"

"I'll deal with it," Sady said, not looking forward to that task. When families provided sons and daughters for service to doga households, they expected them to be safe.

"What sort of person would do this?" Merni said, whirling around. She cast a furious look at the southerners, none of whom met her eyes.

"Merni, please."

"It's because of them."

Sady sighed. He rubbed his hand over his face. Mercy, he was tired. "Let's be rational. I don't know what happened and why." But the man they caught *was* a southerner, and he could fully understand her anger. "All I know is that we can't turn it back. We have to ride the cart we bought."

She gave him a hard look. Yes, that's right. She didn't like old sayings.

"Besides, we caught the killer. He is likely an escapee from the camp. He will be questioned and dealt with." Last night, Farius had confirmed that the man had not been with the family when they arrived at the house. "Meanwhile, please treat these people as you would like to be treated yourself. The woman has lost her baby. I doubt that was her choice. Give me some bread and I'll take it to her room."

"I'll do that," Merni said, meeting his eyes squarely. She sounded offended.

"Then do it soon," Sady said. "Please, look after her as you would if she were my sister. They are our guests."

Merni grumbled and went to get a tray.

Sady drank his tea. His eyes pricked.

He turned his attention to his bowl, filled with a gluggy substance with bits of grain.

Cooking roccas was Lana's specialty. Merni had left the grains in the water for too long. The skins had burst and the grains were no longer separate and juicy.

The grain had gone like jelly, was hard to scoop up, and stuck to the inside of his mouth. Trying to swallow made him gag, and he had a distant memory of being forced to eat a plate like this as a young boy at his grandmother's house; she had been a particularly careless cook.

Merni watched him, and said nothing. The southern family at the other end of the table sat like statues, pretending not to be there. All three of them had eaten Merni's attempt at roccas, no doubt out of politeness.

But he wasn't so afflicted. He shoved the bowl aside. "I'm going to work."

From the fire into the war zone.

The truck was waiting outside the gate by the time he left the house, and, by the looks of things, had been there for some time.

Sady got into the van, with an apology to the driver and guards. Orsan sat in the front passenger seat. He was ones of these people who could survive on hardly any sleep, and right now, Sady would give everything to be like that.

The vehicle drove through the near-deserted streets under a cover of low clouds. Wind whipped fallen leaves, still green, and dust and rubbish through the streets. Doors and windows were closed and obscured by boards or curtains, as guidelines for a level one sonorics warning dictated.

He tried to force his thoughts to the problems at hand. As he had become accustomed, someone in the office had left a folder with important items on his seat. They were documents on the financial crisis, which was a bad enough problem by itself. Several senators were pushing for a criminal case to be brought against the doga's chief accountant, who had allowed the missing books to leave the building. Destran said, of course, that he'd never taken the records out of the building and had returned them. But they were nowhere to be found.

Today, those problems seemed minor. While the truck drove through the streets, he kept reading the same passage of the document over and over, and could not stop the memories playing through his head.

Lana in the kitchen, smiling as he came in. "I heard you won!" Her eyes shone. "Congratulations, Proctor."

Lana, with her open smile, with her hearty laugh. She wasn't pretty or seductive, and had accepted her role as housekeeper, while she should have been his wife. Never mind that she wasn't from the right family. She lived for him. She never looked at another man. She had, once, even covertly suggested that he sleep with her.

It was a few days after Suri's funeral, when Sady had come home from staying with Milleus and Milleus looked unlikely to follow her in killing himself, and all the fuss had died down. They were in the kitchen. Just her and him, and they'd been talking about Suri and how desperate she would have been to take her life, and if only he'd known, he could have told Milleus. He had trouble keeping his emotions down. Lana was making tea, and she lifted the kettle with boiling water off the stove. Through the steam, her eyes met his. She said, "If it would help you feel better, Sady, I can stay with you tonight."

He remembered saying, "But you already stay with me every night," when he realised what she meant. It shocked him so much that his reaction had been immediate.

"I would never ask you to do such a thing."

She had turned back to her task without saying anything, but all night he'd lain awake wondering about the strange remark, and about her silence following his too-sharp, shocked reply. She had never mentioned it again, and he'd often wondered what would happen if he'd said yes, or, after one of their late nights talking politics in the kitchen, instead of waving and disappearing out the other door, he'd come up to her, and put his arm on her shoulders. Would she shrug it off, or would she turn up her face so that he could kiss her if that was what he wanted? Which he probably would.

Now it was too late.

Two women he loved gone without ever having felt his touch. That was what was wrong with him: he never made a move when he should, always trying to think up excuses as to why a relationship was inappropriate. With his brother's wife, or with his housekeeper.

People might say he just chose the *wrong* women, but both of them had led deeply unhappy lives because of him, because he kept them on an emotional leash, giving them hope, but keeping what they wanted just beyond their reach.

And now it was too late.

Too late.

The truck jerked to a stop, and Sady, deep in thought, lost grip on his documents. They slid onto the floor. He scrambled under the bench to retrieve them.

The driver opened the door. "You're all right, Proctor?"

Sady rose, the dishevelled papers in his hand. "I just dropped these." He climbed down from the cabin, feeling the driver's questioning gaze on him.

Mercy, he was in no state to run his household, let alone the country.

He clamped the papers under his arm and, accompanied by Orsan, he entered the gates to the doga building. The guards at the gate to the forecourt greeted him with salutes. Honest, open faces. They expected him to have all the answers. He crossed the courtyard and climbed the steps. In the hall, he gave his cloak to the wardrobe boy and turned towards the stairs, where the sound of many voices echoed in the high hall.

What was the ruckus up there? The crowd was halfway down the stairs.

Someone yelled, "It's the proctor!"

The shout was repeated up the stairs all the way to the foyer in front of the office.

Sady said, in a low voice, "I thought we had set up a process for people to submit their complaints or issues in the morning." He'd hated how the citizens used to crowd in front of the proctor's office shouting like they were at a camel auction.

"I warned you that a lot of people had come to see you," Orsan said.

So it seemed. Guards shooed the people to the side so that Sady could pass.

Sady met the eyes of a man on the side of the stairs, and the next moment, the man had shoved a dead bird under his nose.

"Look what they did," the man said, shaking the carcass so it almost touched Sady's robe. It had duck feet, but no head. The feathers on the belly were bloodied. "This isn't the only bird. We lost six, all with their heads chopped off."

"Same here," a woman said.

And another man added, "We lost a goat. I took the others inside, but you can imagine the wife isn't too happy with animals in the house."

"And the infuriating thing is that whoever did this just left the bodies there, and didn't even bother to eat them."

"It's vandalism, that's what it is."

"Wait." Sady held up his hands and the people fell quiet.

"We caught someone last night," Sady said.

The audience erupted in cheers and applause.

"Good for you, Proctor."

Sady held up his hand again, and silence returned. "This person attacked my house, and killed four people there." His eyes pricked all of a sudden.

Several people gasped.

"It's an attack on our government," a man said in a low voice.

"I very much doubt this person knew who he was attacking," Sady said, fighting his emotions. "We went and chased after him, and found him not far from my house. The credit for capturing him should go to Orsan and my personal guard Farius. The killer is in the courthouse prison."

"Who is this criminal?"

"We can't be sure. He said nothing. It looks like he's an escapee from the camp, but he doesn't seem to be right in the head."

"None of them are right in the head," a woman said.

A rotund man growled, "A filthy southerner? The prison's too good a place for him."

Several people agreed.

Sady thought of the man's strange hollow eyes, and his horrific scars, and the blood on his hands. "Secondly, has anyone seen the latest sonorics figures? Last I'm aware, the bell rang once on the hour. Unless something has changed that I'm unaware of, you should go inside your houses and stay safe. The madman will not kill again."

The news of the killer's capture travelled faster up the stairs that Sady could walk, and by the time he had arrived in the foyer, most people were making their way back down the stairs towards the entrance, many of them smiling at Sady and giving him victory signs.

Some hollow victory. If the man was mad, then how could he gain any satisfaction out of condemning him to death?

Sady went into his office, and heard from his secretary that Viki was waiting for him with the weather reports Sady had asked for.

At least someone was organised.

His former student sat in the visitor's chair, having spread maps and graphs all over Sady's desk, all over his papers and neat piles of documents. Whatever remained of the student too shy to say boo?

"Uhm, Viki?"

"Oh." Viki jumped up and took a number of rolls of paper from Sady's chair. Two of them tumbled out of his arms.

Sady picked them up, put them on the desk and sat down with a sigh. "Viki, do you always need to carry your entire office around with you?"

"I need to be prepared for every question." Viki sat down again. To Sady's shock, he had not shaved himself since Sady had last seen him and his chin sported a rough cover growth of hair.

"How long have you been here?"

"Uhm—I thought I'd come early . . ."

"I mean—have you been living in the office?"

"It's been very busy and there's a lot of work to do."

"All right. How does it look?" *Sonorics stabilising, still locally high, in the vicinity of the camp, but tapering off . . .*

Viki hesitated. "I don't understand what's happening."

"Show me." But it did not sound like the result he'd hoped for. Sady didn't like that little catch in his reply at all.

Viki rolled out the latest pressure map on the table. Normally, in this time of the year, an area of high pressure sat over the south, pushing a band of clouds into southern Chevakia, which manifested in a continuous progression of low-pressure cells. Instead, there was only one pressure cell, and it sat over the southern platform. Since Sady had last looked at a map, it had deepened and appeared to be moving, no—expanding—north. Sady stared at the crowded isobar lines.

"I've never seen anything like this before. Have you checked the records?"

"Yes, but I can't find any precedent."

"How many data points did you use for these maps?"

"Not as many as I would have liked. All of these measurements are from recovered balloons. A lot of the ground stations are out, or their reporting is unreliable."

"What measurements are we still getting? Twin Bridges?" He thought of the group of scouts he'd sent there.

"Yes, Twin Bridges, but most of the southern stations have stopped responding."

"Mekta? Solmeni?"

Viki shook his head. "None of those. Ensar, too." He pointed at the map. "Look, the storm front has moved into the southern regions and likely lines are down. People are reporting wildfires."

"In this weather?" Mercy, why hadn't he dragged Milleus home with him?

"There is a lot of wind, and some of those forests are very dry before the spring rains."

"What about sonorics? Have you mapped those?" They knew for certain that the barrier at Fairlight had shattered, but it might still be in tact elsewhere, never mind that there didn't seem to be a way of finding out.

"I have. And that's even more strange." Viki rummaged between his rolls of paper, pulled one out and unrolled it on the desk. Lines of sonorics were superimposed over a map of the city and surrounding areas.

There was a bright hotspot with many lines around it.

"That is the location of the camp," Viki said, unnecessarily.

"I thought we'd decontaminated them."

Not well enough, obviously, and another thing: if this very low level of sonorics showed up, what had happened to the base level— Sady checked: nothing. Sonorics levels were below ten motes per cube, lower even than normal for the time of the year.

He pulled the map onto his lap and studied it.

After a long silence, he said, "This is strange."

"I said so."

"Really, really strange."

"Anyway, that's last night's readings. Look at the difference this morning." He passed Sady another map with—mercy—levels as high as hundred and ten motes per cube at the army balloon base to the south of the city.

Sady put one map on the desk and the other on his lap and looked from one to the other.

"What caused such a sharp change?"

"Do you want the honest answer?"

"Is there another kind?"

Viki met his eyes, and his expression said, *One we don't tell the citizens*. Sady nodded.

Viki averted his eyes and looked down. "I don't have a single *fucking* clue."

Coming from his mouth, the expletive was doubly shocking. Shy, even-tempered Viki, who wouldn't even know how to harm anyone. Yet the strain was visible on that young face as were the bags under his eyes.

Sady reached out and touched his student's arm. "Viki . . ."

"I don't have a clue, all right? Sack me if you want. I don't know! Everyone expects me to know. I don't!"

"Calm down, Viki."

Viki took slow deep breaths.

"Have you asked Alius for advice?"

Viki gave Sady a look that said, *Do you think I have suicide tendencies?* Yes, that was right, there was some sort of issue why Viki was terrified of his tutor.

"Mercy, Viki, one hundred and ten, just outside the city. Enough to cause minor harm with long-term exposure. Have you sent out any warnings?"

"Warnings?"

"Sending out warnings is part of the Chief meteorologist's job. Those levels are high enough to justify two rings of the bell."

Viki's eyes were wide. "I . . . uhm . . ."

"Go, order it." That was part of the job, and Viki had nowhere near the training required to do it and while he had the confidence to do the technical part of the job, he had none of the skill with people.

Viki rose and scrambled to collect all his rolls of paper. He scurried for the door.

"And Viki?"

The young man froze. "Yes, Proctor?"

"What's with the face hair?"

"This?" Viki rubbed his hand over his unshaven chin, dropping a roll of paper. "Something different. I thought it looked good." He bent to pick up the paper. "Beards are very popular right now. I thought—"

"You look like you have a hairy caterpillar plastered on your face. Look, tell me this: what's with the group of men who wears beards?"

"Group of men. . . ?" Viki frowned.

"Yes, they hang around with Alius and other people from the Scriptorium. Some senators, too. Please tell me who they are and what they're about?"

"I . . . I have no idea what you're talking about."

"Then will you please shave yourself before someone assumes you to be something you are not?"

"Uhm—yes, Proctor. Surely." Viki went red in the face and scurried from the room.

Sady slumped in his seat and sighed, feeling an ache for his old job and the anonymity that came with it.

Instead, he lead a country that faced a sonorics crisis of uncertain nature, with financial irregularities that would sink a few political careers in normal times, with a huge population of refugees with whom no one could communicate, while a large group of prominent citizens appeared to be conspiring against the doga. At least they had caught the killer.

CHAPTER 11

*L*ORIANE AWOKE from the first good sleep she had for days to a sound of a door opening. For a moment, she thought she was at home in her limpet, but then she saw windows and curtains and she realised that she was not, and not only that, but she was no longer pregnant, and she was in Chevakia.

Dara was crossing the room to her bed, carrying a tray. "How are you feeling today, Mistress Loriane?"

Her voice sounded hesitant and uncomfortable, and Loriane remembered snatches of an argument last night, of Dara shouting, *I can't stay here like this!* somewhere in a corridor, while a young woman helped Loriane wash herself in the bath.

"The Chevakians gave me this to bring to you for breakfast," Dara said.

She set the tray down on the bed and backed off a few steps. Ontane and Myra had followed Dara into the room. Ontane left the door open as if he was prepared to flee at short notice.

Breakfast consisted of a bowl with a jelly-like substance which contained many little brown balls, like fish eggs, except it didn't smell like fish, and a cup of tea, which at least smelled like tea.

Loriane slid the tray onto her lap. The scent of food made her stomach churn. She had hardly eaten anything yesterday.

She poked at the sticky substance in the bowl. The little balls resisted being scooped up by remaining firmly stuck in the jelly. The Chevakians called this food? "What is this?"

"I have no idea," Dara said. And after a silence added, "These Chevakians don't know how to cook."

"I didn't mind it," Ontane said.

"You'd eat anything."

Loriane managed to hack some of the substance off and put it in her mouth. It was so gluey that it stuck to the roof of her mouth, which made it hard to swallow.

She swallowed the mouthful, with difficulty, and poked about in her bowl for a bit that wasn't so gluey. By the skylights, she couldn't eat this.

"The Chevakian didn't eat it either," Myra said. She patted Beido on the back. Loriane hoped he was hungry, because her breasts felt like rocks.

Ontane said, "Yeah, but he is the head of the household, and not some murdering refugee from a hated country."

Dara glared at her husband with something like a look of warning. He shrugged and crossed his arms over his chest and glared back at her with a look that said *What?*

Dara muttered something under her breath that sounded like, *We agreed not to mention it.*

Not mention what? If they had anything to say to her, they should say it. No doubt it had something to do with being the mother of a monster that had killed four people. As if she could help it. Damn Tandor and his machinations.

Loriane poked the spoon at the bowl's contents, ignoring the tense silence. She tried a couple of the round grains, but the jelly-like substance that coated them made her feel sick, and her anger made it worse. She flung the spoon in the bowl and shoved it aside.

"The tea is good, mistress," Dara said, her voice timid.

Loriane blew out a breath and met Dara's eyes. "Look, just what is going on?"

"Nothing. You need to recover, mistress."

"Nothing? And you're all behaving like I have some sort of disease?"

"We're . . . we're sorry about the babe." Dara averted her eyes.

Myra clutched Beido to her chest, her eyes wide.

"We have to do more than just be sorry. We have to find it."

Dara said, "You'll need time to recover, mistress. Let's not worry about it now."

"We should worry about it. That monster killed four people. It's out there somewhere."

Her only response was blank faces.

Then it clicked in her mind. "You don't believe me, do you?"

Ontane said, "Now, mistress, that be a big thing to say. You maybe confused, that's all."

"Confused? It's true!"

Ontane hesitated, shrugged and said, "All we heard were that the little mite was born and then you tried to strangle it."

"Because it is a monster, a hybrid. By the skylights, you don't think that I killed those people?"

More silence. It was clear they did. Loriane's heart thudded in her throat.

She remembered somewhere in her haze of pain after having arrived at the house, Ontane declaring his dislike of "women's business". That he was going to wait in the other room. Myra had wanted to stay, but the Chevakians wouldn't let her.

"I din' say that, Mistress Loriane."

"But you believe it."

"I din' say that either."

But Dara believed it, judging by the look on her face.

"You have to believe me. This is the truth: I didn't kill anyone. I *tried* to kill the child before it could do any damage, but I didn't. It's out there somewhere, threatening all who come across its path." She met their gazes one by one, feeling increasingly cold. They had travelled with her, they knew Tandor. If they didn't believe her, then what chance did she have with the Chevakians?

The uncomfortable silence lingered.

Eventually, she asked, "Whose house is this?"

Ontane said, "Someone Chevakian. He be rich."

Dara shot him an angry look.

"What? He is. All the other people be his servants."

"Where is Tandor?" Loriane asked.

"Tandor's still in the camp," Myra said, softly. Little Beido was making happy baby-gurgling noises. "You were right. Tandor was being controlled by Ruko, and we broke the bond by separating the two, but Tandor made such a fuss that the Chevakian guards took him out of the tent. We haven't either of them since."

"You left him in the camp?"

"It wasn't our choice. The Chevakians took him away. I have no idea where to."

"And no one thought to make sure he came with us?" By the skylights, Tandor was the only one who knew what was going on. He was the one who had wanted her child. If he was free, he could go and complete whatever evil plan he had cooked up. Use icefire to kill the Chevakians, seize the throne, kill the Knights. Whatever. And the child had a place in his machinations. If he could find it, which he probably could. Maybe he already had.

She threw the blankets aside. "I need to know where Tandor is." She rose.

Dara said, "You should stay in bed. You're still recovering."

"By the skylights, I won't. I'm going to find that monster." But a spell of dizziness took her and she had to sit on the edge of the bed.

"See? You need more time to recover."

Loriane looked around. "Where are my clothes?"

"The woman left some bandages in the bathroom."

"I'm not talking about bandages. I want my clothes. Where are they?" Not on the chair next to the bed. Not on the two chairs near the hearth. Maybe in the cupboard?

"You shouldn't get up yet."

"Why not? I've never stayed in bed. I've had ten children."

Dara's eyes met hers. Loriane thought she saw disapproval. "Look, I'm not staying in bed, and I'm not crazy. I need to find Tandor. Please give me my clothes."

"Uhm, I think they went to the laundry."

"Then get me something else."

"Yes, I'll ask."

The family left, and Loriane sank back onto the bed with a deep sigh. Dara was right in one, no, two things: one, the tea was really good, and two, she did not feel up to walking around much. Her backside hurt. It had not been a normal pregnancy and neither had it been a normal birth. Just trying to get up exhausted her.

By the skylights, what would she do? She would have expected at least some support from the family.

Her memories from yesterday were so distorted, she had trouble to tell what was real. It had to have something to do with the stuff the Chevakians had used to knock her out.

She knew that she'd suddenly awoken to a sharp pain, that she had jumped off the stretcher, because she could not possibly push out a child while on her back, that the Chevakians—and what were they doing here anyway?—had tried to stop her. That it was much too late for all of that, because she could feel the child drop into position between her legs.

She *thought* she'd run from their grasping hands before they could put her back on that table. She was in a strange room with no memory of how she'd ended up there. She'd opened a door—which turned out to be a cupboard—got in, shut the door and crouched in the corner. She remembered that overwhelming feeling of pressure. Unable to do anything else except push that damn child out. And push, until she was short of breath.

She remembered reaching down there and her hand meeting something slime-covered that wasn't any body part she recognised. And panic, and that overwhelming urge to push. This thing was happening to her and she had no way to control it.

She clearly remembered that the Chevakians yanked the door open and she was standing there, leaning against the back wall of the cupboard. They tried to pull her out. She screamed at them. What was it with these people trying to interfere with a woman giving birth? They backed off. She felt the burning pain of the head crowning, knelt down in that pitch dark cupboard, and reached for the child down there where she couldn't see. In the palace, other women would do this for the mother, like she had done for Myra. Usually, there would be a group of women sitting around the birthing mother, chatting and offering drinks and words of courage, ready to pass along the items the midwife asked for. These Chevakians were men and had no idea what to do, they didn't offer any help. They just watched.

She remembered, as the child came out and she tried to get hold of it, reaching awkwardly around her belly, grabbing something that felt like the child's shoulder. The skin was rough, and the bones were too sharp and poked at the skin. The little arm came free and felt not-so-little anymore. It *flapped*. A gust of air wafted past her thighs wet with birth fluids.

She'd been scared and shivery with panic, but could do nothing except what her body told her to do.

But by the time the child was out and she'd sunk down on the floor, and the Chevakians shone a light into the cupboard, the thing in her arms was just a baby.

A girl.

The Chevakians brought blankets, and helped her out of the cupboard, dripping blood everywhere. They chatted and seemed happy. A woman brought a cold drink. Loriane sat on the bed when the babe squirmed in her arms and opened her eyes. They were nothing like she had seen before. They were blue and she *looked* at her. Normal newborns didn't look. Their eyes were hazy, black and barely open. They were certainly not bright blue. And as she watched, the babe's nails became like little kitten's claws, digging into Loriane's skin. Her chubby little shoulders became less chubby, the limbs grew ad extended into large leathery wings—

A demon creature.

She shouted and grabbed the child by the throat, pushing it into the mattress.

The Chevakians rushed to stop her. Everyone in that room was shouting.

She remembered the feel of the child's skin under her hands, and that the soft neck grew in size and roughness even as she was trying to throttle it, and that the arms grew into huge wings, that she lost her grip, and that the demon-like thing grew and hissed and pushed her onto the floor. And that the two Chevakians, and some other people, had tried to restrain it. She remembered the vicious slashing of claws, spraying blood, screams. Hiding under the bed, on her knees, while blood dripped onto the floor. The demon-like creature prowled around the room, ripping up everything in its path. It hissed and slashed and growled. And then it charged straight at the window, smashed it and disappeared into the yard.

After seeing the bodies on the floor, she'd run out through the broken window, to hide in some other part of the house and waited … and waited, shivering and bleeding, her back against a cold wall.

That was where the kind Chevakian had found her. And he was the only one who had been nice to her all day, even though she couldn't understand him and he couldn't understand her.

Loriane finished her tea and had another go at getting out of bed, slowly. First, he legs over the side. Then sitting on her knees. The pad against the bleeding felt thick and wet between her legs. She would have to change that. Then, one foot under her, her hands on the side of the bed. She pushed herself up. By the skylights, her muscles hurt.

But she didn't feel dizzy this time.

Very carefully, she padded to the window, which looked out onto a courtyard surrounded by a stone wall. On the other side, she could see into a neighbour's yard with neatly-clipped hedges and statues and a bench where a child had left some toys. Wind whipped the bushes and blew leaves around the paving. Nothing moved; the curtains of the house were closed.

She ran her hands along the window frame, but didn't understand how it opened, if it opened at all.

She opened a few cupboard doors. There were blankets and pillows inside, but no clothes. Did this man really live here by himself?

One of the doors had a mirror on the inside. She lifted the night gown and wished she hadn't. Her belly was floppy, with a skin flap hanging down from below her navel, and wrinkled and cris-crossed with bruises and angry red marks. At least she didn't have a husband who had to pretend that she was pretty.

She'd had ten children, and where were they now? Where was Isandor? She couldn't imagine anyone having survived in the City of Glass.

On a top shelf in the cupboard, she found a box that contained coloured books with pictures. Children's books, with simple pictures of everyday objects, and words written next to them. She supposed that those letters said *house*, and those ones *mother*. She spent some time leafing through the book and made a decision: if Dara and Ontane weren't going to help her, she'd learn to say what she needed in Chevakian herself.

*

By the time Loriane had finished inspecting every item in the room, no one had come and she had heard nothing outside, so she decided to go for a walk. The nightgown was gossamer thin, but in the bathroom she found a towel or some sort of cloth to wrap around her lower body so that anyone she met wouldn't see her bandages and floppy belly through the fabric.

The corridor on the other side was familiar to her—she had been taken this way last night. If she remembered well, the main area of the house was to the right, down a flight of stairs.

The door to the room next to hers stood open. Inside stood a large bed with fine silky sheets rumpled and hanging off the side. A man's shirt lay on the floor and a couple of mis-matched shoes stood half under the bed.

She hesitated near the door, both embarrassed to see this and eager to tidy the room up. One of the people killed had been a woman who had been kind to her yesterday, someone who was probably a housekeeper here. Maybe the younger, unfriendly woman was a daughter who hated having to do this work as well as trying to cope with her loss.

She continued down the corridor and came to the staircase, where her footsteps echoed in the cavernous hall. A huge metal structure with lots of oil lamps hung from the ceiling. She counted twenty-one lights. The stairs themselves were made from a white polished stone with carved railings. A mosaic in different types of stone, depicting a man riding an animal of some kind took up most of the floor in the hall.

By the skylights, and she had thought that the large hall in the palace in the City of Glass was a display of splendour. Just how rich were these Chevakians?

The sound of voices drifted from downstairs, so Loriane descended the steps and remembered the way to the kitchen.

Inside, she found Myra washing dishes. Sounds of hammering came from elsewhere in the house.

Loriane sat down at the table, thankful that Myra's parents weren't here.

Myra gave her a scrutinising look. "You're feeling all right?"

"Yes." This insistence on asking about her wellbeing was getting annoying. She'd given birth to ten children. Why should she *not* be all right?

Except with this one, there hadn't been a happy father taking the child away, and she'd received no money. The child had just . . . vanished and was out there to threaten everyone, wild and dangerous. Except no one would believe her.

"Where are your parents?"

"Ma is cleaning the room we were in yesterday, and Da is in the garden."

"The Chevakians let you do work?"

"They're busy fixing up the mess from yesterday. It's the least we can do."

Loriane nodded.

"Do your parents speak any Chevakian?"

"Not much. Just a few words."

That was still better than Loriane. That annoyed her to be dependent on someone else to make herself understood. "You speak some Chevakian."

"Only a very little bit."

"Better than your parents."

She shrugged. "I guess . . ."

"Could you teach me?"

"I don't know that much either. Most of the things people say I don't understand. They speak so fast."

"That's more than I understand."

"True."

There was an uneasy silence. Loriane looked at her hands.

"Myra, your parents don't believe me, right?"

She turned away from the washtub, and shrugged. "I guess not. It's hard for them to believe that something like that could exist."

"Do you believe it?"

Myra's eyes met hers, direct. "I believe you're a good woman, Mistress Loriane." Which was not an answer, but close enough.

She sighed and went back to her washing up. "My parents, and everyone in Bordertown, was scared of Tandor. He paid us, but no one understood why."

Loriane nodded. That was pretty much the deal with Tandor.

"We, the Imperfect kids, thought he was the best thing ever. He brought us presents and sweets. He let us have parties, and boys. He also showed us all these old books. We thought he was weird." She paused to tip the water out of the tub. "Anyway, some of those books showed winged creatures. We asked about them, and he said they were real. He said they were powerful, and he also said that they were on our side."

"What is that supposed to mean?"

"I don't know, mistress Loriane. I really don't know. I thought his talk was boring. I wished I'd paid better attention. He was clearly trying to tell us something, but I have no idea what it was, and if he meant that winged creatures were going to take over, I somehow prefer the Eagle Knights."

Loriane nodded.

There were voices in the hall outside the kitchen, and the sound of footsteps.

A woman's voice, not familiar.

Then the door to the kitchen opened and the cranky housekeeper Merni came in, together with a woman Loriane hadn't seen before. She had white hair and a face lined with age, but walked straight in the manner only someone of high birth can. Like the nobles in the City of Glass. In fact, she was very much like the nobles of the City of Glass, down to the richly embroidered robe that was surely too warm for the Chevakian climate.

She advanced into the kitchen and turned to Loriane. Her eyes were dark blue.

"You're the Pirosian?" she asked.

It clicked in Loriane's mind. This was Tandor's mother.

Loriane returned the woman's stare. What business did she have asking questions like that? *You're the Pirosian?* As if that was all that mattered about her.

She returned a mock bow. "I am very well, thank you."

"You *are* the Pirosian." The woman's gaze went to her belly, and her eyebrows rose. "Where is the child?"

"I'm sorry. I didn't catch your name."

In a few steps, the woman stood in front of Loriane and grabbed her chin. "Where is the child?"

"Why do you want to know?" Loriane swiped her hand away. She was *not* a naughty child. "Please don't touch me. The child is contracted to a man called Yanko in the City of Glass."

"The child is my son's."

"Can't. He's got no dick and no balls."

"Rude language doesn't suit a simpleton like you. Where is the child?" The grip of her hand tightened, and she now also held the front of her nightgown. For her age the woman was surprisingly strong. Loriane struggled to pull away, but didn't want to yank too much for fear she'd rip the nightgown that belonged to the kind Chevakian man. They had already wrecked so much in his house.

"I don't have to tell you or give you anything. I don't recall Tandor ever speaking of you."

"You're a Pirosian whore, that's why. What my son has to say is of no concern of yours."

"Stop insulting me, and leave. The child is mine and I don't see why I should tell you where it is."

The woman said something in Chevakian, and a hulk of a man whom Loriane hadn't noticed entering the kitchen came forward. He grabbed her shoulders and pinned her to the wall with one hand while holding a dagger under her chin with the other.

Loriane yelped.

The grumpy housekeeper stood in the door that the man had left open, yelling at someone in the hall. Myra just stared.

Tandor's mother pulled a medallion from under her clothes. On it was depicted a creature the size of an eagle, but with wings of skin. Loriane had seen this creature before, on the cover of one of the books Isandor was fond of reading. It was the crest of the Thilleian house, the dacon. She'd always tucked those books away quietly, without commenting on them.

"Does this look familiar to you at all?"

"Uhm . . ." Loriane said. The tip of the dagger pricked in her skin. "I'm not going to tell you, and you can't kill me, because then no one can tell you."

"You insolent—"

People ran into the kitchen.

"Keep your head down, Mistress Loriane!" someone yelled near the door. Dara.

A blur in a brown shirt—Ontane—shot through the kitchen, knocking the guard half off his feet. He stumbled back. The dagger clattered onto the floor. Ontane scrambled to pick it up.

"You idiots. You don't know what you're playing with!" Tandor's mother held up the medallion.

Clearly, it gave off light or power of some kind, which Loriane couldn't see. Dara shouted.

Myra clapped her hands over her eyes.

In the corridor, the housekeeper screamed.

Loriane glared at the woman. "That thing can't harm me. I can't see icefire, and it has no effect on me."

"Me neither," Ontane said, brandishing the dagger. "I be fed up with this darned sorcery. You are going to leave Mistress Loriane alone. Or you will have to deal with me."

The guard clambered to his feet, clutching his shoulder with one hand. He didn't meet anyone's eyes. He took the woman's arm and together they left the kitchen. When they had gone, Ontane shut the door and stuck the dagger in his belt.

Dara and Myra stared at him with wide eyes.

Loriane whispered, "Thank you."

"I protect my women, even though they don' always deserve it and don' appreciate it." He glared at Dara, who glared back at him. "There be no use in freedom, woman, unless we get rid of all self-righteous idiots, not jus' the ones we disagree with."

CHAPTER 12

CARRO DIDN'T DARE mention the visions to his father, or the figures he had seen made from fire at the time when he and the hunters had been trying to get back to the City of Glass, before they knew about the explosion. Heck, he didn't know himself what was real and what was a vision, and his father wouldn't like it if he heard that his son saw things. Carro was still waiting for the punishment he would inevitably receive for failing to meet his father's expectations.

So he trudged off and went to find Farey and Jeito in the dorms. Nolan, already aware of the task ahead, followed silently.

Under the jealous eyes of a few fellow Knights, who stood guard in the courtyard and who had been cooped up in the farmhouse for days, they went to the stable. The eagles started protesting as soon as he entered wearing riding gear—they had probably heard the tinkle of the metal rings the moment he'd left the farmhouse.

They, too, had been inside for days—to stop Chevakians in balloons seeing them—and didn't like this situation. They stood in semidarkness in the musty smell. They were all snapping at each other, and hissed at Carro as he walked past. His own eagle bent its head low down, spread its wings and fanned out its tail feathers, a strange mating behaviour that the females displayed if they were begging their riders for food or attention.

Carro scratched the animal on the head and untied the leather straps of the head gear. The bird jumped up and flapped huge wings. The giant wing feathers brushed Carro's hair. A couple of other birds squawked. Carro's eagle hissed.

A stable boy scurried out, but Carro whistled hard and the birds calmed. In a very pleasing way, it surprised him. It seemed he *had* learned, even though the hunters still thought him a clumsy fool.

Jeito and Farey's eagles stood at the far end, eyeing Carro's bird. Compared to all these fresh, skittery birds, they looked sleek, but well-used, and care-worn, and rather blasé about their surroundings. Jeito and Farey needed only snap their fingers and they came strutting through the stable. Jeito hissed back at a bird that tried to peck at her eagle's feathers. Her hiss could almost pass for an eagle's.

"Trouble is those birds don't get out enough," Nolan said.

"Tell us something we don't know," Farey said.

They led the birds outside in complete silence. Carro's eagle took large steps and lifted its feet high, and tilted its head this way and that to look at the surroundings. Carro held tight onto the reins even as it tilted its head all the way back to inspect the sky. Rider Cornatan stood watching, his arms crossed over his chest.

Carro met his father's eyes and a chill went over his back. This wasn't just a simple mission to find this army, or Rider Cornatan would have sent someone else. As for every one of Carro's tasks, there was a message in it. If only Carro understood what those messages were.

Carro mounted his bird and for the first time in days, rose to the air. The breeze through his hair reminded him painfully of his races with Isandor. The hunters were close behind.

"Better make some headway before daytime," Farey said.

At first daylight they had progressed deep inside Chevakia's central district, an area of farms and little villages interspersed with bits of land too rugged or steep to farm.

In an embarrassing way, Carro was glad to stop flying. Because they didn't want to be seen, they had to fly very high, where it was cold and squally winds tried to unseat them from their birds. It was hard to make out where they were going because a blue-grey haze hung over the landscape, turning the landscape into a grey soup. At times, Carro thought he could smell fire, but he was sure that was only his imagination playing tricks with him. He sat hidden deep within his cloak and spent a lot of time fighting visions.

When the night had become a grey and listless dawn, they made camp in a cave in a rock wall overlooking a river. They went through the usual routines. Nolan made the fire while Farey plucked the bird that Carro had shot. He was proud of the kill—using a dart in mid-air —although he half-suspected that it had been an escaped domestic bird.

His next job was to haul water from the river.

He half-slid down the steep incline, holding himself on whatever trees and bushes were available. The water in the river was murky brown and churned in little eddies. The current carried sticks and leaves.

Carro dipped the bladder into the water and held it under until it was full. When he was putting the stopper back in, a tree trunk drifted past, its surface black and charred from fire. He noticed other blackened branches, too, washed up on the banks. And his mind went back to those apparitions of fire. These burnt tree trunks proved that there *was* a fire out there, up on the southern slopes.

He did not mention the burnt wood when he returned to the others. They had seen the same things he had, and would have the same worries, save that they didn't have memories of people made of fire. And even those worries wouldn't change the task they'd been given.

Nolan had the fire going and Farey had plucked the bird. Jeito sat a little apart from the others. She held a map, but wasn't looking at it. She sat staring into the hazy morning air. Carro poured water in the pot and put it on the fire to the side of the duck which was already dripping fat and starting to smell good. Farey added the bird's wings and feet to the water. All this without anyone saying a word.

Carro sat down with his back against the rock wall of the cave. When he'd bent to get water, the Pirosian medallion around his neck had dangled free from his clothes, and now Farey glanced at it. Carro put it back under his clothes. Increasingly, Farey and Jeito's silence and looks made him nervous. Nolan tried to make small talk, joking about certain commanders at the farmhouse, but even he fell quiet until all that could be heard was the whistling of the wind around the cliff face and the occasional distant rolling of thunder.

Carro felt alternately hot or cold depending on the direction of the wind. Dark visions clouded at the back of his mind. The Outer City. Limpets on fire, the staff with the sink in his hand, the feeling of frost biting into his hands as the stone absorbed icefire. He tried to push those images away, and he must have drifted while staring into the fire because suddenly Nolan exclaimed, "I don't get it! What are you two on about?"

"Shut. Up," Jeito said.

"But you're behaving like idiots. We know we can trust him."

"He was the one who fucked up when we almost had them."

Carro was fully alert now. He met Jeito's eyes, which burned like furious coals. No, he didn't belong with this group, and had never truly been part of it.

"It was an honest accident," Nolan said.

"Oh, shut up, pup."

"What? Now I'm the pup?"

"You behave like one, so you get called pup. You have no idea what I'm talking about."

"Then enlighten me."

Nolan crossed his arms over his chest, his nostrils flaring. He was probably half a head taller than Jeito and twice the width.

Jeito snorted. "Anyway, I don't care if it was an accident or not, I don't want him with us if he's likely to fuck up again."

Farey said nothing, but he likely agreed. Nolan spread his hands, his eyes pleading, most likely for Carro to say something like, *but it was really an accident.*

But it hadn't been an accident, and Farey and Jeito would always know that.

Carro rose. He felt like he was trembling all over.

"I could leave, if you don't really don't want me along," he said.

"Leave?" Nolan said, his eyes wide.

"Yeah, go somewhere else. I've thought about leaving a lot."

"Deserting?" Nolan squeaked. "Your old man would go mad."

Carro nodded. "Sure he would." Rider Cornatan probably wouldn't rest until he was found, and punish the hunters for letting him go. Both Jeito and Farey were looking at him with wide eyes. He had them. They listened to him.

"Why by the skylights would you do that?" Farey asked, now no longer angry. "You got your career mapped out. You will go straight into the upper command."

"Only because of my father."

Their silence surely meant agreement.

"Do you know the motto of the Knights?"

They frowned at the change of subject.

"Course we do," Farey said.

"Say it for me."

"Obedience, honour, honesty, humility and silence." Farey's voice had a recalcitrant tone, a tone that said, *Why should I do this? Just get on and tell me what this is about.*

"The Knighthood is a proud institution," Carro continued. "We uphold the law in the City of Glass, we guard the Queen, we protect the citizens. We are what young boys dream of becoming, what young men sign up to join."

He let a silence lapse. Jeito and Farey's faces looked grim as if they knew what was coming. Nolan just looked puzzled.

"You don't have to answer this question, but what is honourable about killing the Queen and one of the citizens we are sworn to protect, when all she has done is to refuse to let herself be fucked by senior Knights? She is not sworn to obey any of us. She isn't in the Knighthood and doesn't even sit on the council."

If possible, the silence grew more intense. Even Nolan seemed to understand now.

"I grew up adoring the Queen. At home, we cried when Maraithe died." Even his merchant father had, he remembered now. "We lined up for half a day to catch a glimpse of her bier being carried to the shore. Our hearts broke for Jevaithi, the little girl in the procession, with her hand held by some stiff-faced maid. The tears on her cheeks were real. I was only eight, but I wanted to go to her and bring her my toys so she would be happy again."

Jeito nodded, her hands in her lap.

"When I joined the Knighthood, everyone spoke of serving the Queen. To us, she was the most beautiful woman in the world, if not the only woman in the world. To be a Knight was to dedicate your life to the Queen. We watched her tower room, we watched the corridors of the palace for glimpses of her. Which Knight has not dreamed of landing a job to escort her?"

No one replied to that question; they all knew the answer. Carro sat down pretending to be calm, but he trembled all over. By the skylights, what had gotten into him? The hunters were likely to kill him for saying all these things. But they were things that had bothered him for a long time. Certainly he could not be the only one thinking them?

In continued silence, Farey removed the cooked duck from the fire and cut it up. When he handed Carro a piece, his eerie grey eyes met Carro's with a burning intensity.

"You know that men have been killed for saying lesser things?"

"Yes," Carro said, although he did not. He was such a naïve fool and these hunters would probably be doubly keen to get rid of him now.

He'd hoped . . . he didn't know what he'd hoped, but all he'd received was silence. And he still didn't know what the hunters thought.

They ate, and tried to get some sleep. Farey and Nolan had no trouble, but Carro found it hard to sleep when it was light. He lay tossing on his mat, feeling the bumps and rough edges of the rock through the thin surface.

He must have fallen asleep, because suddenly, it was much later, and a shadow crouched over him. In one fluid movement, he rose, grabbed his knife and slammed the person into the ground, with the "oof" of breath being forced from lungs. It was Jeito, pinned under him. He was heavier than her and in this position, she could do nothing.

"My, I think the pup learned something," she said, her voice low.

"What the fuck were you doing, sneaking up on me like that?"

In a flash movement, she pulled him down by his shirt, and rolled over so that she sat on top. Her face was so close that he could feel the heat of her breath of his skin.

"Do you want to fuck me?"

"No."

She seemed taken aback by that reply, then one corner of her mouth went up. "You prefer boys, huh?"

"No."

"What's wrong with you?"

"Nothing." He looked into her puzzled face and added, "If, however, you think the things I said are true, I do appreciate your support. You are a good fighter, and I'd like to trust you as a friend."

"A friend, huh?" She gave a crooked smile. "I thought I was way too bitter to have any friends. Friends are for children."

"Are they?" Carro could stop a memory of Isandor, and their innocent friendship.

Jeito crawled back to her sleeping mat, giving him strange looks.

"You're weird."

Carro nodded. He had come to accept that.

But as Carro lay back down, he still couldn't sleep. In a roundabout sort of way, Jeito's odd behaviour must have meant that she approved of what he'd said, but may have been too afraid to say aloud.

CHAPTER 13

THE MORNING in the Proctor's office had the feeling of being at least two days long. Sady was fighting to stay awake, never mind concentrate, while reading through financial reports. The only thing that kept him from putting his head on the books and falling asleep was the sheer magnitude of the mess. Had no one ever given the budgets more than a cursory look? Not only was expenditure vastly bigger than income, columns hadn't been added properly, or not at all, entries had been left out of the total, and large amounts of money just vanished in between being transferred to different departments.

He didn't understand how Destran could have let all this happen, and he couldn't imagine how Destran would not have known about these problems. Or—and the thought brought an increasing chill—was Chevakia in such perilous financial state that Destran had no choice?

Sady leafed through the books, found large chunks of data missing, and with every page he turned, things seemed to get worse.

There was a knock on the door and his secretary came in. "Uhm, Proctor, General Finnisius is here for you."

Sady frowned. "Did I forget an appointment?"

"No, but, uhm—" He lowered his voice. "He doesn't look happy."

What now? "Send him in."

The secretary vanished and a moment later, the general strode in

with big steps, stopped in front of Sady's desk and gave an exagger-
ated bow.

He wore his dress jacket, with its many shiny buttons and medals
of decoration.

"Good morning, Proctor," he said, in a tone as if measuring his
words out precisely.

"Sit down," Sady said.

The general did so, placing each hand precisely on the corresponding
knee. Catching the light that fell through the window, his hair looked
more silver than grey. The general was closer to Milleus than Sady in
age, and had led the army into Arania; a man of intimidating experience.

"About the refugee camps," the general said, and his voice sounded
tense.

"Yes, tell me how the situation is there."

"We're withdrawing from the camps."

"You're—what?" The army was needed to distribute food, and to
transport other supplies, and . . .

The general fixed him with an angry look. "There has been unrest
amongst the refugees. Overnight, the southern fence was breached
and a large number of people came into the camp—"

"Into? Who in mercy's name would want to—"

"—Chevakians, from the Ensar Road. They appear to be refugees
from the border region, who thought the camp was for them and had
been waiting on the other side of the fence. They'd run out of food,
and got so angry that they cut through the fence."

"But what were these people doing there? There should have been
signs on the Ensar road."

"I don't know. The fact is that those people were there and
assumed the camp was for them."

"I told you to put up signs—"

"I'm running an army, not the roads department."

A tense silence followed.

The general breathed out deeply through flaring nostrils and
continued, "Anyway, once they came in, we tried to turn the
Chevakians around, but some refused to do so. The road behind
them is so crowded that they can't turn their vehicles and if they
could, there is no way for them to get out. More worrying, the camp's

youth took the interruption as a sign to riot. There were fights overnight. They lit fires. Chevakians were injured."

What? "So you've lost control of the camp?"

The general gave him a hard look. "We have not *lost control.* We have set up a perimeter around the camp, because we can contain the site from there. There have been no more fights since dawn. We have also made a temporary road to allow the refugees on the Ensar road to leave."

"And, there is a problem? It seems to me that you have the situation under control."

"We have the situation under control and we are passing the responsibility for the camp to the city guards. My men are not equipped for this. Our duty is to protect the borders."

What was this? "We have criminals escaping from the camp. I want that perimeter to be completely closed."

The general nodded. "Done. The city guard is looking after it."

"I want all Chevakians out of that camp. Use health warnings to get them out. The southerners may have been decontaminated, but Viki has just shown me evidence that sonorics levels in the camp are still high."

"Proctor, there are two things you have to understand. First: the primary task of the army is to defend the country. We have a balloon base to run and an army to keep on its toes in case the south tries something funny. I'm sure you are aware of the rumours of a rebellion against the Eagle Knights. Last time something like that happened in the south, it spilled over the border. It is our priority to concentrate on that, and I do not want to take any more personnel from that task than absolutely necessary."

"Yes, I understand." Sady was getting irritated, and he felt irritated about being irritated, too. He should not let anyone get under his skin like this, but why did the man have to behave like such a patronising boor?

"Further, as I mentioned, a significant number of Chevakians came into the camp by their own choice. They remain in the camp *by their own choice* despite our directions for them to leave. They're demanding to be housed there, because they have nowhere else to go."

"They can't stay, for their own health. They are going to have to leave and come into the city. We'll process them here and—"

"They will not. They have their own tents and animals. They want a place to camp. Some of those refugees are quite violent. They are already angry with the doga for having forgotten about them. They have joined forces with the southerners. There will be fights."

Sady spread his hands. *You're commanding an army, for mercy's sake!* "Is that a problem?"

The general gave Sady a hard look. "Yes, and that is the second, and more serious issue. My people are soldiers, trained to fight the threat of war from outside our borders. My soldiers do not fight fellow Chevakians."

Sady looked at him in stunned silence, knew that the general was right—incredibly right—in principle, and knew he'd just made a monumental mistake that would cost him whatever respect he had with Finnisius, if there had ever been any respect in the first place.

The general was sure to think of him as a complete idiot now.

He would think a lot clearer if he wasn't so *fucking* tired.

"Then . . ." He paused to order his thoughts and found they were all over the place. Riots in the camp, murderers loose in Tiverius, no money to do anything, and strange sonorics patterns. "Tell me, what would you do?"

The tiny smile around the general's mouth was triumphant. No doubt he'd come here to tell Sady he was an idiot and succeeded, above expectations. "We have already isolated the camp and the wider area around it, so there is no risk to the citizens of Tiverius—"

"No risk? Tell me then why one of those southern refugees, a madman, is in the courthouse prison after having killed four people at my house?"

He had shouted much louder than intended, and Finnisius looked taken aback.

". . . killed?"

"Yes, two surgeons and two domestic staff. Orsan, one of my private guards and I managed to catch him. He's a southerner, an escapee from the camp."

"Are you sure?"

"I don't know where else he would have come from. He's either escaped last night, or during transfer."

The general looked as if he'd just been robbed of an argument.

After a short silence, Sady continued, "So, what do you suggest we do about this problem? The one that the city guard is so brilliantly coping with?" And what was the general's mandate to pass major jobs like this onto the guard without the doga's approval?

General Finissius' expression was hard. "Increase the number of people. Look, that is a matter for the high command of the guard."

"The city guard is not equipped to deal with large-scale riots." Sady glared back at the general.

"And I told you: we have a country to protect—"

There was a sharp knock on the door and Orsan came in. "I'm sorry to interrupt—"

Finnisius rose. "That's all right. I'm just leaving."

No, he was not. "I haven't finished."

"But I have." Finnisius left the room in complete silence.

Orsan stared after him, his eyebrows raised. His expression said, *What was all that about?*

Sady felt like saying, *Well, Orsan, that was about Finnisius being a prick and having assumed authority he does not have, and challenging me to put him in line.* And he didn't have the people to put Finnisius in line, and likely Finnisius knew that, too. The question was: who runs Chevakia? Between the army, the city guard and the doga, Sady wasn't sure he could answer that.

Orsan closed the door behind him, leaving an uneasy silence.

Sady sighed. "What's the matter?"

"Uhm, we just got a message from Farius. If you could please come home as soon as possible."

"From Farius?" He'd left the young guard with the southern family this morning. "Did he say what it was about?"

"No, sorry. It was a courier, not Farius himself. The message was only short, but it said it was urgent."

What had happened at home now?

"All right." He rose from his desk, while the fear of last night reached cold fingers into his heart. Walking through his house in the dark, finding bodies surrounded by puddles of blood. Intestines spilling out. Lana's face ripped off—

Orsan left the room with him. As soon as he entered the foyer, people wanted to speak with him, including someone from the courthouse prison, presumably to talk about the interrogation of the prisoner, but Sady waved them all aside and left of the building, into the truck.

While the driver scrambled to build pressure in the boiler—usually he had notice of when the truck would be required and could prepare in advance—Sady wracked his mind about anything that might have become an urgent problem: Merni's grumpiness towards the southern family. Their quiet apologetic presence in the kitchen. They'd eaten all of the terrible roccas Merni had made just to be polite. They'd said nothing.

The woman Loriane, he hadn't gone to check up on her. Maybe she had collapsed. Maybe she had done something silly. Maybe there was something wrong with her. But no, what would she do that required his immediate attendance? Anything of that sort required a medic.

All he knew was that he had no time for domestic crises. He would have to send these people back to the camp as soon as the situation there was stable. Much better for them to stay with their kinsfolk—

The driver cursed fluently and hit the truck's brakes with force. Tyres slid over the pavement with a screech.

Sady had to hold onto his seat to stop himself being flung onto the floor.

The vehicle skidded sideways and came to a halt. The driver cursed again. Orsan flung the door open and jumped out of the passenger seat.

Sady scrambled up. "What was that?"

"A child crossed the road in front of me!" The driver opened the door and let himself out of his seat. "She didn't even look."

"Did you hit her?"

"I'm not sure. She is only a tiny thing."

Feeling sick, Sady followed him out of the truck, his head reeling. A child. He seemed to fall from one disaster into another.

A small girl sat on the pavement directly in front of the truck. She couldn't be older than two or three at the most. She had her knees drawn up to her chest and her chin leant on her knees. Sleek black hair fell to her shoulders. There was no sign of blood. That was something at least.

"Little girl, are you hurt?" he asked.

She didn't reply. She clutched her knees and rocked backwards and forwards in a way that chilled him. "Why is a child like that alone in the street? Where are her parents?"

"I have no idea. She just ran onto the street." The driver looked around. His voice sounded shaken.

They were on the main street that ran to the hilly part of the City where Sady lived. The walls of the doga complex were to the right, the Chevakian Archive and the Scriptorium Library to the left. This street did not normally get busy with ordinary citizens; today, it was deserted.

Orsan knelt next to the girl. "It's all right. We won't get angry. We're just glad you're all right. Where are your parents?"

The girl looked up. Her eyes were bright blue.

The look on her face reminded Sady of the knife-wielding madman they had caught last night.

"I think she's too young to understand you," the driver said.

"She's southern," Sady said. Those eyes gave him the chills.

Orsan frowned at him. "From the camp?"

"Where else?" Anger flared inside him. That pompous idiot of a General Finnisius. If even a toddler could get out of the camp, then the army was doing a poor job indeed.

Sady held out a hand. "Come, I'll take you somewhere safe." How had she found her way here all the way from the camp? Did she even understand Chevakian?

She ignored his hand. He rummaged in his pockets, but any sweets he kept in there had long since been eaten.

"Come, I'll take you home."

As he touched her shoulder, she jumped up and retreated until she stood with her back against the truck.

"Whoa, I'm not going to hurt you."

She crouched on hands and feet, like a wild animal, and made a hissing noise that made the skin on the back of Sady's neck crawl. He retreated a few steps. Belatedly, he noticed how hot her skin had felt

"Whoa," Orsan said.

Sady said, "Don't be scared. I know people who can talk to you." Curse him. He'd been to the City of Glass twice, and had not learned one word of their language.

She ducked and ran, between Orsan and the driver's grasping hands, into the street.

"Mercy." Sady straightened, watching her cross the road without looking. Her black hair bounced over her shoulders.

"What was that about?" Orsan said.

"I'd like to know what southerners do to their children to scare them that much," said the driver.

"At least the truck didn't hurt her," Sady said.

Orsan said, "I'd like to know what she's doing here alone and why our men can't even keep a little girl in the camp."

"Good question. Make some inquiries."

When he climbed back into the truck, Sady could still see the wild look in those blue eyes. All through the incident, the girl had uttered not a single sound.

The driver dropped Sady and Orsan at the gate to Sady's house not much later. Sady was relieved to see that the house was still there. There had been no fires, the windows were all still intact and, when he entered, there were no dead bodies in the hall. That was at least something. Strange how expectations changed in a matter of days.

He walked into the hall. "Farius?"

There was no reply but the sound of a male voice came from the kitchen, so he went in.

Farius sat at the table, opposite Merni, who leaned her head in her hands.

"Oh, there you are." Farius' voice sounded relieved. He got up from the table and came to Sady's side.

Merni didn't move.

"What is the matter?" Sady shrugged off his cloak. "I'm extremely busy at work." He found himself getting quite annoyed. He hoped this emergency was at least as bad as dead bodies in the hall, because he seriously had much better things to do.

"What is the matter?" Merni screamed, while she rose from her seat, pushing the heavy bench so hard that it wobbled. "You better ask what isn't the matter." Her eyes were wild.

"Merni, Merni. Calm down."

"No. I'm not putting up with any more of this. First we have a murderer attacking our house, then these people take over my kitchen, then this woman just barges into the house and tries to drag people out—"

"What in all of mercy's name do you mean?"

"That southern freak!" Merni buried her face in her hands and sobbed.

Sady frowned at Farius. "Does she mean Loriane?"

"No, we had a visitor. It was the southern woman who lives on Merchant's Hill."

"Lady Armaine?" The question was futile. There *was* only one southern woman in the merchant district.

"Yes, she came to the house, demanding to see our refugees. I said no, as you told me, but she had a private guard with her, and with Orsan being away, and Serran . . . I'm sorry— but there was little I could do to stop them. They came in anyway. The southerners were in the kitchen. The lady made straight for the woman Loriane. There was some sort of an argument with the woman, and the next thing the old lady attacked her."

"She attacked Loriane?"

"Yes. I don't know what either of them said. But I think she wanted Loriane to come, and Loriane didn't want to come, and then the old lady used her sorcery—"

Merni jumped up. "In my kitchen! Sorcery in my kitchen! Magic!" Her voice rose to a screech. "You always said there was no magic. But I saw it. In *my* kitchen."

"Shh, Merni, it's all right now. I'm sure there is a logical explanation."

"No, it isn't all right. I don't care for logical explanations. Whatever it was, that was no natural thing that she did. Next time she'll use it on us, like they did to poor Lana and Serran. And you expect me to sit here and wait until she comes?"

"It wasn't Lady Armaine who killed Lana and Serran. We caught the killer."

"How do you know that? As long as there is magic, they'll come and kill us. I don't care who they are. They're all evil. I'll tell you, either these southerners are leaving the house right now or I am going—"

"You want to turn them out into the street?"

Her face blazed with anger. "You care more about them than about us, that is clear to me. I've had enough. I'm going back to my mother's house." She untied her house apron and threw it on the table. Then she stormed out of the room.

Sady rose. "Merni!"

But she was already halfway across the hall. She opened the front door, went through and slammed it behind her.

Sady slouched back to the kitchen, slumped at the kitchen table, leaning his head in his hands.

"I could have told you that was going to happen," Farius said. "She was extremely shaken by the events—"

"Farius, we are all shaken. Do you see me screaming at people?" Tears pricked uncomfortably close behind his eyes.

Farius sighed. "I'm sorry. I guess. I'm not sure she was all that well-suited to the job."

He was right, and although it felt wrong to admit it, he had employed Merni because Lana thought highly of her, and not because he liked her. "Suited or not, I don't think she'll be back."

Farius shook his head.

Sady sighed. "To be honest, I've had enough of people who blame me. If she doesn't want to work here, I don't *want* her back."

"I hope that doesn't include me."

"Include you in what?"

"People who blame you."

"No." Sady sighed. "Sorry, Farius. I'm just . . ." *not coping very well.* Tears pricked behind his eyes. He wiped his face with the back of his hand, but that only made it worse. "I'm sorry."

Farius nodded, silently, and made a show of staring at the table. Sady wiped his face again, the back of his hand wet with the tear that tracked over his cheek. He cleared his throat, attempting to get control over his emotions. "I'll need a new housekeeper."

He sighed into the silence that followed. "Do you know anyone?"

Farius shrugged. "I'll ask." Still looking at the table. "I have a cousin who may be interested."

"Tell her she'll have to deal with disruption, murder, and . . . magic."

"He."

Oh, all right, whatever. Farius' young cheeks had gone red.

There was a small noise in the hall. Loriane stood in the doorway, holding a bowl. She was still wearing the night gown Merni would have given to her. Through the gauze-like fabric, he could see the outlines of her swollen breasts.

Had she been walking around like that all day?

"Farius, see that she gets something more appropriate to wear." And while Farius nodded, he gestured to her. "Come."

She came, and put the bowl on the table. There were brown crinkly things in it, like thinly-sliced, over-fried meat.

She said something and gestured at the bowl.

"What's this?" he asked.

"I have no idea," Farius said. "But it's not bad. The southerners made it this morning. I guess they didn't think much of breakfast."

"I guess they were not the only ones."

A small smile played on Farius' lips. "They used the big frying pan and almost set fire to the stove. They also used up a lot of salt, part of why Merni was so upset, but they cleaned it all up when they finished. And whatever they call this stuff, it doesn't taste bad."

Sady eyed the stove, but couldn't see a sign that it had been used. He took a piece from the bowl and bit a tiny corner off.

A tang of salt, and sugar exploded in his mouth. He put the rest in his mouth and took another piece.

"It's quite good," he said.

Loriane smiled at him and sat down on the other side of the table. Her blue eyes were intense, with long, dark lashes. The skin around her eyes showed some wrinkles and he guessed that she was in her early forties. Her top lip curved into two distinct peaks, and her bottom lip was full and round. She had let her hair out of the bun and it fell in a cascade of dark curls over her shoulders, except at the temples, where white hair mingled with black.

"Thank you," he said.

She attempted to repeat his words, which sounded foreign in her mouth. So she had been the reason that Lady Armaine came here? Lady Armaine wanted something from her? How did Lady Armaine even know that she was here?

From under her arm, she produced a book that he hadn't noticed her carry into the kitchen. He recognised the worn front cover in an instant. *Toki takes the train.*

He used to read this to his little nephews when they visited, when Milleus was doing the job he now did. Suri would bring the boys, and she would sit where Loriane now sat, watching the boys fidget and bounce while he read. He could still see their bright eyes and hear their voices. *Can we read Toki?* Over and over. They loved that book to death. When they stayed overnight with "Uncle Sady" and slept over in the room that Loriane now occupied, they'd take it to bed.

Loriane opened the first page. Sady didn't need the text.

"Toki got up early one morning. He was very excited. Today, he would take the train with its shiny red locomotive and its three carriages." Mercy, the memories. Two little boys and their lonely mother. Brown eyes and honey-coloured hair. Soft cheeks and a pale-skinned neck that he'd often dreamed of touching. Soft lips he had never mustered the courage to kiss. He fought to keep his composure.

Loriane said something, pointed to the written words and her mouth.

Farius said, "I think she wants you to teach her Chevakian."

"I know," Sady said, but his voice wouldn't cooperate. He cleared his throat, but the tide of grief had broken through the dam. Tears streamed over his cheeks.

From the corner of his vision, he noticed Farius rising. "I'm sorry, uhm, Sady, but I should be at the gate. I'll ask Orsan to come and take you back—"

Sady held up his hand. "Just leave me . . . for a bit." He took a shuddering breath.

"As you wish."

Farius scurried out, and Sady leant over the table, tears streaming over his face. It was a blessing for young men to be so unacquainted with grief that they felt embarrassed by the sight of an older man incapacitated with it. Suri, Lana, the young boys who used to love him and were now prickly adults. Milleus, who was still missing, who he should go and find instead of being Finnisius' pissing post.

He should never have challenged.

He should have kissed Suri, or Lana.

He should have brought Milleus home with him.

There was a gentle touch on his shoulder. Loriane.

He turned aside, meeting her blue eyes, sincere, with not a sker-rick of shame or embarrassment in them. She reached out and wiped a tear from his cheek, and said something, her voice soothing. The corners of her mouth turned up.

"Thank you," he said.

She repeated, "Thank you." It sounded close enough.

Then she rose, and, like Lana would have done, poured him tea.

Sady patted the book. "Tonight, we start."

CHAPTER 14

TANDOR HAD no idea how long he'd been in that cell when there was a sound of footsteps, and more unusual—voices —coming down the stairs at the far end of the corridor. A light came closer. Someone holding a torch and shining it in each of the cells. Soft voices, in Chevakian. At least one man and a woman.

"This is the one," a man said. The glow of the torch showed a guard's uniform, but not one of the regular prison guards.

A light was directed into Tandor's face. His eyes saw only white. He tried to scramble into a standing position, but his hands were still tied and his side was too sore from where the guard had kicked him. His pants were soggy and wet and the skin underneath felt raw.

Someone stuck a key in a creaky lock. A bolt slid back with a metallic clang. The door opened. That was new. The prison guards only shoved the food into the cell using a long stick.

"Phoo, he stinks." This was a woman's voice.

A man laughed. "What did you think?"

They came in, and shut the cell door behind them.

"How are we this morning?" another male voice asked in a mockery of friendliness.

"You're here to interrogate me."

"Good guess."

The guard slid the torch into the wall bracket, and slid a light sock over the flame, making the light spread more evenly.

Now Tandor could see who had entered: a guard, a man in the grey robe of the court and a woman wearing a light blue medical outfit. She had brought a bag which she had set on the bench against the side wall. She was taking things out and setting them on the wood. Glittery, shiny things with sharp points.

A chill crawled up Tandor's spine. "Whatever you have me here for, I didn't do it."

"You had a knife and blood all over you. The court will decide if that is enough evidence." But evidence never held much sway with the Chevakian courts. Someone was dead, so someone had to pay the price. Now that four people were dead, the price would be so much quicker. Chevakia didn't have large or many prisons for a reason.

The man stopped opposite him. "But we want to question you about something else."

He glanced at the woman and the array of metal instruments in the tray, one of which a glimmering needle.

Tandor's chill increased. Some of the Chevakian poisons messed with your mind. There was way too much in his mind that could do a lot of damage to him, his mother or her cause.

The woman took a bottle with a clear fluid and filled the syringe from it. She tapped the reservoir to rid it of bubbles.

No, please.

She approached and knelt in the straw next to him. She was young, but with a hard set to her mouth. How many prisoners had she killed?

He flinched when she touched his arm, but it was only to wipe the skin clean.

"What are you doing to me?"

"We need some answers."

"You could just ask me."

She smiled, as if she enjoyed hearing the fear edge his voice. "The only reason you haven't already been trialled and sentenced is that we need to know where the missing baby is. What you say now may be important for your sentence. If you speak the truth, the court may give you a more lenient sentence."

Yes, like hack his head off with an axe instead of hanging him? "If you release me, I can go and find this baby for you."

"Wouldn't you like that?" She gave a mock laugh and held the syringe up to the light. A drop of poison glittered at the sharp point of the needle.

Tandor flinched involuntarily.

"Where is the child?"

"I don't know. I didn't touch it. I didn't touch the others. I didn't kill them—argh!"

Quick as lightning, the woman had jammed the needle into his arm, and she held it there with one hand while pushing the plunger down with the other.

A sharp, tingling pain spread from his upper arm.

"What is it? It hurts." Already, he started feeling light-headed. "Argh, what is this for?" Part of some new Chevakian torture method? Sweat ran down his back.

She put a cup-like device over his nose and mouth. It had a soft rim that sat snug on his face and sealed it off from the outside air. The inside smelled stuffy. He tried not breathing, and turning his head away from the thing, but the guard came to stand behind him and held his head still. He kicked with his feet, but that brought the pressure back on the manacles holding his upper arms and they hurt so much that he forgot that he wasn't going the breathe and he screamed inside the mask. The poison made his mouth burn. He yelled and coughed, and coughed some more. Strings of phlegm coated his lips.

"What do you remember of last night?" the woman's voice sounded far off. His vision had gone funny, his tongue tingled.

"I don't know." Tandor closed his eyes to stop the world spinning around him. "I know nothing, do you hear? I didn't do it. I didn't kill anyone. I have never killed anyone. It was the monster." Chevakian didn't have a word for dacon.

"What monster?" the female voice came from far away.

By the skylights, he hadn't meant to say that. Why was he speaking Chevakian anyway? Weren't you meant to return to the language of your birth when layers of consciousness were stripped away?

Tandor struggled against the tide of dizziness, feeling himself being pulled away. He coughed, and the burning in his throat increased. He tried to shake his head away from the mask. "Take that thing away from me." He coughed again, big hacking coughs. He couldn't stop coughing.

The woman said something, and her companion withdrew the mask. Tandor drew deep wheezing breaths.

But the world he saw was not that of the dank prison cell. He was outside, in a field under a threatening sky.

He was Ruko, and he came to a halt at a ridge top that overlooked a patchwork of farm plots, roads, hedges and a scattering of houses. A wall of smoke hung at the horizon, black roiling clouds that hid the presence of the beings within.

He knelt in the dirt and pulled his dagger from his belt. He held the weapon out before him on flat outstretched hands. Strands of icefire danced along the blade. It was so strong here.

He balled his fist at the horizon. "What are you waiting for? Come and avenge what's been done to you."

For a moment, the clouds parted, and revealed a giant figure made of orange flame within. Yes, they were here.

First Ruko pulled his shirt over his head. Then he took off his pants. Last, he unstrapped his artificial leg. He bundled these things together and flung them downhill, towards the fire. "Sisters and brothers, I am here. Time has come for revenge!"

A shrill voice cut through the roar of the wind and popping of fire. "Come to me!" His girl. She was there, amongst the inferno. *She was here.*

The ice-cold wind buffeted his naked skin. It pimpled into goose-bumps. The power, the majesty of it. And he was stuck in this stupid half-baked body. The girl had done a piss-poor job of turning him back into a young man. The stupid women then did an incomplete job of freeing him of the sorcerer's hold. The sorcerer was still inside him somewhere. He longed to sever those links forever. Life was better when he didn't have a heart.

He gripped the dagger more tightly, his hands trembling. The touch of icefire aroused him to the point of pain. Strands of blue whipped out from the menacing clouds and stroked his skin like a long-forgotten lover. He longed to jump into that ecstasy.

Could he do it?

He eyed the dagger again. In this form, he could never survive being swallowed by that cloud. In this form, his gratification would be a short one. Like the male spider, he'd risk his life to have sex once, and be eaten by his mate. That was not how he wanted to die.

Deep breath in, and he plunged the dagger into his own chest. Pain lanced through his body. Blood flowed over his hands, rivulets of it running over his naked chest, into his pubic hair. It hurt, it hurt, and it was so good. He lifted the blood-stained dagger and stabbed again, deeper this time. Blood dripped onto the ground and pooled around his legs. Icefire crackled along the edges of the puddles. He watched in in a pain-filled haze, the dagger buried into his chest up to the hilt.

"Come to me!" he screamed, his voice hoarse.

They came, towering figures made of icefire, with hollow eyes burning with anger. Smoky hands reached out of the wall and grabbed him. Drew him within. She was there. Her fiery body engulfed him, dug into his chest to lift out his heart, dripping, and still beating. She flung it away. He would never have a need for it again.

He looked into her fiery face and said, "I'm yours." He grew and became one with the fire, and one with her. They tumbled over the countryside, eating up farms and forests and crops in the wake of their fight of love. And then he found release, and they lay, exhausted next to each other while flames digested their loot. With each breath, she grew fatter and rounder and more glowing and powerful. When the little flames had burnt all they could burn, she clambered to her feet in the middle of the blackened earth. She was enormous, her belly huge and gravid. She spewed a gout of fire that engulfed him with its power, and spewed again, and again, great globs of fire that moved, grew little legs, and coalesced into little fire people. She spewed and spewed, and the little people grew. Hundreds, thousands of them.

Tandor fell, and fell through darkness. Wisps of mist rushed past him, shards of voices, people screaming and calling out for him.

He screamed.

The dank prison cell returned, and immediately before him, the face of the woman in the light blue medical suit.

Reality returned. Ruko had joined his kin. They were on their way to avenge what had been done to them. They were after him, and the Knights.

"Interesting," she said, and she straightened. And then again, "Interesting." He had no idea what she found interesting.

He looked up at her, his vision dimmed with pain.

"Let me go."

She laughed.

"Let me go, or you will all die."

"I don't think so."

"I'm serious. There is a great wall of evil coming this way."

She ignored him and started packing her things. Then she rose and nodded to the guards. They left the cell, locking the door behind them.

Tandor screamed after them. "Let me go. Let me go."

A rough voice came through the darkness. "Hey, new guy. We all tried the madman trick. Didn't work."

CHAPTER 15

*L*ATE IN the afternoon, when the light filtered by the cover of clouds was fading, a handful of people gathered on the windy hillside on the eastern fringe of Tiverius. Women, mostly, those Lana had maintained contact with during her life. Her sister, a middle-aged woman with a heavy brow, and a cousin Sady remembered sitting in the kitchen at times. Only six of them to watch the bier, with the cloth-covered body, be swallowed by flames in the fire pit, standing a bit further away than usual, because the wind was particularly fierce and carried gouts of flame up the fire pit wall each time the wood popped.

The funeral celebrant from the Central Tiverius morgue—Sady made sure she got the best one—was unused to ceremonies with so few attendants. She seemed awkward, glancing from Sady and Orsan on one side to Lana's family on the other.

She spoke the rites. A woman Sady didn't know had tears running down her cheeks. How had she known Lana? The other women were glaring at him.

He stared at his hands, clasped before him. He felt too empty even to cry. He remembered the times—too many to count—that he'd come home late and he and Lana had sat in the kitchen. They'd talked about the doga, about Destran, about the weather.

They had never talked about *her*. He had known so little about her life. The celebrant spoke of a warm woman, with time to help everybody. Who had Lana helped, other than him or people in his household? Sady had no idea.

He had accused Milleus of being distant, but he was just as bad. Worse maybe, since he had never attempted to share his life with anyone, but had expected his household to serve him and him alone. Who was he to judge his brother's marriage? What made him remotely suitable to run the country? He was not. Even Viki, in all his inexperience, was doing better than he was. Sady had failed everyone in his personal life, and only did a marginal job of running the doga.

The wind whipped Sady's hair. In the city down the hill, the clock tower played its regular tune, and then the bell rang, twice. It chilled him.

He remembered the sonorics warnings as they had been drilled in to him when he was young. There was a children's rhyme based on it.

Once rings the bell and we stay inside,
Twice rings the bell and school is out,
Thrice rings the bell and we find the shelter,
But when it rings all the time, we run.
They should be inside on this day.

When the ceremony was finished, Sady and Orsan left with the small group of women. Past the walls that held little alcoves which contained the ashes of many great Tiverians of the past. Somewhere out there was the han Chevonian alcove, with the remains of poor Eseldus, and the remains of his parents who had such great hopes for both of them. They'd seen Milleus' rise as proctor, but had never seen how he was deposed.

The truck waited outside, and before climbing in, Sady turned to Lana's sister.

"Be well. I'm sorry we have met again under such sad circumstances."

He was not prepared for the vicious look in her eyes. "You should be sorry." Her voice was full of venom. "My sister looked after you with everything she had, and what do you do? Invite strangers into your house who kill her."

"It wasn't—"

"Just stop your politician's talk, all right? Barely a month into the job, and you're just as bad as the rest of them. Empty promises, excuses for sitting on your backside. Leave us in peace, and don't pretend that you cared for her, because you didn't."

Sady felt like shouting, *Woman, I've been working for my country and my eyes are about to fall out!* But that would only sound like a complaint. He *had* volunteered for the job, and in case he needed reminding, he had to ride the cart he bought, because there was no money for another one. And time could not be wound back.

The constant demands on his time, the constant crises. And now people were starting to accuse him. His time in the job would be short indeed.

He left quickly for the comfort of his truck.

On the way back, Orsan sat, silent, opposite him. Sady was painfully reminded how not even Orsan was a true ally. Orsan would never reveal all he knew. Working for the doga, he would be privy to other senators' schedules and appointments. All those people meeting at Lady Armaine's house. Why were there so many influential people in a setting that was almost worship? He bet Orsan knew who they were.

His household had been violated, his brother was still missing, despite the fact that the mire of the Ensar Road refugees was almost cleared up, and all people housed in the city or camped in a field next to the Balloon base. Milleus' absence was like a hole inside him.

Spending resources on trying to find him would be considered inappropriate. Ensar itself was still not responding. If Milleus had been too stubborn to leave, he would now be dead.

The truck stopped at the house, and Sady could hardly carry himself up the stairs, he was so exhausted. Mentally, emotionally. He hoped that Farius had been able to find another housekeeper, and that no more crises had erupted since he'd left the house.

When he opened the door, it was to voices from the living room, which Sady hardly used these days. There was also a sound suspiciously like the banging of a hammer. Sady went into the room, where he found Farius and the southern man Ontane. Farius balanced precariously on a ladder in front of the window while hanging up what looked like a curtain rod.

"Oh, good afternoon, Sady," Farius said. He held a hammer.

"What in all of mercy's name are you doing here?" asked Sady, spotting on the floor a pile of old carpets which, judging by the musty scent, came from the store room. Some of those were from Milleus' old house, before he moved to the farm.

"There was a level two alert," Farius said, his face red. "Ontane says all the windows make our houses vulnerable to sonorics, so we're putting up stuff to cover them. Look." He climbed down the ladder and picked up a piece of paper. It had diagrams with writing in an unfamiliar scrawl and unreadable script. "He says that once sonorics motes get into a building, they bounce around the walls until they've lost all their energy. But now that energy is in the walls, radiating it back onto the people inside. It's less safe inside than it is outside. So that's why you board up the windows. If the house is closed, that makes a cage that the motes won't penetrate so easily."

That made a lot of sense in a warped sort of way. Through his fatigue, Sady regarded the southern man Ontane, who stood holding a box of nails. A scruffy sort of fellow, who strangely reminded Sady of his father's brother, who had never had much time for pomp and ceremony. It was a painful memory, after that funeral service. He fought to keep those thoughts away; tears were closer than any time during the service. He had never cared enough about his family. "But . . . you're putting a carpet up over the window."

"We ran out of boards. We figured this room was less important than some of the others, since you don't use it very often. We've already done all the important rooms. I thought you'd approve."

"I guess I do." Here they were, two complete strangers, making a home for themselves. "I'm just extremely tired." He shrugged, fighting tears. Lana's presence was everywhere in this house. "Do whatever you see fit, I'm going to bed. Just don't make any loud noises." Although he suspected that he would sleep through those as well. Belatedly, he added, "Thank you."

He turned for the door.

"Make sure you go past the kitchen," Farius said. "The women have been cooking."

The women? Did that mean he'd found someone to replace Merni?

"All right." Then he recalled that he had promised Loriane to start teaching her Chevakian.

Mercy.

Sady left the room. In the hall, he almost bumped into Dara scrubbing the floor.

"Oh, pardon me," he said.

She said something in her language. She looked busy and red-cheeked, so he side-stepped the wet patches as much as he could.

He went into the kitchen, where many oil lamps and candles lit the room. It was quite warm in here, contrary to the rest of the house.

"Uncle!"

One of Milleus' granddaughters in the kitchen. Reili was only eleven, but she was already as tall as an adult, albeit half the width. She was wearing one of Lana's aprons, and gave him a soap-scented hug.

"What are you doing here? Didn't you hear the ringing of the bell? Twice. You should stay inside."

"I am inside." She held herself straight with all her aristocratic righteousness. "I came here to bring roccas because Farius said this morning that Merni can't cook, and found a friend."

Myra stood at the stove and smiled at her.

"What about your mother? She'll be worried."

"She knows I'm here. Really, uncle, do you know how old I am?"

Yes, he knew, and eleven wasn't old enough to make her own decisions.

Sady walked to the stove and lifted the lid on the pot that stood there. It contained a concoction of strips of meat, beans and turnips. "What is this?" Sady asked. It smelled considerably nicer than it looked.

"I don't know. Myra made it."

"Is this what they eat in the south?"

Reili laughed. "No, silly. It's what we could find in the kitchen. You really should do some shopping."

Food supplies would be low. Sady had told Lana not to go out when the bell rang.

"If you would let me, I could—"

"No, Reili."

"We have suits, if that bothers you." Most families would have old suits stashed away somewhere.

"No. You should be home." It disturbed him how lightly the young generation took sonorics threats.

"But I'm bored."

"Your mother . . ." He didn't have a good relationship with Milleus' daughter-in-law. She frequently accused him of giving the girls strange ideas. Besides, he had no energy to argue with anyone right now.

The house was clean, and safe, and there was food on the table. What more did he want? Let his niece and her mother sort out their differences at home.

He sat down at the table next to Loriane. Someone had found her a simple woollen dress. Sady had no idea who it had belonged to— one of the past servants maybe—and the thing was probably horribly out of fashion, but it was elegant dark red and looked gorgeous on her. She wore her curly hair loose, combed over her shoulders.

Toki Takes the Train lay on the table in front of her.

"Give me the book," he said, holding out his hand.

He dragged it over the table and opened it at a random page, which showed the boy Toki's house. "What's this?" he pointed.

"House," Loriane said. The word sounded strange in her mouth.

"And this?"

"Train."

"I've been teaching her some things. She's smart." Reili elbowed Loriane in the side. "You say it."

"You . . . want . . . tea?" Her blue eyes met his.

"Yes, I would love some."

She rose to get a cup. Her hair hung to halfway down her waist, which was quite narrow despite her recent pregnancy. Her hips were broad, and her backside round and full.

Farius came into the kitchen and sat at the table. "Doing well," he said in answer to Sady's questioning eyes. "My brother will come to help me with the guard duties."

"Thank mercy. No sign of the baby?"

"No."

Loriane stood at the porcelain cupboard, staring at the two of them.

"We'll find the child," Sady said, speaking clearly, so she could understand.

She came back to the table with cups. "I must warn," she said.

"You mean plead?"

"No. Warn."

"For what?"

"I don't know. She's been talking about this all day," Reili said while she emptied the wash tub. Then she glanced at Myra. "The others don't like it when she brings it up. It's like they're embarrassed by what she's trying to say."

"Why?"

"I have no idea."

Sady took tea and cradled the cup in his cold hands. "Has Loriane been very upset?"

"Not that much."

Sady knew that southerners had strange family arrangements. Loriane was probably what they called a breeder, who bore children for other people. Judging by her age, it was unlikely to have been her first child

Loriane said, "Warn. Get away."

Get away. From what? "I don't understand," Sady said.

Reili said, "I've been saying that all day. It's something to do with the child."

Loriane's eyes were intense. "Yes. The child. Girl. Danger."

"Yes, we are trying to find the baby for you. We'll do our best."

But when he met her intense expression, he felt terrible. Chances that they'd find the child alive were very small.

He continued to go through the book with Loriane. His niece brought more tea, and then dinner, and they all ate around the table by the light of many candles.

They were a strange assortment of people. Farius seemed to get on quite well with Ontane, and it was comical to see the two discuss building methods—Farius' father was a builder—without a common language between them. Reili was disturbingly interested by Myra's baby, and she rocked the boy on her knee while Myra ate. Seeing the Myra struggle, Sady resolved to find out how much it would cost to give her a claw hand.

They talked, and laughed through awkward language mashups.

The mood was rudely broken up when Reili's mother came to the door. She not only scolded her daughter for staying out so long, but proceeded to tear a strip off Sady for allowing her daughter to interact with *these people,* so that she had to come and rescue the girl *in her state* and poked out her six-month-pregnant belly. Whatever Sady protested, it mattered not. She dragged her oldest daughter out and left Sady to stand in the hall. There was a soft noise behind him. Loriane stood in the doorway, backlit from the kitchen. Imagine what *she* had gone through, coming here on that disgusting train just moments before giving birth.

Sady suddenly felt very tired.

"Going to sleep," he said and mimicked sleeping.

"Good night."

"Goodnight to you, too."

He slowly climbed the stairs, and re-assessed his earlier plans to return the southerners to the camp. Maybe what Lana's memory needed was for this house to be as much as a home as he could make it, in her spirit. And a house needed people. He quite liked these ones.

CHAPTER 16

*J*EVAITHI WOKE in the comfortable nest of furs and the familiar feeling of soft leather against her naked skin. She wondered why she had awoken, because it was still pitch dark. The breeze made the sides of the tent billow inwards.

There was a small noise close by, without a doubt inside the tent. She reached out to the other side of the bed where Isandor had climbed in some time long after she had gone to bed. The spot was empty, but the furs still warm.

"Isandor?" she whispered, straining to see.

The noise stopped.

"Go back to sleep," he said.

"What are you doing?"

"Please, go back to sleep."

She sat up, drawing the furs over her naked skin. The tent cloth flapped with a gust of wind that made her shiver. Something jingled that sounded like the clasp of a cloak being done up.

"Isandor, please. Let me know what's going on." She rose from the bed and padded across the earthen floor where she sensed Isandor standing. She touched his chest, and her fingertips met the warm fur of his cloak. "You're going outside?" She went to kiss him, but he brushed her off, just like he had earlier that night, after finally coming to bed. It opened up a big hole of uncertainty in her. This was the third day that he hadn't made love to her. Did he not love her anymore? The thought closed on her like a vice. Everything had changed since she'd gone back to being Queen. They should never have come here, but stayed on Milleus' farm.

"Where are you going?"

"There is something I need to do," he said.

"I'm coming."

"No. It could be dangerous."

"I'm still coming." She grabbed her clothes and started to pull them on, humid and dirty as they were. "Do you think nothing we've done so far was dangerous? We were going to stay together. You promised. And any trouble you make I will have to deal with anyway."

"All right." He snorted. "Don't tell me I didn't warn you."

She finished dressing and followed him out of the tent, where two shadows fell in step with them.

Isandor said, "These are Kenna and Zito. We can trust them."

At least whatever he was doing wasn't secretive enough to do so without guards. That comforted her, a little.

After the Chevakians had withdrawn, people had re-arranged the tents in more familiar pattern of circles. The open space of the circle that included their tent was deserted. The fire in the open-sided cooking tent had died to a feeble glow. Jevaithi could still smell the scent of the animal that had been roasted for dinner, and could still taste its tangy meat which stuck between the teeth.

They walked into the night. The cold and humid air bit into parts of her skin not covered by the cloak. The only sound was the whistling of the wind through the guy ropes and the occasional flap of canvas.

Isandor led the group into a narrow alley sheltered from the wind. At the end, they came to the large tent where Chevakian trucks had brought supplies that afternoon. Isandor pushed aside the flap and disappeared inside. The guards and Jevaithi followed, into in darkness. One of the guards lit a torch, a small pool of orange light. Jevaithi was surprised how young the boy Zito was. He would have been no older than fourteen. The other guard Kenna was a young woman, probably in her twenties. She bowed when meeting Jevaithi's eyes.

"I'm honoured to serve, Your Majesty."

Isandor bade them to be silent. The boy held the torch aloft, and its long flapping flames lit stacks of boxes around the tent's perimeter. Isandor walked around and studied them all, before selecting one and using his dagger to pry it open. Jevaithi didn't dare say anything, but wondered what he was doing. The Chevakians had brought these things, why should they contain anything other than food and clothing?

Isandor said, "Come on, if you want to be of any use, give me a hand."

She took the dagger Zito offered her and carefully inserted it in the crack in the wood between the lid and side of the crate. She had no idea how to do this type of thing, and felt awkward, afraid that she was going to make a noise and bring *someone* down. The Brothers most likely, since they had overseen the unloading of the trucks.

They worked quickly, and when Isandor lifted the lid off the crate, the torchlight hit . . . the metal barrels of Chevakian guns.

She looked into Isandor's face, sweaty with the effort. "Did you know this was in here?"

He met her eyes, his expression grim. "I wasn't sure, but I had a suspicion. You know how the Chevakians brought in supplies earlier today? Well, I saw Simo talking with one of them and he seemed to know this person. I thought it was odd, because why would he know Chevakians? Also, this happened when the other Chevakian truck drivers were arguing with Milleus and his group. While that was going on, these few Chevakians were unloading these boxes from the truck. I suspected there was something odd going on."

Jevaithi had seen that, too. With nothing else to do in the camp, and a plethora of guards stopping her going to see Milleus, how could she have missed the supply trucks coming in? However, she had not thought there was anything unusual going on.

"But why—"

Then there was a noise. Isandor froze. Kenna yelped.

A huge man stood behind her and clamped a hand over her mouth. "Be quiet." His voice was rough, his clothing black and beard big and bushy.

Three other men pushed in through the tent flap and moved into the light. Two of them were equally huge. The third man was Simo.

"Well, well, what do we have here?" He started off in his usual sarcastic voice, but then he noticed the open crate with the guns, and he glared at Isandor.

For a moment, no one said anything. Jevaithi held her breath, expecting Simo or one of his hulking henchmen to lash out at Isandor. She shuffled closer to him. If they wanted to harm him, they would have to harm her first, and she had a feeling that they might *want* to harm her, but couldn't afford to do so. She felt Isandor's warmth behind her and felt for his hand. Their hearts beat in unison.

"So, we have two children snooping around in places where they are not allowed."

Isandor said, "You trade weapons with the Chevakians behind the Queen's back."

Jevaithi tightened her grip on his hand in the hope he wouldn't try to do something stupid. The other man still held Kenna and Zito stood, wide-eyed and white-faced, clutching the torch. Fortunately, it hadn't occurred to him to use the dagger at his side, because if he had, it would only have led to disaster.

Simo laughed. "You're surprised that the world doesn't revolve around you?"

If Jevaithi had been uncertain about Simo's loyalty to her, she was certain now. To him, her turning up had been a nuisance. The common people's adoration of her was a hitch in his plans.

She said, "Actually, a lot of the world of the refugees does revolve around us."

Simo took a few steps towards her. Side-lit by the torchlight, she could see the pores on his face. His mouth quivered. Jevaithi braced herself to be hit in face, but he breathed out forcefully, and retreated. He gave a mock bow. "Your Highness, how long would your popularity last if through your actions, the people went hungry?"

She glared back at him. "Is that a threat?"

"If you choose to see it that way." He flicked his eyebrows in *see if I care* way. "We have Chevakian supporters who bring us supplies we need, rather than starvation rations."

"Is that so?" Isandor said. "I guess we can also eat guns. I think we might complain to the Chevakians that they delivered some wrong crates."

Simo snorted and spread his hands, rolling his eyes at the ceiling. "Why am I even arguing with a couple of children?"

"Because you need us."

Simo whirled at him. "I don't need you."

To Isandor's credit, he didn't flinch or back away. "You do need us, because most people in the camp are curious about you, happy that you're not Knights, but don't support you outright either. They do, however, support the Queen."

That was the truth, and Jevaithi read it in Simo's face. If the Brotherhood had wanted power, they'd failed at making clear what they stood for.

"Who are these Chevakian supporters of yours?" Isandor continued.

"Private Chevakian citizens."

"Chevakians, helping us? Why would they do that?"

"There are plenty of reasons. Maybe to help an overthrow of a regime they don't like. Maybe some of us, whose families were killed, fled to Chevakia." Simo's voice had a distinct sneering, shut-up-you-little-boy tone.

"The old king's family, you mean." Isandor's voice was cold.

Simo glared.

"Say it aloud, if you dare. It's an ill-kept secret that the family of the old king fled to Tiverius. These are families of people who thought it was fine to murder anyone who didn't agree with them, and reign with terror through heart-less servitors. People who terrorised the City of Glass. These are the families who want to see that regime re-instated!" Isandor was yelling now, and more people rushed into the tent.

"Isandor!" Jevaithi grabbed his arm, but he paid her no attention. His muscles were tight as a spring.

"No," he said, brushing her off. "This needs to be said. Because you know what? We are the old king's family, too. And we never agreed with what he did, and neither do all the people out there."

Simo's eyes narrowed. His voice was low and threatening. "What are you? A spy for the Knights?"

"I'm a Knight, not a spy. I'm a Knight committed to the honour of the Knighthood, not to the murder of innocent children, the raping of new recruits and the imprisonment of the Queen. Jevaithi and I are a full-blood Thilleans more pure than any of you. We are also sick to death of this clan business, which hasn't done the City of Glass any good for the last fifty years, if not longer."

"You are a traitor."

"Not me. You will be a traitor if you accept help from people who haven't lived in the City of Glass for fifty years, a traitor to your own country. The people of the City of Glass don't *care* about the perpetual arguments between Pirosians and Thillei. They want peace. They want this stupid vendetta to be forgotten. Buried. Never to be resurrected."

"How dare you say that to someone whose family was murdered by Pirosians?"

Isandor grabbed Simo's black cloak and drew him so close that their faces almost touched. "Pirosians almost killed me, but the woman I call my mother is Pirosian. A Thilleian sought to turn me and Jevaithi into servitors, but Jevaithi is pure Thilleian and I love her. Let people be judged by their actions, rather than their blood. I've had enough of this stupid clan stuff. Enough!" He let go of Simo's cloak, and Simo stumbled back to keep his balance. His eyes were wide. Clearly he had not expected such strength in a *child*. "I'm going to let the Chevakians know that these weapons are here, so they can take action against whomever from Tiverius brought them. Having heard about the Chevakian laws, I am sure that inciting rebellion is an offense punishable by death."

Simo eyed Isandor as if sizing up his chances in a fight, but decided against it. "You, boy, what do you think you are?"

"I am Isandor. I am Thilleian. I am an Eagle Knight. I am a butcher's assistant from the Outer City. You can choose which of those reasons you want to use to justify killing me, but I am what I am, and I want the clan fighting to stop."

Simo looked like he was about to explode.

Isandor turned to the man who was still holding Kenna. "Let her go. This achieves nothing."

To Jevaithi's surprise, the man did as Isandor said.

He continued, "We're in a foreign country, and none of us know where the main body of the Knighthood is, whether they're still alive, and if so, whether they'll come to join us, and if they'll come peacefully. One thing I know, if they come to fight, none of us stand a chance."

"What did you think the weapons were for?" Simo said.

Isandor nodded. "Point made. But when they turn up, we're better off to talk to them. A lot of Knights adore Jevaithi."

Simo said nothing. Jevaithi didn't think that he liked making bargains with *children*. On the other hand, he didn't disagree either.

"Come," Isandor said to the two young guards.

They left the tent, to find that a huge crowd had gathered outside in the dawn light.

A voice came from somewhere at the back. "Mercy, I leave you for a day, and you already create trouble."

"Milleus!" Jevaithi let go of Isandor's hand and threw herself in Milleus' arms. He smelled of goats and smoke and engine oil.

"Now, now." He patted her hair. "Come, you two, let's get some milk."

Some time later, the three of them sat next to Milleus' truck clutching cups of warm milk. Milleus told them of how the soldiers had refused to let the Chevakians out, and Isandor told him of the weapons.

Milleus' eyebrows rose. "You were sure these were Chevakians? Why would Chevakians send weapons?"

Isandor looked over the rim of his cup. "I can think of only one reason: to fight the Knights."

"But there are no Knights here," Jevaithi said.

"They are somewhere. Maybe the Chevakians know where they are."

"Still, why would Chevakians care?"

"I think," Isandor said and let a silence pass as he sipped. "I think that the survivors of the royal family who fled to Tiverius have somehow managed to get a lot of supporters. I think that the Chevakians preferred dealing with the old royal family. They might have been bad to their own people, but they were more open to the Chevakians. Back then, there were ambassadors, and Chevakians came to the City of Glass wearing strange suits. After the king fled, the Knights had this idea to solve the fertility problems in the City of Glass by bringing Chevakian girls. We were told they came voluntarily, but the Chevakians know otherwise. The Knights haven't attempted to trade or even talk to Chevakia. I think it's understandable that Chevakia would support anyone who tries to get rid of the Knights."

"Mercy," Milleus said. His eyes were wide and in wan dawn light, he looked pale. "Mercy," he said again. "I think you could be right. And I think I know exactly who you're talking about."

"Tandor," Isandor said.

"His mother," Milleus said.

"Are you kidding?" Jevaithi said. "She's not even a real princess. She married into the royal family."

"Those are often the worst," Milleus said.

Isandor met Jevaithi's eyes. "They forget one thing: we are old king's great-grandchildren."

"We?"

She met his eyes, and was shocked to see them overflowing with tears. His heart beat in her chest like crazy. Then he said, "King Caldor's son the crown prince was married to Tandor's mother. She was pregnant with Tandor when she fled to Chevakia. Through Tandor's machinations, the baby daughter of the queen installed by the Knights was swapped for Maraithe, who had a lot of Thilleian blood. Tandor posed as merchant and fathered her twins. You were one of those. I'm your twin brother."

CHAPTER 17

CARRO AND the hunters packed up their camp at dusk. They rigged their gear to the eagles' saddles and mounted their birds, still without many words spoken. Jeito who had studied the maps, led the way, over the valley through which the muddy river with the burnt logs wound its way, and over the slowly-rising farmland.

The sun came out right on sunset, a rare occurrence with the recent heavy cloud cover. The sky turned deep red with the haze that seemed to have gotten stronger. Lit from below, the menacing bank of clouds in the south looked menacing, as if edged in blood.

By the skylights, it looked like the worst of the weather was still to come.

Soon, the town of Twin Bridges came into view, a loose scattering of houses at the place where two rivers joined. From here, the road split, with branches going off in two directions, each with its own bridge. The railway line did the same, following the road. The main track went to the west and would join with the Fairlight line and the other branch kept going into the ranges, where it would go as far as a town called Solmeni.

From Carro's height, the train tracks were easy to spot, unnatural straight lines cutting through the landscape. The metal occasionally glistened between the trees. The roads were harder to see, narrow, and often overshadowed by trees.

They circled over the town a few times while Jeito was squinting down trying to get her bearings. There was meant to be a narrow forest road leading towards a timber town long since abandoned.

The town of Twin Bridges itself looked peaceful. Sparse lights lit the street and smoke curled from chimneys. The forest to the south was a black mass of trees.

Jeito whistled. She had found the track and they set off in the direction of the highlands, rugged hills with rocky outcrops.

The forest underneath was now so dark it was almost black. The tiny lights of the town faded on the horizon.

It grew dark and the air became very cold. Occasional gusts of wind brought images to Carro's mind, shadows moving beyond the edge of his awareness. There was icefire in the air, he could feel it. He lashed the reins around his wrists, hoping they'd find the hidden army before he got any full-blown visions.

Those clouds on the southern horizon looked very scary, worse than blizzards in the City of Glass, worse than the worst weather he had seen. Occasional flashes of lightning flickered within the cloud tops, and endless series of anvil-shaped protuberances jutted from the top.

Jeito whistled and sent her eagle plummeting towards the dark forest. Carro and the others followed.

At much lower height, he could make out a forest clearing with dark shapes that looked like buildings. The abandoned logging settlement. There were no lights.

They brought the eagles down in the middle of the clearing.

Carro's bird skittered, its wings held wide as if ready to take off again. He had to hold tight onto the reins to stop it doing so. It pulled the straps, uttering *kek, kek, kek* sounds, the eagles' alarm call.

Farey lit a torch.

Nolan's bird was also protesting, hissing in a low crouch, with its wings spread. Farey's magnificent male gave it a disdainful look.

The pool of light cast by Farey's torch showed nothing more threatening than a forest clearing with a few dilapidated shacks. The roof had collapsed in one of them. Another had sagged sideways. Thick layers of moss grew on the timber beams. This did not even deserve the name *village*.

The grass underfoot was short with longer clumps, a sign that the field had held animals at some time in the recent past. The air was thick with haze and smelled of fire. The wind whipped the treetops, making branches whistle.

Carro shivered. "Where is everyone? You're sure this is the spot?"

Jeito snorted. "Who got the directions, you or me?"

Carro's eagle gave another alarm call.

"Shut that bird up, will you?" Farey said.

Carro threw the long end of the reins around the eagle's beak and pulled the head closer. It strained against his grip, its eye rolling.

There was one major thing that alarmed eagles: unfamiliar other eagles, often wild birds, which would sometimes attack intruders into their territory. But they were far outside the Aranian border ranges where wild birds lived.

A gust of wind blew all his hair to one side. Voices whispered in the air. Isandor, his mother, the merchant, his sister's whiny voice, Caman and Jono's sneering, the Tutor berating him. All those voices yelling at him, or quietly scolding him. *You had the chance, why didn't you say anything?* or *You're a coward.* Yes, he was a coward, and all those people in his past life could tell.

"Over here," Jeito called from the darkness, jolting Carro from the edge of his torment.

They went into the forest, where huge trees towered above them, their straight majestic trunks rising out of reach of the pool of light from Farey's torch.

The eagle, still with the leather strapped around its beak, was growling and pulling so hard at the reins that it cut off the circulation in Carro's wrist. On top of whatever disturbed it, eagles disliked being in enclosed spaces. They were birds of mountaintops and open plains, not of forests.

Jeito stopped and whistled.

Further up the slope, someone returned the whistle.

It was a single man, in a Knight's shorthair cloak, but wearing a Chevakian-style shirt and trousers. He carried a Chevakian oil lamp, with glass sides that stopped the flame being blown out.

He called, "Who are you?"

Carro wrestled through the shrubbery to pass Jeito, pulling the Pirosian medallion on top of his clothes. On this mission, talking was his task. The man was taller than him, with southern grey eyes, and carried a southern-style crossbow.

"We've come from Tiverius. We assume that you didn't get the Supreme Rider's message?"

The man's gaze rested on the medallion. His face remained strangely blank. For someone having lost contact with the rest of the army, Carro would have expected joy at hearing from other countrymen.

"You'll want to speak to the command," the man said. "Come."

He turned and led the group further up the slope. The shrubbery grew dense here, and the eagles snapped and hissed at passing branches. Carro's eagle uttered sharp calls that eagles used to establish each other's presence. Even though he couldn't see them yet, there were definitely eagles here.

The path became more steep and led up to a rocky outcrop, under an overhanging rock. Underneath, a single light marked the entrance to a cave. The ground was dry, sheltered from the weather, and marked with many eagles' footprints.

The cave was much larger than he had thought. Rough walls suggested that it had been enlarged by people. Carro's eagle skittered and pulled at the reins. It yanked so hard that Carro almost lost grip of it.

"The birds go in here," the man said, indicating a dark entrance to the side. It smelled like birds, too. A young boy came out with a basket containing hunks of meat. All of a sudden, the eagles were all over him, pushing each other to get to the food.

By the skylights, those birds had no principles and manners at all. So much for being scared of confined spaces.

The man led Carro and the hunters further into the mountain, along a hewn passage where occasional lights flickered on the walls.

"Who made all this?" Carro asked, and his voice echoed in the passage.

"This used to be an outpost for the Chevakian army," the man said. "Back in the day when the border regions were still independent."

Carro didn't know that much about Chevakian history.

"The army had to hide here, because the border regions had strong armies, and morale amongst the Tiverian army wasn't always high. They used these caves to hide their supplies and give their troops a comfortable life to stop them from starting a mutiny."

They arrived at another opening where soft light slanted into the passage. Inside a low-ceilinged chamber, a camp office had been set up, with proper furniture and other things that must have been here before the group came.

Farey, Jeito and Nolan remained at the door.

Carro and the Knight headed across the floor, with people stopping their work and looking at them. Many fell silent and followed the group with their gazes. Again, Carro had expected the Knights to be cheerful at their arrival. And what were all these people writing anyway? No, they weren't all writing. A group of Junior Knights sat around a lamp, sewing fur pelts together. Another group was using twine to lash mesh made from sticks to the bottom of sturdy poles. Those looked like snow walkers.

They came to a halt at a field desk at the far end, where a Senior Knight sat. Carro recognised his short, grey-flecked hair, his alert face and penetrating eyes: Eminent Rider Barton, a member of the Knights' Council.

The man who had brought him here retreated. Rider Barton rose and greeted Carro, his gaze on the Pirosian medallion—Carro started to wish he'd put the damn thing under his clothes—and they both sat down.

Carro spoke into the uneasy silence. "I am glad that we find you well. Just as well we had instructions. You would have been hard to find."

"This is a dangerous area," Rider Barton said. "We were forced to hide. The Chevakian army probably suspects that we're here. There are many balloons during daytime. You took a great risk coming here."

"We didn't see any balloons."

"You were very lucky." Yes, Carro remembered this man from the eyrie. Highly ranked, softly-spoken, but had a reputation for being merciless on his enemies in that same, kind voice.

"You didn't receive prior messages from Tiverius?"

"No, we haven't received anything."

"Rider Cornatan sent a messenger. You've seen no sign of him?"

"We've seen no one. What was the message?"

"Rider Cornatan requests that you come to Tiverius."

There was a small silence and the Rider Barton said, "Certainly. We were already preparing for that mission."

With furs and snow walkers, certainly. But Carro let it rest. It was not in his power to question, and it wasn't in Rider Barton's interest to discuss the unit's intentions with a messenger.

They went on to discuss the route Carro and his companions had taken, and if they'd run into any Chevakian army outposts.

"We'll leave tomorrow on dusk," Rider Barton declared. "I'll ask the men to put you up in one of the dormitories. It'll be crowed, but dry, safe and out of the wind."

On the way back through the chamber, many gazes followed Carro. No one smiled. When he was in the passageway, the men continued what they'd been doing, never mind that those activities would be futile.

The hunters waited for him, but because they still had a guide, Carro couldn't ask the hunters for their impression.

First call was the eagles to get their packs. Now that Carro's eyes were better attuned to the dark, he guessed there were well over a hundred eagles in the chamber. The poor birds were chained up at very close quarters and some had already been biting at each other's feathers. He was glad his own bird would not need to stay here for more than one night. With no air coming in, it stank of dead meat in here. His eagle was tied up with a couple of local birds which were all jostling and hissing at each other. Carro stroked the feathers on his bird's neck to calm it. Then he noticed that one of the birds in the cluster next to his wore a harness. It was well-made, of the type that hunters often wore. His father would have used hunters as messengers.

He stared at the bird, contemplating the meaning of this. Did it mean that Rider Barton had lied about the messenger not having arrived? If so, then why and where was the man? And why would Rider Barton not want to obey Supreme command orders?

The answer seemed clear from what he had seen in the chamber: because they had been planning to return to the City of Glass.

Here, within hearing distance of the stable boys, he dare say nothing, but while another man led them to the dormitory, he held Farey back.

"We'd do well to make sure one of us stays awake at all times. I wouldn't be surprised if Rider Barton is a traitor. I think the messenger arrived, but was killed."

Farey said nothing, but nodded, his expression grave.

The dormitory was indeed crowded, and there was barely any room for extra sleeping mats. Carro's mat ended up being next to an Apprentice with a face so young that he could not possibly have any violent intentions.

Carro remembered how he had joined the Knights, probably similarly fresh-faced and innocent. It seemed such a long time ago. He asked the young man how long they'd been here.

"Too long. The only time we get to go out is for hunting and the older Knights mostly do that." And he added to it, "Sir."

"I'm Carro."

The young man blushed.

"Before we came, you were planning to return to the City of Glass?"

He shrugged. "That's what the command said where they thought we'd go next. Many of the older Knights wanted to go, you know, because there'd be people there who might need our help. We heard of people burnt and all. Can't just leave them to die, can we?"

Carro nodded, and saw his family—the family he had grown up with, bleeding and dying in the street of the Outer City, while he slept safely.

These were good men, and his message put them in a difficult position.

But Rider Barton was a true Knight, and he obeyed.

CHAPTER 18

"OVER THERE is my house." The old lady pointed a crooked finger past Sady's nose.

The truck turned the corner into another deserted street and stopped in front of a well-maintained house in the merchant district. Orsan got out and opened the door for Sady, who climbed out and assisted the old lady down to the pavement. He took her arm and helped her through the gate and up the path. A middle-aged man opened the door, watching this high-profile visitor to his house with an expression of great surprise. From his clothing, Sady judged him to be a merchant, already in the long trailing dust robes merchants wore in the warehouses, and he presumed he'd dug out this clothing for sonorics protection, because, failing protective gear, residents had been urged to cover their skin as much as possible if they needed to go outside.

"My son-in-law," the old lady said. She shot the man a triumphant look that hinted at a disagreement about her visit to the Proctor's office.

The man bowed. "Thank you, Proctor, for honouring us with a visit."

"I apologise for the lack of warning and I wish it were in better circumstances," Sady said. "Can you show me the scene?"

"Follow me." The man turned and went down a corridor, his wide robes brushing the walls.

The house smelled of cooking. A couple of young children ran to a doorway, giggling. A woman's voice scolded them to be quiet. They watched, wide-eyed, as Sady and his entourage passed. Sady could only imagine how bored they were. School had been closed since he ordered the bell to be rung twice.

Rooms on either side of the hallway were richly furnished with warm touches from loving family members. How empty and cold was his own house, how devoid of life. Although, without Merni's crazy antics, this morning's breakfast had been an improvement, if a linguistic muddle. Loriane was up to naming the items in the kitchen. That dumpy woman Dara turned out to be a pretty decent cook. He'd sent Farius on a shopping expedition while Ontane guarded the gate. It was a strange combination, but it worked, for now. As a bonus, Ontane didn't need to cover up for sonorics protection.

They went through the laundry, and then the man preceded him into a courtyard and stopped. "This is where I found him."

Amongst a bucket of spilled grain and uprooted hedges lay a blood-covered body, an old man, on his side. His clothes had been slashed to shreds, and the skin underneath torn open as if he was a fruit, showing ribs in the gaping cavity. Chunks of flesh lay on blood-soaked paving, and other chunks had been dragged off, as evidenced by trails of blood.

Feathers stuck in dark red puddles. There were at least two bloodied carcasses of ducks. The front of the duck house had been smashed in, and the remaining birds, about twenty or so, waddled around in a tight group, backwards and forwards along the court-yard's back wall.

"I'm sorry that you have to see this, Proctor," the man said. His voice wavered for a moment. "I don't understand why anyone would harm him. He was frail enough. Wouldn't hurt anyone."

"I know," Sady said, placing a hand on the man's shoulder. And he did know. He tried to push away memories of that night in the guest room. Finding Lana . . .

The rest of the family remained in the doorway: a younger woman, presumably the merchant's wife, and the old woman who had come to get him, his mother-in-law and the dead man's wife.

Orsan walked around the courtyard, careful not to disturb anything that could be of use to the city guards. Each time he came close, the knot of ducks ran, quacking loudly, to the furthest corner behind their wrecked duckhouse.

"When did this happen?" Sady asked. It felt like a big hole had opened up inside him. He had been so confident they had caught the murderer.

"Early this morning. I saw pa when he went to feed the ducks, as he always does. We started breakfast and wondered where he was. I went into the garden to check and then we found him like this."

"Did you see anything unusual?"

The man shook his head. "Nothing unusual. That's why no one worried earlier."

"Nothing at all? No sounds?" Surely, somebody would have screamed. With the ripped bushes and spilled grain, the signs of a struggle were everywhere.

"If there was, none of us heard anything. The dining room is on the other side of the house. Pa always feeds the duck, and he usually comes in while we're having breakfast." He wiped away a tear. Sady had to fight to keep his own emotions in check. He knew exactly how the man felt.

His wife said, "There was a little girl in the front courtyard this morning when I went to pick up the fruit box from the gate. A scruffy little thing. I tried to talk to her, but she ran off."

"A little girl? A toddler, about four years old?"

She shook her head. "Older than that. At least eight or nine."

"What did she look like?"

"Dark hair, dirty. Dressed in a large shirt, probably stolen. No shoes."

"Southern?"

The woman nodded. "Not that it has anything to do with this, but it was strange."

It was. Did that mean there were two little girls running around, or had either of them mis-guessed her age? Then again, who would mistake a toddler for a child of eight?

He shook his head. "I'm afraid I have no idea what's going on." But he felt cold inside. Mercy, he thought they'd caught the killer.

There was nothing more he could do for the family, but the merchant said that they appreciated his visit and offered him tea. Sady declined, because the City Guards and other relatives arrived and it got busy at the house. Besides, he had something he wanted to do before going back to his office and Viki's maps of continued wildly fluctuating levels of sonorics and his continued inability to raise responses from the southern districts. Or, failing that, his inability to find the missing financial records. Or if that was not enough work, Alius still hadn't replied to Sady's request for the pills, and in fact he hadn't seen Alius at all for a number of days.

The courthouse was one of the places in Tiverius where Sady least liked to come. The pompous splendour of the building, with its large dome-capped hall, intricate mosaic floors and crystal chandeliers, belied the decisions of life and death, but mostly death, that were made inside. Since the sonorics alarm had suspended all court cases, there was little going on this morning, just a few guards milling about, two of them on either side of the courtroom door. Both of them dressed in heavy winter gear.

The doors were open, giving Sady a glimpse of the interior of the courtroom, an equally richly appointed room in which people with a lot of money decided over the lives of many with none.

Although he understood better than anyone about the tightrope that Chevakia walked—of having enough food or not having enough —he felt deeply uncomfortable with the ease with which the city guard condemned to death anyone who had committed a serious crime. And even more so that this was done in the name of giving the country's scarce resources to those who deserved it most. In this way, the killing of prisoners tied back to meteorology—if he predicted more rain, the court would feel less pressured to cull the "undeserving" and criminal poor.

When he was twelve or thirteen, he had attended a court case as minor witness—he'd seen the accused run from the house where he was said to have tried to rape one of the daughters. He remembered the man's cries, his scruffy hair and pleading eyes. The prisoner had admitted to breaking in and stealing—he lived on the street and had no money—but had sworn that he would never lay a hand on a girl. The counter-witness was the girl's mother. She claimed to have seen what he did.

The girl herself had been quiet.

The audience had cheered when the judge pronounced the death sentence.

When the session had finished, Sady had asked his father how the judge could be certain that the girl's mother was right, and his father had said that they couldn't. And then Sady had asked what they would do when they discovered the man wasn't guilty after all.

He still remembered his father's uncomfortable look. They had been standing there, next to the pillar outside the court room.

Sady couldn't remember what his father said next, only that he had never answered the question. The smell coming out of the darkness of the courtroom brought back those memories. This was a place of death.

A guard met Sady and Orsan on the other side of the hall. He was one of the designated courthouse guards, dressed in blue, with the courthouse symbol of the two crossed swords on his shirt. The man bowed several times, and Sady explained why he had come.

"But Proctor, do you need to go into the prison yourself?"

"I want to speak to this prisoner. I presume he's not going to meet me anywhere else."

"Uhm—no, but the man is out of his mind. What he says is complete nonsense."

"I still want to hear what he has to say. I will decide if it's nonsense or not."

The guard gave him a blank look, and bowed. "Of course, Proctor."

"Good then, let's go." Sady led the way into the corridor and off the side down a set of stairs, sliding his hand over the railing. The prison guard trailed behind him.

"But seriously, Proctor, don't take him at his word. The man is an idiot. Sometimes he seems to make sense, and other times he is clearly out of it. You don't know when he speaks the truth even when he seems sane. Maybe he's killed in his insanity but I'm not even sure about that—"

Sady whirled. "Enough. I want to talk to him, and I'll draw my own conclusion. I'll not be accused of ignoring things I should have been told."

"But we have no information from our questioning. The man

keeps telling us how we're all going to die from some invasion of creatures of damnation. If we bothered you every time someone predicted the end of the world, you'd have no time to do anything. He's as mad as a ground squirrel in heat. The man is a waste of space."

"That may well be, but do you want to go and talk to the family of the old grandfather who was murdered this morning? I suggest you go and look at the body. It's not pretty."

The man's eyes went wide. "You mean—there are still people being killed?"

"Yes. That's exactly what I mean." That was right, Sady never liked how these guards made up their minds about guilt and motives before the court decided. They were known to coerce confessions from beggars, only because the Tiverians liked their streets clean of anyone who did not look up to their standard.

When all this was over, he should really do something about the court system and the prisons.

Mercy, now he was angry.

At the bottom of the stairs, he turned right, past the entrance that led to the gallows room, and past the little cells that held criminals awaiting trial. The air here was breathless and stank of damp and sweat. As he passed, there were stirrings and curses in the dark cells behind the barred metal doors. Sady guessed many of the inmates had still been asleep.

The prisoner in question was in a solitary cell at the end of that corridor. Sady grabbed the bars of the door and rattled it. "Open it."

Metal chinked against stone as the prisoner moved his arms.

"But we need—"

"Open it." Need to have another guard present, sure. This man was shackled and wouldn't go anywhere. Moreover, he might be mad, but most likely *wasn't* a murderer.

"Sure, Proctor. Immediately." The man inserted the key in the lock, his hands trembling. The door creaked open, and Sady charged in, bracing himself against the smell of excrement and dank rot.

The prisoner sat bound and shackled against a crate that stood in the middle of the cell, a room normally used to house several prisoners. His skin was grey with filth and shiny with sweat. The only thing on him that looked clean was the golden metal of his claw hand. It was a beautiful thing that was clearly of Chevakian origin. In the light of the oil lamp the jailer carried in, his burned and scarred head looked like a skull. His eyes met Sady's, furious. Brown eyes.

Sady was taken aback. When he saw him last, the man had blue eyes. Had he remembered wrong?

He made a show of sitting down on the bench next to the door to give himself time to think, but nothing came to him that could have explained this strange phenomenon. Brown eyes, blue eyes, there was no way he would have seen wrongly. Blue eyes were southern. He remembered very clearly judging that the man was southern. He remembered the skull-like appearance of his head, the tightly stretched and scarred skin, the patch of hair around one ear. This was the same man, and his eyes had changed from blue to brown.

The prisoner's gaze followed his every move.

Sady said, "We caught you with a knife and blood on your hands near the place where four people were gruesomely killed. When we caught you, you did not speak to us and led us to believe that you didn't speak Chevakian. If you want to walk free, or indeed if you want to live, we will need an explanation."

"I am a citizen of Tiverius." His words were clear and measured, and without accent. "I was defending the country."

The guard at the door snorted. "I'm touched by that patriotic statement. Excuse me if I don't believe it."

Sady glanced over his shoulder. That guard was most irritating. Did all courthouse guards have such a high opinion of themselves? Had Destran really exercised so little control over the courts, and for that matter, the city guard and the army?

Sady leant forward, his elbows on his knees, and fixed the prisoner's gaze.

"I will need to know who you are, your name, your home, whatever you can tell me to prove that you're telling the truth."

"You don't remember me?"

"No," Sady said, staring, puzzled, at the man's scarred scalp.

"I remember you." He gave a chilling chuckle that turned into a phlegmy cough.

The guard moved to hit the man, but Sady held up a hand to stop him.

"But you do remember me, although I may look a bit unconventional. The unassuming Chief Meteorologist has made a promotion from watching the bully beat up a defenceless boy."

Bully? Defenceless boy? When had he ever been involved in beating up—

Mercy, this was Lady Armaine's son. The southern spy. "What was your name again?"

"Tandor."

Yes, Sady remembered. But now he was certain: the boy had, or he was certain he used to have, blue eyes. He remembered the boy standing against a wall in a back alley in the merchant district, crying, unable to move backwards or forwards because older and bigger boys surrounded him on all sides. They pushed and kicked him and called him names. Even though he was older, Sady had been too small and skinny to do anything, if he had wanted to, which he hadn't, just in case the bullies would turn on him instead. Most of the tormentors were now influential men and had probably long since forgotten the incident. And if he was a good and strong leader, he should forget the incident, too. Except he couldn't.

"You remember," the prisoner said, and succumbed again to a bout of coughing.

"I cannot see what this has to do with the accusations against you."

"But it does. Because I am southern, you assume guilt."

"I think it rather had something to do with a bloodied knife. What were you doing in that yard and whose blood was on your hands?"

"I did not kill anyone. I was trying to stop people being killed. There is a great evil coming this way. You can either let me out now or you will beg me for help you when it is too late."

The guard snapped back, "Don't push your luck. If you're as Chevakian as you sound, you know where the gallows are. You've never answered where the baby is."

"I tried to stop it." He spat in the straw, and the guard jumped forward again. Sady again held him back. "Tried to stop what?"

"Your murderer. The baby. The dacon."

"The what?"

"He's been talking about this a lot," the guard said. "It's pure non—"

"Please, let me be alone with him."

The man retreated as far as the door. Sady felt like shouting at him to mind his own business. The city guard was another world of its own. Chevakia had splintered into far too many worlds like this, where leaders were kings of their mini-kingdoms and where everyone else had to abide by their rules, or pay bribes.

Orsan pushed himself off the wall and semi-casually went to stand by the door. He was taller and broader than the guard, and the man seemed to get the message. He retreated. Sure there would be questions about this in the doga later. Sady could already hear the complaints. *Any senator wishing to visit the prisons should file a request with the appropriate authorities.* Well, hang the authorities. Any elected senator of the doga should have that authority by default.

Sady rose and faced the prisoner. The lamp light made the weeping sores on the man's face glisten. His eyes didn't close properly, and wept involuntary tears over his cheek. He said, "You're here because the killing hasn't stopped, aren't you?"

"Can you answer my question, please? What is the thing you need to save us from?"

"Have you seen the girl?"

"Girl? Just answer my question." He lowered his voice and glanced at the door where he had no doubt the prison guard would be laughing.

"There is a little girl with the blue eyes who wanders around the city streets."

How did he know about that? "What if there was?"

Tandor laughed, and his laugh descended into a phlegmy cough. "See, you've seen her. She's not a girl; she's a dacon. She is your killer and can be our saviour if you let me out to catch her."

"Just a little girl?" Sady did his best to sound sarcastic, but wasn't entirely successful. She hadn't been *just* a little girl, had she? For one, she was southern, and with the strange look in those unnatural blue eyes, he had to admit that she was far removed from *just a little girl*. There were places—madhouses—in Tiverius where people like that were looked after. The thought of her piercing eyes still chilled him. And then there was the question of her age, and how she would have escaped the camp.

Tandor looked at him with an intense gaze. For a moment, it seemed like a brown layer over his eyes became transparent and the blue underneath shone through. Sady blinked but the eyes were as brown as ever.

He re-settled on the wooden bench next to the door.

Tandor spat again, and Sady suspected it had to do with his injuries and not because he was trying to be rude. Tandor's upper arms were raw from the shackles. He could move his upper arms just enough to reach the crate next to him where the guards would put his food. His clothes were so filthy they were crusted with dirt and who knew what else. This man was ill. Even without death penalty, he would not live long. He *seemed* crazy, but on the other hand . . .

"Tell me about this girl," Sady said.

"That girl is not a girl. It's a dacon. And she is hungry. She will grow a year in age with every day, so she needs lots of food. If you let her roam, she will kill a lot more people. If you let me tame her, I could save Chevakia."

CHAPTER 19

By THE SKYLIGHTS, this truck made a lot of noise. And it bumped and jerked, and it *stank*. Loriane sat on the velvet-covered seat, her back straight, her hands clasped between her knees. She was hot in the stuffy cabin. The dress that the young man Farius had brought was very thick, unusually tight in the waist, and her belly was still flabby from the pregnancy she thought would never end.

Outside, the streets of Tiverius slid past at disconcerting speed, huge houses with walled yards, like Sady's house.

The two men in the front seat seemed relaxed, the driver and the huge dark-haired and dark-eyed guard in his stiff uniform.

He had come to the house especially for her. She'd seen him before, briefly, in the corridor and shadowing Sady when he went out. And this morning, she been sitting in the kitchen with her Chevakian book, and this man had come in and had demanded that she come with him. He mentioned Sady, but not much else of what he said made sense.

She worried about being taken back to the camp, where surely the child could easily find her and kill her. She should have let Myra cut it from the womb, this instrument of Tandor's. It was out somewhere, and if not killed, it would kill again. The thing was a predator, living off raw flesh.

At a time that now seemed long ago, Loriane had seen the mis-shapen foetuses in jars in the palace birthing rooms. Demon-like

187

creatures with *wings*. She'd thought such children were born dead, but the awful truth was that sometimes, they lived.

Dara and Ontane didn't believe her.

The Chevakians had no idea, and how she could possibly warn them of this thing was a mystery to her. These people with their machines, with their refined tastes and beautiful houses. The people were so rich and so far removed from her. They knew nothing about icefire, and worse, seemed unwilling to believe that such a thing existed.

The truck stopped in front of a building with tall columns at least two storeys high. In the dark space between the columns, Loriane spotted two guards standing on either side of a door. Another guard, in similar blue uniform, came around the side of the truck, opened the door and helped her out. She caught a glimpse of herself in the reflection of the glass. The Chevakian dress didn't look bad on her. It just felt hot and tight. Her hair was still loose from combing it this morning. It hung in a curly mass halfway down her shoulders.

Sady's guard took her arm and led her up the steps between tall columns into the building. This looked like some sort of official building to her. She wished Sady were here, and would feel a lot better if he was.

They entered a high-ceilinged hall, circular, with columns around the sides and a domed ceiling above. The floor underfoot was smooth, with a mosaic of different-coloured tiles. Patterns of leaves and vines slid by underfoot.

They went through the hall into a corridor on the other side, and from there down a staircase. It grew dark here, with oil lamps casting little pools of orange light over rough stone walls. She didn't like being under the ground. By the skylights, this place reminded her of the dungeons in the City of Glass.

The smell was the same, too, of human misery and suffering. A hand of panic clamped around her chest. Were the Chevakians blaming her for the deaths of their citizens? Was she to be locked up?

She turned to the guard. "Can you tell me what is happening?"

But the guard didn't understand and her Chevakian vocabulary didn't yet include the words "prison" or "I did not kill them." She thought her innocence was clear. She thought Sady understood. After all, he wouldn't have allowed her to sleep in the room next to his if he believed that she had killed four people.

Or would he?

They arrived in a corridor where the stink was worse than on the stairs. Metal-barred doors lined both sides of the corridor.

Dark presences rustled in cells off the side. She thought she heard ragged breathing and the rough whisper of a male voice. Leering.

At the end of the corridor, a light burned in a cell where there were silhouettes of a number of people. The guard led her inside. To her immense relief, one of the people was Sady.

He smiled at her.

She returned his smile, her heart still thudding. By the skylights.

Then she spotted the cell's prisoner. Shackled to a wooden crate, his ankles bound. With pale, scabbed skin and his shoulders wasted to bony protuberances, he resembled a skeleton more than a living being, and a disgustingly filthy one at that. But she recognised his scarred face.

"Tandor!"

He squinted in her direction, but she was unsure if the watering eyes saw anything. Brown eyes. She thought he could only use disguises when there was icefire?

He smiled, and coughed. "Loriane, my love."

"I am not your love." She shuddered with revulsion. Was there ever a time that his mysterious craggy face and lilting voice had seemed exotic to her? She'd been stupid for believing that he would carry her off to a more exciting life. Riches, living like a princess, travelling to foreign places, what a load of rubbish.

She turned to Sady. "Where . . ." And then found that all Chevakian words had fled her mind.

"You talk to him," he said, and mimicked talking. "We go outside." He pointed at the door.

"No."

"All right. I watch from here. Talk to him." He leaned against the metal bars of the door. One of the other Chevakians crouched in the corridor. He had a slate with paper and was making notes.

"He wants to check out what I told him," Tandor said. "And the other guard understands what we're saying. But I'll tell you the same I told him already." His Chevakian accent, always very slight, seemed to have become stronger. He chuckled, and then coughed and spat in the straw. A dribble of brown slime ran down his chin.

By the skylights, he was disgusting. This wasn't Tandor. Not as she knew him. This was the evil that hid underneath the disguise of an alluring, mysterious travelling merchant.

"So what happened then?"

He coughed. "Well, they played with something that was too big for them. And it blew up in their faces, huh?"

"The Knights?"

"Who else? They played with icefire but they couldn't see it. They had no idea what they were doing."

"So, whatever you did that was your plan, when we went into the palace with Myra had nothing to do with the explosion? Am I supposed to believe that?"

"Whatever you believe makes no difference." His voice lowered. "It is what we do now that can doom us or save us. The Heart has come alive. When I reached their prison, the children who were captured by the Knights had been tampered with. They wouldn't listen to me. The Knights' tampering had turned them into living sinks and they were attracted by the Heart. They absorbed all the icefire from it and became living evil constructs of icefire. Ruko has gone to join them. He has become more dangerous, having returned to his servitor state. His temper was always a problem, but he was a proper servitor and I had him under control. He's been free since the explosion. I managed to keep some control over him, but it took all my wits to do so. Often, I was controlled by him, not the other way around. By removing him from me, you and Myra set him free and allowed him to return to his peers. He is the most dangerous of all the children. He should never have been allowed to escape."

"So now it's all my fault?"

"Loriane, if you only listened—"

"If I'd listened? If I'd listened to my concerns I would have given you up to the Knights years ago, and if I had, I bet that none of this would have happened. Whenever I asked you about your plans, you never told me anything. It was always later, or, when it's all over. But I see now. First everything that was wrong with the world was all the Knights' fault, and the stupid people from the City of Glass who let the Knights rule. Then it was Isandor's fault, and mine, for letting him sign up. And it was the Chevakians' fault, and your mother's. And the Knights' fault again, and the Brotherhood of the Light. Now, finally, the Chevakians are going to make you pay for your own failures."

"Loriane, please, I need your—"

"You don't need anything that I could give you. Because of you, I've lost all I have. My house, my position, my son . . ." Her voice grew unsteady. She glanced at the man in the corridor, writing down everything they said. "I'll tell the Chevakians that you're evil and should never be released."

His voice cut through hers. "Loriane, listen to me!" He coughed and spat on the floor.

His expression was intense. For a moment, the brown illusion of his eyes wavered, and the blue came through. Royal blue.

From the corner of her eye, she noticed Sady's concerned look.

"I need to get out of here, you have to tell them that. Whether or not you believe in my guilt doesn't matter. I need to find the hybrid child." Tandor cleared his throat and spat again. That began to get on Loriane's nerves. "Where is it?"

"I don't know, and that is the truth."

"It hasn't come back to you?"

"No. Why should it? I'll kill it if it comes back."

"Kill it? The most valuable of all your children?" He laughed.

"This is not the time for stupid jokes!" A wave of anger came over her. She lashed out and her flat palm connected with his cheek with a satisfying slap.

Tandor cursed, and met her eyes, his nostrils flaring. His cheek was going red.

"This child is part of your machinations, isn't it? You are the king's grandson, and you wanted to put yourself back on the throne and return the City of Glass to what it was before the king left. I thought that all that stuff about Thilleians and Pirosians was over, not important anymore. You said so. But that's what this is all about, isn't it? Isandor is Thilleian and that was why he was an experiment, to see if I could live with him, and . . ." She saw something now. It was part of the experiment. The misshapen foetuses in the palace had not died because they couldn't live, or because the Knights had killed them, but they had died because their mothers had killed them. How often, at the start of the pregnancy, had she felt that she wanted to kill the child? How carefully had she planned for Myra to cut the child from her womb and strangle it? But she had hesitated, because the hybrid's evil blood had already mingled with hers. Seeing the baby girl, having suffered for so long carrying her inside her body, she knew she could never kill it. That was Tandor's experiment: to see if, in the face of evil, a Pirosian would kill her own child.

She continued in a lower voice, "Me and Isandor were part of this evil experiment. I know how you did it. He is the hybrid's father."

His eyes widened to show that she had guessed correctly. And some part of her had still hoped that she was wrong. Tears pricked in her eyes, and she couldn't have told if they were from anger or grief. Where was Isandor?

"I'm sorry about all of it, Loriane. Help me out of here, please. You're my only hope. I love you."

"You don't love me. You only wanted to use me. Even now, you're lying and grovelling. Anyway, even if I knew where the child was, you are not getting your hands on her. I'm through with your only hopes. You've said this so many times that I don't believe it anymore. I could have died from giving birth to that thing. All you ever think about is yourself." Tears pricked in her eyes. She wiped them away, angrily.

"Just let me explain."

"No. No more explaining. I'm through with you." She turned away.

"Come join me, Loriane. Tell him to release me. Help me find the child. Come and be my queen. We will rule the City of Glass."

"There is no more City of Glass, because of you. You didn't love me back then. You don't love me now. You never loved me. I do not want to be with a man who made the entire country suffer. I hate you. I hate you." Her voice would no longer cooperate. She buried her face in her hands and sobbed.

Sady said a few soft words and put an arm around her shoulders. She leant into him.

Tandor snorted. "Look at that. You have yourself some powerful friends." He said something in Chevakian and Sady replied in a sharp tone. Tandor spat in the dirt.

The guard sprang forward and thrust the point of his dagger under his chin.

Tandor spat again, on the man's uniform. "Tell your powerful friend, if he listens to you. Tell him that he'll come and beg me for my help sooner, rather than later. Tell him that he'll need the hybrid to stop the icefire storm coming for me."

Loriane clamped her hands over her ears. "Stop this nonsense. Stop it. I don't want to hear it anymore. I'll tell them to hang you and shoot the child."

A gust of wind tore through the cell. Loriane's chest grew tight as if she could barely breathe. She clutched her throat, her breath wheezing. "Tandor. What are you doing?"

Chevakians were shouting around her, evidently some saw something she did not. Her chest grew tighter. She could barely move. Black spots danced before her eyes.

Sady grabbed her shoulders and pulled her away from Tandor, shouting angry orders at the Chevakian guards. Before he dragged her to the door, she noticed between the bodies of the guards, two men pouncing on Tandor.

Loriane could only properly breathe when she had left the cell. Sady was looking at her with a concerned expression. "I'm fine," she said in her best Chevakian, but she was still trembling. Sady shook his head, speaking soft words, and holding her.

She stood like that for a while, with his arms around her, feeling his comforting warmth and breathing the clean smell of his clothes. It struck her in a way she had not realised before, how much she hated everything to do with the royal family and the City of Glass. The secrecy, the fear of who was watching whom. All her life, she'd pretended to be unaffected, because she couldn't see icefire, but icefire affected the lives of everyone. None of it had ever done anyone any good.

Sady let go of her and started moving again, leading her down the corridor and back up the stairs.

"I help you," she said. Help him deal with Tandor, help him catch and kill the monster child. Help him guide the refugees from the south to a safe and better life.

He smiled. "Thank you." His eyes were kind and honest. He would not betray her.

While she walked back to the truck with him and his guards, the warmth of his touch lingered on her shoulder. She accepted his hand in climbing in and sat opposite him in the cabin. He was finely-built, with close-cropped hair threaded with grey at the temples. His intelligent eyes were light brown, his skin several shades darker than hers with a smattering of freckles over his nose and forehead and a small black mole under his right eye.

Cute, both freckles and mole.

Then he looked up, noticed that she was looking at him, and she feigned interest in Tiverian architecture.

As the city buildings slid past the window, she berated herself. Men were no good, and only wanted to further their own aims. At the very best, they only wanted sex. At the worst, they wanted to destroy her and everything she loved. It had started with the Senior Knight when she was sixteen. She was innocent and naive. He had only been kind enough so that she, starry-eyed with his attentions, came willingly to his bed. She had hoped he would care for her as a lover and companion, but he didn't. She had hoped he would love the child she suffered so much for, but she understood Knights never looked after their own children. She had hoped Tandor would care for her, but he didn't, either.

Men didn't care.

And she hated getting that warm feeling inside whenever she met Sady's light brown eyes. She hated feeling giddy when he smiled.

Damn it, Loriane, you're too old and grumpy to fall in love. She'd seen it all before. Love was for suckers. Not to mention that it was the wrong time and the wrong person and by the skylights, she couldn't even talk to him.

But he liked her. And he seemed open and honest, everything Tandor was not.

Yeah, all right, she liked him. But that didn't mean anything.

CHAPTER 20

CARRO SQUINTED, fighting an acute attack of yawning. He took up a stance with his legs slightly spread and his hands behind his back. Yes, he understood that it was a privilege to be allowed to listen in on the Knights' Council meeting, but how much longer did he have to wait for this meeting to start? He'd been up since dusk last night and was struggling to stay upright, and the stuffy air in this room didn't help.

The three Senior Knights in attendance sat in easy chairs in the large room that his father used for special occasions and had been able to keep free of beds or stored gear. Ever since Carro had arrived with the extra Knight Division, the farmhouse had been bursting with people. But the large previous formal room had remained solely Rider Cornatan's domain, which he used for meetings.

Carro had been given the task of bringing the men drinks from his father's drink cabinet. The men spoke in low voices. Silhouetted against the light was Rider Barton, who had led the unit into Tiverius. He had cleaned up, brushed his shorthair cloak and polished his buttons. The other two Senior Knights Carro knew only by name. Rider Barton was easily the youngest of the three.

Rider Heston was a wrinkled old man who used to look after maintenance at the eyrie, and whom Carro had never spotted going outside. Rider Ataro led the special service division: spies and hunters and other kinds of specialised groups. He had a sharp face and unsettling blue eyes that felt like they could do all the spying work his men did just by looking through people's skulls.

Rider Cornatan was yet to arrive.

Carro had seen him briefly after returning to the farmhouse with Rider Barton and his unit, but after greeting Rider Barton, he had gone to some place from where he had not yet returned. The three members of the council did not seem to mind; they found plenty to talk about. Rider Heston complained about the state in which they had found the farm. Rider Ataro spoke about contacts in Chevakia and then the two of them marvelled over the fact that some of those contacts were still alive. Apparently it was a long time since anyone had used them.

Then they started discussing building styles. Chevakian city buildings and Chevakian rural architecture. By the skylights, it was boring.

Carro tried not to yawn too much.

Finally, there were quick footsteps in the hall, and the jingling of a riding harness and Rider Cornatan came into the room. He carried his cloak over his arm, his face looked red, his hair windblown, and Carro suspected that he had just flown in from that mysterious place where he'd been. He winked at Carro, and smiled, and said, "Shut the door, will you?"

Carro did, while Rider Cornatan took his place at the one remaining chair.

"Drink?" Carro asked him.

"Just some water, thanks."

Carro took a glass, but there was no water in the room, only spirits, so he had to go to the fountain in the hallway to get some. When he returned, Rider Cornatan had maps spread out over the table. He took the glass without comment and without meeting Carro's eyes.

Carro returned to his previous position and took up a wide-spread stance, his hands clasped behind his back. At least he felt a little bit more awake now.

". . . We have this side covered," Rider Ataro was saying, gesturing at the map.

"There are likely to be a lot of Chevakian troops on this side," Heston said. "We *are* close to the main base of the Chevakian army, and they do have balloons."

Rider Cornatan nodded. "Rather a lot more than we suspected. We'll have to be quick. And we'll have to take birds."

"The Chevakians won't care. They won't use their army to defend a camp full of foreign citizens," Ataro said, his voice scornful.

"You never know with Chevakians." Heston said, taking his glass in a gnarled hand. "They jump in strange directions."

Rider Cornatan said, "They will defend the camp because if it looks like we're trying to occupy it, they will consider that as an invasion of their territory." He gulped the water down and held the glass up for Carro to give him more.

"What is on your mind, Barton?" Rider Cornatan asked, when Carro had retreated. "You look like you have a better plan."

Rider Barton folded his hands on his knees and sighed. "I'm wondering if a full-scale invasion of the camp is wise."

Both Ataro and Heston stared at him.

"What do you mean—wise?" Ataro asked, his voice reserved.

"For all we know, most of the camp's residents are citizens. Ordinary people. What do you think the men will feel about fighting our own people?"

Rider Cornatan raised his eyebrows.

Rider Barton continued, "Many of my men have lost family, or are uncertain of their fate. They were expecting orders to go back to the City of Glass to see if we can find any further survivors—"

"That would be idiocy. Icefire is far too strong. There are no survivors. Any who survived are likely to be in the camp under the thumb of the Brotherhood."

There was a small silence. "Do we know how many Brotherhood men are in the camp?"

"We can't be certain, but they have support from within Chevakia. We have to break that link. We can fight the Brothers, but we cannot fight the Chevakian army."

Rider Barton let a silence lapse that seemed rather long. He cast the briefest of glances at Carro, and nodded. Carro didn't think he looked happy.

Rider Cornatan moved a glass out of the way so he could spread another map. Carro rushed to take the glass and returned it to the cabinet.

Behind him, Rider Cornatan continued, "Right, so let's get this underway. We have the units at the farmhouse, and the ones to the east of here, a total of two thousand men and well over a thousand birds. When I give the order, we start on this side of the camp with Ataro's unit. We'll have half the unit push into the camp, over land, and the other half stationed out here with birds to ward off any curiosity from the Chevakians."

"The Chevakians will view this as an attack on their country," Rider Barton said.

"We can deal with that." Rider Cornatan rose. "Do you mind if I open the door. I find it rather hot in here."

Carro could see that Rider Ataro probably wanted to object, but Knights lived in much tougher conditions in the City of Glass, and complaining about the cold in Chevakia would not look good for him. So Rider Cornatan opened the window and a blast of cold air blew in.

Rider Ataro dived for the map which was about to blow from the table. "By the skylights, the weather is like the City of Glass."

Carro stands in the cold hall, facing the Knight. He feels small and insignificant.

So, you want to serve our Queen? the Knight asks.

Carro nods. He's nervous about this. No boy from the Outer City is accepted into the Knighthood. It's a noble place for noble sons. Men of honour.

Serving the Queen is the highest thing he could do. The Queen is his goddess.

"Son, I could use that drink now."

"Yes, sure." Carro's heart was still thudding. Was there a more awkward time for those visions to return? It was the open window, he realised, the air laced with icefire. Rider Barton met his eyes in a piercing way as if he knew what was going on. Carro's cheeks felt hot.

Carro went to the drinks cabinet and took a fresh glass, his hands trembling. Where was that bottle of imported bloodwine? He rummaged between the empty bottles and found various bottles of spirits that were not his father's. He also found a box of playing dice and a little slate with scores. At the top was written *Queen's Wolves*. Much as he despised the wolves and what they stood for—honestly, were all men obsessed with sex?—those men still considered themselves loyal to the Queen. Did they know that their leaders in the council were discussing her death? Did they know that these men were discussing an attack on their families in the camp?

He shifted another empty bottle aside and came across the stoppered jar with the blue poison crystals tucked at the back of the shelf. By the skylights, what was that still doing out here?

A gust of wind made the curtains flap.

Carro stands at the back of the empty shed. He just saw the older boys go in there, with a younger boy who they always tease. It's pitch dark inside the shed, but he can hear their voices.

Come on, do it, or I'll beat you up.

Someone is crying. Carro assumes it's the younger boy.

Come on, we made a bet. You said you can eat shit. Do it.

A silence, and then a wail.

I said I'd hit you.

Carro's hands grow cold. He should come forward and tell the boys to get out of his father's warehouse, but he's afraid they will turn on him instead. They already call him names. Tattletale, they call him.

The bloodwine almost went over the rim of the glass. Carro stopped pouring just in time, but now he had a too-full glass and it wasn't acceptable to fill the glasses up that much. He tried to pour some wine from the glass, but it ran down the side, making a mess on the top of the cabinet.

Not knowing what else to do, he sipped from the glass until the level of fluid was more acceptable and wiped the glass clean with the end of his sleeve. While he was doing this, he noticed the bottle with the poison crystals again. How careless to leave it here. He could so easily open that bottle and drop a few crystals in his father's glass. How long would the poison take to kill him?

He returned to the table with the glass, feeling light-headed and sweaty.

"Come and sit here, son," Rider Cornatan patted the armrest of his chair.

Carro sat, under the gazes of the three Senior Knights.

"I wanted to discuss how we will take control over the camp and weed out the Brotherhood element. It is very fortunate that we have all the refugees in one spot. There has been unrest in the camp, and if we move quickly, the Chevakians will thank us for getting them under control. Meanwhile, we take the opportunity to get rid of the dangerous elements."

"How do we know who is dangerous?" Carro asked. Isandor and Jevaithi were in the camp, he knew that for sure.

"Some Brothers identify themselves clearly. Any others, we don't know. Any Chevakians in the camp will be suspicious."

Rider Barton said, "Any Chevakians in the camp should be removed and allowed to leave to avoid nasty situations with the army."

The two met each other's hard gazes across the table. Rider Ataro still tried to find something heavy to weigh down the map.

Another gust of wind came into the room.

Carro hears Isandor's voice, sees Isandor's blue eyes. *Then fight back. Tell him what you think.*

Rider Cornatan said, "You will take this unit, son, and come in from the east."

Carro licked his lips. "Me?"

"Yes, you heard me. We have a shortage of commanders I can trust. I'll give you the command of a hundred men and birds and you will lead the air attack."

And Carro says to his merchant father, *I'm not going to stand here all night. Tell me why you wanted to see me or I'll go back to my study.*

"We need to make sure the Chevakian army doesn't have any balloons ready," Rider Ataro said. "I'll send some of my spies."

Rider Cornatan nodded at Carro. "Those hunters of yours will be good."

"I'll tell them," Carro said. He was nominally still in charge of the hunters. Whether they would listen to him . . . probably, if they wanted to live. The lives of so many, in his hands. Knights who had signed up for a job knowing that it might kill them, many more citizens, whose only crime it was to have survived the disaster.

And then Isandor asks again, *What do you think, Carro?*

Carro thought nothing, ever. Carro obeyed orders. His step-father's, his father's, his Tutor's. Isandor's even.

What did he think?

He thought nothing of Nolan's affections at night.

He thought nothing of his father's mindless praise that came regardless of whether he did well or badly.

He thought nothing of his father's plan to force into the camp and fight miserable, unarmed refugees. He thought nothing of being given a division to lead. Rider Cornatan made Carro nothing but a front for himself, someone to blame if things went bad. He put Carro in charge because he *knew* that things would go bad.

His father didn't really *care* about him.

He thought nothing of the Knights' insistence on discipline on the one hand and continuous breaking their own rules on the other. The Knight's mantra was worth nothing.

It was all hypocrisy, and fake. No one really cared.

What did the Knights want? A world in which everyone would continuously be afraid of everyone else?

But he was powerless against the machine of war.

He had nowhere to turn. He had nowhere to flee. Not like this. Not alone. And he had no idea where to turn for help.

The penalty for treason was death. And he wasn't even sure that what he felt amounted to treason. Mutiny, yes, the word was mutiny. The penalty for mutiny was death, too.

Rider Barton watched him, his eyes blinking. As if he could read the warring emotions in his mind.

CHAPTER 21

SADY DROPPED Loriane back home. She sat in the cabin opposite him, still pale after Tandor's attack on her. She said she was fine, but a few diamond drops of sweat collected on her upper lip. He deeply regretted having called her into the prison. Deep inside, he'd known that Tandor was crazy and the incident with Loriane only proved it, and he felt terrible about having inflicted this on her; he had not learnt anything new from the exchange.

He made sure he escorted her into the kitchen, where Myra was feeding her baby.

Loriane told her that she'd seen Tandor, and some discussion ensued. Myra seemed cautious, and Loriane frustrated, but the long process of trying to get her to explain what she knew would have to wait until he came home. As it was, one of the prison guards had a rudimentary understanding of the southern language, and had made notes. The report was already on his desk when he returned to the office, but he had no time to look at it. He was already running late for a special doga session, and he ran in to the hall, poorly prepared, where all the senators had been waiting.

General Finnisius would be there, and he hated waiting.

Viki presented the latest sonorics situation. While the levels in the city continued to fluctuate wildly, the shattering of the barriers had allowed a large area of the southern provinces to become contaminated to a level dangerous to Chevakians. How far this area reached was uncertain. Viki's instruments relied on telegraph lines, and many were out. The fate of the people in those areas also remained uncertain. There might well be pockets still safe or people still holding out with suits and shelters. If they had suits.

There were questions about Alius' pills. Not even the army had enough suits for all its troops, and those pills would come in very handy if the army would have to conduct rescue operations.

But no one appeared to have seen Alius for days, and he ordered another senator to inquire.

Why couldn't they send southerners into those dangerous districts, someone else asked, and many thought that was a good idea, but others thought that the southerners were too much of a risk, because they might steal from the abandoned houses or take over Chevakian farmland.

And so the debate went. But in all this one thing worried Sady most: no one had any accurate maps of the sonorics cloud and how it was likely to disperse. It could be that the main farming areas were going to be out of bounds for most of summer, which would mean no crops, and the country would face a winter of shortages.

Even if they could send southerners to farm the land, and if the crops would grow, they could well be too contaminated for the Chevakians to eat.

No, definitely the pills sounded better all the time.

They discussed the camps and what to do if the refugees needed to stay for a longer period. The authorities needed a register of all people inside, of their allegiances, and the people who did not riot and had behaved well could be released to farming districts.

To which a senator from the Fairlight district said that the south had no vegetation and southerners didn't know how to farm. That was definitely a problem.

And so it went on.

When Sady eventually returned to his office, his head was spinning. He had a quick look at the report that the prison guard had delivered. It did not contain anything he hadn't heard before, and that concerned him, too. A flying creature with mysterious power, evil creatures embodied a sonorics storm. He'd better not let the magic-believers see any of this. Either the prisoner was not as mad as everyone thought he was, or he was consistently mad. He ordered some tea and set about making a list of things that needed to be done. Urgent, less urgent and long-term things.

Urgent:

Find out sonorics situation (requires weather balloons)

Make list of camp inhabitants and their names and skills (requires reliable translator)

Catch murderer (requires . . .

Whatever it required. More guards, which he didn't have at his disposal. But . . . a winged monster? Surely that was some sort of southern superstition. And frankly, Loriane looked far too smart for superstition. Or at least, he hoped she was, which was not at all the same thing. It worried him. That, and the business with the girl and however she had gotten out of the camp

Sady, keep your mind on your work.

Urgent: take stock of current food warehouses.

Assess how much cropping the north could stand.

His urgent list was growing rapidly while his long-term list was still empty.

There was a knock on the door and the secretary stuck his head in. "Excuse me, Proctor. There is someone to see you urgently."

Every demand on his time was urgent lately. "Send him in."

The secretary retreated and a moment later, a man stumbled into the office in slow and awkward gait. He met Sady's eyes, and bowed. The movement destabilised him, and he had to hold onto the back of the chair so as not to fall. Sady would have thought that he was a drunk beggar, save for the fact that the skin on his face was covered in weeping blisters. He wore a Chevakian army uniform caked in so much dirt that Sady hadn't recognised it at first.

Mercy.

Sady gestured for him to sit down, and he did so, gingerly as if his backside hurt him.

"Reporting back, sir." His voice was husky.

"Back, from where?"

"Twin Bridges. You sent us with the woman from Solmeni to investigate."

Sady had, and had almost forgotten about it with everything else that had happened. "Where is the rest of the patrol?"

"I *am* the patrol, sir. They're all gone. I'm pretty sure they are. Solmeni is gone. Twin Bridges is gone."

"How?" His heart thudded against his ribs. Twin Bridges was closer to Tiverius than comfortable.

"So we went with the woman on the train. When we arrived at Twin Bridges, it was already very smoky, and the air smelled of forest fires. We reported to the local unit that we wanted to go to Solmeni with the woman, but the area officer told us that the line was cut because of fire, so we decided to stay in Twin Bridges and wait. The local meteorology officer said that there was a very bad storm coming and warned people to stay indoors. But they must have changed their minds because later the town guards came around warning people to evacuate the town. We reported to the area commander to offer help and were ordered to go to the station."

A chill went over Sady's back at the memories of another station, another time. This was starting to sound awfully familiar.

"When we got there, many people were already waiting for us on the platform. There were some folk from further up the plateau, and they had burns all over their skin. The stationmaster ordered all trains out of their sheds, even the really old ones. Two of them left, but even while we were loading the third train, the storm front came into town. The sky went so dark that it was like night. The clouds were black like smoke, and when they parted, there was fire inside. You wouldn't believe it if you hadn't seen it. The black clouds rolled over the town and started eating up the houses one by one. It was the scariest thing to see, houses exploding in big balls of fire."

The soldier wasn't looking in Sady's eyes anymore. His gaze had dropped to the area of Sady's mouth or chin, but he wasn't looking there, either. Sady was quite sure he didn't see what was in front of him. Instead, he was seeing the scene he was describing. "There had been some people who didn't want to evacuate and wanted to stay behind to ride out the storm, stubborn as they were. When we went to their doors, they had told us they were scared that looters would come in and steal their possessions when no one was in the town. Those people now came running from their burnt houses, covered in sores and peeling skin. Many fell while trying to get to the platform. Everyone was cramming to get onto that third train. The driver panicked and the train started moving while we were halfway through loading. People jumped on if they could. So many could not . . . or they fell off. But the train left, and just as we were about the pull out, the front reached the station. It was the scariest thing I have ever seen, this huge wall of black smoke, flames leaping into the air, trees and houses exploding. And the noise, you wouldn't believe it unless you've heard it. Roaring wind, snapping wood. But the strange thing, Proctor: the wind was cold. The fire was not hot, it was cold." He shuddered.

"The train gained speed. We were all screaming for it to go faster. People were blocking the windows with anything they could find. The train was going faster and faster, but it was getting colder and colder, and we weren't going to make it—and then the engine exploded. It sent such a shockwave through the train that it leapt right off the tracks. The carriage I was in was thrown on its side. The side wall splintered and people were crawling out over each other. I think some of the younger ones had already died, but I wasn't going to stop and check. We were crawling over bodies. I managed to get out after pushing another fellow through a crack. His shirt had ripped, and he was bleeding. He took a few steps and fell on his face on the rails and didn't move again."

He raised a hand to rub his face but obviously thought better of it even before touching the blisters and, slowly, lowered the hand to his lap. "I was starting to wonder why I was still alive. I started running, and running, but I still heard the roaring behind me. I reached a house in a meadow. I was so tired that I couldn't run anymore. I thought I might try to hide in the house, so I ran up to the door and I made the mistake of looking around."

The soldier's gaze, like his voice, had been dropping steadily, but now he looked up, into Sady's eyes. "You wouldn't believe if you hadn't seen it, but there was a wall of fire following me, reaching to the sky. I could see nothing but smoke and fire. And then, in that fire, something moved. It was a huge thing, shaped out of fire, the figure of a person. I don't know, but I think it saw me. I knew that was the end for me. And then all of a sudden there was a cry of a beast from the other side and I was yanked right off my feet. The next thing I knew, this huge bird landed next to me. There was an Eagle Knight on its back. I would not be here if not for the bird." He frowned. "Did you know that the Eagle Knights have women in their ranks?"

Sady hadn't known. Then again, many balloon pilots were women, too.

"She dropped me off just outside town, probably didn't want to be seen."

That, too, made sense. There had been few Eagle Knights sighted, but some were sure to have fled. They would not be keen to be spotted.

"Did you check if anyone else survived?"

"They couldn't have, Proctor, honest."

Sady met his eyes, watering and cloudy with pain.

"Can I be excused now, proctor. I am not well."

"Go," Sady said. "My staff will take care of you."

The man rose, leaving a wet patch on the edge of the chair. Sady went after him.

"Orsan, take him to the hospital."

Orsan nodded, but his face was grim. This man would probably not live long.

CHAPTER 22

FROM ISANDOR'S point of view, the situation in the camp did not improve, but did not deteriorate either. Simo treated Isandor and Jevaithi with suspicion, Milleus came to see them freely, which he said drew odd looks from the Chevakians, who had re-established their small Chevakian enclave in the camp, and many of the southern refugees were oblivious to the tension between the Brothers, their Queen and the Chevakians, and went to get milk from the goats and eggs from the chicken farmer to supplement the bland army rations brought in once a day by the Chevakian army.

On the morning of the third day, Isandor and Jevaithi sat with Milleus in the big tent, when a man came running in. He skidded to a halt and dropped to his knees in front of Jevaithi.

"There's a lot of soldiers arriving," he said, still panting.

Isandor's heart jumped. Yes, things had been too easy. He translated for Milleus, who said, "Doesn't surprise me. Chevakians don't like messy situations. They weren't just going to leave things like this. They will have brought more specialised troops."

"What will they do?"

"Split the camp, probably. Allocate the healthy people to farms to work."

That made sense, except . . . Isandor met Jevaithi's eyes; she looked worried, too.

"Where are these soldiers?" she asked.

"At the camp entrance," the man said.

"Are you sure they're soldiers?" Isandor asked. Chevakians about to sort people into smaller camps wouldn't send soldiers; they'd send administrators.

The man bowed first to Isandor and then Jevaithi. "They're wearing uniforms. There are a lot of them, Your Highness."

"Let's have a look." Jevaithi grabbed her cloak and rose from her seat.

Isandor and Milleus followed Jevaithi outside.

The windy hillside was covered in a grey-blue haze that whipped over the city from the west. The air smelled of burning fire bricks and reminded Isandor of the days in the Outer City that butchers did all their smoking. With all the southern voices around him, he was suddenly reminded of home and all they had lost. His home, his mother. He wished he knew where she was.

At the edge of the tent city, a group of people stood at the remains of burnt-out barricades, watching the camp entrance, which was wide open, and where a number of trucks were coming into the camp. The sound of the engines carried on the wind. The man had been right to warn them. This convoy was a lot bigger than the usual few trucks that came to bring the daily supplies.

The trucks stopped, a door opened and a man in Chevakian uniform came out. He walked around the back, opened the doors, and men jumped from the back, one after the other and arranged themselves into a neat pattern of straight lines. Like Isandor would have to line up as Apprentice Knight. He shivered.

"There's so many of them," Jevaithi whispered.

She was right. At least twenty lines, of at least twenty soldiers each.

"I don't understand," Milleus said, squinting over the field. "Why do they need so many people? It looks like they're getting ready to fight a ground war."

A Chevakian soldier came out of the tent which had become the sole Chevakian army post in the camp, and went towards the trucks. Judging by his gestures, he ordered the trucks to go back.

A couple of the soldiers detached from their neat lines and approached him. He held up his hands and retreated. Two men grabbed him and twisted his arms behind his back until he cried out.

A number of the refugees gasped, and Isandor could feel the chill going through them. He could draw only one conclusion. "They're not Chevakians. They're Eagle Knights disguised as Chevakians."

Jevaithi made a scared noise and clamped her hand over her mouth. Other people cursed.

Two of the Chevakian soldier's mates came out of the tent, only to suffer the same fate as their colleague. The three of them were bundled into the back of a truck. The door shut.

A woman somewhere behind Isandor said, "How could that be? There weren't any Knights on the train. Where did they come from?"

Isandor said, "The Knights know how to save themselves. They've got eagles."

A man said, "With Newlight, the Knights should all have been at the eyrie. They would have died with the nobles." Or so everyone had hoped, clearly. Although even some nobles had survived, those who had been partying in the Outer City.

And of course, a lot of Knights hadn't been at the eyrie either.

"This proves they knew about this disaster beforehand," Simo said, his voice angry.

"They've organised the explosion to get rid of us," another man, also a Brother, added.

Isandor said, "The Knights have outposts and missions away from the city. There were riots in the Outer City and there were Knights to attend them. Those men would have survived and would have gathered at one of their safe houses."

They all looked at him. He saw meaning in their eyes and stared back defiantly. He used to be a Knight, and was proud of it, too. There *were* Knights who were honest and trustworthy, although he agreed with Simo that he suspected that those honest Knights were not the ones now pouring from the trucks.

"I'm not going back to being constantly afraid of them," someone said, and a lot of bystanders agreed.

"Yes, we're going to fight," Simo said.

"We have to call up all able people to fight them." This was one of the young Brothers. "We have to protect the Queen."

"We have no weapons," someone said.

"It doesn't matter," another said. "We make weapons. We erect barricades."

"We have weapons," one of the Brothers said. "Anyone who volunteers will be given them."

Some cheers went up.

Isandor thought of the Chevakian guns in the crates in the store tent. He held his arms around Jevaithi. She was very quiet, white-faced, and shivering.

Simo said, "Come, Your Highness. We must take you to safety. We'll build our barricades around your tent."

"I will fight, too," Jevaithi said.

Milleus was shaking his head and muttering in Chevakian. "This is ridiculous. How can Destran allow this? Being attacked by a foreign force in my own country . . ."

They went back up the hill, where youths were already stacking anything they could find into new barricades. A Brother had come out the large supply tent with one of the crates, and was handing out guns and ammunition to eager southern men.

Milleus grumbled. "For mercy's sake, do they know how to use them?" And he stomped off to deliver an impromptu lesson on powder guns.

Isandor and Jevaithi had already received that lesson, and Isandor had actually used the gun a few times, so they watched.

"What else can we do?" Jevaithi asked, her eyes wide.

Isandor didn't know. These events were bigger than him, bigger than Jevaithi, bigger than their family. Milleus might have been able to help, but he was stuck here, too.

It didn't take long for the Knights to mount the first attack on the tent city. They came in with flaming torches which they lobbed into the barricade in a hail of fire. Crates, tent fabric and whatever the Brothers had been able to gather made eager food for hungry flames. The wind fanned the inferno, sending clouds of sparks over the surrounding tents. Some of them caught fire, too.

Fortunately, the Brothers had everyone leave the immediate vicinity of the barricade, but many people would now have nowhere to sleep, all crammed in a few large tents in the middle of the camp.

Isandor stood in the second line of defence, amongst men in

Brotherhood black, ordinary peasants, men and women, old and young holding whatever weapons were available. Isandor had a gun. Milleus stood next to him. He had retrieved his gun from the truck and stared at the scenes of mayhem at the lower barricade with a look of determination that made Isandor feel scared.

Milleus had seen battle. Isandor has assumed that the first he'd see action, it would be from the back of an eagle. Instead, they would probably face eagles soon. He knew what those birds could do.

And all he could do was watch. Powerless, and angry.

Tents burned, sending palls of smoke over the hillside, punctuated by the sounds of battle. People screaming orders. The discharge of guns. It was impossible to see what was going on and who was winning. Too much smoke and chaos. Groups of people running past, all still camp inhabitants.

The low clouds finally delivered on their promised rain. It came down in freezing sheets, whipped by the wind.

"Hey, relax," Milleus said next to him.

Isandor made a forced attempt to diffuse tension. "Is it always like this, when you're in a war?"

"Fighting is mostly waiting for things to happen. And then things do happen, either it's confusing or scary, or it's over so fast that you wonder what happened. You have no idea if you've won or lost. No idea where to go. You may have lost your unit, or they may be dead. That's what it's like for the soldiers on the battlefield."

Isandor nodded. He didn't like this feeling at all. And he thought that, given who he was, he should have more of a say in the situation. But respect needed to be earned. Milleus had said that many times.

They waited.

The Knights posted guards downhill of the barricades and went to sit in their trucks.

A squall of wind brought sheeting cold rain that made the camp inhabitants run for cover. Isandor grabbed Jevaithi's hand and ran for one of the large tents, pulling his cloak over his head.

Inside the tent, everyone sat down, and people shuffled out of the way to make room for Jevaithi.

"Where is Milleus?" Jevaithi asked.

"He was just . . ." Isandor looked over his shoulder. Milleus was not behind him anymore. "By the skylights. He must have gone back to the truck."

"I hope so," she said, and there was fear in her eyes.

"Sit here, Your Highness." Someone had spread a cloak on the ground.

They sat. People watched Isandor and their gazes made him feel uneasy. He thought they should listen, and they probably thought he should do something. But what?

A Brother walked around, doling out dry chunks of bread.

Simo prowled at the far end of the tent, shaking his first and shouting slogans like *We're winning this battle*. It seemed to cheer people up, but Isandor knew enough about the Knights to see that this wasn't a victory at all. The Knights were likely happy to have established a presence in the camp, ousted the Chevakians, and would send in the birds tonight. Then the real battle would begin.

Isandor sat amongst smelling bodies, chewing his dry bread, and wondering where their next meal would come from and what the night would bring.

CHAPTER 23

$\mathcal{S}$O WHAT WAS going on with sonorics levels?

Sady went to the meteorologist's office—his old office, but he no longer thought of it that way—and he and Viki studied all the available maps. Even though human-collected data from the south of the country was lacking, some of the barygraphs were still working. They showed the low pressure cell in the south still deepening.

Sady stared at the map, and its white area where they had no data.

"It's as if something is still feeding this system," Viki said.

Sady nodded. "But how reliable is this likely to be?"

"Can't be sure, but the barygraph in Twin Bridges was still operating normally yesterday."

Sady had a vision of a machine busily taking measurements in a town where all people lay dead in the street.

"Based on how long the sonorics spike took to get from Fairlight to Twin Bridges, how long before we'll see it here?"

"A day and a half, two days maybe, if the wind eases off."

Not much chance of that happening, Sady knew. Not in this time of the year, not with a low pressure cell this strong.

"So what do we do?" Viki asked. He had shaved his beard, but his cheeks looked hollow.

"Go home. Find a place in a shelter."

"But—"

"Go home. No one can do anything without measurements. We don't have measurements, and—"

"We have to do something!"

"Yes. Look after your elderly relatives. Get them to safety. Get them comfortable. Eat something yourself while you're feeding them."

Viki's eyes met his. Sady didn't like the expression. It was one that spoke of worry and deeper problems. Resistance against sonorics varied wildly, even amongst Chevakians. Children, elderly people and some adults were already feeling the effects of sonorics. What if Viki was one of them? Mercy, he should have thought of this possibility before getting angry with him.

He lowered his voice. "I understand your devotion to your work, but—"

"It's nothing to do with devotion." Viki's voice spilled over. "We're all going to die if we do nothing."

A deep and uncomfortable silence followed. It was a truth that had remained unspoken.

Sady sighed. "Possibly, but you've not been doing nothing. You're a wreck and you're not functioning properly. Your family needs you. Go home. I'm going to sit here until you do."

Viki sighed and rose from the desk. He moved slowly, supporting himself on the desk like an old man, and when he put his jacket on, his hand trembled.

"Shall I ask my driver to take you home?" Sady asked.

"I'll manage." Viki shuffled to the door and opened it.

As he turned and met Sady's eyes, Sady had an overwhelming and irrational fear that this would be the last time he'd see Viki. This disaster was bigger than all of them, and there was nothing he, or anyone, could do about it.

Even without a doga session planned for the afternoon, the news of the demise of Twin Bridges had spread quickly, more quickly than it should, had everyone heeded warnings to stay inside. When Sady came back to his office, there were large crowds outside the foyer, and he had to take the painful step of restricting public access to the doga building. There were people wanting to know what had happened to their loved ones, people demanding that the army go over to check, and strangely enough, a lot of boys wanting to sign up as soldiers.

Sady despaired for the younger people, who had never experienced a sonorics crisis. All these people should be at home boarding their windows. They had no concept of the threat, although some of them were probably already feeling some effects.

He was chilled to think that the prisoner Tandor had foreseen this. And he, who had been at pains to take everything into consideration, had ignored it. Because the prisoner spoke of magical beasts. Because Chevakia didn't just ban the use of the word magic, it actively erased the word from common speech. There was no magic, Sady had heard that repeated from the moment he was old enough to speak. Magic was a superstition held by poorly-educated people from backward regions.

Southerners believed in it, but southerners were crazy anyway.

But Tandor's prediction had been true. And the soldier, who could not have known what Tandor said, had seen these fire creatures.

Sady wondered how much of what Tandor said was true. A magical beast flew over the city, and as it did so, it absorbed sonorics. And outlandish as it sounded, it was the only explanation Sady had heard for the wildly fluctuating sonorics levels. Yet he could not, with all the will in the world, bring himself to take it seriously. There had to be a rational explanation

In his days of working as a meteorologist, he would have launched an investigation into air currents, tornadoes and their links to the myths and habits of the southern people. Even old Chevakian mythology was rife with weather phenomena personified into spirits. He would have asked at the Scriptorium; he would have tried to find books on southern mythology. But there was no time for any of that.

All they could do was hide.

So he wrote notes that ordered halls and cellars to be turned into shelters. By some cruel twist of fate, the courthouse jail would be one of the safest places in the city. He ordered the city's thick-walled, marble buildings to be opened up to those who had no shelter. The library, the Scriptorium hall, even the doga's assembly hall. He went to deliver those directives to the guard station downstairs personally, and when he came back to his office, it was to find that someone had delivered a stack of large boxes to the foyer.

Sady prised open a corner. Inside were countless vials stacked one on top of the other, all containing little white pills.

Alius' pills. Not a moment too soon.

"There are a lot more of them in the store," the secretary said.

Sady could have cried with relief. They might actually survive this crisis.

"Distribute these immediately to all troops and all people who have a need to work outside. Then give one each to each family."

"Yes, Proctor." The man went into the next room and called for help.

While the staff carried boxes away, Sady he slipped one vial in his pocket. For his family and Farius.

In the large kitchen, Sady regarded the people gathered around the table. It was late afternoon, still light outside, but the boards over the windows made it dark inside the kitchen. Persistent wind crept through gaps and cracks and the draught made the flames on the candles flap. Long shadows danced over the table.

Andrean looked out-of-place in the kitchen in his finery. His business was doing well; he'd gotten quite rotund in recent years. His wife, he said, felt too tired to come. Likely, Sady thought, she refused to come to his house with *all those foreigners*. Reili had come with her father, and she had the presence of mind to make tea for everyone. She was so much more mature than her eleven years. She smiled at Myra and stroked little Beido on the head.

Her father watched, and she met his eyes. She had Milleus' stubborn set of her mouth, and all of Suri's exuberant beauty.

Kalius sat alone and brooding at the other end of the table. With every year that passed, he resembled his father more, down to the hawkish suspicious nature of him. Of course the fact that his wife had walked out on him recently didn't help.

As oldest, he was old enough to remember his mother before he was bundled off to boarding school. He proclaimed to hate his father, but they were so much alike it was scary. His glace went to

Ontane, who had shaved, washed and cut his hair and wore a work shirt, all of which had taken ten years off his age. He looked very respectable, down to the pouch with tools which he had put on the table.

Myra sat next to her father. She had introduced herself politely to the visitors, and while Andrean had been polite in return, Kalius just glared. She had removed their sonorics suits and hung them up in the hall.

Loriane had been friendly to Andrean who had fumbled through a resemblance of a southern greeting, but hadn't bothered with Kalius. She sat at the far end of the table, her arms crossed over her chest, glaring back at Kalius whenever he deigned to look in her direction. That woman took no nonsense.

"I'm sorry to call you all together like this," Sady began. "But I don't have the time to visit each of you individually. As you will probably know, a sonorics-related fire front has reached Twin Bridges, and is expected to come this way. The Most Learned Alius and his colleagues at the Scriptorium have produced a medicine that helps your body deal with the effects of sonorics. I want you all to take some of these." Sady took the bottle of pills out of his pocket and put it on the table with a soft clunk.

Kalius picked it up and frowned at it, before giving it to his brother, who gave it to Myra.

Loriane took it from her, opened the lid, shook a pill out onto her hand, looked at it, sniffed it, and said something to Myra.

"And what else are we supposed to do?" Kalius asked, still glaring at Loriane.

"Do go outside. Board up the windows. Hide in the safest place in the house. Hope that this will be over within a few days. Take the pills, once a day."

"Have you heard anything from Father?" Andrean asked.

Sady had to shake his head. Wasn't game to say that Ensar was out of communication. He hoped Milleus had been able to save himself. He had hoped Milleus was somewhere in the traffic jam on the Ensar road, but it had been cleared from behind and there had been no sign of him. Milleus was resourceful and able to look after himself, but Sady was beginning to fear for his brother's safety.

Reili divided the content of the bottle into three piles: a small one for Kalius, a large one for her own family, and a medium-sized pile for Sady and his household. She put each pile into a small container.

Kalius gave a sniff, pocketed his portion and rose. "Anything else?" His voice was distant and businesslike.

"No." *Except...*

Sady's thoughts went to the children's book on the shelf. They surely would have thought he'd lost it if he asked them, *Can we read Toki one more time?*

Kalius was out the door almost immediately. Andrean worried about his wife. Could she take the medicine without it harming her unborn child?

Sady didn't know. Wanted to say, *Does that matter if we're all going to die?* But instead, he said, "If there was a problem with unborn children, Alius would have said so."

Did Andrean even comprehend the seriousness of sonorics contamination? It did permanent damage to your body. The more exposure, the more damage. Some of it took many years to show up.

Andrean left, dragging Reili, who wanted to stay. "But, Dad—"

"No. You've spent enough time here. You have to help your mother."

"But all she does is ask me to fetch cups of tea." The sound of her protesting voice faded in the corridor.

Sady sighed, meeting Farius' eyes. The young man sipped from his tea, trying to look as if he wasn't there. Mercy, they were so terrible at doing family things.

Myra, Dara and Loriane were studying the bottle, talking in low voices.

Myra said, "Loriane wants to know what you do with this?"

"It's a medicine to stop the effects of sonorics."

Myra translated, and Loriane's frown deepened. She exchanged some words with Myra, who shook her head. Dara put a pill on her hand, sniffed it, then broke a piece off and put it in her mouth. She said something to Loriane, who nodded. Dara laughed.

"What?" Sady asked, his heart thudding in his chest.

Loriane said, "This is simple medicine. We use for stomach cramps. This will not help you at all."

"You're kidding, right?"

Myra said, "Loriane knows about these things. She helps many people with medicine. This you can take, but it will not stop the icefire. It is not medicine. You cannot take medicine for icefire if icefire make you sick."

The bottle now went to Loriane, who also rolled a pill out onto her hand. She sniffed it, put it between her front teeth and bit half off. Chewed. Frowned. Shook her head. She handed the bottle back to him. Her light blue eyes met his. Sad.

"But . . ." He turned his own bottle around in his hands so that the pills rolled against the glass. This medicine came with Alius' guarantee. He'd just distributed thousands of these across the city. The army's support relied on these pills. Alius had an entire team working on this.

If this medicine was useless, why had Alius given it to him? Why had he distributed it throughout the army? If the men took it and believed they were protected, it would kill thousands of them.

Finnisius was going to kill him.

They were all going to die.

Why, Alius, why?

CHAPTER 24

RAIN PELTED down on the tent roof, whipped up by the wind.

Inside the tent, people sat huddled together in too small a space. Milleus ached all over. The ground was cold and his old limbs unsuited to sitting in such cramped conditions. If he leaned forward, his hips ached, and if he leaned back, someone behind him kept poking an elbow into his side.

Earlier on, he had wanted to go to the truck, but men dressed in black stopped him at the tent entrance. They talked, but he didn't understand them. None of them spoke Chevakian. No one left the tent.

He had given up the idea that he could control any part of what was happening. He should have listened to the soldiers and left the camp when he still could.

Artan and his wife sat next to him, huddled under a blanket. She was crying, and talked about some relative or friend whom they should try to contact.

"Please, just be quiet," Artan said. "What do you think we can do from here?"

"But if we asked—"

"We cannot ask anyone. They don't speak Chevakian."

"Surely they would have someone—"

"Maybe there are people who speak Chevakian, but I don't see anyone. I'm just trying not to get killed. I can't see what any of us can do."

She fell quiet, but Milleus could hear her crying. He could not begin to imagine what it was like for them, never having experienced war. In the Aranian war, his soldiers had been scared enough, and they had volunteered and were trained.

So he sat, said nothing and shivered.

He worried about Isandor and Jevaithi. It was too dark in the tent for him to see who was there, but they would have heard his voice earlier, and would have come to him, if they were here. Maybe the Knights had already found them and killed them, and maybe all his efforts at hiding them had been for nothing.

Why hadn't they told him earlier who she was? Yes, he knew why. Still, he worried about them.

Then he worried about the goats out there in the weather. They had been panicked enough with all the fighting and shooting. They'd need milking and feeding soon. Maybe the Eagle Knights would kill them for meat. And that thought sent shivers down his spine.

From outside, there were shouts and bangs of guns discharging. Someone splashed past the side of the tent and stopped there.

The people in the tent fell quiet. The flapping torch in the middle of the tent showed anxious faces.

It was so quiet that Milleus could hear the man's breathing. He shouted something that sounded like an order. A second man replied, further away. The Brothers at the entrance stiffened and gripped their guns. One picked up the torch from the stand. Ready to fight. A child started to cry and despite its mother's attempts to keep it silent, only cried louder. The Brother at the entrance mouthed insults at her.

"Keep your head down," Milleus said to Artan.

The tent flap was thrown back and in the light cast by the Brother's torch stood . . . an Eagle Knight in uniform, the characteristic grey short-hair cloak, made from the skin of the South's curious-looking Legless Lions, and underneath, the thick maroon shirt, without visible markings of rank. He was only a young man, with a characteristic narrow southern face and his sleek black hair tied at the nape of his neck.

Behind him stood another Knight. Two more were coming up,

and behind them Milleus could see outlines of birds, and more Knights with crossbows.

The young Knight spoke a few sharp words that sounded like an order. The Brother with the torch replied, his tone angry. He moved the torch in an arc as if to indicate all the people in the tent.

The Knight repeated the same order, but the Brother just glared at him. A second Brother at the back of the tent rose from between the seated people, and then a third one.

"This is not going to end well," Milleus said to Artan, in a low voice.

The two Knights came into the tent, stepping over legs towards the Brothers at the back. The Brother with the torch shouted at them, waving the torch about. Its light glinted on a metal object in the hands of a man close to Milleus.

He had a gun. And so did another man, a bit further. Milleus had his own gun, but it was tucked inside his belt.

First lesson in survival in an armed conflict: when you were in a minority was not a time to start wielding guns, not unless you were in a position from which you could inflict serious damage.

This was going to be a blood bath. He had to do something. The only thing Milleus could think of was *create a fuss*. Surely the Knights would not like any Chevakian witnesses, especially on Chevakian soil.

He pushed himself up. "Hey, you!"

Artan hissed at him. "What are you doing?"

Milleus yanked his trouser leg out of Artan's grip.

The nearest Knight turned; his eyes fixed on Milleus. As most southerners, he had cold, light-coloured eyes. His eyebrows flicked up.

Milleus continued. "We are Chevakians and we don't belong here. You must let the Chevakians leave, or the doga will consider this an act of war against our citizens." He felt ridiculous. The Knight gave no indication that he understood any of his words.

The Knight spoke in his language, and another, older, Knight gave a sharp reply. A few of their mates came into the tent, several of them with southern crossbows strapped into position. All of them looked at Milleus.

"Sit down, if you want to live," Artan hissed. "See those crossbows? They're bad news."

"I know." He remembered years ago, back when he was still in the army, trying a southern crossbow just for fun, and having difficulty, even as trained soldier, pulling the spring back. When he missed the target, the bolt hit a tree at a distance that matched the range of a gun.

"My name is Milleus han Chevonian, and I used to lead the doga," Milleus continued, and a kind of reckless feeling took hold of him. There was nothing else he could do, and if the Knights decided to shoot him, well, there was nothing he could do about that either. But he suspected they wouldn't do that, given the disturbed looks they shot one another. Oh no, they hadn't expected any Chevakians in the camp, that much was clear to him.

So he went on, recklessly, "I know many people in the doga, and if any of us, or anyone else is harmed, I will let the proctor know. They will consider it an act of war against the Chevakian state. So, please leave the camp before anything happens that would cause me to let my friends know."

It was rubbish, and utter bluff, but it confused the Knights, and while they conferred with one another, someone at the back of the tent ripped a hole in the fabric with a loud tearing sound.

One of the Knights shouted.

Someone at the back made a remark that sounded like an insult.

Two Knights charged across the tent, stepping over legs. People scrambled out of the way.

A shot exploded. Milleus could not see from where. The Brother dropped his torch. It went out and the interior of the tent was plunged into ink darkness. All around Milleus, people were getting up and pushing towards the entrance or the hole at the back of the tent. Milleus could do nothing but go with the flow. He grabbed what he thought was Artan's arm.

"Hold each other," he said somewhere near where he thought Artan's shoulder was.

"I've got Kara. I don't know where the other Chevakians are."

"Over here," someone shouted in Chevakian, but with all the other people shouting and pushing to get out, Milleus had no idea where the voice came from.

He could see nothing, and had no idea where the Knights were. People trod on his toes, and poked elbows in his side.

He shuffled with the stream towards the entrance, through the tent flap, out in the rain, on the muddy field that had been some sort of central point in the camp. The dark silhouette of one of the large communal tents loomed ahead. Milleus didn't know which. He was unsure where his truck was. Uphill, that was all he knew.

There were fires everywhere, even in the rain, screams, rioting groups of people, fortunately still further away. Over all the noise came the occasional loud bang of a gun being fired. The orange glow from fires showed the white-feathered bellies of flying eagles streaking low over the camp: more Knights arriving. Hundreds of them. How had all those men been able to come into the middle of Chevakia unnoticed?

"This way." He led Artan to the dark cover of a large tent, which could be the cooking tent, or one of the dorms, but wasn't the tent where Isandor and Jevaithi had slept. That one was further up the hill ... and on fire.

A vice of panic clamped his chest. Where were the youngsters?

He couldn't see his truck, which might be a good sign—at least it meant it wasn't on fire. But how to get there? People were running past at high speed, both camp residents and Knights. People were throwing rocks and other projectiles.

He gasped when a couple of dark forms ran around the corner and almost crashed into him.

"Shh, Milleus," a voice in Chevakian said. Isandor, with someone else, a thin figure, smaller than him. Mercy, it was the youngsters, both of them, safe.

"Milleus." Jevaithi gave him a shivering hug. She felt cold, wet and thin.

"I'm so glad you're alive." He was embarrassed how his voice faltered. He wanted to hug them and carry them off to a safe place.

She huddled in his arms. "Please help. They're looking for us."

"If we can reach the truck, they won't find you there."

"They'll search the entire camp. They know that we're here."

"They will not touch the truck when I'm in it. They know that the Chevakian doga will see action against Chevakians as an act of war."

"I hope you're right." But she didn't sound convinced. "But we must get help from outside. I don't know who else can still help us other than the Chevakians."

"Let's go to the truck first."

While they sneaked through the shadowed alleys between the tents, Milleus considered their options. Hide in the truck and then what? Jevaithi was right. The Knights would find her. His threats to warn the doga were empty. The doga would never find out that there had been Chevakians in the camp if none of them got out of the camp.

Which meant they had better get out, and also that the Knights would have no hesitation in killing them.

He could ram the fence with the truck—the fence wasn't that sturdy anyway—but then all of the Eagle Knights would be after them. Eagles flew much faster than the truck could go and he could never reach Tiverius in time.

The Knights had a group of citizens rounded up sitting on the ground in the rain.

As they passed, a woman rose and ran. Two Knights went after her, caught up, pushed her on the ground. She screamed at them and one Knight kicked her.

Mercy, was that how they treated their women? No wonder the south had fertility problems. No wonder the youngsters had fled.

Further up the hill, the black-clad young men of the Brotherhood were throwing fire bombs at the Knights. Milleus spotted a man with a cloth covering all parts of his face except for the eyes on top of a stack of crates, shooting at random. Smoke billowed between the tents. A line of Knights stood there holding shields against flying rocks and burning sticks that flew towards them.

They reached the truck, an island of safety in this crazy world. Fortunately, there was no sign of activity uphill.

"What can we do now?" Jevaithi asked.

"Be ready to move," Milleus said, opening the cabin door.

Isandor offered to get the steam going.

Milleus went to check on the goats. They were bleating and jumping around. They were probably hungry, but there was no time to look after them.

A couple of loud bangs echoed over the hillside. Isandor froze, and met Milleus' eyes. No words were necessary. The fighting was coming up the hill.

Isandor flung wood into the furnace. The water level was quite low, so Milleus grabbed the goats' water trough and emptied it in the reservoir. The water would be dirty and might clog the steam nozzles, but he'd sort that out later. Damage to the truck was worthy price to pay if they could escape.

Isandor was trying to light the fire, but the wood was wet and his hands cold and clumsy. The small pilot flame would not ignite the kindling. His hands trembled.

"Here." Milleus opened the lid to the first aid box, which contained a flask of spirits. Isandor tried to screw the top off, but couldn't get it, then he slammed the bottle against the metal barrel so that the top broke off, and splashed the fluid over the wood. With a *whoosh* from the pilot flame, the fluid turned into an inferno.

Then they clambered in the cabin and the wait began. Milleus closed all valves, hoping that none would burst, and settled in to wait.

A couple of men marched up the hill, weapons drawn. Milleus ran his hand over the barrel of the gun that leaned against his leg.

"Hide behind the seat!" he told Isandor and Jevaithi but they already huddled there. He threw the bag that contained the tent over them. Watching the pressure needle move.

Come on, come on. He wasn't sure what he'd do. Ideally, he would have wanted to ram the fence on the lower side of the camp. Going to the higher side meant that he would have to backtrack along the Ensar road, and it would take quite long before they'd get to Tiverius. That was if no one punctured the tyres. After the last mishap, he had no spare. The lower fence, however ...

This warming up was too slow. The shouts were coming closer. And closer. He was irritated that he couldn't see anything for the smoke, the darkness and the steam.

A number of figured resolved from the mist, running towards the truck.

Finally. With a hiss of steam, he dropped the truck into gear. The vehicle shot forward, but still didn't have much speed. They were going uphill and the truck was heavy. He should have disconnected the trailer, but he cared too much about his goats. They were not going to make it. Or maybe they were. People ran next to the truck, and the truck was slowly inching ahead.

A huge shape descended from the sky.

"Eagles!" Isandor called from the back seat.

More shapes swooped down, so close that the truck rocked with their passing. Milleus peered into the sky, but couldn't make out where the eagles had gone.

The heavens opened in all earnest. Milleus could hardly see anything for the water that ran down the window. There were screeches outside. The eagles were following. Damn it, they were not going to make it—

A series of shapes loomed up out of the rain. Trucks. Milleus slammed on the brakes, but the weight of the truck sent it skidding in the mud. Milleus yanked on the wheel.

The truck slid, sideways, missing the other vehicles by as little as a handwidth, and came to a stop. Milleus gunned the engine, but the tyres slipped in the mud and didn't find traction.

The engine hissed steam. Rain pelted down on the roof.

Milleus wiped his face.

"What happened?" Isandor asked from the back seat.

"We're stuck!"

A couple of figures came walking through the rain, men with cloaks. "Shh, don't say a word." His heart was still thudding.

One of the men outside shouted something, and gestured for Milleus to come outside.

There was nothing for it. Milleus half-opened the door. Cold and humid air gusted in, mingled with rain drops. He debated taking the gun, but decided against it. It was only a hunting rifle, and would bring more anger from the Knights than protection against them. The best thing he could do was create or hope for another diversion. And stay within reach of the gun.

As he clambered from the vehicle, slowly, to win time, a group of people caught up with the truck and positioned themselves around it.

They were ordinary people, not Brothers, not fighters, but young people and old people and children, their mothers, fathers and grand-parents, about fifty of them.

A young boy he guessed to be about ten carried a gun. Water

dripped from his hair into his eyes and his clothes were soaking wet, but his face showed determination.

These people knew where Jevaithi was and were ready to protect her.

Eagle Knights were coming from all directions, some of them leading their birds, until the refugees were surrounded and huddled around Milleus' truck.

Lightning flashed.

Milleus could do nothing but watch. In all the wars he'd fought, he'd never felt so helpless. He had no army to command, no idea what was going on, and why there were no Chevakian soldiers here. *They* would have listened to him. Now all he could do was wait while the Knights inspected everyone, and hope the doga would do something, but with Destran in charge, he didn't hold out much hope.

They would find the youngsters, and then what would he do?

CHAPTER 25

IN THE EVENING, under the cover of growing darkness, the main tower of the Scriptorium was like a ghost town. Since Sady had ordered the bell to be rung, there had been no more lessons, no more students talking quietly in alcoves, no more bows and whispers as an academic passed. Just a solitary door attendant on the ground floor who assured Sady that yes, the Most Learned Alius was in the building.

Sady made his way from the ground floor entrance hall up the spiral walkway that circled the inside of the tower. A soft red carpet absorbed his footfalls, and the rich hand-crafted book cases along the walls spoke of history and knowledge contained in this place.

Orsan walked behind him like a shadow. Under normal circumstances, anyone bearing arms was not allowed in the Scriptorium, but the gatehouse guard had waved Orsan through, because "it was not as if anyone's here to notice".

Sady knocked on the door of the familiar office. The sound carried in the eerie silence. He pictured Alius sitting behind his desk that always overflowed with books and papers, slowly getting up and walking to the door. And he found himself in that mental space he had occupied during most of his own studies. Even back then, most of the students saw Alius as a god, quoting his words at every opportunity. Back then, Alius was working on the barrier, and he was Chevakia's hero.

Why did he take so long to open the door?

He knocked again. "Alius, it's Sady."

Sady held his breath

But nothing happened. He looked around, but the mezzanine gallery and the hall below were empty except for Orsan, who leaned against the banister, his face without much expression.

What to do? He really needed to talk to Alius about these pills, and he didn't have the time to chase Alius all over town. Where did he even live? Sady had no idea.

Maybe there was some clue in the room where he would have gone. A note about a meeting or something. The thought *Lady Armaine's house* came unbidden. Her house had been like an impenetrable fort protected by a wall of excuses uttered by the guards at the gate.

Come on, Alius!

Sady tried the handle, and the door opened with a creak. It was dark in the room, and an odd kind of musty smell wafted out, as if the room had been closed for a long time. Slowly, Sady walked in.

A lamp against the far wall was sputtering the last of its flames, gilding piles of boxes just inside the door, identical to the ones that had been delivered to Sady's office earlier. The room smelled musty and damp, and there was a cloying sweet scent that he couldn't identify.

Sady nearly tripped over a book that had been carelessly flung onto the floor, its pages open.

What was going on here?

He grabbed for the lamp and turned the wick up so that it gave more light, and held it up.

All through the room, books were spread over the floor, yanked off shelves and left open, pages ripped. Alius' desk stood by the window against the back wall. The high back of the chair faced the door. Alius often complained about the room's layout, necessitating the placement of the desk facing the window. Today, the chair was empty . . . no, it wasn't . . . Someone with grey hair lay slumped over the desk, his head on the books.

Mercy.

"Alius!"

Sady rushed across the room, tripping over more books. He set the lamp down with trembling hands.

Alius' head lay sideways facing away from the door, on the open pages of a book. The eye that stared into nothingness was open, glassy. A trail of blood had dribbled from his mouth onto the book, but it was already dry and black. Some little insects were crawling into his open eyes and nostrils.

His hand, gnarled and aged, clutched a pen. The other lay on his lap.

When Sady touched the Most Learned's shoulder, the flesh was rigid and unyielding under his hand.

Above his head lay a wooden box, the lid open, with inside a tiny glass vial, empty. The matching glass stopper lay on the desk.

Sady had to stand back. The body gave off a cloying scent that suddenly became too much. He ran to the gallery, feeling dizzy and struggling to keep control of his stomach.

"Orsan! Orsan, quickly!"

Orsan had wandered a little away from Alius' room and came rushing back.

"Proctor?" His face was concerned.

"Look!" Sady gestured into the room.

Orsan looked, and swore. He walked around the desk without touching Alius. Sady followed, covering his nose with the sleeve of his robe. That cloying smell was the beginning of decay.

Orsan looked up. "He's been dead for a while." He picked up the wooden box. "What's this?"

"Careful of that box, whatever is in it."

Orsan put it down carefully. "Poison?"

"Looks like it."

Orsan's brown eyes went from the box to Alius' unmoving body. "Why would he do a thing like this?"

"I gave the pills he made to our southern guests. Both Dara and Loriane said the medicine had been made from a common herb, and would offer absolutely no protection against sonorics."

Orsan frowned. "And you believe them over Alius' word as academic?"

"Neither of the women knew what the pills were meant to do. Both are familiar with herb lore, and offered their opinion without knowing any of the story behind these pills. I cannot see why they should lie."

"But why would Alius send us medicine if it doesn't work?"

That, of course, was a very good question.

But Sady got a cold feeling. There was no medicine. That was why Alius had been late delivering it, why he hadn't wanted to promise its delivery nor talk about it, why he had looked nervous or evasive, and had been unhappy that Lady Armaine had mentioned it. He never had a working sonorics medicine.

Why Alius?

Sady glanced at the shelves to the side of the desk. The books were all ones he'd expect to see in an academic's room. Medical volumes, fat books with titles with long, academic words, the meaning of which Sady had long forgotten. There were so many books, so much information in this room.

"Have you seen this?" Orsan asked.

Sady turned. Orsan was pulling a sheet of paper from under the book under Alius' head.

"What is it?" Sady took the paper from Orsan. It was, in fine script that Sady recognised as Alius' handwriting, a letter, addressed to him.

It said,

To the honourable Proctor of Chevakia.

By the time you read this, I will be dead. I have deceived my country and the country will be better off without me. There is no excuse for what I have done. I'm afraid that I've let myself be distracted by politics in a time where I should have been working harder for Chevakia.

It is well over ten years ago, when I was unhappy with the way your brother was unseated, that I made some political comments that led Destran to cutting money for the Scriptorium. It was a necessary thing from his point of view. The wars had drained a good deal of our money, destroyed a lot of factories and converted others into making weapons. A lot of people came back from the wars needing care and housing. These were important issues for the doga to address. The Scriptorium was less important and lost a lot of its funding. Nevertheless, I believed, perhaps foolishly, that the doga should invest in knowledge for the future. The doga did not share my views.

In a public speech, I made no secret of my anger, and afterwards, a woman came to see me at my office. I didn't know her, but she said she heard my plea and offered to pay for some of the work I would no longer have the money to do. I asked her motives, and she said she had come into money and wanted to spend it on a worthy cause. She acted innocent and although she clearly had southern blood, I thought she was well-intentioned but naïve. My work was to find better ways to protect humans against sonoric rays. How could I refuse? That decision has haunted me ever since.

Sady felt cold. Just by pure chance, and a less desperate situation, he had avoided making the same decision. He wondered what would have happened had he not insisted that Lady Armaine's contribution to his travel expenses had been registered as non-political. It had been more dumb luck than anything, that he'd had the presence of mind to ask that. He continued reading.

Over the years that followed, she continued to fund a larger and larger proportion of my work. She encouraged me to work on using sonorics as an energy source. Since our forests are suffering from our need for wood fuel, I thought that was an excellent idea, providing we could find a way to protect ourselves from sonorics.

She said there were ways in which sonorics could be made harmless, and brought me into contact with this group called the Brotherhood of the Light. She told me that when the City of Glass was plunged into the dark ages by the Knights, the Brotherhood kept knowledge about sonorics alive. I soon learned that the Brotherhood wasn't made up of just refugees from the City of Glass. Many of its members are rich Chevakian merchants, disgruntled with the doga, and lured by the prospect of cheap energy and new technology. Many of those merchants had been in close contact with the City of Glass under the royal family, and had lost much trade when the Eagle Knights took over.

They saw an opportunity to regain what they had lost. They knew that the Brotherhood and its supporters planned to bring down the barriers and they supported that plan, providing a way could be found to protect Chevakians from sonoric rays. This is where I came in. There were some hopeful results from a new ingredient, they said.

I was given a huge stack of material. I don't think they expected me to go through it as closely as I did. I might have been gullible, but I will not be accused of substandard work. In the pile, I found results from experiments done on Chevakians who we know to have been forcibly moved to the City of Glass, all of whom had died horribly. The research, while macabre in nature, was interesting, but the main ingredient of the pills I was to make, from a plant that grows in the borderlands, had not been used in any of those trials.

How was this meant to help me find a medicine, I asked, and I was told that there should have been data about another experiment, which they would provide. You have to understand that none of these people were academics and their knowledge of the subject matter in question was rudimentary at best. They would not have realised that these were the wrong trial results they had given me. I asked for the correct results. They promised me to send them. Except they didn't, and every time I asked, they gave me some excuse that seemed plausible, if annoying.

Just make the pills, they told me, and we did, because if we were going to test it, we would need them anyway.

Next thing I knew, Lady Armaine had told you about this medicine.

I should have walked out at that point in time, but the problem was that I had no other way of paying all the students I had taken on and I couldn't leave the project without major loss of face, both to myself, my staff and students and indeed all of the Scriptorium.

And there was another, deeper, problem, namely that of deeply-rooted corruption. If I walked out, a lot of my colleagues and friends and others in the higher echelons of power would have lost their positions. In the beginning, when she first came to me, Lady Armaine had used her own money to fund my work. However, she fled the City of Glass with only the clothes she wore, and married Darius han Lavani, who was always much better at gambling than at merchanting. He was well-off but never as rich as his father and grandfather had been. Then of course he died in suspicious circumstances, and there was no more money coming in.

So she used her ground army of Brotherhood supporters to keep politicians in office, and demanded payment from them in return. Then she recycled those bribes by paying us. We were paid with money that had mysteriously vanished from doga accounts.

If I had walked out, all that would have been exposed to great upheaval in the doga. Lady Armaine repeatedly let it shimmer through that if I walked, she would harm my family, and they are innocent and know nothing of this.

So they forced me to bring out the medicine regardless of my objections. I can no longer live with the guilt.

Please, Proctor, the medicine does not work. Do not believe anyone who says otherwise. Please evacuate everyone from out of the path of this storm.

Once the storm has passed and Chevakia is safe, please take the book underneath this message to the doga. It contains everything they need to know. I believe in Chevakia. I believe you are by far the best leader the country has ever had. I will not have any more Chevakian deaths on my conscience.

With trembling hands, Sady opened the book.

There were columns of financial data. Sady recognised references to the books that had gone missing. Those books Destran appeared to have deliberately hidden. Alius had received *how much* money from Lady Armaine? She had received how much from Destran? And the money had gone where? To an account in the City of Glass, for *what*?

Lady Armaine's riches were paid from money scammed from the doga. Mercy. He met Orsan's eyes.

"Did you know about any of this?"

But Orsan, proper as he was, didn't answer the question. If they came through all of this, he must remind himself to pass a ruling that doga guards could be questioned about this matter.

Who was involved? Worse—who wasn't involved? He stared at Alius' lifeless body, his heart thudding. The entire doga was short of money. Every senator had been a target for Lady Armaine's group. Any of them might betray him. Any of them might still believe that the pills worked.

He'd run out of ways to protect the country. He'd given the orders for people to find shelter. Now he could only go home and prepare his own house for the inevitable. He wished there was something else he could do. And in the back of his mind, he still heard the rough, pain-laced voice, *You will beg me to help you by the time it's too late.*

In the cosy darkness of the kitchen, Sady ordered everyone in this house to sit down for dinner. He'd deliberately left Orsan at the gate, so that Farius and Ontane could be inside. Young Farius sat next to Myra. They talked in low voices and judging by their coy looks, he had a suspicion there was something going on between those two.

Dara had finally stopped fussing with pots and pans and sat down at the head of the table. Reili had shoved her study books out of the way of the plates, and it was as if everyone understood that the spot next to Sady was reserved for Loriane. She had come into the kitchen quietly. Myra said that following the family meeting, she had gone with Andrean to look at his pregnant wife, because Andrean had complained that with the sonorics warnings, no one would come to see a patient unless they were about to die. Sady suspected that Andrean was bluffing, and that his wife was perfectly fine, but Loriane had gone and come back looking impressively professional. Myra had confirmed that apart from a breeder, Loriane was a midwife.

The soft light from the plethora of lamps and candles around the kitchen gilded her hair and made two bright spots of reflection in her eyes. Her broad-lipped mouth curved into a smile, and Sady noticed that she had little dimples in her cheeks.

"How was my niece?" he asked her.

Loriane waggled her hand. "Not time yet."

Thank the heavens for that. Sady might not like his nephew's choice of wife, but he could hardly think of worse times to have a baby as in the middle of a sonorics emergency.

"Mother is just bored," Reili added.

It struck Sady how normal life continued in the face of danger, and he hated to shatter that small bubble of normality.

He said, "I don't know how much of this you will understand, but I'm going to need your help."

They all looked at him.

"Reili, Farius, please help me explain if anything is not clear. The medicine doesn't work. It seems it was part of a conspiracy to assure Alius' cooperation with a group called the Brotherhood of the Light." He used the southern term.

Myra repeated it in the way it was supposed to be pronounced, and said something else. Dara nodded.

"You know these people?"

It was Loriane who spoke. "They have . . ." She stopped, and said something to Myra.

Myra said, "Schools? Is that word for place for children?"

"Where children learn?"

"No, they live. With no family."

"You mean orphanage." As far as he knew, the City of Glass didn't have schools.

"Yes." Her eyes lingered on his. "Brotherhood of the light have orphanage. In City of Glass."

"What do people in the City of Glass know about the Brotherhood?"

Myra quickly translated the question.

Ontane said something, spreading his hands and rolling his eyes at the ceiling.

"Father says they crazy."

Dara nodded.

Loriane looked more pensive. She spoke to Myra.

"Loriane says that in City of Glass Brotherhood teaches about icefire. The have old books from king."

"Caldor," Sady said.

She flinched.

Sady understood the situation with a clarity that should have been obvious long ago. Fifty years ago, the City of Glass had been prosperous. He had only been a very young boy, but vaguely remembered the envious talk of his parents and grandparents. At the time, there had been a regular trade between Tiverius and the City of Glass. But, while the Tiverians were both enchanted and fearful of the south and its technology, within the country, a revolution was rising of people who had been abused for the sake of that technology. This was the part that Chevakians in border regions called magic, and that academics in Tiverius had always denied existed.

The resistance against the abuse of magic—let's call it side effects of sonorics—led to the rise of the Eagle Knights, who blamed the icefire technology for their ills and banned it. At the same time, Chevakia was developing steam technology, and found out how to build the barrier to stop sonorics. But all of the southern sonorics technology, their "magic" and Alius' barrier were part of the same academic discipline, and in both countries, those who saw good in the power of sonorics were driven underground. They had formed one large cross-border alliance, which, in Chevakia with its eternal limitations on cropping and land use, had drawn strong support from influential people.

And now, the sonorics supporters had done something to the source of the power and it had gone badly wrong.

"So, here is the situation: a large storm is coming this way, clouds heavy with sonorics—-icefire. The Chevakian who knew most about sonorics is dead. Without shelter, many of us will die. Since we had the barrier, no new shelters have been built, and they are not big enough to hold the entire population. There is no time to build more shelters. Many people will die. Except, the prisoner Tandor claims that this . . . dacon . . . thing is the only way to reduce sonorics. My question is: do you think there is any merit in what he says?"

Acknowledging the potential existence of the magical being felt like making a hard confession. He would have preferred to ignore the issue if another option had been available. Which there wasn't.

Myra said, "I don't know what the creature is."

Loriane shook her head. "Is real. I seen it."

Dara said something in a harsh tone. Loriane replied, equally harsh. Myra loosened the sling and took Beido out. Ontane glared at Loriane from the corner of his eyes.

Loriane glared back at him.

"Is real," she repeated. "Is kill people. Baby."

Dara made another sharp comment.

"She says Loriane is not good in the head."

"It's true!" Loriane said, her eyes blazing with anger, and then she added something to Myra.

Dara snapped back at Loriane, and Ontane said some soothing words.

Myra rose. "Have to do work now. Make the house safe. Tandor is crazy. Bad."

When Sady came in, they had been working on the bathroom, which Farius had determined to be the safest part of the house, and supplies and beds were being moved in.

Everyone left, except for Loriane. Sady now understood the argument he'd sensed the morning after the killings. Mercy, if even the southerners were unsure of Tandor's words, then how much hope did he have? A small part of him had wanted Tandor's story to be true, because he wanted to be able to do something.

And Tandor said that this *creature*, if it existed, could be used to reduce sonorics, but he had no control over it, and neither did anyone else, and Sady could not see what else he could do to stop the sonorics cloud reaching Tiverius, with or without people made of fire —that detail hardly mattered anymore. Thousands of innocent citizens would die, and he could do nothing to stop it.

He let his shoulders slump. They'd go into the bathroom when the storm came. He'd put on his suit, and accept any family whose house did not have a safe place, and hoped they would survive, and if they survived, hope that they'd still be able to grow food, and that the farm animals had survived. *If* they survived, and that was a big question.

He blew out a heavy breath.

A hand moved into the field of his vision, and closed over his.

He met Loriane's eyes, their strange colour mesmerising. She didn't look away and didn't smile, but continued to meet his eyes with a steady expression. "Sorry," she said.

"You can't help it," he said. He shrugged. He hated being power-less. He had done all the right things, prepared the people as best as the situation allowed, re-opened the shelters, he had settled the refugees and given them food. He had settled the Ensar people, and ordered the army to be ready for an attack. Except this wasn't the kind of attack that could be fought.

"What do you want me to do? Just sit here and wait until we can die?"

He was unsure Loriane understood.

"Chances are that when this storm has passed, you will be the only ones alive in Tiverius."

Maybe that was what this Brotherhood had wanted all along, and gullible Chevakian businessmen had bought into the dream of free energy while being told lies about the side effects.

"You will live," Loriane said in the oddly disjointed way of a foreign speaker. "You are a good man."

"This is not about good or bad."

"You are good."

Her hand slid up his arm. That must be a southern thing, because Chevakians didn't touch there, unless . . .

Her steady gaze did not waver from his.

Sady's heart was thudding. When had the atmosphere changed from one of comfort to something overwhelmingly suggestive?

He lifted his hand to cover hers, feeling her skin, soft, but with bumps and calluses on the fingers, under his hand.

How long had it been since he had last touched a woman like this?

"Loriane, I . . . don't want you to think that you have to do anything to stay in my house. I require no payment of this kind."

She didn't react, but continued to meet his eyes, and smiled. Her lips curved and her lips drew back to make little hollows at the corners of her mouth. Her cheeks dimpled.

Woman, don't do that or I'll . . .

Do what?

It hardly mattered if they were all going to die.

Would he go to his death regretting not having shown his affection to three amazing, brave and beautiful women in his life?

He reached out and touched the soft skin of her neck, threading his fingers through her hair. It was lush and bushy and smelled of flowers.

"I won't do this if you don't want me to."

Who was he kidding? Who was the most scared here? Twenty years, thirty years, since he had last kissed a woman.

He was scared to death that she would get up and walk out. That she would slap him in the face. He was waiting for it.

But nothing happened.

And then slowly, he closed the remaining handwidth distance between them and kissed her, fleetingly, on the lips. Giving her the opportunity to back out.

She didn't. Still meeting his eyes in that intense look, she slid her hand up his arm, to his shoulder, and pulled him closer.

He kissed her properly, and she kissed him back, unleashing a flood of feelings deep inside him. Relief, regret, desire. She was an amazing woman, strong in the face of incredible hardship, and if he had only night left to live, he was going to spend it with her.

For a blissful time, he forgot about the problems. He wanted to hold her and never let her go. He wanted to take her by the hand and shout *Look, I found the best woman in the world and she's mine.*

He had never, ever, been in love. Oh, he'd liked Suri, and had dreams about her. He'd liked Lana, as companion, but there was a reason why he'd never taken any intimate steps with either of them: because he hadn't wanted to.

The kitchen door opened, and someone said, "Sady—oh!"

Sady let go of Loriane, his heart still thudding.

It was Orsan at the door, dressed in a cloak dripping rain, his eyes wide.

"Uhm—I'm sorry for interrupting your—uhm . . ." His cheeks had gone red.

"You have interrupted. Tell me." Sady was surprised at how unapologetic he felt.

Orsan pushed down the hood of his cloak, still watching Loriane. Oh, yes, he disapproved.

"There is fighting in the refugee camp. The camp commander confirms that his men were overwhelmed by Eagle Knights."

Sady's first thought was *Fuck the camp and fuck the Eagle Knights*, but managed not to say that. He took a deep breath, still tasting and smelling Loriane and wanting, oh so badly, to take her upstairs. His second thought was *and Finnisius said they had everything under control*, but he didn't say that, either. His third thought was very different. "Orsan, tell me what the *fuck* are Eagle Knights doing in Chevakia?"

"Uhm—General Finnisius sent me to report. I don't know the details."

"What is General Finnisius doing?"

"He asks for advice."

Sady pushed himself up from his seat and grabbed his suit. "Well, I'll give him some advice. He's been giving me nonsense about these camps for days. Withdrawing from his job. *We don't fight civilians.* I bet my life that there is someone, or several someones, inside that camp who attracts this kind of weird behaviour." Likely the Brotherhood had infiltrated the army. "Come." He grabbed Loriane's hand. "Get a cloak. It's raining."

And as he followed Orsan out of the kitchen, another thought came to him: supposing this mythical creature existed, and supposing it roamed wild in the Tiverian skies, turning from a little girl into a flying monster at will, the only place they could find someone to tame it was amongst the southern refugees, and maybe that someone was a person with experience in dealing with large flying creatures and they had none such people in Tiverius.

CHAPTER 26

CARRO DID NOT want to go out. By the skylights, the weather was awful. Rain lashed the metal sheets of the shed, which creaked and rattled with gusts of wind. Carro stood at the central bar, fussing with his eagle's reins. The bird snorted and shook its head, scattering bits of down, and gave Carro the evil eye. It had been asleep, beak tucked in its feathers, when the order to fly out came.

It looked like it wanted to do this just as much as Carro did. No piece of clothing would keep him dry in weather like this. The eagles hated it, and hated it even more because it was dark.

All around him, Knights were saddling up their birds to go out, part of the second wave of attacks, as Rider Cornatan had ordered. They had word that the trucks were in the camp, now it was the Eagle Knights' turn to fly in under the cover of darkness and flush out Brotherhood leaders and find the Queen. She was to be brought back to farmhouse. Alive. Rider Cornatan had vacated and prepared a room for her, a store room, without a window, with a heavy lock on the door, and a large luxurious bed with satin sheets.

Anyone defending her was to be killed, and the Queen brought back to this prison, where she would again be paraded out to the people as mascot, and where the Junior Knights would again talk about her puppies. Except this time, Rider Cornatan would waste no time in getting her pregnant.

And when the Brotherhood was defeated and its members killed, and the Queen safely imprisoned, the Knights could go on being just as dishonourable, disrespectful and disobedient as they wanted. Nothing would change unless *someone* changed it.

As Carro stood there, surrounded by eagles, unnecessarily fiddling with the harness, he was struggling to hold visions at bay. Icefire was strong tonight, and it made him alternately shiver or feel hot.

Jeito glanced at him. She had been doing this ever since they had started preparing, as if looking for an opportunity to do something unexpected, like stick a knife in his back. Since their conversation at Rider Barton's hideout, she had not spoken to him.

Farey had told him that Jeito's mother and sister were likely to be in the camp.

Carro thought, *My family could be there, too* until he remembered that the merchant was no longer family, and that the scornful dumpy girl wasn't really his sister, and never cared about him . . . except he remembered walking through the streets holding her hand. And he remembered her walking up the stairs to his sleeping shelf carrying broth. He'd been sick for days, and the soup was the best thing he'd ever tasted, even though he would never tell her. He remembered her wanting to dress him up in some garishly-coloured thing she had made with offcuts from her father's fabrics. He remembered screaming at her, and his mother telling him to be nice to her. He remembered yelling, *I hate her!* And his mother boxing him around the ears for being horrible to his sister, after which he had screamed that he hated his mother as well. He enjoyed looking at the hurt expression on her face.

At one point, his family had cared about him.

In later years, they had given up caring, because he had never given them a reason to care for him. He liked it when people hated him, because he could stay angry.

The world had hated him, because he had expected the world to hate him. By hating himself, he had made himself be hated. Except for Isandor who had, in some way, seen through the hate.

Whatever had possessed him to tell on his friend? Why had he cared about Rider Cornatan's approval?

Rider Cornatan didn't care for him. Perhaps his real father cared for him less than the merchant had. Rider Cornatan didn't care for the any of the people of the City of Glass. Rider Cornatan didn't care for the Eagle Knights' mantra, or their task: to keep the order and protect the Queen.

And he *did not* want to go into the camp and fight other people from the Outer City. But everyone around him was getting ready with grim determination.

Knights were already taking their eagles out into the rain. The birds made protesting noises.

Farey jerked his head in a *let's go* kind of way.

Carro nodded. Several pale-faced Knights under his command looked scared. They didn't want to fight either.

He turned around to needlessly adjust the saddle on his eagle's back—and met Rider Barton's eyes, intense.

Why were they all staring at him? But he knew why. If there was ever someone who could stop this, he was that person. Rider Cornatan would not listen to anyone else.

With trembling hands, he re-tied the eagle's reins and crossed the stable. At the open doors, groups of birds were taking off into the stormy night.

Rider Barton met his eyes in silence. His face was exceedingly blank, as if he was afraid to show any of his thoughts.

Carro said, "I noticed at the meeting that you were reluctant about sending the men into the camp."

"My excuses. I didn't mean to question the Supreme Rider. I was merely voicing the feelings of my men."

"Loyalty and Honesty." Carro forced a smile.

Rider Barton nodded and returned an equally forced smile.

"You backed off because you didn't want to push the Supreme Rider for what you feel is right."

Rider Barton flicked his eyebrows. "I don't know what that is supposed to mean."

Carro met his eyes, and felt like screaming, *Come on, give me some help, I know that you don't like this either*, but he said nothing, and Rider Barton said nothing, and Carro couldn't be completely sure that Rider Barton's remark about his men expecting to go back to the City of Glass in order to rescue people meant that he disagreed with Rider

Cornatan's order. He was trembling so much that he couldn't think of anything safe to say.

Rider Barton nodded. "I'm sorry. I have a unit to lead." He clipped the loops of his riding harness together.

"Yes, sure. Let's go."

Trembling, Carro went back to his eagle. Now what did that mean? That Rider Barton distrusted him? That he didn't agree? That he was scared of being found out as dissenter?

He led his bird out the stable, feeling that an opportunity had just passed him. By the skylights, if he wanted to reinstate the Knights' honour, if he wanted to lead a movement, a rebellion, a *mutiny* against the upper command, he would have to be more bold than this. Yet, he needed numbers. Jeito and Farey might support him, and some of their friends, but he needed Rider Barton. Rider Barton's men might support him . . . but he couldn't see who they were in the dark and chaos of the shed where half the men had already left for battle. He had no way of reaching them.

So he grabbed the eagle's reins and followed Rider Barton outside. Rain pelted down, freezing and biting his skin. Not even his thick cloak was going to be enough to keep him warm in weather like this. He was already shivering.

They took off over the forest. Driving rain cut into the skin of Carro's face and hands and he could barely see.

First was the darkness of the forest that separated the farmhouse from Tiverius, and then some fields and dotted lights of farms.

He was nervous, shivering. Worried that Jeito or Rider Barton had been told to act as they did in order to test his loyalty and that either of them would run a dagger through his heart as soon as they landed.

Worried that they might think that he was a spy for Rider Cornatan.

He could already see the glow of fire on the horizon, and palls of smoke rising into the night air. He didn't have long to think about what to do.

Carro stands in the emerald room where he first met his father. The door rumbles open and three men come in. They stop a few paces inside the door and stare at him. They're Knights, of a fashion, but their standard of uniform would never be approved inside the eyrie. One wears a faded shirt, the other non-standard trousers. They wear shorthair cloaks, and are just recognisable as Knights, but clearly not ordinary Knights. One of the men he recognises. It's the tall and skinny Farey who he met in his father's bathroom, the one with the Aranian face. A second man is quite young, with a head of honey-coloured curls. His eyes are light brown. The other is slight of build, with sleek black hair and piercing eyes.

Uhm—I'm Carro, he says, and the small man glares at him in a way that says, *See if I care.*

The men must obey you, his father had said. If they do not, punish them until they do.

Punish these men? Rider Cornatan has to be kidding.

The camp was closer now, and Carro could make out burning piles of wood and people running. Shouts and screams. The first Knights had gone into the camp in trucks, to despatch the Chevakian soldiers. There were the trucks of the Chevakians which people had said were in the camp. There were the trucks that had held the first wave of Knights. He peered into the stinging wind. Where were all the camp's inhabitants? Where were Isandor and Jevaithi? What if they had already been captured?

The eagles landed on a field uphill from the tents. Knights jumped off and formed groups according to orders, while the stable boys looked after the birds. Everyone with their unit. Carro found Jeito, Nolan and Farey in the dark. He was cold, wet and his muscles were stiff, so his steps were awkward. Men shouted orders. Someone lit a torch, which almost flapped out in a strong gust of wind. Carro pulled the sides of his cloak closer against the rain and shouted to his command to follow him.

The Senior Knight walked back and forth in front of the lined-up men. "At the moment, most of the fighting is on the other side of the camp. We are going to come in from this side. We will get everyone out of the tents and line them up. We search the tents to make sure no one hides. First pick of beds tonight for the unit that finds the Queen. Go, go, go."

Kick him, the boy says.

Carro looks up from the boy who crouches, sobbing in the snow to the bully standing next to him. The bully is older than him, a head taller and almost twice his width.

Come on, kick him, he says.

Carro wants to ask, *Where?* Or, *How?*

He doesn't need to ask why; he knows. Because if he doesn't, the older boys will hit him. Not that he really wants to kick the boy, but it's easy because he's younger and smaller than Carro, and he's too scared to fight back.

Carro glances at the door to Isandor's house. Isandor would tell the big boys to go away, but Carro hasn't seen his friend all day.

He swings his leg backwards and kicks the boy. Not as hard as he can, nor softly enough for the older boys to notice that fact. He hates the soft feeling as his boot connects with the young boy's back.

By the skylights, this was not a time for visions.

The first Knights were already marching into the camp. Carro followed. He was wet and freezing. He couldn't see anything through the mist and smoke. He no longer knew where Nolan, Farey and Jeito and the rest of his command were, because the torch had been doused and everyone around him reduced to dark silhouettes.

Ahead, Knights arrived at the first of the tents. A man threw a tent flap open and shouted for the people to come outside.

They did, slowly, into a pool of light of a torch held up by a Knight. There were old men, women, children, some making pleas to the Knights. Many of them sported bandages. A man spat at the Knights at the entrance, and retreated when one of the Knights lashed out at him. A woman screamed.

They weren't Brotherhood people, men dressed in black with beards, but ordinary citizens, most of them from the Outer City.

Carro tried to find familiar faces, but most people pulled their cloaks over their heads and hid in the darkness underneath.

Rain came down in sheets.

The Knights made all the people sit in the rain, and went to the next tent. Carro looked over the group. Some people attempted to sit on their knees so they wouldn't get wet from the ground. Mothers took children on their laps.

He couldn't see Jevaithi or Isandor, but it was only a matter of time before they were found. And what would he do then?

He stood there, avoiding the people's gazes, and shivered, and wished something would happen that would make all this go away. He wished he knew where Rider Barton had gone, or even that Rider Barton had given him a less ambiguous reply about who he supported.

He wished he never betrayed Isandor, and he wished he'd had the courage to tell Rider Cornatan that he wanted nothing more to do with him.

The Pirosian medallion burned against his skin. He longed to take it off and fling it as far as he could.

But that would solve nothing, because everyone would continue doing all these stupid things without him. Pirosians versus Thilleians, was that what it all came down to? It was stupid, stupid that people would die for this vendetta. Stupid.

NOT MUCH LATER, Sady and Loriane arose from the truck at in General Finnisius' field office while rain pelted on the roof. The canvas sides of the tent billowed in with gusts of wind and the flapping of the fabric, and the rain, almost drowned out the sound of the truck idling. Sady had ordered Orsan and the driver to wait. From further away came the blasts from burners which kept a unit of balloons in perpetual readiness.

Sady had shed his hood, but had kept the rest of his suit on, dripping water all over Finnisius' chair. Loriane wore only a cloak over her dress. If he understood correctly, she was of the type of people on whom sonorics had no effect whatsoever and could not see it. She didn't seem to be cold either.

Finnisius came to the table with a map, raising his eyebrows at Loriane. "These talks are confidential," he said, meeting Sady's eyes.

"If there is an answer to the problems we're facing, it will be with the inhabitants of the camp. We'll need to talk to them and we'll need southerners for that."

"But she doesn't need to be here now."

"She will not leave this tent. You, Lady Loriane, and a handful of others are the only people we can trust, and I wish you'd stop being such a precious prick about my judgement." He wanted to rub in that it was Finnisius' poor judgement that had left the camp under-protected, but could not afford an argument right now. He glared at Finnisius, and

Finnisius glared back. Sady had no idea what sort of relationship Destran used to have with the general, but he guessed that, as the city guard and the courthouse guards, Finnisius could do pretty much as he pleased.

Sady continued in a milder voice, "Now, tell me what is the situation?"

General Finnisius blew out a breath through his nose. He spread the map out, on which someone had outlined the field of the refugee camp and the perimeter around it.

"A number of trucks arrived here," Finnisius said, stabbing at the place on the map where the lower camp entrance was. "My men thought they were supply trucks, but there weren't any supplies scheduled. When they went to speak to the drivers to find out what was going on, a great number of Eagle Knights came out of the back and overwhelmed my men."

"You're sure they were Eagle Knights?"

"Oh, yes, no doubt about it. They were in uniform."

"Where did they come from?"

"A farmer saw the trucks turning onto the road a bit north of the camp. They came out of the forest. Other than that, we have no information. We need to get airborne to find where their base is but we can't see anything until daytime."

By which time there were probably more important matters to take care of, such as seeking shelter against sonorics.

Sady glanced at the map. The perimeter checkpoint was closest to Tiverius. It was probably the last place anyone would expect an attack.

General Finnisius hit the table with his flat hand. "Eagle Knights, performing military operations inside our borders. That's an act of war."

"That, it is."

Finnisius' eyebrows rose. Maybe he had expected an argument. "If the Eagle Knights take over the camp prior to the storm, they can move under cover of the weather, and who knows we'll find ourselves occupied by the time we can come out of hiding."

"I agree completely."

"We will not tolerate any southern occupation of any part of our country."

"And we will not tolerate any political foreign influences to dictate our decisions."

"We seem to be in unusual agreement. Tomorrow, I'll apply for permission of the doga to retaliate."

"You have permission now." That was it. Declare war. Sady had never envisaged it to be as easy as this.

"Now?" Finnisius frowned.

"Immediately. The sooner, the better."

"But the doga has to vote—" Normally, the doga would have to approve any military action by vote in the emergency council.

"The doga will be disbanded at the next sitting."

In a few sentences, Sady told him of the medicine and the content of Alius' letter. Finnisius listened without speaking a word, an increasingly stunned expression on his face. "So the pills don't work at all?"

"No. We have less than a day to stop the Eagle Knights, or anyone else, invading the city. That's even with suits. By tomorrow morning, I want everyone in the shelters."

"The entire doga could be affected with this corruption."

"The entire doga *is* affected."

"Is there anyone we can still trust?"

"No. Just you and I, and Viki and Shara Diadoro. And Lady Loriane. I declare emergency rule until this crisis is over. We tell no one of this decision and carry on as normal, but meanwhile, all decisions are taken by us. And we're going to go into the camp."

A small smile played around Finnisius' lips. I seemed this was what he had wanted to hear. "You'll have access to any of my soldiers who have sonorics suits."

"Thank you." The question remained if the suits would be up to protect the soldiers, but no one could answer that. "Prepare to go into the camp as soon as you can. I want the Eagle Knights to be evicted from the camp or taken into custody. I want to make it clear to them that I consider this invasion an act of war. The refugees are here by our invitation and are on Chevakian soil."

The general gave Sady a calculating look, as if he was already working out the logistics in his head. His expression showed reluctant respect. Sady thought of the words in Alius' letter. If the Most

Learned had really thought he did such a good job, why hadn't he said so earlier? He wouldn't have made so many mistakes.

He said, "It is also important to remember that not all southerners in the camps support Lady Armaine or the Brotherhood."

"There is no time to find out what's going on and who everyone supports. My men will fight anyone who creates trouble."

"I want you to do more than that. I want you to dismantle the camp and take everyone out to supervised shelters. Consider as hostile anyone who resists. Take the ordinary citizens and guard them elsewhere in the city. Gather the people who identify themselves as belonging to the Brotherhood and lock them up separately. Take everyone's names. Employ southerners to help, but don't tell them what it's for. Do not accept money—bribes—for anything. The Knights themselves . . . when you have defeated them, I'll talk to their leaders."

"Certainly, sir." Finnisius strained his legs as if to get up.

"Wait, I haven't finished."

Finnisius sat back down, all his attention on Sady.

"Do you have a courier here?"

"Yes." The general's voice made it sound like a question.

Sady dug in his pocket and took out the symbolic key to his office. "Tell your courier to take this to Senator Shara Diadoro."

Finnisius stared at him, horror written on his face. "You're resigning?"

"No. I'm giving this to her in case."

"In case of what?"

"I'm going to go into the camp with you. In case I don't come back."

"No way," Finnisius said.

"Yes, and my decision is final. We'll travel in one of the rear balloons, out of the way of the likely site of battle. I won't sit on my hands while you are fighting."

"It's my job to fight, not yours."

"Nevertheless, I'm coming. There is nothing more for me to do except hide and hope that some of us will survive. There may just be someone in the camp who can help us. The lady here will come with me."

CHAPTER 28

*I*SANDOR RAISED his head enough to see over the back of the front seat.

Outside the truck, Milleus faced the Knights across at least ten paces of muddy ground. Only a few drops of rain were still falling down. The wind chased wisps of mist and smoke past him.

The Knights stood quiet, holding crossbows. They had all the time in the world. They had the refugees surrounded and wouldn't do anything that would risk their advantage.

Jevaithi looked at him with wide eyes, her face a pale oval in the sparse light.

The other refugees were still under or behind the truck, forming a living wall between the Knights and their queen. Isandor could hear their voices. Even so, Isandor didn't think their presence would be enough to stop the Knights if they set their mind to reaching the truck—which they would if they knew who was aboard.

Lightning flashed, showing the fence line where, a few days ago, the Chevakians had cut through into the camp, desperate for *something* to happen. Milleus was right, he should have told him who Jevaithi was before entering the camp.

Now that fenceline, and freedom, might as well be miles away. They could never reach it.

Thunder rumbled in the distance, and the sound of a bell ringing, a thin and high sound carried by the wind. Milleus had explained about the bell and what it meant to Chevakians. Milleus should be inside. If he stayed out here, he would be exposed to icefire levels high enough to do short-term and long-term damage.

But Milleus didn't move. He stood straight-backed, with his hands in his pockets just like he did when looking at the goats. In fact, the truck rocked with the jumping of the goats. They had been inside for most of the day and Milleus' smell probably made them think that he was about to let them graze.

The Knights didn't move either.

Milleus said, projecting his voice so the Knights would hear, "We ask to be let out of the camp. I am Chevakian. These people are ordinary citizens who do not support your conflict. Let them go so they don't get hurt."

The Knights said nothing and showed no sign of having heard Milleus' words.

"They don't know Chevakian," Jevaithi whispered. "He's wasting his breath."

"Some will understand." Knights came usually from the upper class families. They had tutors. More than a few would have a basic knowledge of the language.

Milleus was still talking. ". . . If you use any violence towards us or anyone else in the camp, the Chevakian doga will see this as an invasion of their territory. If Chevakians are killed, they will declare war. So, if you let me go, I will take this matter to the Chevakian doga and we will negotiate—"

A voice shouted a harsh order.

One of the Knights marched up to Milleus. The man was almost a head taller, but Milleus faced him defiantly.

"He's so brave," Jevaithi whispered.

She was right. Through all of their trip, and before that, Milleus had faced any risk. He might be old, but Isandor felt a twinge of jealousy. Why couldn't he stand out there and tell the Knights to go away?

Because they wouldn't listen to him. Respect had to be earned. He was an exiled junior apprentice who had run off with the queen.

A Knight gave an order and a number of men marched forward. Milleus took up position between them and the truck, but there were too many of them and they simply walked around him.

"Why doesn't he shoot?" Jevaithi asked.

But Isandor knew that would make matters worse. If Milleus did, the Knights would kill him instantly.

The refugees tried to bar the way, but they had no weapons. The Knights pulled people out from underneath the truck or trailer.

"They're coming for us," Jevaithi whispered. "They know we're here."

"We're not giving up that easily." He grabbed Milleus' walking stick and pressed it into her hand. "Here. Mind the door on that side."

She took the stick from him, and then pulled him close. Her breath came fast and her skin felt sweaty. It was so good to feel her against him, to feel their hearts beat in unison. It felt like coming home. Then he thought of his mother stirring concoctions on the stove in the limpet that was his home, her warm hug. He could smell the faint scent of herb extracts that always hung around her. Those feelings made him so angry. Yes, he would fight for Jevaithi and his mother.

Jevaithi stroked his hair. "I love you."

"I love you, too."

"I don't care that you're my brother." She pressed her lips on his for a fleeting kiss. The smell of her was intoxicating.

"Don't give up," he said. "Whatever happens, we never give up."

She nodded, het face pale. "My mother always said that. Our mother."

That hit him harder than expected. He'd never thought of Queen Maraithe as his mother before, but she was his mother, and she had withered away in the luxurious prison the Knights had created for her.

"We owe it to our mother to fight. To our mothers."

Jevaithi settled in next to the door holding the walking stick aloft, ready to strike at anyone who came in.

Isandor took Milleus' shovel and waited by the other door.

Voices yelled outside. Something hard struck the side door with a thunk. A squall of rain lashed the window.

Then the door opened on Isandor's side. A blast of icy wind came in. Isandor swung the shovel at the dark silhouette. It hit a hard object with a clang. The handle jarred in his hands and he almost dropped the shovel. The Knight went down without a sound. Immediately, a lot of people ran to the truck, shouting. It was too dark to see who they were and who was fighting who. He could only guess that refugees pulled the unconscious Knight away. More Knights ran onto the scene and fistfights fights broke out everywhere. Refugees crammed around the truck.

Two Knights dragged a woman away. They dumped her on the ground, and then one Knight stabbed her. She did not move again. The Knights now had hold of a smaller person. Several other people were screaming.

By the skylights, the Knights were going to kill everyone just to get him. Where was Milleus?

Isandor shouted for him.

His voice was lost in the tumult. Behind him, people were trying to open the door to Jevaithi's side of the cabin. She hung onto the door handle with all her might.

"Wait." Isandor slammed and locked the door on his side and scrambled over to help her. "Lock it."

"I have." Her voice spilled over with fear. "They'll break the door." The truck rocked with the efforts of the Knights yanking at the door handle. Hard objects hit the window. There was already a big crack in the glass.

Then the door burst open and a Knight climbed into the cabin

Jevaithi screamed and flung herself in Isandor's arms, but the man pulled the back of her shirt.

"No, no, Isandor, help me!" She grabbed his arms.

Isandor put his arms around her and wedged his feet at the back of the driver's seat. The Knight half-climbed into the cabin and pulled on her legs.

She screamed, "Keep your hands off me!"

The door on Isandor's side sprang open. A cold breeze went through the cabin. Large hands grabbed Isandor's shoulders and yanked. He tumbled backwards out of the truck. Jevaithi slipped from his grip. The Knight dragged her out the other side of the cabin.

He could hear her scream, "Isandor! Isandor!"

People jostled him. He managed to get upright, and yanked his cloak out of the Knight's hands. People were attacking the man from all sides.

Milleus' gruff voice came from somewhere Isandor couldn't see.

"Mercy, let go of them. It's a disgrace. How do you dare against a couple of children."

Isandor shouted, "Milleus! Milleus, where are you?" It was so dark, and there were so many people fighting, and the rain was running into his eyes.

"Over here!"

Isandor spotted Milleus standing on the beam that connected the trailer to the truck. He wrestled through the crowd. Milleus stuck out a hand and hauled Isandor up.

"You hurt?" Milleus asked.

"Jevaithi. They took Jevaithi." Panic clawed at his insides. All around, people were fighting hand to hand. He stuck his head out to look at the other side of the truck, but it was too dark to see who was who. Too dark to see any trace of Jevaithi.

Isandor screamed, as loud as he could, "Jevaithi!"

A couple of people took up the chant. "Jevaithi, Jevaithi."

"Shut up, everyone. She's missing! The Knights took her."

More voices now chanted, *Jevaithi, Jevaithi. Peria, Peria!*

Isandor climbed on top of the trailer. "Shut up everyone."

Several people made shushing noises.

"Hey, who are you?" a man asked.

There was nothing left to say except the truth. "I'm Isandor, Jevaithi's twin brother. The Knights just took her. They'll kill her if they get the chance. They've been trying to kill us ever since we escaped from the palace."

There were gasps.

A man shouted, "Revenge! Revenge!"

"Glory to the queen and king!" someone else yelled. Other people repeated those words. Isandor cringed. He was no king, and the south definitely didn't need another king. He only wanted Jevaithi to be safe. He had failed her.

When he saw the Knight behind him, it was too late to run.

CHAPTER 29

THE WORD CAME from somewhere uphill, and went through the Knight army. "We've got the Queen!"

While many around him cheered, Carro went cold inside. He'd know this would come, but had hoped that it wouldn't, that Isandor and Jevaithi had found a way out of the refugee column and were safe in Tiverius. He wanted to ask if the report was true, and if anyone knew anything about Isandor.

His eyes met Jeito's by the faint light of the impending dawn. Jeito's face was grim, and Carro thought of Farey's words. Jeito had family in the camp.

He followed the others up to the commotion on the hillside.

A ring of Knights who had cornered a group of at least a hundred citizens and a truck with a trailer. Carro's heart skipped a beat. This was the truck of the old man who had given Isandor and Jevaithi shelter, and a couple of Knights marched downhill with a struggling prisoner who he recognised a moment later as Jevaithi.

She was cursing, her hair was tangled. As they passed, her eyes met Carro's in a fleeting moment. There was mud on her face and her simple Chevakian peasant dress. The hot anger in her expression shook him.

Next came a couple of Knights carrying a blanket with a blood-covered body. A deep cold went through Carro. Isandor was dead? Was this the end of it? Jevaithi back under the influence of the

Knights and her lover murdered? The only person who had ever cared about Carro without any motive other than friendship?

His head reeled.

Knights bustled around him, but he hardly noticed. Up on the hill, voices took up a chant. *Peria, Peria, Peria!*

That was the name of the southern land under the reign of the old king. Carro had never heard anyone say the name aloud and didn't realise that anyone still used it. This was the Brotherhood's doing. But why? Why revive a regime of a tyrant who tortured his people?

What were the Brotherhood fighting for? The right to torture again?

The conflicting emotions became too much for Carro. He clamped his hands over his ears, wanting to shout, *Enough!*

Most of the refugees were not Brotherhood people, they were ordinary citizens who cared nothing about the feud between the clans. Most of the Knights were not Pirosians. Many could see icefire and knew how dangerous it could be.

The Pirosian medallion burned against his skin. He and his father were spurring on this war by their very existence. The people were fighting just because they disliked the Knights' hold on power, not because they wanted the Brotherhood to rule.

Enough, enough, enough. This war had to stop.

Carro's heart jumped when someone put a hand on his shoulder. "Can you do something for me, son?"

His first, stupid, reaction was to salute.

The hand, of course, belonged to Rider Cornatan, and he laughed at Carro's hasty salute, but his eyes showed concern. "Are you all right, son?"

"Uhm—yeah." Carro's heart beat furiously against his ribs. That had been a stupid thing to do. "Uhm—tell me what you want me to do." By the skylights, what would his father do when he found out about all those thoughts Carro just had?

"I need someone reliable to stand guard. Come." He led Carro downhill where two Junior Knights stood guard on either side of the entrance to a large tent. While going in, Carro met one of their gazes, wide-eyed. Was he going crazy or did he see fear for his father in everyone?

Inside the tent, a couple of Senior Knights stood around a table on which they had tied a woman.

Filthy and blood-smeared, Jevaithi was still the most beautiful woman he had ever seen. They had tied a gag around her mouth, but she growled insults that needed no explaining. Her grey eyes were vicious.

"I want you to make sure no one comes in here," Rider Cornatan said in a low voice.

Carro nodded, his gaze on the Queen, and the way the torchlight gilded her skin.

"No one, right?" Rider Cornatan held up a finger. "Not even any other Knights, especially from the Council."

"Yes," Carro said, trying as hard as possible to appear calm and careless. He glanced around, but couldn't see the blanket with the blood-covered body.

"There are subversive elements amongst us," Rider Cornatan continued.

Carro's heart skipped a beat. "There are?" His mouth felt dry.

"You heard Rider Barton at the meeting. Don't trust him. Don't let him into the tent."

"Uhm—sure."

Rider Cornatan gave him a penetrating look, then held the tent flap open. Carro went outside, where it had started raining again, and took up his position with the two Juniors.

He could only think one thing. Rider Cornatan knew that he had reservations. He had no idea how his father knew, or whether it was only a hunch, but he knew nevertheless. This was a test of his loyalty. He'd be watched. There would be spies somewhere.

But no matter how much he looked—and he didn't dare crane his head too much—he could only see the two terrified Junior Knights, scrunching their faces against the biting rain.

Rider Cornatan had gone back inside the tent and left the flap open. Carro could see the queen's legs through the gap, and the filthy cloth that held her ankles to the table.

His father said something that Carro didn't catch, and next followed a scream and barrage of swear words from Jevaithi.

Rider Cornatan laughed. "That is uncouth language for a young lady, let alone our Queen."

She spat. "If you think I'll go back to living in your prison, you're mistaken." Carro shivered with the anger in her voice. "I will rather die than help you."

The Junior Knight next to him shifted, and his boots made squelching sounds in the mud. Carro glanced aside, but the young man was staring intently at the next tent.

Rider Cornatan said, "Then be prepared to die, Your Highness."

The young Knight took in a sharp breath, noticed that Carro was looking at him, and turned his head so that Carro could no longer see his face. When he turned around, the young man on his other side did the same.

"I hate you," Jevaithi said.

"You make one mistake, Your Highness." Rider Cornatan's voice was mocking. "You seem convinced that we need you alive."

"I don't care if you kill me."

"I had something else in mind."

There was a sound of fabric ripping, a snarl and then a hard slap of a hand on naked skin. Carro cringed. That *had* to hurt.

An angry growl, also from Jevaithi. And Rider Cornatan's chuckle. Carro shivered.

"Rape me, if you cannot get what you want elsewhere, you disgusting old man. I will never, ever give you the pleasure of seeing your daughter on the throne."

Rider Cornatan laughed in his dangerous, amused voice. "We'll see about that." And a bit later. "Take her away."

The tent flap rustled and Rider Cornatan came out. He stopped and smiled at Carro. "Good work, son. Another job for you. Take her to the farm."

"Er—how . . . er . . ."

"Don't be so shy. Grab these young men, and one of the drivers. Someone will look after your bird." He turned to leave, but turned back. "And feel free to teach her a lesson in humility."

"Er . . . sorry?"

"My dear son. Do with her whatever you want. You do remember how fuck a woman, don't you?" He laughed, and then he was off.

Carro remained in front of the tent while the Knights were still fighting rebels in other parts of the camp. He could hear the cries and shouts, the pop of fire and the firing of Chevakian powder guns.

He turned aside to see that the young Knight was staring at him. He went into the tent, where a lone oil lamp flapped a sooty flame.

Jevaithi lay on the table. The ripping cloth he had heard had been her skirt. She was now completely naked. Carro stared at the rising mound of her pubic bone and the mussed-up black hair that covered it.

By the skylights.

The remains of the dress had fallen onto the ground and had been trampled into the mud. He picked the cloth up, but it was wet and disgusting.

One of the Junior Knights was peering into the tent. He met Carro's eyes, flinched.

"You have a cloak or something I can borrow?" Carro asked.

The young man took off his cloak and handed it to Carro, who approached the Queen.

She turned her head, the only thing she could still move.

"I'm not afraid of you." The anger in her eyes made him shiver.

Carro wanted to say, *There is no need to be afraid of me,* but he figured the less said, the better. He draped the cloak over her. A small frown crossed her face.

Carro's hands trembled. The breeze that came in through the tent flap carried alternately warm and cold air. Dark figures moved at the edge of his vision, but he forced himself to think of other things. He had no time for hallucinations. If he was going to act, he had to do so before Rider Cornatan came back. It scared him witless, but there was no option. *Mutiny.*

He gestured at the Junior Knight. "Come inside, please."

The Junior Knight did, his eyes wide, no doubt wondering what he had done wrong.

"What is your name?"

"Minno, sir."

"Minno, do you want the Queen to be killed?"

The young man's widened even further. "I . . . I don't know, sir." His gaze flicked to the table behind Carro, and acquired a telltale glitter.

Carro answered the question for him. "You don't want the Queen to be killed. Do you want the Queen to be raped?"

"Uhm . . ." The glitter became more prominent.

"No, Minno, you don't want the Queen to be raped. No matter that she's Thilleian."

The man looked at the ground and shook his head. "No, sir. I don't want the Queen to be raped."

"Serving the Queen is one of the honours of the Knighthood."

"Yes, sir, it is."

"Minno, were you happy with what you were ordered to do here?"

"It's not up to me to say, sir. I follow orders."

"But if I asked you, as a man, not as a Knight?"

The man's eyes widened. Carro thought he understood. Again, the less said, the better. "Minno. This is important. I want you to go and get Rider Barton for me. Tell him that he knows what this is about—"

"But what about my orders to guard the tent?"

"Fuck your orders. We're going to do what I should have done a long time ago. Run. Quick."

Minno's whole attitude changed. He smiled. "Certainly, sir." He ran out.

Carro turned to the table, freeing his dagger from its sheath.

Jevaithi's eyes were wide. She said nothing—probably too scared —but surprise did not need words to show itself.

No time to explain. He bowed. "I'm sorry, Your Highness, but I'm going to have to touch you." He lifted the cloak, inserted the dagger between the wood and the fabric that tied her ankle to the table leg and sliced through in one movement. Then the other leg, her upper body and her arms—her stump and her wrist on the other arm. She sat up, stiffly, her stump rubbing her shoulder. Her feet were bare, and he would have to carry her.

"Keep the cloak. You'll need it when—" Splashing footsteps sounded outside. "Ah, there is—"

The tent flap rustled and in came . . . Rider Cornatan. He stopped. His gaze went from Carro to Jevaithi seated on the table.

"You told me to move her," Carro said, trying to sound as innocent as he could. His heart was thudding against his ribs.

Rider Cornatan's hand moved so fast that Carro didn't see it until it, and the staff with the sink at the end, hit his face. He reeled back. When he wiped his face, the back of hand came away covered in blood. It ran from his nose down his lip and chin, from where it dripped onto his shirt.

"Fight, you coward. Straighten up." Rider Cornatan poked the staff in his side.

Carro straightened, his head still reeling. He licked his lip, but new blood trickled down almost immediately.

Rider Cornatan had taken up a fighting stance, with his legs apart and both hands holding the staff. That thing didn't work here in Chevakia, did it?

Carro stumbled a few paces so that Jevaithi was at his back.

"Stand aside so I can take the girl, if you're not going to do it."

"She is the Queen."

"She's a just dumb girl. Stand aside."

"No." Carro was trembling. He clutched the hilt of his dagger so tightly that his fingers hurt.

"What's this nonsense? Instead of incompetent, are you now dumb as well?"

"No," Carro said, louder this time. "I am a Knight and swore service to the Queen—"

"I recall that I just say you could service her—"

"Don't talk of her like that!" Carro lunged, raising his dagger. It was an automatic gesture, learned while hunting Chevakian creatures for roasting on the fire.

Rider Cornatan swung the staff just in time. It hit Carro's hands and dislodged the dagger from his grip. It bounced over the muddy ground before coming to rest under the table where Jevaithi still sat, wide eyed.

Rider Cornatan came closer. "My dear son, just *what* are you up to?" His voice was cold as a blizzard.

"I am a Knight. I have sworn to the Knight's pledge: Obedience, honour, honesty, humility and silence."

"And you will obey me."

"There is no honour in attacking our own people. There is no honesty in ordering your slaves to kill the Queen. There is no humility in encouraging rape, and there may be silence in not saying anything about any of these despicable things, but I am sure that this is not the type of silence the motto intended." He was angry, oh, he was so angry that he trembled all over.

Rider Cornatan's voice lowered. "Do I hear that right? You dare challenge me? I have done so much for you. Given you a good home. Fished you out of the cesspit of the Apprentice Knights . . ."

Carro wanted to say that the merchant had not provided a good home, that the merchant had mistreated him, but he had not. The merchant had hit him only a few times, when he was little, and when he deserved it.

He fought images of the merchant coming to the table in the central room of the limpet, bringing the box of dice for a game. Carro loved those word games.

Rider Cornatan put a hand on his shoulder. "Come on, son. Let's just forget about this. Let's stop this nonsense and take her—"

"I am not your son! Here . . ." With trembling hands, Carro fumbled under his clothes and pulled out the Pirosian medallion. He flung it onto the table, where it came to rest against Jevaithi's leg. "You can take that back. I don't want it. I thought the Knights were about honour and courage, but they're about repression and thuggery, about serving yourself at the cost of others. That is not the Knighthood I joined, or one I want to be part of."

Rider Cornatan's face hardened. "All right, if you want to play like that." He retreated a step, and swung the staff. A hissing trail of steam zipped over the ground.

Carro jumped aside. By the skylights. He'd thought it didn't work here. If Rider Cornatan attacked him with that thing, he was as good as finished. He tried to back away, but the edge of the table bit into his back.

If only he could reach his dagger . . . He lunged for the table.

"Not so fast, boy."

A stream of light cut through two of the table legs. As if in slow motion, the table lurched, and Jevaithi started sliding off. She crashed into him and they both fell on the muddy ground. Jevaithi scrambled onto her feet, holding the cloak around her naked body.

Rider Cornatan laughed. "So, you think we served you badly?"

Carro glared up at him while on his hands and knees in the mud. He pushed himself onto his knees, picking up one of the severed table legs.

"So, you think no one noticed all the mistakes you made, clumsy pup? The fact that through your bungling, I lost two very good men. The fact that you had to tread on a stick to let the Queen escape?"

"I am no ace fighter. You had all the right to tell me off and made sure I wouldn't do it again. You could have returned me to where you found me. I didn't want the attention. I am a scholar or an accountant." He never thought he'd say that, but he knew how much he meant it. His stepfather, no, the man he knew as his father, was a cold, hard bastard, but if there were any ethics to be taught, he was far better at it than any Knight had been.

"You're right," Rider Cornatan said, and his voice was cold. "I could have done that. Yet, I did not. Time and time again, I gave you a chance. I sent you with the hunters—"

"To murder my best friend!"

"I gave you a patrol—"

"And told me to rape them!"

"I gave you a job at a desk—"

"So that I could take the blame if something went wrong!"

Carro runs home through the street. The snowy ground is lit by orange light from the blazing warehouse fire behind him. The ground shakes from explosions. Fires in the Outer City are always dangerous, but this, in a tanning warehouse, is worse than usual.

People are running through the street, while burning debris rains down from the sky.

His mother stands at the door of their limpet, holding his sister. His father is looking anxiously into the crowd of people fleeing.

Then his eyes meet Carro's.

He smiles. He opens his arms.

Carro runs, stumbling over his feet as another explosions rocks the ground.

Into his father's arms. The familiar smell of his fur cloak. The smell of his shaving cream. His hands ruffling his hair.

Tears pricked in his eyes. His father cared. He was harsh and at times unreasonable. He never showed his emotions except in rare occasions, but he cared. Why had Carro taken so long to remember that?

In all the memories of bad things, this was what really mattered. There was nothing wrong with his family. It was him. He was a whiny, ungrateful kid who didn't appreciate what he had.

And now the merchant was dead and his real father would kill him soon with a weapon that used icefire.

Rider Cornatan laughed. "And I had great hopes for a son of mine. You're a pathetic weakling, too fragile for the Knights. I should simply kill you when you're off-guard, but I'm going to give you a chance. Come on, stand up straight and fight."

He swung the staff and Carro thrust out the table leg. He had no great sword skills and the move was as inelegant as much as to protect himself. The staff hit the wood with a great clunk. The table leg jarred in his hand and he almost dropped it. He stepped backwards, and almost tripped over the remains of the table. But something was pressed against his back.

"Take this." Jevaithi, with his dagger.

He freed one hand without taking his eyes off his father. "Give it."

Jevaithi put the dagger in his hand, blade first. By the skylights, what use was that? He needed to hold it by the hilt. And he needed two hands to change his grip, and his other hand needed to hold onto the table leg.

He gestured to Jevaithi. "Your Highness, turn it around."

The moment Carro glanced aside, a hissing beam of air shot through the air. He ducked, without knowing where the beam was. Lightning crackled.

Carro lunged, his dagger poised. Rider Cornatan put up a hand and the blow deflected. The blade of the dagger ran through the sleeve of his tunic.

Carro regained his balance. By the skylights, he was no fighter. He was going to lose this badly, even though Rider Cornatan was now bleeding from the cut in his arm.

He held the staff in front of his face. The metal was rimed with frost.

There were splashing footsteps. The tent flap opened, letting in a blast of icy air. Minno came inside followed by—thanks the skylights —Rider Barton.

Rider Cornatan glanced over his shoulder.

Carro pounced. He could only see Rider Cornatan's weak spot: his throat. He'd learned to hunt large animals with a dagger. He knew how to cut a throat. The movement was mechanical. Rider Cornatan toppled backwards onto the tent fabric and Carro fell on top. He drove the dagger down and sliced. Blood spurted everywhere.

Carro scrambled up, unable to tear his gaze from Rider Cornatan's convulsing body. Blood had drenched the front of his pants. It was sticky and cold. The fountain of blood weakened until it was a mere ooze. The body twitched a few times and finally lay still.

Rider Barton bent and retrieved Carro's bloodied dagger and returned it to its owner.

Much calmer than he felt, Carro took it with blood-covered hands, wiped the blade and stuck it back in his belt.

Rider Barton gave a Knights' salute, which was only ever performed to superiors. "I am glad you read my signals." His voice was soft. "Let's get the south back to being a respectable country."

Then he knelt before Jevaithi, who stood there muddied and covered only in a cloak, shivering.

Carro also sank to his knees. A feeling of relief washed over him. The fight had left him exhausted. He swelled with the enormity of his actions. This was his decision.

Rider Barton said, "I am an Eagle Knight bound by honour to serve the royal family of the City of Glass with fairness and obedience to our laws. I, and my men, are at your service."

Carro picked up the medallion that lay in the mud and put it in Jevaithi's hand.

She studied it, and then met Carro's eyes. "You're Rider Cornatan's son?"

Carro nodded, pressing his lips together. He'd gained a father, he'd lost a father. Maybe he'd never felt like Rider Cornatan was his true father.

"It is time that this feuding was forgotten," Rider Barton said.

Carro put a fist on his chest. "It is time that the Knighthood behaved according to its motto."

"Agreed," Rider Barton said. "Give the order, Your Highness, and I and my men will carry it out."

Jevaithi said, "Stop the fighting between our people."

Rider Barton bowed. "At your service."

He turned on his heel and left the tent. Carro followed him.

CHAPTER 30

THE FORMATION of balloons had left the army base and was making its silent and deadly way over the outskirts of Tiverius, under the cover of menacing clouds and occasional squalls of rain. Seated in the centre of the gondola, in seats normally reserved for ground troops being transported, Sady was uncomfortable in his sonorics suit. He hadn't worn the suit since his trips to the City of Glass, and the smell of those trips lingered inside. The rank scent of meals consisting of nothing but meat, the restrictive atmosphere, the claustrophobic feel of hearing his own breath echo back at him.

Chevakia was in uncharted territory now. No one knew how bad sonorics was going to get, and how long it would last, how far it would reach and whether or not anyone would survive.

Sheets of rain lashed the side of the gondola, rocking it from side to side. Sady pulled his legs as close to the seat as possible, to keep them out of the way of the crew who were running around opening and closing flanges. Every now and then, the pilot would shout an order, or would start up the burners with a roar that echoed over the landscape.

Sady felt cold and hot at the same time. He couldn't see the ground over the edge of the basket. The feeble light from the vessel's bridge only reached to the railing to allow the armsmen to see. The gunner in the corner closest to him scanned the sky with binoculars

277

attached to his weapon. He wore an army-issued khaki sonorics suit that was so badly scuffed on the knees that Sady wondered if it still worked.

On the empty seat next to him stood a portable sonorics meter and a rack of gel-coated measuring tubes. He'd taken on the task of taking air samples in a sampling balloon, blowing the air through the tube and inserting it into the machine, because he knew nothing about military action and this was something he did know well. But he might as well have given up on the measuring thing. Each time he shoved another tube into the meter, the measurement was wildly up or down. He'd plotted a graph, but it was all over the place. There was no logic to it. In the back of his mind, he wondered if that meant the flying creature was about.

Loriane sat on his other side, wearing a Chevakian army outfit. The trousers were too big for her so she had rolled up the hems. The shirt and jacket fitted better. She had her hair tied at the back of her neck, but did not wear a suit. She stared into the darkness, clutching the safety belts over her shoulders. Occasionally, their eyes met. For someone who had never seen steam engines until a few days ago, she was holding up well.

She also cast regular glances at the balloon's pilot, a sturdy woman of about Loriane's age, who bossed the crew about in a loud voice.

General Finnisius had been adamant that Sady travel in one of the support vessels at the back of the column. There were about twenty balloons ahead, an army of menacing dark bubbles punctuated by tiny lights in each gondola and the occasional flare of a burner. Already, the merest of dawn light silvered the horizon.

"You see that, Proctor?" The pilot pointed.

Sady pushed himself out of his seat, and quickly crossed to the railing to keep out of the way of the crew. The floor rocked with the wind.

They were flying over the farm land immediately to the south of the city, neat rectangular plots interspersed with roads and farmhouses. The southern forest started on the crest of the hill, a dark mass of waving pine trees.

The pilot pointed at the blackness of the clouds threatening to the south, which had grown into a huge roiling wall with the occasional flash of lightning within. It chilled him deep inside. Sady had never seen anything like it. He even doubted that this used to happen in the days before the barrier. This weather cell was deeper and more vicious than anything this country had ever seen.

"How long before that is here?" the pilot asked.

Sady eyed the clouds, trying to remember Viki's maps. "Half a day, I guess."

"We'll need to be out and packed before that hits."

Sady nodded. Having balloons packed away would probably be the least of anyone's worries once that storm front hit.

"Has the wind carried the sonorics away yet?" the pilot asked.

"The sonorics levels are all over the place. On average, it's probably not safe to go without suits."

"I feared as much," she said. "Much as the men hate wearing them. Anyway, we're almost there."

They had come over a ridge and the camp was easily visible, the source of firelight and smoke. Up here, dressed in the muffling suit, Sady couldn't hear anything, but there were people running between tents with flaming sticks.

The balloon's signaller was waving lights to communicate commands. General Finnisius travelled in the next balloon and his gondola was a frenzy of flashing lights. Sady understood a mere fraction of their coded meanings.

A number of dark shapes rose from a spot uphill from the camp.

The pilot cursed. "Eagles incoming."

Both gunners, one on each side of the gondola, already had their weapons aimed.

"Everyone to their stations! Everyone else, out of the way!"

Sady rushed back to his seat and buckled up his safety belt with trembling hands. He met Loriane's eyes which were wide with horror.

He took her hand. "We're safe here."

She nodded, pressing her lips together, but she looked scared more than anything.

"Watch it. Here come the eagles," called the gunner. He swung the gun around, following a huge dark shape swooping past.

Bangs echoed over the hillside from the firing of the gun on the other side of the gondola. Gunners in other balloons were firing as well. Loriane clapped her hands over her ears.

Sady put an arm around her shoulders, shielding her with his body as much as he could.

The birds lost their formation, swooping between the balloons. When they had passed, one fluttered to the ground.

One balloon appeared to be losing air, but the rest held formation. The eagles had disappeared into the darkness. The gunner searched the sky for them through the binoculars.

Sady didn't dare move. His muscles felt rigid as if he'd frozen in place. Loriane trembled under him. He had volunteered to come, had even demanded it, but he regretted his decision now. He was no soldier.

A squall brought stinging rain from the sky, lashed against the side of the balloon's gas bag. Even the suit could not keep out the fingers of cold.

One of the gunners shouted. A flash of lightning blinded Sady.

The birds returned, huge flying shapes plummeting towards them, with menacing claws outstretched, accompanied by the war cries of the riders on top.

The balloon shuddered when a bird hit it. The gunners on both sides were shooting into the air, the pilot screaming orders at the crew. One of the men jumped onto the ladder and scaled the side of the air bag. He vanished out of sight. A moment later, two loud bangs echoed, the balloon jerked and huge wings flapped past so close that Sady could feel the air rushing past, even through the suit. The basket swung from side to side. A crew member slipped on the wet floor and hung onto the railing until the movement stopped.

Loriane stared, her eyes wide.

"How did we come through? How many of them are there?" Sady asked.

"I've counted at least twenty." The pilot peered into the sky.

"That's not many."

"They won't have their entire force active, with this type of attack."

"Looks like they're in trouble," the gunner said looking ahead.

Sady pushed himself up in the harness high enough so that he could see where the man pointed. An eagle had its claws stuck in the netting that covered a balloon at the front of the formation. Its huge wings flapped as it tried to take off with the balloon struck to its claws swinging violently underneath.

Light signals flashed between the remaining balloons. *Hold fire.*

It would be easy to finish off the eagle, as it was a pretty large target and well within range for the crews close to it, but bringing it down would unbalance the entire balloon and would endanger the men in the gondola underneath.

But it managed to free itself, releasing the balloon with such force that it swung almost vertical. Something fell out—Sady hoped it was not a person—and it swung a few times back and forth before it stabilised. The eagle flew off slowly before it was shot from two different directions. It fell, soundlessly.

Meanwhile, the other birds came back around and unleashed an attack of arrows. This time, Sady's balloon was in the firing line. The shield netting deflected the crossbow bolts, and one fell into the basket next to Sady, a southern thing made from bone and feathers. The two gunners on either side of the gondola were going gangbusters, swivelling their guns on their mounts as they followed the eagles swooping past. A small projectile pierced the balloon skin above Sady's head. Hot air whistled out. The pilot fired the burners with a roar.

Then the eagles were gone for another fly around. Sady made a quick inspection of the balloon's crew and found them all unharmed. Two other balloons had now sunk so low that they weren't going to make the camp. General Finnisius was busy signalling commands to these men, and a bit later a third balloon went to join them, presumably so that they could lead an attack from outside the camp. Sady suspected that this had been a potential strategy.

There was a shout, and the eagles were back, silhouettes against a flash of lightning in the nearly black sky. There were a lot more than twenty this time. A thunderclap shook the ground. Sady could hardly see anything after the flash, but heard the lashing of rain against the side of the balloon.

The guns went off again. There were soft pops of things bouncing off the balloon netting. Another eagle went down, a flutter of feathers and claws that plummeted past. Sady kept as still as he could. Loraine clutched onto his suit.

General Finnisius' signalling light changed to red, indication that they were going down.

They were now so close to the camp that Sady could see the people running between the tents. Huge bonfires, fight. Shouts reached up to the balloons. The three balloons were already down outside the camp, their crew having jumped clear of their deflating gas bags.

The eagles swooped again. New volleys of arrows came from below. Sady sat as still as he could, feeling the thunking of the arrows hitting wood under his feet.

Many people down there were cheering, too, but Sady couldn't see what was going on. Now that they were almost on the ground, the eagles couldn't attack anymore.

The first balloons touched down, and their fighting crew jumped out before the basket rose again once their weight was no longer inside. Each balloon would hover for as long as they could, given the prevailing wind, containing a pilot and gunner to help defend those troops on the ground.

Sady's balloon was one of the last to come down, and by that time, the soldiers had secured that area, holding back a crowd of refugees.

General Finnisius yelled, "Hold your fire for the proctor of Chevakia, by whose grace you are in this country and whose food you're eating."

Sady clambered out of the basket, accepting a hand from one of the men and then helped out Loriane, into the circle of Chevakian troops.

The people behind the troops were all southern refugees by the look of their clothing, and more of them crammed from behind. Loriane studied their faces.

"Do you know anyone?" Sady asked.

She shook her head.

Jammed in between a wall of soldiers, Sady couldn't see anything. Fights raged on the other side of the closest tents. He couldn't see who was fighting. He couldn't see General Finnisius. Eagles flew over. Shots rang out. Smoke billowed, reducing visibility to a few paces. How had he ever thought of finding something of use here?

He would have been better off hiding in the shelters.

CHAPTER 31

AFTER THE KNIGHTS had gone with both the youngsters, first Jevaithi and then Isandor, Milleus slumped against the side of the truck. He felt sore and tired, and incredibly *old*.

The refugees stood huddled around the truck. A man leaned on another's shoulders. A woman cried. What were the Knights going to do with the youngsters?

He could sit down and cry himself. He might have been half-decent at running a wartime army, but ever since, he had failed everyone he cared about. Suri, Kalius and Andrean, Sady and now the youngsters.

He stuck his hand through the bars of the trailer and scratched a hairy flank. His goats were the only thing he had left.

The Knights had retreated to a position from where they could watch the truck. He could see six of them, watching like silent statues, silhouetted against the threatening sky. The southern horizon was a broiling mass of black clouds. If he had been at home he would have said there was a snow storm coming.

But first things first. The goats needed milking or they would dry up or their udders would become infected. He had run out of hay and he would have to set up the pen so that they could graze whatever grass had not yet been trampled into the mud. But it would have to wait until the situation calmed a bit. Milking couldn't wait.

So he climbed in the trailer. The animals bumped and jolted him. There was barely enough room for him to sit. The goats pushed him. They nibbled his clothes. The bucket fell over twice. A couple of animals dunked their heads in the bucket and drank their own milk.

When he finished, he had only half a bucket left. He poured some in a container for himself, and was just distributing the rest to the refugees the ground shook with a roar. Several of the refugees ran for the cover of the truck. A young girl squealed.

But Milleus would recognise that sound in his sleep: the sound of a burner. And indeed, there were the dark shapes of balloons in the northern sky. The Chevakian army had turned up. There was hope yet. Destran wasn't half-stupid after all.

Milleus put away the bucket and climbed over the trailer railing. The goats bleated and pushed him.

"I'm sorry, ladies, but 1 don't have anything for you." He would have to do something soon because the poor things were going crazy.

The Knights had gathered in a group, and looked uncertain as to what to do.

Milleus wanted to be ready to move, as soon as he had the opportunity. Join the Chevakian troops, tell them what was going on here. Get them to free the youngsters.

He checked the furnace and threw in a couple of logs. The boiler was still full of steaming water.

The first of the balloons had come down on the downhill side of the camp, to sounds of shouting. Groups of Knights were running down the hill. The refugees around him were getting restless. Milleus closed the escape valves, allowing steam to build up in the boiler.

A Knight came up to him and said something.

"You can say whatever you want, but I'm going to join my countrymen."

The Knight didn't move. He flapped his hands and gestured. Milleus had no idea what he meant.

"Look, I am Chevakian, and it is my right—"

The man gestured again, more angrily now.

One of the goats in the trailer behind Milleus stuck its nose between the bars of the railing and managed to get hold of his shirt. It pulled, hard. "I need grass for the goats. They're hungry."

He was sore, tired and hungry, too. And angry.

The man yelled. A couple of refugees argued back. Over their heads, Milleus could see smoke rise into the air. A number of Knights came running back up the hill, took positions behind tents and aimed crossbows.

"Come on, Mister. I'm Chevakian. I don't understand. I don't want to get out." He pointed uphill.

The Knight repeated the same command and pointed to his right, where there was a dark and empty field. Go there? No, not likely.

Burners roared. Gunshots rang out. Tents went up in flames.

The goats were jumping and pushing in the trailer.

The Knight raised his crossbow . . .

And Milleus pulled the pin out of the trailer's tailgate. It fell down with a clang and an avalanche of goats burst out. The Knight was caught in the middle of the stream of hairy bodies, waving his arms to stay on his feet. They jumped against him, pulled his clothes. He screamed, pushing the animals away.

The refugees cheered.

At the same time, a number of Chevakian soldiers surged onto the hillside and took possession of the terrain like a well-oiled machine. Most of them were wearing sonorics suits. There were a few warning shots, but they outnumbered the Knights on the side of the camp by at least ten to one, and guns were more effective than crossbows. Some Knights whistled—presumably for birds—but none came and the Chevakians rounded them up.

Strangely, the goats had settled to graze peacefully amongst all these goings-on. Well, at least someone was going to get a good meal today.

A group of five suited people came up the hill towards Milleus, four khaki-suited men surrounding one man in a civilian suit. Their khaki suits sported the insignia of the proctorial guard. The man in the middle was too short to be Destran . . . Besides, he couldn't imagine Destran coming into battle.

"Milleus!" The voice sounded muffled inside the suit, but it sounded like . . .

"Sady?" What in mercy's name was he doing here, with the proctorial guard no less?

"Milleus, you're safe!" Sady ran, and took Milleus into a hug.

Milleus hugged him back. "Mercy, Sady. I am glad to see you." And he was.

"I was so scared for you. I should never have left without you."

"And I should have come with you."

"I should have realised that you were one of the people trapped in the camp when we didn't find you with the Ensar road refugees."

"Don't blame yourself. I'm here now, ready for whatever you want me to do. You know I still have that damn letter. We'll show Destran, huh?"

Sady didn't respond to that and an uneasy silence followed.

The four guards had positioned themselves in a rectangle around them. There was something eerily familiar about the way they *watched* Sady.

"Sady, what is going on?"

"Well . . ." Unease crept into Sady's voice. "I wanted you to challenge, but you weren't there and . . ."

All of a sudden, it became plainly obvious. Sady, his little brother, was doing the job he had asked Milleus to do. The job Milleus had come back to do.

Then the second shock. Sady had allowed the traffic to build up on the Ensar road? Sady had under-staffed the camp? Sady had made this mess?

"Milleus?"

"I'm . . . happy for you." He couldn't possibly challenge his brother.

He would never have expected Sady to consider himself for the job. His brother always had his nose in maps. Sady, run the country?

"It has nothing to do with happy, Milleus. We're in a major crisis. I need your help. I need the help from every person I can still trust. Are you with me?"

"Yes, certainly."

"Well then, listen. The only reason I am here is because there is a huge front of sonorics coming this way, none of us can do anything about it, we don't have enough shelters, Alius was supposed to have given us a medicine against sonorics, but it never worked, and Alius had killed himself, and all there is left for us to do is hide and hope we survive. We have until midday, and I'm not going to spend that time doing nothing. You've lived with the southern people. If there is anything or anyone who can make a difference to our survival, no matter how small—"

"Did you know I was here?"

"No."

"Surely you haven't come here just because of some vague hunch. I know you better than that, Sady."

"Well—uhm—no." Sady hesitated. "This is going to sound like I've gone crazy, but, it's like this: I'm trying to find a giant winged creature called a dacon."

Milleus' first thought was that his brother had gone crazy. Then he remembered the book Isandor had shown him, and he remembered the screech in the night, and the warm air.

He said, "Larger than a southern eagle?"

"Yes." Sady's gaze was intense. "Please, can we leave the mockery until this is over?"

"I'm not mocking you. I've seen that thing. When it flies over, the air that follows it is warm."

"Where did you see it?"

"Exactly where I'm standing now. It came from the direction of the city and went over there, to the forest."

Then he told Sady of Isandor's book, and the spark on Isandor's hand, and when he finished, Sady swore loudly.

"What?" It chilled Milleus. Sady never used such language.

But Sady turned to one of his guards. "Can you contact the prison urgently, and tell them to release the prisoner."

The man bowed and left.

The battlefield had quietened.

By the weak dawn light, Chevakians marched Eagle Knights off to repossessed trucks, which Sady said the Knights had stolen from farms. Their birds were harder to control, because none of the Chevakians knew how to control them.

A group of soldiers approached. Their suits hid their faces, but they stopped and the first man saluted.

"Proctor, the situation is under control. We defeated the Knights, and more than half of them switched sides."

Milleus recognised that stiff voice: General Finnisius.

Sady said, "Good. Sweep the camp and ask anyone who has ideas about our safety to come forward. Make it clear that they will be rewarded."

Finnisius gave a small bow. "Certainly, sir." And he was off again.

Milleus stared after his retreating back. Finnisius was a self-important, arrogant piece of work. If Sady had him acting like this, his brother must be doing something right.

CHAPTER 32

IN THE DARKNESS of the eternal night in the prison cell, Tandor could tell day from night by the number of meals brought by the guards. During the day, there would be three meals fairly close together, followed by a long time without any meals. Also, during the day, guards came and went, jangling keys, and taking prisoners away, to the courts or the gallows room. Every time someone left, other prisoners took bets as to whether he would be back.

But today, they'd received only two meals, and no one had come to get the prisoners. In fact, no one had come yesterday either. The other inmates went into a frenzy about this. They said the guards never skipped a meal, and sentencing went on every day, even during festivities.

With his knowledge of Ruko and the other children, Tandor feared that this was the beginning of the end. The guards didn't come because either they were too busy trying to organise people into shelter or, and that was worse, they were all dead, and in that case, the prisoners would starve to death in this hole.

What a way to end a life that should have ended in triumph.

When a guard finally did show up, he marched past all the doors, to loud protests of the inmates.

"Bring our bread."

"We're hungry!"

The guard walked past all of them, while the patch of light from

289

his lantern moved down the corridor. He set the lantern down at the door to Tandor's cell, extracted keys and opened the door. He picked up the lantern, and set it on the bench inside. He didn't close the door. By then, Tandor knew.

"I told that idiot of a Proctor that he'd beg for my help," he said, and coughed. "He still wouldn't believe me. So what's happened now?"

"The Eagle Knights have attacked, and there is fighting in the refugee camps. A large sonorics storm approaches. Someone seems to think that you can do something about it."

The guard knelt next to Tandor and unlocked the shackles that held his legs. "Don't get too cocky. Also, don't think that this means that's you're innocent."

"I don't think my innocence or guilt matters."

The man swore under his breath. Next, he unlocked the shackles that held Tandor's arms, then quickly backed off.

Tandor let his arms rest by his side, relishing the feeling of freedom.

"Come on then, go," the guard said. "Before I change my mind. I don't like this order one bit."

"Good for you then you didn't have to give it." Tandor struggled to his feet. He was stiff and sore, and clumsy. In slow, shuffling steps, he walked past the guard into the corridor.

Prisoners stirred in their cells.

"Hey, they let him go."

"What about us?"

"You can ask him," Tandor said, jerking his head at the guard. "But I doubt he'll be in the mood. To be honest, you'll be safer down here."

It cost him much effort to climb the stairs.

The courthouse corridor was deserted and lit only by a few flapping lamps along the walls.

There was a guard just inside the building's entrance, looking bored at a temporary guard station that would normally be outside. Tandor half-expected to be challenged, but it seemed the order to release him had been genuine, and the guard only watched him.

He opened the door and walked onto the porch of the building. Cold air buffeted him in the face, and with the wind came a familiar tingle. He drank in the icefire, and searched the sky for the flying dacon. He didn't see it.

To the south, the sky was pitch black, a dark mass of roiling clouds with the occasional flicker of lightning within. The base of the clouds glowed orange. That was the direction of the camp, where all the action was taking place. But he was too stiff and sore to get there in a hurry.

He moved in a kind of shuffling run. Through the merchant quarter past the houses of families he knew. The sky was dark and ominous punctuated with flashes of lightning.

The wind whipped around corners, sometimes warm, sometimes cold. Sheets of rain lashed his face. When his muscles cramped, he stopped and studied the sky, but never did he see a dark form fly over, not an eagle, not the dacon. Where would it have fled?

Finally, he stumbled up the steps to his house. The windows at the front were dark, at least those he could see over the wall.

The doorman stuck his head out of the gatehouse and called, "Halt, what are you doing here?"

"Don't be stupid, let me into my house."

The man came out, carrying a torch. He shone it into Tandor's face and stared, his mouth open. "Master?"

"Open the gate, you idiot. I don't have all night." In fact, it was almost morning.

"Yes, yes, sure." The man unlocked the gate and pushed one half of the solid metal gate aside.

There was light on in his mother's back room, and he heard voices.

"But it was your guarantee that none of us would be harmed!" said a male voice.

"That depended on your work." That was his mother. "You didn't do the work I required."

"No, that was not what I heard. This medicine was to protect us all from sonorics."

"You lied to us!" Another voice.

"You are responsible for Alius' death."

Tandor opened the door and went in.

His mother sat at her desk, surrounded by her rich Chevakian men, the ones she had convinced to support her. Their clean and cultured faces twisted into masks of horror. Tandor could only imagine what he looked like to them, dirty, with his hair burned off, his face scarred so that he could barely close his eyes and his clothes filthy from the prison.

The rule was that when family turned up, guests left, so the men rose and left the room. One of them was the former proctor Destran.

No one said anything until the door closed.

His mother gave him a cold look.

As he took his time sitting down, he noticed that his sisters were also in the room.

Rosane wrinkled her nose at him. "You stink."

He felt like telling her off, the arrogant cow. Always thought she was better than him, and never did any of the hard work.

But his mother glared his sister into silence. She regarded him from behind her desk, her elbows leaning on the surface and the tips of her fingers touching each other. "You took your time turning up."

"Yes, well I got held up."

He hadn't expected sympathy and got none. She flicked her eyebrows; her gaze lingered on the hairless part of his skull. "Where is the dacon?"

"That's why I'm here."

"I don't see it. You were meant to bring her."

"I *will* bring her, but I need a vehicle. I can't chase anything like this."

His mother's lips twitched. "Very well, but I'm coming. I'm not letting you ruin a perfectly good truck." She rose and retrieved her cloak.

"Thanks for the confidence," Tandor muttered.

His mother crossed the room in a few steps and held a finger under his nose. "Look, without me, you'd be nothing, and if you ask me, you're still nothing. What is so hard about bringing a newborn baby here?"

"If you'd come to my help, you would have found out. But no, you let me deal with the escaped servitor by myself, and now you blame me for all that's gone wrong."

"You never knew where the baby was."

"I did, but she turned before I could get to her, and I tried to climb on her back, but she wouldn't obey me."

His mother stopped. "What? Isn't the dacon meant to listen to Thilleians?"

"She didn't listen to me."

"Where is it now?"

"I don't know. I haven't seen it, because the Chevakians caught me and put me in the courthouse jail. Where were you? Why didn't you check on me?"

"I had other problems. Alius decided to jump sideways on the issue of the pills. He stalled and stalled bringing out the pills until it was too late, and then he killed himself rather than issue the medicine to keep everyone happy. Next thing, all our supporters have questions."

"Why?"

"They say that people have warned them that the pills don't work."

"And—do they work?"

He had trouble transporting himself back to the situation before he left: his mother in discussion with Chevakian business people about opportunities that would open up with increased icefire. The barrier was silly, she said. There were better ways for the Chevakians to protect themselves.

"That hardly matters." But he saw the answer in her eyes. She didn't care about any of the Chevakians who had given her money. "We need to control this beast or the entire country is going to demand the death penalty for us. We need to find it. I'm coming with you. Two of us will be stronger than one."

CHAPTER 33

ISANDOR STRUGGLED, but the Knights bound his arms behind his back and dragged him away from Milleus' truck. He yelled out, "Jevaithi!" But his voice did not rise above the screams of the people, and the hiss of engines.

People chanted, "Jevaithi, Jevaithi!"

A lot of people were screaming, and over the noise, there was a thunderous roar that shook the ground and made the air vibrate. The Knights stopped behind a large tent, with Isandor suspended between them, hanging from their grip on his upper arms.

"There," one of the men, a Knight Leader, said, his gaze directed downhill. At least twenty huge dark objects were floating down into the camp, massive round silhouettes occasionally punctuated by a flame and another roar.

Balloons. The Chevakian army.

A volley of arrows flew from the camp but most fell well short of the baskets, which were bristling with soldiers.

There was a moment of eerie silence before the first bangs echoed over the hillside: Chevakian guns.

Voices on the ground screamed orders.

The balloons landed.

The Knight Leader shouted, "Everyone, come with me. You two, take him away. We don't need him."

Isandor felt a surge of fear. *Don't need him* was a Knights' way of

295

pronouncing a death sentence. He struggled, but with his hands bound, he could do nothing. The two men dragged him across muddy ground. More balloons were still coming down and the sounds of battle changed as the Chevakians joined. There were people cheering. Groups of Knights ran downhill towards the scene of the fights. A flash of lightning turned the whole camp white and a moment later, a clap of thunder shook the ground.

The air tingled. For a heartbeat, he thought he could see icefire strands in the clouds. Blue and pulsing

They arrived at a couple of trucks guarded by one single Junior Knight standing on the steps into the cabin peering over the camp. "What's going on down there?"

"Trouble. Chevakian army has turned up. Go join the unit."

The Junior Knight saluted his superiors and left Isandor with his executioners.

They looped a rope under his arms and tied it so he stood with his back against the truck. Then another rope around his legs. Isandor kicked, but they were too strong. The ropes were really tight and cut circulation in his hands, but he suspected that he would not have use for blood circulation for much longer.

Please, let it be quick.

"Now, let's see how brave our boy king is."

"I don't want to be a king." The people had called him that and it embarrassed him. The people of the City of Glass feared kings, and he was no king.

He glanced at the sky. Where were those balloons? Where was Milleus? If he whistled, was there a chance that his eagle would turn up?

The Knights laughed. "You're a worm, nothing but a worm, from the Outer City. You really thought you could defeat us with your pathetic rebellion?"

"We will defeat you." Although he wished no part in the rebellion. By the skylights, he had to keep them talking, until someone, *someone* would see him.

One of the Knights lashed out with a rope.

A sharp pain exploded across his legs, as if someone burned a glowing rod into his skin. Isandor bit his lip to keep in the scream. He braced himself for the next hit, which came soon enough, and the next one, on his stomach. Each felt like it dug deeper into his skin. With the fourth hit, he screamed.

"Change the tone of your cockiness now?"

"We will win!" He turned his face to the sky, and with all the breath he had left, whistled for his eagle.

He had to keep believing, or all was lost. Believing that Jevaithi was alive, believing that Milleus would find him, that the Chevakians would defeat the Knights.

He lost count of how many times the Knight hit him. With each hit, his anger grew. Once he had respected the Knighthood, but these men were rotten, evil.

His shirt felt wet, with blood, he guessed. The icy rain was probably the only thing to stop him feeling the pain. Because there was no pain, only anger.

With each hit, he screamed. "Fuck you!"

The rope lashed him. "Shut up, you worm."

"Never!"

Again.

"Never, You'll have to kill me first."

Again. His throat was raw from screaming.

"Never."

There was no next hit. The Knight stood before him, his face shining with sweat, his chest heaving.

"Getting tired, huh?" Isandor said. His skin was itching like crazy.

"You are a tough bugger." The Knight grabbed the collar of his shirt and pulled him up, dragging at the bonds that held Isandor to the truck. "You like playing games, huh?"

Isandor spat blood into the man's face. Behind the Knight's head, roiling clouds parted, and something *moved* between them, blazing blue icefire. "By the skylights, what is that?"

"Trying to distract me?"

"No, look!"

But the clouds had covered the crack again. The first Knight stared. He had seen it; Isandor had seen it, but the second Knight had not.

He said, "Looks like the Chevakians are beating the stuffing out of our boys. Come, we got to help them. Just get on with this job."

"I hear ya." The first Knight unsheathed his dagger, but he still looked nervous.

Isandor screamed, "Jevaithi! Milleus! Mother!" But a gust of icy wind tore past him and carried any sound his voice made. It was so cold that it hurt. All around him were flurries of . . . snow?

His mind drifted off into a place where he kept his secrets, a place where he and Carro sat on mounds of snow and read old books, a place where he led Jevaithi by the hand in the warehouse where they had changed each other's hearts. And a small hunting shack in the Aranian mountains where he had first made love to her.

The dagger came down.

One moment, it glittered in the light, the next it plunged into his chest. He screamed without making a noise. The clouds burst open and released a lightning bolt of pure icefire. The world stopped moving around him. He felt no pain, and no sense of having a body.

The Knight stumbled back, wide-eyed.

Voices, thunder and battle sounds went quiet. Was he dead? He tried to move, but his arms were still tied to the truck. Not dead, then?

A screech above the camp made all the hairs on Isandor's neck stand up. The Knights shouted at each other and looked up.

A waft of warm and humid air went over the camp. The air wove into blue strands that were sucked up into the sky.

Isandor had only felt something like this once before: in the City of Glass, when he tried to escape through the Outer City with Jevaithi, and when Carro and his patrol had attacked him with an icefire sink.

Isandor sensed a lot of people running up the hill. There were cries and screams.

A huge shape came plummeting out of the air. At first Isandor thought it was his eagle, but it was much bigger than that. The thing —whatever it was—landed on top of the truck, where he couldn't see it. He tried to twist around, but his arms were still tied to the truck. His back hurt, his legs hurt, his chest hurt. His movements dislodged the dagger from his chest. It fell into the mud at his feet. A strand of icefire played over the hilt and the blade, which had withered to a useless stump.

The animal behind him snorted, and no, that didn't sound like an eagle. It didn't sound like a camel, or a bear, or like any animal he knew, but it was a large-animal snort. A very large animal. He felt the warmth of its breath. The icefire strand on the dagger curled itself into a little coil and sprang off, over Isandor's head, to the creature on the roof of the truck.

A woman's voice screamed, "Look! Look at it!"

The truck wobbled at his back. There was a thud of a heavy weight landing on the ground, and then the thing came around the side of the truck. It was . . . a girl.

She was about his age, dressed in a dirty men's shirt and trousers held up by a rope. She stood, bare-footed in the mud. Her cheekbones were strong, but her cheeks rounded. Her hair was curly and deep black, like mother's hair, before it started going grey. Her eyes . . . were deep royal blue, like his own. She was strange and alluring and the most beautiful and most wild girl he had ever seen.

"Who are you?" *What are you?*

She didn't reply, but her eyes remained fixated on his. She came closer and ran her nose over his shoulder, like an animal sniffing its master. Her breath was so hot that it made him shiver.

She reached out a claw-like hand, with long and pointy nails, and ran it over his blood-soaked shirt. The blood dried, turned to powder and blew away on the wind. His skin burned and itched. She ran her hand down both his thighs and the skin there itched, too, *knitting* back together. Then she hooked the long nail under the rope that tied his arms to the truck and ripped it.

Oh, the freedom.

Oh, fuck, the pain.

She ripped the rope that tied his hands together, too.

While he cursed with pins and needles, the girl knelt at his feet and ripped the bonds to his legs as well. Her back was unusually broad for a girl and triangular in shape. Her backside was not full and rounded, like Jevaithi's, but muscular and strangely asymmetrical, and her legs—wait, what was the snake-like thing that curled around her upper leg? She had a tail?

"What are you?" he asked again.

She rose and bent over him, and kissed him on the forehead. He leaned into her warmth. She smelled like home, as if he had known her for years. If there were any good spirits, this had to be one.

At the edge of his consciousness, a truck engine roared. People shouted.

"Give her to me!" a rough voice yelled.

Someone stumbled towards him. The man looked like a living skeleton, dressed in filthy clothing, with a skull-like head devoid of most of its hair. The face had suffered horrific injuries, burns probably, and the skin was stretched tight over his forehead and cheeks. The lidless eyes were permanently open. But the irises were royal blue.

By the skylights. "Tandor."

Was this girl creature a slave of his?

Tandor stopped, panting. "You're in great danger. Stand very still and don't speak, and I'll come to take that creature away. I know how to deal with it." He inched closer, his hand outstretched.

The girl turned her head, and gave a low hiss that made the hair on Isandor's neck stand up.

"Why should I give her to you? She seems to like me a lot better."

"She's a dacon."

A magical shapeshifter, the symbol of the Thilleian house. Isandor wouldn't have believed it if he hadn't seen the girl. "Why should I give her to you? You lied to me about everything else." Isandor was surprised how quickly his anger resurfaced. "You lied to me about who you are, and what you wanted, and about everything. About my sister. You used my mother—"

"Come now, there is no time for talk."

Isandor laughed, an action that made his stomach hurt. "Everyone is watching. These two tried to kill me. And you're just going to walk out of here?" He noticed an elderly woman having come out of the truck. That was the Lady Armaine, daughter-in-law of the old king?

"We're not going to walk. We're going to fly," Tandor said. He had come even closer. His left eye didn't close properly and was weeping. By the skylights, what had happened to him?

Isandor laughed again. "We'll fly because I'm a magical being since someone just stabbed me and I should be dead?"

"You stupid boy. You're a servitor, that's why."

A servitor that couldn't be killed unless the master died. When the master died, the servitors died. Which meant that no one could kill him when Jevaithi was still alive, and that he died when Jevaithi died.

And that no one could kill Jevaithi while he was alive. That thought filled him with hope.

Tandor continued, "We're going to tell that beastie to turn into its dacon form and take us out of here."

"You can't tell her what to do. She doesn't even understand you, or doesn't speak."

"Come, you stupid boy." He grabbed Isandor's arm.

He yanked himself loose. "Let me go, you don't own me."

The girl snorted and shook herself like a bear did. She positioned herself between Isandor and Tandor, jamming Isandor up against the side of the truck. Her body was much hotter than a normal person would be. It . . . grew. The skin became rough, the body became thicker, the shoulders extended. The clothes ripped. Hands and feet became huge claws. The head elongated like a bear's snout. Ears and hair vanished into the leathery skin. And the snake-like thing against her leg grew into a huge tail.

Lastly, protrusions on her shoulders unfolded into giant leathery wings.

The creature turned its head towards Isandor. It had retained the girl's blue eyes.

"Watch it!" a male voice yelled. One of the rebels, with a gun, pointed at the creature's head. He wore the black of the Brotherhood, and Isandor recognised Simo, wild-eyed. "I'll kill the abomination!"

"No, don't!" Isandor jumped forward, but his muscles were still sore from being hit. A mighty wing swooped over his head. There was a bang.

He vaguely heard Milleus shout. The next moment, a rain of burning embers came down. The creature hissed and spread its wings. Simo fired again, and this time, Isandor saw the bullet hitting some kind of invisible shield in mid-air. It exploded into millions of glowing fragments. The dacon hissed. Simo fumbled with the gun that would have to be reloaded.

"It's a construct of the old king!" someone yelled.

"It's a servitor."

"Kill it! Kill it!"

Isandor held his hand on the creature's neck. He could feel muscles relax under the hot skin. The creature understood the insults? It had nothing to do with the old king, and was not a servitor.

It was something of icefire itself, some poorly-understood part of it, some part that, possibly, the Brotherhood denied for fear of frightening the people. The Brotherhood desperately wanted icefire to be a positive force. And it was not.

The creature bowed its head and breathed out a cloud of warmth. As the air stroked past his skin, he could feel a sense of longing, and a savage hunger.

She finds nourishment in icefire, Isandor realised. And he also realised what he could do to save Tiverius from the same fate as the City of Glass and the southern Chevakian towns.

"You fly, huh?"

She crouched and held out her wings.

By the skylights, they were massive.

He grabbed a handful of leathery skin, put his good foot onto a bony protuberance that might be an elbow, or a shoulder, and heaved himself onto the broad back.

The huge body under him felt warm, and *right*. This was what he did best: working with animals.

He bent over the long neck. "You ready?"

The giant wings flapped and he rose into the air.

CHAPTER 34

"THE IDIOT!" Lady Armaine cursed, and Tandor was unsure if she meant him or Isandor, who had become a black speck of ever-diminishing size in the sky. This was something neither of them had considered: the dacon could only be controlled by its Thilleian parent.

He stood a little apart from his mother and her retinue.

The Chevakians were returning to their balloons, ignoring hundreds of bodies in Eagle Knight uniforms. Chevakian commands rang out over the camp. *Quick, quick, get to the shelters.*

It was futile. Not even the shelters would be enough to weather this storm. The front was already at the next ridge, and whenever the clouds parted, human-like forms made from icefire peeked through.

"So." His mother spat. "The storm comes. We all hide. Tiverius is destroyed, and everyone who manages to survive is convinced that icefire is the worst thing in the world. No one will want to support us anymore. Our family is ruined. Can you think of a worse outcome?"

Tandor held his silence. As a matter of fact, he *could* think of a worse outcome, one in which Ruko destroyed all of Chevakia. Even his mother didn't understand the depth of the boy's anger.

"Come, let's get out of the weather." His mother walked towards her private truck. Tandor followed, for lack of inspiration of what else to do.

Loriane had the Chevakian senator. His children despised him.

His mother had never loved him, and both his countries disowned him.

They joined the long column of Chevakians going into the city. The camp inhabitants watched the vehicles roll past. These people would all die, even though they thought they could survive the icefire cloud. They were people like Loriane, most from the Outer City, most innocent, tired, injured and confused by the succession of battles fought in the camp. Tandor couldn't bear to look at them.

Isandor was flying a zigzag pattern over the city, creating a lacework of icefire in the sky. It was as pretty as it was futile. A stupidly brave boy. Given some training and a few hard life lessons, he and his sister would make a good king and queen. The Knights were defeated. He'd even heard rumours of a rebellion from within. Rider Cornatan killed by the hand of his own son. The younger generation was taking over.

"Why don't you ever listen to what I'm saying?" his mother said.

She sat opposite him in the lavishly appointed cabin.

Old money. Old values. Corrupt values. After the mistakes he made—and they were his mistakes—the survivors from the City of Glass would never accept him as their ruler. His mother certainly didn't deserve to get that position. The throne belonged to Jevaithi, or Isandor, or Loriane even, people who cared.

And as his mother talked about hollow victories and corrupt plans, and as the doomed city that was his home slid past outside the window, one thing became clear to him: it was never too late to make a stand. Even if it would be his last.

He knocked on the glass that separated the driver compartment from the rest of the cabin. "Stop the truck."

The driver did. His mother stopped halfway through her rant. Tandor rose from his seat and opened the door.

"What are you doing?" His mother spoke as if he was a small child.

Tandor didn't answer. He let himself onto the pavement and slammed the door shut. The truck didn't move, but he walked away from it. His mother opened the door and shouted, "Tandor, come back!"

But Tandor kept walking. There was one reason that Ruko still sought revenge, and he was that reason. He walked into a side street and shouted at the sky, "Ruko! Come and get me if you dare."

CHAPTER 35

ITH A FEW lazy wingbeats, the dacon turned and flew back over the city. He loved flying on her broad and muscled back. Her movements were majestic and powerful. He had never flown a stronger mount.

The wall of smoke loomed before him, a mass of broiling black clouds. Fires consumed farm land and forest, thick smoke spreading from the fire front. Wind whipped the trees on the ground, throwing up eddies of dust. The air tasted of smoke and grit. And icefire. It streamed through the air, forming ever-strengthening cords that danced over the dacon's skin. Isandor felt none of it; she drank it all in, like a camel in desperate need for water. With each wingbeat, muscles became more powerful and confident. With each wingbeat, she came closer to the front.

Soon, tendrils of smoke detached from the clouds and reached for her, long strands of wispy substance, whirling with grace that belied the violence within. Isandor's skin tickled with their power, and these were only offshoots that escaped the dacon's skin. The cold was biting, and he wasn't dressed for it.

The dacon swooped back and forth, feeding from the roiling clouds, *halting* their progress. This was then, how the storm could be beaten, unravelled from the outside like a ball of knitting wool.

Back and forth, back and forth.

But when the outer layer of grey-black peeled off, the inside of the clouds glowed an angry fiery orange. Shapes of blue icefire moved within. By the skylights, something lived inside those clouds, shapes that knitted the outer layer back together. Shapes that picked up entire trees and hurled them at the dacon. She managed to evade their projectiles, but Isandor felt the whooshing of wind of the force with which they were thrown. The burning projectiles fell amongst farms yet unaffected, and started new fires. The fire front roared and billowed outwards. Lightning cracked and thunder shook the ground. The dacon absorbed power, and flew backwards and forwards.

It was not enough.

Not enough to stop the fire, not enough to halt the progression of the front towards Tiverius.

We are going through the clouds, Isandor thought at the creature. If we break apart the storm, it may lose coherence.

He sensed a measure of glee. *Finally. Why did you wait so long.*

She banked sharply and plunged into the roiling mass. Blackness closed all around him. The air was so cold that his hands became stiff. Wind buffeted him. Icefire grew much stronger here. Blue strands of light zapped through the darkness without notice. They struck the dacon's back, its head, its wings. She absorbed all the power without flinching.

Angry orange flames lit up, and a human-shaped figure made of flames rose from the fire. It had dark holes for eyes, and gouts of fire for hands and a mouth that blazed with white icefire.

Attack it! he thought at the dacon.

She dived into the fireball. Air crackled around Isandor, protecting him in a cage of sizzling strands. Flames pulled at the cage, but wherever they broke though, the cage knitted back.

The fire-being hefted a burning tree and swung it around as if the dacon were an annoying fly. Sparks flew off the burning wood. The trunk hit Isandor's protective cage with a juddering crack. Some of the strands broke and re-knitted around the burning tree. Isandor was lifted off the dacon's back with his protective cage when the fire-being swung the tree in the other direction. Sparks rained down on him, freezing onto his skin and clothing.

He screamed in his mind, *Help!*

He couldn't see the dacon anymore.

The fire-being roared triumph. Isandor crawled as far into his cage as possible, but the fire-being wasn't roaring at him. The dacon had taken hold of its arm with its mouth. It shook its head like an eagle trying to kill a larger animal by shaking it, and sparks of fire rained from the fire-being's arm.

It dropped the tree. Isandor fell, and fell . . . and was snatched up just before hitting the ground by the dacon, carrying the icefire cage in its mouth.

It flew at crazy speed, dodged and twisted. At least twenty other fire-beings had come to the first fire-being's aid. It was shouting at the sky, sparks spewing from its mouth and still leaking from its injured arm. Icefire streamed from its damaged form into the dacon.

A second fire-being tried to grab the dacon, but it swung its tail, unleashing another shower of sparks from the fire-being's side. Isandor understood. The sparks were blood, and once the skin of the fire-being had been broken, it didn't easily repair.

"Put me down!" he yelled over the roar of fire and wind.

The dacon did, and Isandor climbed onto its back, anchoring the icefire cage to the dacon's shoulders.

As he did so, he noticed how the skin of the dacon had darkened . . . and wrinkled. As if she sensed his thought, she turned her head. Her eyes, once bright and blue, had clouded. Eyelids sagged, wrinkles surrounded her nose.

She looked . . . old.

He understood. "By the skylights. Taking in icefire makes you age quickly."

Her eyes were sad. How long did she have?

The lumbering fire-beings were coming for them, and there were a lot more now. The idea was to injure them. Two were already 'bleeding', one staggering aimlessly leaking sparks from its side, the other now kneeling on the ground, and much smaller than it had been before.

Isandor unsheathed his dagger and held it to a strand of icefire to imbue the blade with it. Then he threw it at the nearest fire-being. Straight into the chest, and out the other side. It left a gaping hole into the fire-being's body. It seemed surprised for a heartbeat or so, and then the sparks gushed out, the being howled at the sky and fell flat on the ground. Isandor cheered. He kneed the dacon around.

Hauled up his dagger on its thread of icefire borrowed from the dacon.

Threw it at the next construct, which it hit in the shoulder. Turn around, and again. The fire-beings were not very smart, if determined to fight to the death. Several lay on the ground, their lifeblood oozing out of them in the form of sparks, re-absorbed into the dacon's skin.

Isandor collected the dagger, threw it, retrieved it, threw it. And the fifth one, he missed completely. His arms were getting tired and too cold to aim effectively. By the skylights, how many of these things were there?

Also, he noticed that the fire front had started moving again. There were only two bleeding fire-beings left on the ground. The others had all come back to life again.

A thought went through his mind. *You cannot kill a servitor until its master dies.*

These were not regular servitors, but what if they had a master? If so, who was this master? How could he find out in the short time he still had?

He became aware of the sound of a voice. Somewhere outside the cloud, a man was calling his name.

No, when he steered the dacon out of the clouds, he heard that the man was calling, "Ruko, Ruko."

It was Tandor.

He steered the dacon to a glide and landed next to Tandor—his father. He screamed, "Do you command these fire beings? Tell them to stop!"

Tandor shook his head. "Sadly, I do not. But I know who does." And he raised his voice. "Ruko!"

A huge being detached from the clouds, with shimmering flames for arms and legs. The body was transparent, and the head a construct of delicate flames. Isandor could see the eyes, hollow and dark, the shimmering flames that formed the hair. The figure, a young man, had a broad, square face and a jutting chin.

"Ah, there you are. Come and get me if you dare." And then to Isandor, "Stand back."

"But he will kill you!" And somehow, that mattered, because Tandor was his father, and there had to be some good in him.

The fire-being that was Ruko bent down, showing Isandor all the intricate detail of the head. Smooth skin, a flat nose with flaring nostrils, heavy brows. With a chill, Isandor recognised the giant who had locked him and Jevaithi into the butcher's warehouse.

"Yes, he will kill me. Revenge is the only thing he has ever wanted since losing his girl. If not me, he'll go after the Knights, or the Chevakians. He'll find a reason to suit his murders. The only way to stop him is to give him what he wants. I'll tell you something I've learned. Servitors are a bad idea, not because they obey evil people, but because they are evil, and you cannot control them unless you're more evil than they are. I was never evil enough to do what would have been required to keep them under control. I must pay for that. Look after the City of Glass, son. It is yours."

The fire-being's hand touched Tandor, and the world exploded in a flash of white. The wind knitted into strands of power that were sucked into a roaring vortex of icefire. Isandor was flung high into the air. The wind sucked him up as if he was a flurry of snow and dropped him on the ground in a whirlwind of dust and leaves. Thunder rumbled. Huge hail stones pelted down, bouncing all around him. He pressed himself into the mud shielding his head with his arms. Those hailstones *hurt*.

Furious as the storm was, it didn't last long. The hail stopped, the torrential rain eased, and Isandor pushed himself up. Somewhere in the struggle, he had lost his wooden leg, and he fumbled in the mud until he found a tree branch to support himself.

The branch had come from a copse of trees next to a ruined farmhouse. Isandor limped to the building. The roof had been blown off and the exposed beams seared by fire. Piles of blacked coal that had once been items of furniture were still smoking. He found no sign of life. Rain drizzled down, and mist and smoke restricted his vision. Where was he?

A soft whimper attracted his attention. On the other side of the farmhouse, he found a duck pen with all the ducks in the hutch, burnt to cinders. The sound came again. The grassy field next to the duckhouse was strewn with burnt wood and splinters, and amongst them, he found an old woman. She lay in the dirt, her back horribly twisted. Her eyes were closed and her lips formed inaudible words.

"I'm here," he said. "I'll help you."

She didn't react. A tear ran over her cheek. Her breath came shallow, although he couldn't see any injuries. The skin on her face was pale and thin as paper. White hair was plastered to her head. Curly hair.

Breath caught in his throat. He knelt, clumsily without his wooden leg. "Can you hear me?"

She turned her head towards him and opened her eyes. They were blue.

With trembling hands, Isandor tried to turn her lower body. If only she'd lie straight, she wouldn't have so much trouble breathing.

But her lower body was limp and he feared that she had broken her spine and he'd be best not to touch her. He took the wrinkled right hand into his. The nails were still sharp, but the skin no longer hot.

"Please, live," he whispered. "For me."

She gave his hand a tiny squeeze. Her blue eyes blinked, once, and remained open.

Isandor didn't know how long he'd sat there when the sound of an approaching truck made him look over his shoulder.

An unfamiliar vehicle had stopped on the farm road. The passenger door opened and someone climbed out.

A female voice called, "Isandor!"

Jevaithi. He struggled to his feet. She rushed to him, jumping over the debris, and came to a halt when she saw the body.

"It's all right," he said.

She didn't look convinced, but ran into his arms, enveloping him with her familiar scent. He was so happy that he pulled her close and kissed her, until he remembered he shouldn't do this anymore, because she was his sister and it was not proper. But there was a time for being proper later. He kissed her again, because he loved her so much. She broke the kiss by pushing herself against his chest.

"Hey, silly. We're not alone, you know." Her chest heaved with deep breaths. Their hearts beat in unison.

"I love you. I don't care what anyone says."

"I love you, too."

"I was so scared for you. How did you escape the Knights?"

"Someone helped me." She turned around and behind her stood . . .

"Carro?"

Indeed. It was Carro, but he looked much older than when Isandor had last seen him. He came forward, glancing at the old woman's body.

He stopped in front of Isandor, and dropped to his knees.

"Your Majesty, could you forgive me? Could you forgive all the Knighthood for the things they have done? Could you accept a new Knighthood of men and women who are honest and obedient for all the right reasons?"

"Get up, you silly," Isandor said. "We're friends."

"*Were* friends," Carro said. "I did great wrongs because I believed that I must do those things to please people in power."

Isandor shrugged, suddenly full of emotion and memories. Him and Carro playing in the snowy alleys of the Outer City, him and Carro leafing through old—and illegal—books. Him and Carro flying in the race for the Queen's Champion. The strange discipline of the eyrie, with its rules and bullying by older Apprentices. Carro had not been given an easy time.

"Can you forgive me? Your Highness?"

"I accept your apology," Isandor said. "But please do not call me that again. I am no king and I have no desire to lead a country."

"But we have to," Carro said. "There are so few good people left. We have Rider Barton, you and the Queen. That's it."

"The Knights of the Council are dead? Rider Cornatan?"

Carro nodded, and looked away. Isandor sensed a story that was too raw yet to be told.

"Come on, silly, you're embarrassing me. Get up." He gave his stick to Jevaithi, grasped her shoulder and held out a hand. Carro took it and Isandor heaved him to his feet while holding himself upright on Jevaithi's shoulder.

"Look at me." Carro laughed. "Helped by a man with one leg. What happened to your peg leg?"

"No idea," Isandor said.

"I'll make you a new one, if you let me."

"I would be honoured." He took the stick back from Jevaithi. And with Jevaithi on one arm and Carro on the other, he clambered into the cabin.

The truck took them to the refugee camp, where a huge cheering crowd had gathered. They weren't just southerners, but also Chevakians, soldiers and civilians, and some Eagle Knights with their birds, which looked none-too-impressed with all the noise.

As soon as Jevaithi helped Isandor from the truck—how annoying was it to be without his damn leg?—a man in the audience called, "Peria!"

Others repeated, "Peria, Peria!" Isandor did not want that name to be used, with all it stood for, but it seemed the name had stuck and there was nothing he could do about it. The southern land one again had a name.

And there was Milleus' truck, Milleus himself, and a younger man who looked like Milleus, and with him was . . .

"Mother!"

Isandor ran-limped into her arms. She was crying, and that made him cry as well. Milleus hugged Jevaithi, and then the younger man, who must be Milleus' brother, put one hand on both Isandor's and his mother's shoulders. "Let's go home. You're all my guests."

Sady took everyone into his house. Milleus, the young royal couple, the Knight commander Rider Barton and his young second in command, who seemed to be the prince's friend.

And not to forget Milleus' goats. The latter much to Farius' chagrin.

They talked and ate, and Viki came past to say that sonorics levels were falling rapidly, and got invited to the feast as well.

Some time when it was almost morning, when everyone had gone to bed, he walked with Loriane up the stairs. He stopped at the door to his bedroom. Dara and Myra were sharing the room nextdoor that had been hers, so that the two Knights could have the other room.

"This means that eventually, you'll be able to go back to the City of Glass."

"Yes." She smiled, but the smile faded quickly. "Is safe for you?"

"I don't know. And besides, I belong here." There was so much work to be done.

She gave him an intense look. "I . . . can stay."

"If you want to go home, I don't want to stop you." He had trouble saying this, and he had to look away.

"Hey." She reached for his face and put a warm hand on his cheek. "What you want?"

"I had hoped . . ." He licked his lips, breathed deeply and plunged on. "I'd hoped that you would choose to stay here."

"With you?"

"With me." He licked his lips again. Another calming breath. "In my house. As lady in the han Chevonian family." Another deep breath. "I've been crazy about you since I first saw you on the platform. I love you. I haven't loved anyone like this for more than twenty-five years."

She stared at him. Her eyes glittered with tears. Sady held his breath. She was surely going to refuse and tell him to quit behaving like a child.

But then she closed him in her arms, and buried her face in his shirt, and cried. Sady turned her face up and kissed her. She clung onto him, kissing him back, while the tears ran down her cheeks and dripped on his shirt.

He broke the kiss. "Hey, it's going to be fine. I love you, that's all that matters."

She wiped her cheeks with the back of her hand, smiled, and her smile turned into laughter. "Shhh," Sady said, putting a finger on her lips.

He opened the door to his bedroom and for the first time in more years than he cared to recount, led a woman into his private domain.

$\mathcal{I}$T RAINED in Tiverius for a further three days, and then the sun came out. The sonorics levels dropped dramatically, people came out of the shelters. The tide of sonorics was receding, but would take some time until the border regions were accessible again, not to mention the southern platform.

When the losses could finally be counted, the figure was staggering. Ensar, Solmeni, Fairlight. Entire towns wiped off the map. In addition, much cropping land had become inaccessible and crops lost through the weather or lack or care. Viki had given approval for all districts to farm as much as possible, and fortunately, the bad weather had delivered more rain further north than usual, but still, this would be a hard winter in Tiverius.

One morning, Milleus left his brother's house and walked to the cemetery. He wandered through the rows with familiar plaques and familiar names. So many of his former senators had already died.

He stopped at the wall that contained the han Chevonian cubicle. There was a small statue of Eseldus, a smaller version of the one that stood in the courtyard of the house. Sady's house now. Milleus could have the guest quarter, Sady said, but after today, he wasn't sure he wanted to intrude on Sady's life. Sady had never intruded in his life either.

Kalius had offered him rooms, since he was living alone as well, but he liked Kalius as much as Kalius liked him, and the less said about that, the better. In all honesty, he considered leaving the city for good. He had his goats, he could set up a travelling farm, taking the animals where the milk was needed and where hay was plentiful. Else, he might follow the youngsters up the platform if the issue of sonorics would indeed be gone forever. He figured they could use someone experienced to talk to.

Today, however, was about family. He had brought a cloth and cleaned and polished the plaque that said Suri han Helonian and put a bunch of flowers in the cubicle. He tried to think of her, but after all that had happened recently, he was ashamed that her face would not come as easily as it once would have. It was so long ago. He'd made mistakes, but there was nothing he could do to change them.

"Father."

He jumped when there was a voice behind him.

Andrean stood there, already in his formal dress. "Uncle said I could find you here." His son's gaze went over Milleus' comfortable woollen robe.

"No, I'm not going to the ceremony like this," Milleus said, meeting his son's eyes. Mercy he looked just like his mother when she used to nag him.

An uncomfortable silence hung between them.

"I just wanted to ask . . ." Andrean hesitated. "What do you think about this marriage?"

"You ask me about marriage?" Milleus snorted. His son had always been the first to condemn him for Suri's death.

A further uncomfortable silence.

"Well, I think that my brother is old enough to make his own decisions. Your uncle has also acquired the responsibility for a large group of southerners, and if history is anything to go by, many of them will never leave. War, sonorics, other disaster, it's happened before and will happen again. I do not see it as a problem that he takes his wife from amongst those refugees. If I'd have been less lucky in winning the Aranian war, we might have been those refugees, trying to eke out a living in hostile Arania, and we would have been grateful for a friendly hand."

Andrean shrugged, opened his mouth as if he was going to say something, but thought the better of it.

Milleus tidied up the cubicle, shut the ornate grille that stopped the ground squirrels eating the offerings, and walked with his son out the cemetery gates.

Neither said anything because that was their way of dealing with each other's differences, but that didn't worry Milleus. The sun was shining, the sky was blue, and all Tiverians had decorated their fences, front gates and doors with flowers, most of them woven from straw for lack of the real thing. Already, people lined the road to watch the parade. Never in living memory had a proctor in office gotten married. And it was a perfect day for a grand wedding.

The next spring:

A soft breeze stirred Isandor's hair as he crested the ridge, a breeze scented with green and flowers. The sky was deep blue above and little streams trickled between the rocks on either side. At the head of the column, he kneed his camel up the last of the slope.

Bordertown.

Blocky houses lay scattered in the landscape, but the southern platform was a far different place from the one they had left. It was *green.* Flowers bloomed in the fields as far as the eye could see. Flowers bloomed even on the roofs of the houses, which had lain abandoned throughout summer and winter, until, finally, it was safe to come onto the platform again.

The line of camels inched into the grass, so green it hurt the eyes. Isandor reached out to his mother. In her white dress, she looked divine. Her hair stirred in the breeze, loose locks falling over her shoulders. It was going grey at the temples. But she looked healthy. Her cheeks glowed. The breeze made her dress flutter about her so it drew taut over her full breasts and slight rounding of her stomach. She had not spoken to him about it, but he knew the signs, even if only in the amusing way her Chevakian man treated her like a goddess. After a life of being a breeder, she would be able to keep the last child she would ever bear.

She had asked to come on the trek, to have one more look at her home land before turning back to Tiverius and her new husband.

The line of camels cut a track through the grass and flowers so tall that the heads grazed the animal's belly. It was slow going, because

Isandor's camel, in the front, needed to tread carefully to avoid obstacles hidden in the grass.

"Eeh-yup!" someone called from behind.

Ontane had steered his camel off to the side to a house with a shed in the front yard. He tapped the beast on the neck to make it sit. After it did so—protesting and stretching and twisting to graze—he slipped off the saddle. The shed door stood half open, broken and splintered, and halfway to the front door of the house lay a hump of dirty fur, from which white spokes protruded.

Isandor made his camel backtrack to where Ontane waited.

"This is your house?" Isandor asked.

"It is, Sire, in none-too-happy condition. The wife will be devastated."

Isandor nodded, but he thought Dara was far too content in Sady's household to ever be serious about returning to Bordertown. Not to worry about that right now.

Jevaithi had also halted her camel to look at the odd arrangement of fur and white sticks. "What is it?"

"I have no idea." But as he said that, he knew what it was. "It's a bear."

Jevaithi's face twisted into a horrified mask. She lifted a hand over her mouth. "The poor thing."

Isandor felt a chill. The poor animal might have been lost or abandoned, hadn't been fed after everyone left, and when had managed to escape the shed had been too weak to find food. Bears were fish eaters. The only ocean here was green with flowers.

The desiccated carcass and the flowers encapsulated what the destruction of the Heart meant for the south. New life, but also the death of some old life. By the skylights, what would the City of Glass look like?

"Well, this is where we leave you." He tapped his camel on the shoulder and it sank to its knees.

Ontane bowed. "Your Highness. I would like to thank you for everything. I'm sorry about your loss, Sire."

Isandor glanced over his shoulder. Behind him, the rest of the column had come up the plain. Two camels carried the stretcher between them that held his father's body, dried and preserved in layers of cloth, as it had been found recently in a field by a Chevakian farmer. Some people had wanted to burn Tandor's body like that of a traitor, but although he had been a traitor, he had also given his life to put it right. As it might well be the only right thing he had ever done. He was a Thilleian prince, and deserved to be remembered as one, for good or ill.

"We will bring him home," he said, staring at the horizon. "We will rebuild the city. We will find a way."

Loriane came to him, her arms wide. She whispered, "Son."

Isandor took her in his arms and smelled her perfume. She was warm and soft, and familiar. She would stay here with Ontane who had promised his wife to bring some of their items from their house and return to Tiverius with Loriane.

Other people from Bordertown already fanned out to their houses, while the majority of the column waited. The packing camels carried supplies to survive the coming months, until they could give the sign that the rest of the people from the City of Glass could return home. Whoever wanted to return home. Milleus had said that if it was safe, he wanted to come.

Isandor hugged his mother. Her eyes glittered with tears.

"Be well, my son. I wish you could stay."

"You'll be very happy," he said. "He's a good man." And she wouldn't be alone. Dara would probably stay, and Myra, too, if Farius' family gave their son permission to marry her.

"I know." She returned a weak smile, and moved her hand to her belly as if scratching it. "If it's a boy, he will carry your name, or a girl, Jevaithi's."

Isandor kissed her on the forehead. "I love you. We'll visit soon."

While his mother hugged Jevaithi, Isandor signalled for the column to start moving again.

His eyes met Carro's. His friend sat atop his camel, wearing full uniform. His face was blank, an expression Isandor had come to accept as normal from Carro. Isandor didn't know what went on in that head, but he knew that Carro, and the new Supreme Rider Barton would serve the royal family for the good of the people, and not to strengthen their own power.

"Well, let's go then." He swung his wooden leg over the camel's back and slid in the saddle. Ouch. This mode of transport had much to be desired, but it would be a while before they could fly eagles again. With no snow, sleds had become useless. Balloons, maybe. Yes, Balloons. He must talk to Sady about that.

He dug his heels in the flanks of the camel and it unfolded its awkward legs—back first—with a howl. At Rider Barton's whistle, the column set in motion once more.

They had a task to do.

If you enjoyed the Icefire Trilogy…

Twenty years later, the world's problems are far from over. Icefire returns, erratically, weather patterns are disturbed, crops fail, the northern desert encroaches on once-fertile land. Sady's daughter Lana and fellow students Javes and Tamerane get one chance to understand, really understand, how the world works, or be doomed to die.

Their store is told in the Moonfire Trilogy

ABOUT THE AUTHOR

Patty Jansen lives in Sydney, Australia, where she spends most of her time writing Science Fiction and Fantasy.

Her story *This Peaceful State of War* placed first in the second quarter of the Writers of the Future contest and was published in their 27th anthology. She has also sold fiction to genre magazines such as Analog Science Fiction and Fact, Redstone SF and Aurealis.

Patty has written over twenty novels in both Science Fiction and Fantasy, including the *Icefire Trilogy* and the *Ambassador* series.

pattyjansen.com

BOOKS BY PATTY JANSEN

MORE INFORMATION:

PATTYJANSEN.COM